ROMMEL, AT WAR WITH THE WORLD AND WITH ONE MAN WHO SOMEHOW KNOWS HIS DEADLIEST SECRETS.

Rommel felt the passing of time, as one gauges his own aging by the maturing of one's children.

I did not let the Italians know my plans, which means that the British spies in Rome did not learn of it. Yet here Speigner is, having left Cairo—when?—a week ago? He anticipated my attack on the border dump in September. Now he has advance knowledge of my counterattack. How? I must be doing something obvious. Something connects us. This is a key. Speigner could cost me a great deal. Was that what I sensed five years ago in America? That my future enemy was Speigner?

ROMMEL AND THE REBEL

"Ingenious . . . solid . . . memorable."
—*Atlanta Constitution Journal*

"High adventure . . . entertaining and fun-filled reading."
—*Baltimore Sun*

"Real excitement."
—*Publishers Weekly*

"Engaging . . . crisply done . . . imaginative, romantic."
—*St. Louis Post-Dispatch*

. . . nd skillful novel belongs
. . . e creators."
—James Dickey

ROMMEL AND THE REBEL

Lawrence Wells

BANTAM BOOKS
TORONTO · NEW YORK · LONDON · SYDNEY · AUCKLAND

ROMMEL AND THE REBEL

A Bantam Book / published by arrangement with
Doubleday & Co. Inc.

PRINTING HISTORY

Doubleday edition published February 1986
Bantam edition / July 1987

*Bantam Books are published by Bantam Books, Inc. Its trademark,
consisting of the words "Bantam Books" and the portrayal of a
rooster, is Registered in U.S. Patent and Trademark Office and in
other countries. Marca Registrada. Bantam Books, Inc., 666 Fifth
Avenue, New York, New York 10103.*

To Dean

And gladly wolde he lerne, and gladly teche.

GEOFFREY CHAUCER
The Canterbury Tales

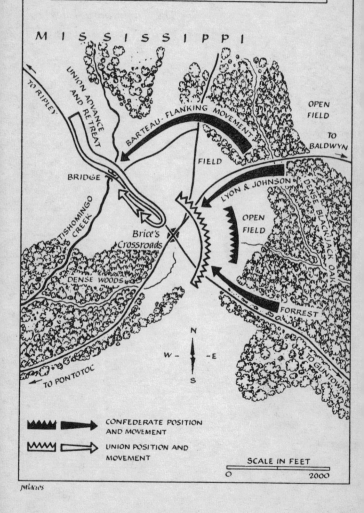

N. B. FORREST—
THE BATTLE OF BRICE'S CROSSROADS
JUNE 10, 1864

MISSISSIPPI

TO RIPLEY

UNION ADVANCE AND RETREAT

BARTEAU-FLANKING MOVEMENT

FIELD

OPEN FIELD

TO BALDWYN

LYON & JOHNSON

OPEN FIELD

DENSE BLACKJACK OAK

BRIDGE

TISHOMINGO CREEK

Brice's Crossroads

DENSE WOODS

FORREST

TO PONTOTOC

TO GUNTOWN

N
W — E
S

CONFEDERATE POSITION AND MOVEMENT

UNION POSITION AND MOVEMENT

SCALE IN FEET
0   2000

palacios

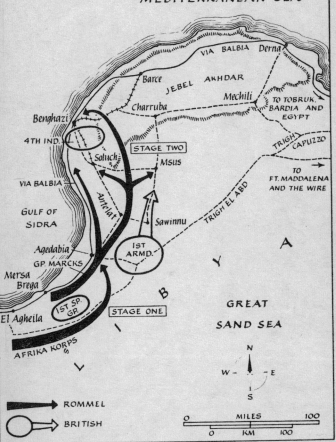

Item in *The Capitol Herald*
Jackson, Miss., July 9, 1937

The Roof Garden of the Robert E. Lee Hotel was the site of a reception honoring German military dignitaries yesterday.

Colonel Robert Adler of Jackson, district military commander, served as host, along with Major Arnold Shoemaker, head of ROTC at the University of Mississippi.

The visitors from Germany are touring Civil War battlefields. In Mississippi, they plan to see the battlefield at Brice's Crossroads, near Baldwyn, where in 1864 Nathan Bedford Forrest defeated a Federal force twice the size of his own.

I

Der Student

I

"*Sie ist eine stolze Königin,*" said Model, who held strong opinions and as ranking officer in the party expected to set the tone.

"*Sie ist königlich,*" Schörner agreed.

"*Eine Göttin,*" said Krüger, the Saxon cavalryman, his eyes fixed on the lady.

"*Die Dame ist eine Kriegerin,*" said Rommel. His companions glanced at him—Model and Schörner competitively, Krüger and Hanke admiringly. Rommel repeated the figure in English, for practice. "The lady is a . . ." The precise translation escaped him, and he searched his pocket German-English dictionary. The sea wind fluttered the well-thumbed pages, and ocean spray dampened the paper. From where he stood on the forward observation deck of *The Deutschland*, the waters of New York Harbor frothed and sparkled like champagne.

". . . fighter. She is a . . . *herrlich* . . . magnificent fighter!"

The morning sun caught the Statue of Liberty full face. Her golden salute seemed to Rommel somehow meant for him alone. Beyond the great statue the spires of Manhattan jutted powerfully as though American energy and confidence had flowed together to explode concrete and steel into the sky. His hooded eyes were bright with wonder.

"And thus," Model said archly, "America is a land of fighters?" Rommel glanced at the monocled colonel. Model was head of the *Abteilung für technische Fragen*, the newly formed department for design and development of modern armament and weaponry. He dealt in cause and effect.

"We are here to find out, are we not?" he replied.

Model's attitude is bad. Why fight an Oberkommando

3

*Wehrmacht order? Take it easy and make the best of it, try to
pick up some useful information.*

At first he too had regarded the unusual assignment as
merely an order to be obeyed. The High Command directive
had come as a complete surprise. He had heard *Generalmajor*
Boetticher lecture at the War Academy on military tactics
during the War Between the States, but that was all. Boetticher was military attaché at the German Embassy in
Washington. A frequent visitor to Civil War battlefields, the
influential soldier-politician had suggested to the OKW that
some of the promising junior members of the general staff
might benefit from a tour of Gettysburg, Chancellorsville, and
Brice's Crossroads. Rommel was unsure why he had been one
of the five officers selected for the tour, but he was grateful for
any respite from the *Jugend,* a liaison assignment which ill
suited his training and aspirations. Once committed, he had
begun methodically to prepare for the new assignment by
reading about Civil War battles.

During the five-day crossing, while squalls beat unnoticed
against his porthole, he had read voraciously in his stateroom,
emerging only at mealtimes, until eyestrain forced him to
moderate his curiosity. The trait he admired most about the
American military was their willingness to experiment, to
deviate from traditional tactics. His favorite generals were the
unyielding Presbyterian, Stonewall Jackson, and the flamboyant and unpredictable Nathan Bedford Forrest. To his own
secret amusement, Rommel found himself looking forward to
the battlefield tour with the eagerness of a schoolboy on
holiday. Historical explanations were just so much abstract
theory until one walked the actual terrain, put himself in
another man's place. Though an infantryman, he relished the
opportunity to wear the cavalry boots of Bedford Forrest.

One aspect of the trip he did not like was the use of
assumed names. Glancing now at his fellow officers, like him
conservatively dressed in business suits and homburgs, he felt
that the OKW mandate to travel under false passports was
unnecessary and even frivolous. Why tempt fate? If, for some
reason, their true identities were exposed, the embassy would
suffer embarrassment at the very least. True, Germany and the
United States enjoyed friendly relations this summer of 1937,
and in the event of exposure, it was unlikely that they would

be charged with spying. (What military secrets could one uncover at Civil War battlefields? An interesting question.) Yet the High Command's penchant for secrecy seemed, in this case at any rate, to have saddled them with a needless risk.

Each of them had retained his Christian or given name, and the false surnames all began with the same first letter as their actual names. Thus, Rommel was Erwin Rilke, Krüger was Walter Kleist, Hanke was Karl Hauptmann, Schörner was Ferdinand Spitzweg, and Model was Walther Meitner.

A funny thing had happened. Upon assuming these names, each of them had undergone a subtle metamorphosis—a shifting of the eye, a delicate defiance, a brazen nonchalance. As if compelled by the novel sound of a false name, each officer had been somehow released to interpret his role as he wished. In his own right Rommel felt an unnerving sense of freedom. As Erwin Rilke he was a world traveler who could climb a skyscraper or fly a kite, a holiday warrior who could fight the Civil War all over again if he wanted to. He had grown wary of himself. Without limitations, anything could happen. The tour was to be a busman's holiday, no more, no less. To condition himself and his companions, he made a point of referring to them by their assumed names—Pass the butter, Herr *Meitner*.

One could not help enjoying Model's brief shock and hesitation. Walther could not forget that his assistants were running the *Abteilung* in his absence. The problem was, were they running it his way? If Model was anxious to complete the tour assignment, Rommel could understand, if not actually sympathize with, his motives. Yet whatever the others' attitudes, *he* had come to America prepared to learn what he could.

"Gentlemen!" Model turned to them with a crisp tone of command. "Shall we prepare to go ashore?"

Rommel tried not to gape at the maelstrom of Times Square. He stared up and down Forty-second Street and Broadway at burlesque houses, peepshows, novelty and newsstands, lunch counters, fruit juice stands decorated with painted palm leaves, theater ticket offices with barkers out front, grandiose hotel and theater entrances, the massive skeletons of electric light frames waiting drably, atop the buildings, for an end to daylight.

Is it true that anything and everything is for sale here?

The consul, a polished and urbane diplomat named Schumann, wasted their time by describing in detail the habitués of Times Square. The ravages of this garish place and its victims were apparently standard fare on his tour. His mild face bore the disinterest of a guide in a wax museum as he pointed out a pimp in a doorway, two streetwalkers window-shopping, the professionally blind with their tapping canes and tin cups. Rommel, with the square jaw, wide mouth, and unblemished cheeks of an ascetic, stood his ground and refused to let Times Square intimidate him. While his companions attended to the consul's description of the Great White Way, he stared up at the belt of electric bulbs spelling out spot news in moving letters around the Times Building. No one else seemed to be watching them. His pointed ears gave him an air of listening to distant voices.

"AMELIA EARHART FORCED DOWN AT SEA—FLOAT-PLANE FEARED LOST 1900 MILES SHORT OF HONOLULU DESTINATION."

Rommel struggled to translate before the letters disappeared around the corner of the Times Building.

"It's a dime a dance in there," the consul was saying. "The hostesses are actually prostitutes."

"Does Al Capone go there?" Krüger asked hopefully.

"CHEW WRIGLEY'S GUM!" a sign on a building commanded. And: "MACY'S JULY HIT PARADE—OPENS JULY 6!"

"The American playboy," said Schumann, pausing to allow them to enjoy the idiom, "finds Broadway a happy hunting ground for beautiful dancing girls."

"Al Capone, he, too?" Krüger persisted. He ducked his head to catch a glimpse of passengers inside a Cadillac limousine pulling up to the curb.

"There's a marvelous Chinese restaurant around the corner," Schumann said. "Everyone ready for lunch?" He led the obedient officers under the Loew's State marquee, which read, "Woman Chases Man—Starring Miriam Hopkins and Joel McCrea."

Americans live too goddamned fast.

Yet Rommel was fascinated with the strange and ordinary details of New York. While his companions ate subgum chop suey and chicken "bird's nest" soup, he stood outside the Chinese restaurant and had a frankfurter at a sidewalk stand advertising "Hot Dog—Red Hot—5¢—Lemonade—Ice Cold —5¢." The frankfurter tasted bland compared to German sausage and mustard. A garbage truck screeched to a stop in front of him and its crew slouched to their work. A derelict stood beside him, speaking earnestly to a lemon. A muscular worker wearing a sweaty undershirt shut off his jackhammer to watch a fire engine clanging past. A boy ordered an ice cream cone from an Italian vendor. In a second-story salon a hairdresser circled his client with the intensity of a bee at its comb. From an upstairs studio came the lament of a saxophone. A ragged woman with a tin cup sang to Rommel about riding to heaven in a chariot of angels. He gave her a dime.

After lunch the *Vizekonsul* took them to the Empire State Building. They admired the modern facade, the polished hallways, the bold vertical stripes on the elevator doors. The design reminded them of home. They instantly obeyed a brassy-voiced attendant who ordered the crowd of tourists to line up in front of the elevators. Rommel's ears popped during the ride to the observation tower. He heard two teenaged girls talk of ramming a bulldozer through something called a Lindy Hop to which they had not been invited.

New York sprawled beneath him, sullen in the afternoon. A splash of yellow caught his eye and he watched a line of taxis weaving between the dark ranks of buildings. To the east, traffic streamed over three bridges positioned at intervals along a dark river. Light aircraft hummed like powerful birds riding the currents above the East River, while passenger planes going in the opposite direction descended in orderly landing patterns. To the north a wide expanse of green ruffed up against steel and concrete walls. Looking below, Rommel saw that on nearly every rooftop ventilator fans whirred, and flocks of pigeons labored upward to their roosts. He recognized the name "Macy's" on the side of a building and wondered about the competitive "Gimbels" glaring from a nearby roof. He moved to the northwest corner of the Empire State and saw cloud shadow drift like ghostly barges down the brown Hudson. Purple shadow bathed the long ridge on the western shore, while the New Jersey flatlands smoked like a burning city under siege. Rommel looked around for someone with whom to share his excitement.

"Magnificent!" he exclaimed to a short, middle-aged

woman in a straw hat. She clutched her purse to her bosom
and edged away from him.

The next stop on their tour was the Metropolitan
Museum. The five visitors carried homburgs in hand as
Schumann, at home in the Metropolitan, led them through
polished halls with arched ceilings. He lectured on the
paintings, sculpture, and artifacts with such authority that
Rommel thought he might be taking inventory for the Reich.
Rommel was soon lost, however, amid the splendor of the
Florentine, Venetian, Dutch and Flemish masterpieces, which
made him feel provincial. He reminded himself that he had
not come to America to gape at the European plunder of
American millionaires. He paid scant attention to Schumann's
esoteric monologue about perspective, atmospheric sense,
spatial composition, oil techniques which superseded tempera
painting—whatever that was. Instead, he wandered the gal-
leries, content to stand quietly behind velvet ropes or brass
rails and look.

He was particularly interested in El Greco's storm-tossed
View of Toledo, guessing that the artist saw the land itself
being torn apart by the Counter-Reformation movement. He
was stirred by the tiny figures washing clothes or fishing in the
river, oblivious to the cataclysmic events occurring in the great
cathedral on the hill. Rommel approved of these humble folk
and of the artist who did not forget them.

In another section of the museum he found a collection
more to his tastes. *"Herr Meitner, kommen Sie!"* he hissed.
Model came reluctantly, unaccustomed to receiving a command from Rommel. Once he saw the ornamental armor,
however, the weapons expert hurried among the glass-encased
displays and wall hangings of axes, maces, crossbows, swords,
shields, pistols, and cannon dating from the fourteenth
century through the mid-seventeenth century.

"Gott im Himmel," Walther gasped, "a treasure trove!
Look how the craftsman dealt with the factors of weight,
balance, flexibility, and tension of materials. Here is the story
of armor until the advent of the cannon, which rendered the
armorer obsolete."

*During coitus, Walther would lecture his wife on the
history of the orgasm.*

Rommel caught up with the rest of the group in a graceful
court. Schumann was holding forth:

". . . the so-called Badminton sarcophagus. Note the tublike shape of the coffin and the sculptured design of Dionysus riding a tiger flanked by winged personifications of the seasons. The meaning, obviously, is that the deceased no longer suffered the vicissitudes of time and change."

Rommel looked at some Roman's final resting place which had proven not so final. He had an irresistible feeling that someone was inside, trying to sleep.

That's what they got for using fancy words like Wechsel-fälle. *The tiger was in control, not the angels.*

"The sculptured sarcophagi," Schumann observed in closing, "literally 'flesh-eaters,' were very popular in Roman burials during the second century A.D. Now, over here we have a bronze of Trebonianus Gallus, Emperor from 251 to 253." The four officers, minus Model, tagged along behind the consul with the self-conscious patience of schoolboys. Rommel discreetly took a folded schedule out of his pocket. Under the consul's letterhead an itinerary was listed:

TAGESPLAN: 3 JULY 1937

8:15A.M.—*Ausschiffung, Die Deutschland*
8:45A.M.—*Abfertigung Amerikanisches Zollamt*
9:15A.M.—*Registrieren* Essex House,
      160 Central Park S.
9:45A.M.—*Kaffee im Konsulat*
10:30A.M.—*Rundfahrt*, Wall Street *Bezirk*
11:30A.M.—*Rundgang*, Times Square *Bezirk*
12:00P.M. —*Mittagessen*
1:00P.M. —Empire State Building
2:00P.M. —Metropolitan Museum
3:30P.M. —Rockefeller Center
4:30P.M. —Museum of Modern Art
6:00P.M. —*Rückkehr* Essex House
6:45P.M. —*Abendessen*, Rudi & Maxl's Brauhaus
8:00P.M. —Radio City Music Hall
10:45P.M. —*Freie Zeit*

We stay inside buildings from here on, Rommel thought with a congested feeling. A man could see more on his own.

"Almost a caricature of the ruler statue," Schumann was explaining. Rommel looked at the nude statue of the short-lived emperor, folded mantle draped over shoulder, hand outflung in rhetorical splendor. "The unusual proportions of small head and large body doubtless derive from the iconographic notion that a thickened thorax was indicative of divinity . . ."

Politicians don't last long.

". . . Gallus became Emperor by betraying his troops in a battle with the Goths in which the Emperor Decius was killed. Gallus, in turn, was murdered by—"

"Betrayal had nothing to do with it," Rommel interrupted. The consul frowned, lips parted in the act of shaping his next word. Rommel continued with an edge, "Decius was killed as a result of attacking an inferior force on superior terrain. He was beaten by a marsh, not betrayal. The Gothic army was drawn up in three lines, and the front of the last line was covered by a swamp. The Romans overran the first two lines but bogged down in the muck. The Goths charged with their long spears and finished them off. Whatever booty Gallus promised the Goths was of minor concern. It was a matter of terrain."

Krüger and Hanke gave a light pattering of applause. With a chagrined expression, Schumann moved them along. "Bust of Caracalla, Emperor 211 to 217," he said briskly. "Note the coarseness of feature corresponding to Caracalla's hunger for power . . ."

As the group moved into another room, Rommel lingered behind and made for the nearest exit. He emerged into the sunshine on Fifth Avenue and looked left and right with the unlimited options of a prison escapee. He headed south, glancing happily at the green, leafy expanse of Central Park on his right, smiling at the pigeons which fluttered away from his feet but veered immediately back to their pecking ground behind him. On impulse, seeing people hailing taxis, he crossed the street and faced north with his hand held up lazily like an old New Yorker. A yellow cab swerved across two lanes with horn tooting and screeched to a halt, causing him to jump back on the curb.

"Heah we are, Bub!" the driver said, leaning over the seat and opening the passenger door. Rommel got in. "Where to, Bub?" Rommel's face went slack. The driver stared impatiently in his rearview mirror. His jaws, blue with beard shadow, ceased grinding a wad of chewing gum. The identification card taped to the back of the sunshade read, "LIEBOWITZ, ERNIE." Their eyes met in the mirror.

"Where . . . you say," Rommel said tentatively.

"You're kiddin'! You hail a cab 'cause you ain't got nowhere to go?"

"*Ich bin* . . . visitor," Rommel apologized.

"I get it. Tourist, eh? Out to see the sights?" With a practiced index finger the driver switched his meter on. "You want my opinion, start off wit' the Brooklyn Bridge. They all like to see it, y'know?"

"Of course, Brooklyn Bridge," Rommel said assertively.

Humming a tune of commerce, the cabby pulled away from the curb and accelerated into the traffic. The yellow cab made its way into the canyons of Fifth Avenue. Rommel craned his neck this way and that, gawking at the magnificent towers. "Dat's St. Patrick's, dere," said Liebowitz. "Over dere's th' Chrysler Buildin', see it stickin' up, dere? Dat one down dere in front of us's th' Empire State."

"Yes, Empire State, I go zis morning."

"You bin dere already! How's the view—great, eh?"

"View . . . terrific!" Rommel leaped off into American space with a broad grin.

"Hey, *terrific!* Now you're cookin', Bub."

Rommel looked at the people hurrying up and down the sidewalks with a lateral energy that matched the vertical dynamics of the skyscrapers. The women—tall, slender—were more self-assured than any he had ever seen. Clipping along smartly on high heels, faces shaded by wide-brimmed hats, they seemed filled with invincible desires.

The yellow cab wound through the maze of Chinatown. Rommel stared at the brightly colored Chinese characters next to "Drink Coca-Cola" on storefront signs, at grocery stores with stacks of crinkly melons in sidewalk bins, brown carcasses of roasted ducks and small pigs hanging from hooks, vendors spreading shiny silk cloth for customers to examine, import shops with ornamental fans spread and taped to their windows.

"*Wo sind wir?*" Rommel asked whimsically. "New York or Peking?"

"Dat's right, Bub. Dis city's got it all."

The soaring steel cables and granite towers of the

Brooklyn Bridge loomed over the buildings of the lower East
Side. Rommel spotted the walkway suspended above the
roadway platform.

"One is able . . . to walk bridge?" he asked.

"Yeah, so?" Liebowitz dubiously regarded his ideal fare in
the mirror.

"I pay you advance, you meet me on far side, no?"
Rommel reached for his wallet and peeled out a ten-dollar bill.

"Hey, Bub, I got all day!" The cabby's square fingers
absorbed the bill as if by osmosis. "See dat subway tunnel
dere?" Liebowitz braked his cab near the subway entrance
which served as pedestrian access to the Brooklyn Bridge.
"You gotta go down before you go up, y'know. Folla da signs.
I'll be outside the subway stop across the river, Bub. Take ya
time."

Rommel descended into the shabby gloom of the subway
and followed a shuffling line of people who pressed against a
row of ticket windows. He watched hands communicate with
each other under metal grilles, exchanging one kind of coin for
another. He noticed a lighted stairwell marked "To Brooklyn
Bridge" and hurried up the stairs toward daylight. There were
few pedestrians on the ramp, and he quickly climbed the steps
leading to the walkway. As he ascended the Manhattan grade
between cars growling bumper to bumper on the adjacent
roadway, he felt an intense elation. On either side of him lay
the shadowy darkness of the old city—markets and gray
warehouses to the south, derelict buildings and twisted streets
of the slums to the north, elevated subway lines rising above
them as though in relief. The higher he ascended, the greater
the view. The Statue of Liberty beckoned from the mouth of
the harbor. Underneath the bridge, barges tended by tugboats
cut white Vs in the gray-green water. On the east bank
Brooklyn waited with a thin fringe of trees like a green apology
for overcrowded red buildings. Bridge traffic passed with an
unending roar. Amplified by the wires, the vibrations sounded
like sirens. Among the competitive taxis and trucks, Rommel
saw a yellow school bus zip along as serene as a swimming
duck. Feeling the sea wind in his face, he turned back to the
Manhattan skyline and was startled to see the blazing yellow-
and-gold buildings he had seen earlier now transformed by
shadow into blue, green and purple. It was a magic sound-and-

light show—just for him. He quickened his pace and broke
into a trot, then a run. The breeze tugged at his homburg and
he pulled it tight. He was soaring above sea gulls and barges.
The walkway began to slope gently toward the Brooklyn side.
He tried to slow to a walk, but his legs refused to obey. Like a
colt under a blue sky, he ran past startled pedestrians, kicking
up his heels.

He reluctantly descended the exit ramp on the east bank
and emerged by the wharves to find the yellow cab waiting as
promised. Liebowitz glanced at him curiously, as if he had
returned from a distant planet. Rommel's cheeks were flushed.
The car radio was playing and he heard a staccato voice say,
"Turner lines to right . . . Ott is under it . . . *takes* it for
the out . . . but Lopez tags up and is going to score from
third . . . he does, and the Bees extend their lead over the
Giants, five to two." To Rommel, the voice had a strange,
musical quality, like the barking of a squirrel.

"*Was ist das?*" he said.

"Dat? Dat's just the Giants and the Braves—hey! You
never seen a baseball game, Bub? Polo Grounds, here we
kommen-Sie."

By the time the taxi reached the end of Fifth Avenue at
the Harlem River, the meter read $5.65. Liebowitz pulled up
to the stadium entrance. "Dere ya go, in time fer th' fifth
stanza. Plenty game left t'see." Rommel opened the door,
hesitated, and extended his hand. Liebowitz's smile faded. He
reached for his coin purse to make change. Then he realized
that the fare wanted to shake hands. He flashed a broad grin.

"Thanking you . . . very much," Rommel said.

"Sure thing, Bub. Take it easy."

Rommel climbed the ramp to the upper grandstand deck,
ticket in hand. The stamping of feet above him had the sudden
violence of a summer storm. He rose to the sound like a bird
drafted by high winds. He felt like running across the
Brooklyn Bridge again, soaring over air and sea without
restraint. He could not remember when he had felt so free,
unless it had happened in the Italian Alps in 1917.

Rommel emerged from the ramp on an upper deck. He
smelled sun-warmed grass, beer and popped corn. The stands
were sparsely occupied. He glanced behind him and saw that
hundreds of seats were vacant. He turned back to the arena, a

green and brown world peopled by men in white uniforms and dark caps who stood and pounded gloves or mitts. With its double tier of roofed stands shaped in a huge U, the Polo Grounds vaguely reminded him of the sarcophagus at the museum—the flesh-eater. A brown diamond had been sculptured out of the green floor and engraved with parallel tracings as though giant fingers had smoothed the dirt.

Rommel paused in the aisle, charmed. On the circumference of the diamond players stood idly, patting their mittens. Their leader, a tall man standing on a mound of dirt, threw the ball to a man squatting behind a white square. This man wore armored shin guards and chest shield. He tossed the ball in a looping arc back to the dominant one on the mound, who toyed with it in his lobster-claw mitt, then reared back and hurled the ball like a bullet. The four players grouped loosely behind the hurler and the three men farther afield—perhaps their reserves—shouted words of encouragement to the tall, long-armed one. The menacing drone of spectators' voices was like the ocean drawing back and gathering itself to batter the shore.

Rommel remembered that he had to find his seat. The numbers on the ticket were self-explanatory. He did not ask an usher for assistance. He carefully counted his way up the numbered steps until he came to his row. Then he counted seats and was astonished to find a man sitting in the place assigned to him. Did Americans not observe their own rules? The man was engrossed in conversation with his companion. Rommel waved the ticket at him.

"Excuse please . . . I think you sit in my place."

The man, a leathery individual with a V-shaped face, regarded Rommel with amusement and surmise. "It ain't like there's a shortage, Mac." He nodded at the empty rows of seats behind them.

"I should sit in someone else's place?" Rommel asked, annoyed.

"Whose place? Nobody's comin'. The score's five to two, and Long Tom's up."

Thoroughly confused, Rommel took the seat behind the two men. The entire row was empty all the way to the far aisle. What did it mean, "Long Tom Zup"?

"Rabbit Warstler leads off for the Bees," an amplified

voice boomed. A tiny figure far below, carrying a wooden club over his shoulder, approached the white square where the armored man crouched. Rommel guessed that the public announcement applied to this figure, who was called a hare, or rabbit, in Aesopian fashion. And who were the "Bees"? The taxi driver had said the Giants were playing the Braves. Bees . . . Braves . . . Brave Bees? The dominant one on the sandy mound leaned forward and appraised the rabbit-man, who crouched over the white square and brandished his club. Then the tall man kicked up his foot and shot the ball toward him. The rabbit relaxed his vigilance. A second armored man dressed in black raised his left hand. "Ball one," boomed the public address system.

Anyone could see it was the first ball.

"Peanuts . . . peanuts . . . peanuts!" a young voice sang. Rommel saw a teenaged vendor exchange a bag for a spectator's money. Curious, he raised his hand to signal the vendor. The youth confidently approached him.

"What is it you sell?" he asked politely.

The youth wore a cap with bill turned backward— obviously a devotee of the armored player. He raised his eyebrows. "You kiddin' me?"

Rommel remembered that the taxi driver had asked him a similar question. Was this a reference to goats? Aesopian idiom? Bees, rabbits, goats.

"We're talkin' peanuts, mister."

"Peanuts, yes, of course. I will purchase a portion. How much the cost is?"

"Nickel-a-bag."

Rommel caught the first part of the compound word and gave the boy a five-cent coin. "Ball two," said the amplified voice.

Yes, of course.

He opened the paper sack and saw that the nuts were contained in their shells. *What could be the acceptable, indigenous method of eating them? Did one bite into the shell, like a rabbit? Did one prise the shell apart with one's fingernails, like a raccoon or otter?* Rommel bit into the shell and then prised it open with his fingers.

He noticed the dugout where the club-swingers holed up like ferrets, emerging cautiously from the shadows one by one to challenge the hurler.

Why not rush him all at once? Are there not clubs enough for all? Then he realized what was happening: one man—one target—to throw at. *Are they trying to hit him and he defending himself with his club? No, it is the white square he defends.*

The man with the club dug his heels into the dirt as if he meant to remain there a long time, pounded the white square, thrashed the air menacingly. Around the diamond, the idle ones were nervously possessive—each of his own domain—strutting this way and that, stamping clods of earth smooth, pruning unruly blades of grass as if daring anyone to ruffle the surface of the diamond.

Then there was the spitting, all kinds of spitting: defiant, insulting, contemplative. Nearly all the players on both teams worked cuds or wads of something between their jaws. They periodically expelled a brown jet as though their juices were pumped to overflowing. Whatever they were chewing was brown.

"Howdja get me t'go slummin' witcha, Al?" the leather-faced man asked his companion. "If the Yankees wasn't in D.C. this weekend, I wouldn't be here wastin' my time. DiMaggio would kill dese bums." Rommel chewed his peanuts and digested these remarks. *Someone would kill them? Americans take their athletics seriously.* The dominant one threw two more "balls," and the rabbit threw away his club and trotted, defenseless, to the first point in the diamond.

"DiMag got his eighteenth today at Washington," the man continued. "Guy's a hittin' machine. Tell me what Joe McCarthy said when somebody asked him if DiMaggio could bunt. Come *ahnnn*, Al, what'd he say? Okay, he said, 'I don't know and I ain't got no intention of findin' out.' Heh-heh."

The tall hurler threw more "balls" to the next challenger, who also dropped his club and ran to the first point, while the rabbit-man moved to the second point. Rommel was beginning to think that baseball, like its British counterpart, cricket, was quite stately, until the leader on the mound threw a ball, rabbit-man scampered, quick as a wink, to the third point. The crowd roared, the sound cascading like breakers onto the flat surface of the arena. The action had come like lightning, without warning. Rommel was excited and also thirsty. He heard a vendor calling *"Bier,"* and he waved his hand at the man.

"What did Lefty Gomez say after Jimmie Foxx slammed one into the upper left field deck? Come *ahnnnn*, Al, what'd he say? He said, 'I don't know how far it went, but it takes forty-five minutes to walk up dere.' Heh-heh."

Americans watered their beer, Rommel decided, after a big swallow. *Is public drunkenness a problem here?* He decided that the leathery man had made a joke, and feeling part of the mass, a drop in the ocean and hence an integral part of its force, he smiled convivially to himself. After a while, the tall man threw another ball away and the rabbit-man ran to the white square. When the crowd roared, so did Rommel, spilling beer on his trousers. On the huge scoreboard, numbers were changed—a 5 became a 6—and Rommel understood that the score had become 6 to 2. He was beginning to master the role of baseball spectator. The thin beer took some getting used to, but it wasn't bad.

"What did Gomez say when asked to what did he attribute his success in baseball? Come *ahnnnn*, what . . . okay, he said, 'Clean livin' and a fast outfield.' Heh-heh."

"Ho-ho-ho," Rommel chuckled over the man's shoulder, and both fans turned startled expressions to the foreigner in the Charlie Chaplin hat.

A high tide of shadow filled the Polo Grounds, and the audience began to drift out of the stands. Rommel stayed until the final out. (He liked that clear-cut distinction, its air of permanence: "You're *outa* dere, ya bum ya!") There had been a flurry of action in the eighth inning (there was a nice term, *in*ning) when the Giants had filled all three bases, or bags (not points, after all), with two singles and a walk (stately designation). Ripple's long fly (lovely) and McCarthy's single brought in two runs (marvelous) to end the scoring. The Brave Bees had beaten the Giants, 7–4, in the only baseball game Erwin Rommel would ever see. He liked the determination with which each player tenaciously defended his own plot of ground, each man fighting on his own hook, and the wily offensive strategy of hits through unexpected corridors. He admired the sacrifice fly and the bunt. Hitler's well-known contempt for the mongrelization of America notwithstanding, Rommel liked the juxtaposition of national origins in names such as Ott, Lopez, Cuccinello, Whitehead, and Schumacher, and the storied DiMaggio he had heard tell of. There seemed to be an understated strength in that alliance, the best of many races brought together by sport.

Rommel himself was no team player. Athletic, trim and fit at forty-five, he was a cyclist, mountain climber, skier, and swimmer. His competition was Erwin Rommel. Yet he appreciated the competitive edge team sports gave a nation in industry, commerce, or war. America, he sensed, was a nation of team players.

He was in no hurry to leave the Polo Grounds, lingering for one last look at the diamond engraved on the grass floor. He followed the crowd out to the street and, without pausing to make a definite choice, got on a bus with the last of the fans. Glancing down the aisle for a seat, he received a mild shock. All the other people on the bus, including the driver, were Negroes. As he searched his pocket change for the nickel fare he asked the driver, "Excuse, please, this bus is . . . *special?*" Perhaps, he was thinking, from Virginia?

"You mean, charter?" the man replied in a rumbling bass. He tipped his cap back resignedly. "Naw, man, this is the Seventh Avenue bus, what you talkin' about?"

"Excuse, please," said Rommel. He found a seat beside a man with a small boy on his lap. The child, who wore a tiny Giants cap, gave Rommel a shy smile from under its bill. Rommel smiled back. The bus headed south for a few blocks, turned west on 155th Street and, after a few minutes, south on Seventh Avenue as the driver had promised. With his unerring sense of direction, Rommel relaxed. He had a feeling that his hotel was situated in line with this southwest course.

It was twilight. Neon lights bloomed like night flowers along a boulevard divided by islands of trees. On either side of Seventh Avenue Rommel observed a drab procession of apartment buildings, stores, cafes, pawnshops, pool parlors, and corner saloons. People aimlessly milled about on the sidewalks as though the sweltering buildings had been waiting for night to draw them out like a cool poultice. Every face was black. He was confused. It had been his impression that American Negroes lived exclusively in the South. Yet here they were in vast numbers, living in their own village inside the great city.

"*Bitte,*" he asked the man beside him, "what is this place?" The small boy looked at him solemnly under the long bill of his cap. The man slid his arm around the child.

"This is Harlem," he said.

A Dutch village for black people. America truly was a land of ironies.

Rommel had an irresistible impulse to walk through Harlem. At the next stop, 125th Street, he got off. He stood on the curb, awash in a confusion of sounds and smells—gasoline exhaust, food frying, a drifting current of musky perfume, a beery effervescence of laughter and a saxophone blaring from the open door of a bar. An elderly man—or was it a woman wearing a man's hat?—pushed a mobile lunch counter into position on the next corner, heating his/her wares—popcorn, hotdogs, roasted peanuts and yams—over a smoky kerosene lamp. As he strolled through the crowds of Negroes, he was aware that eyes followed him each step of the way. He remembered Hitler's snubbing of the American Olympian, Jesse Owens. Germans had been forced either to defend or ignore the action. Unwilling to involve himself, Rommel had chosen the latter course. Now, with hundreds of black eyes on him, he hoped no one could tell he was German.

When he reached 115th Street, he noticed that most of the people were female. Dressed in tight-fitting skirts and halters, they stared not in accusation but invitation. A young woman hovered at his elbow. He automatically tipped his hat to her. Her perfume surrounded him like overripe fruit. In her spike heels she was taller than he. She had an attractive, narrow face with lustrous lips, high cheekbones, and shining eyes with unusually prominent lashes. Large gold earrings dangled from her ears. Wrapped around her shoulders unexpectedly was a worn fox stole. The glass eyes of the fox seemed to wait with indifference for his reply. He understood that an offer had been made, but he procrastinated over doing something about it.

"Lookin' for sump'm special?" she said. Her voice was husky and wild like a pigeon cooing.

Sump'm special? Meaning—as the bus driver said—a charter?

"You a doll baby," she said. "Where you goin'?"

"To *meinem* hotel." His throat was dry.

"Where is it?"

"The Essex House," he said without thinking.

One should not reveal his address to a perfect stranger.

"I heard of it. How much it is a night?"

"*Bitte?*"

"How much it cost?"

"Seven dollars." They were strolling almost arm in arm. *What would Lucie make of this!*

"*My* place is just two dollar any way you like it all night long."

He lengthened his stride, and she stretched her long legs, matching him step for step. Her stole slipped from her shoulder and she flung it back, hips swinging, perfume exploding around them. He could hear her silk stockings sigh as her thighs brushed together. Her white teeth gleamed as she waved to people watching from windows. Rommel looked up and saw an entire family—father, mother with infant, children—all crowded into a single window, leaning into the night with slow-burning desperation.

"Where are you going?" He tried to change the subject. "On your way to work, perhaps?"

"Work? You kiddin', honey? Why doan you say sump'm sweet like, 'Now, where kin I git me a goodlookin' ho' on a nice night like this? Say, *here* one is! Lucky me.'" She smiled at him and paused to windowshop at a liquor store with barred window. While her back was turned Rommel slid his hand into his pocket and drew out his miniature German-English dictionary, riffling quickly through the pages and holding it up to the light from the store.

hoe [hou] 1. Hacke *f*; 2. hacken.

A farm implement? I thought she was a prostitute. She does not look like an agricultural worker, though she is sturdy enough.

She saw him glancing at her and raised her eyebrows.

He swung his gaze away from her shoulders and breasts. They continued to walk south along Seventh Avenue.

"Do you work in the fields?" he remarked and was amazed at her reaction. She squared off before him with feet spread apart and fists braced on her hips.

"I doan do it in no fields, man! God *damn*."

The fox head nodded accusingly as she strutted away. Two young girls playing cards on a stoop looked up from their game with interest. Rommel followed her with a neutral expression, watching her hips work under her skirt. She was waiting at the next corner but did not look at him until he spoke.

"I am seeking Central Park."

She regarded him with hip-shot exasperation. A boy whistling a merry tune sprang from a doorway to tap-dance in front of them with his palm outstretched. The woman swatted at the youth with the back of her hand and he danced out of their path.

"It three block thataway, but doan you go walkin' in there after dark. It ain't healthy." She knitted her eyebrows prettily. "Say, what fo' you come to The Market, you ain't int'rested in what's fo' sale?"

"What market is this?"

"You kiddin' me! You be *in* it, from hundred-tenth to hundred fifteenth. Say, where you from?"

He glanced around, to see if anyone was within earshot. "Germany," he said in a low voice.

"*Ger*-many? Oh, yeah, Yorkville, East Eighty-sixth—venal snitzers, sour krauts, and funny pipes. I seen it a few time. We doan git too many you peoples up to The Market. Doan know why that is. I 'preciate it if you spread the word down there. I got blond, red, brunette wigs, every kinda underwear, and a nice Victrola play Dixieland and Caruso. We *want* yo' bizness."

"I think," he blurted, "your people live in the American South."

"Who? My fam'ly?"

"Your people . . . your race."

"You mean the coloreds?" She cocked her head at a quizzical angle.

"Excuse?"

"Colored, goddamn!" She pointed at her face. "Comprendie?"

"Yes, I mean the 'coloreds.'"

Seeing his confused expression, she relaxed.

"Where you be gettin' yo information? My fam'ly go back three generation in Harlem." She held herself erect. "Wouldn' ketch none-a *me* down South, doll, unh-uh, no *way!*"

They had come to the end of the boulevard. Central Park

stretched before them, a lake of darkness with island chains of light cast by streetlamps.

"This be as far as I go, doll." She added hopefully, "Ain't got a cigarette, do you?" Rommel patted his empty breast pocket to signal that he did not smoke. He reached into his hip pocket, took out his wallet and extracted a dollar bill.

"Thanking you for your . . . directions," he said almost shyly. She shook her head and took a step backward.

"We jest took a walk together, doll!" she exclaimed. "Ain't no charge for *walkin'*. You jest tell all yo' frien's in Yorkville we wants they bizness, hear?" With a lazy grin and a flounce of her hips as if to show him what he was missing, she turned back to Seventh Avenue.

Rommel watched her go, sighed in relief, and entered the moist darkness of Central Park. His solitary footsteps echoed along the walkway. Lighted buildings rose like sparkling cliffs over the treetops. The great city hummed around him like a dynamo and yet he was alone. He was at peace with New York. He was almost sorry they had to leave for Gettysburg in the morning, but he could feel the pull of that hallowed ground where Lee would remain forever blind without Jeb Stuart; where Longstreet would forever chafe against his commander's doomed plan of attack.

Would Jackson and Forrest, on a German tour, have window-shopped along the Kurfürstendamm or taken the air at Tiergarten, or would they have made a beeline for Clausewitz's ancient battlefields?

Night insects droned above the muted roar of the city. A half moon was rising. Off to his left was a glimmering pond where frogs drunkenly hiccupped and belched, hiccupped and belched. Beyond a fringe of trees on his right was a wide playground where city lights vied with the moon for dominion in the shining grass. He felt rather than heard someone walking behind him.

Before he could turn around, a figure emerged from the shrubbery in the dark void between islands of streetlamps. Rommel slowed his pace. The man kept his hand in his coat pocket. As Rommel came within a few steps of him, the man flicked his wrist. There was a metallic click, and a silver blade glinted dully. The man moved into the center of the pathway, blocking him, while two more men appeared on either side.

All three men were black. There was a gamey odor of raw alcohol. The dynamo of the city continued to hum impersonally as if nothing out of the ordinary were happening. It seemed impossible for a man to be so alone with thousands of people seemingly within shouting distance.

"Gimme yo' wallet," the man said. He presented the razor in the time-conscious manner of a streetcar conductor. In the half-light the man's eyes were opaque, as devoid of feeling as a reptile's. Rommel felt the familiar surge of battlefield tension. Adrenaline burned away all emotion, leaving his mind clear and cold.

He let his senses grow, appraising possible avenues of escape. Beyond the man, who watched him hungrily for the first sign of fearful acquiescence, the intermittently lighted and dark sidewalk was empty. To the left, thick shrubbery prevented him from seeing the lay of the land. To the right, a gentle slope fell away into darkness, but he was aware of a curving street at the foot of the hill. The faint glow of headlights signaled the approach of a car around the curve.

"I ain't gonna ask agin." The man shook the razor for emphasis. Rommel noticed that he breathed in shallow pants, possibly asthmatic. The men on either side of him were taller than he. They tensed to seize his arms. He mentally rehearsed the English words before he spoke.

"I am with . . . park police," he said in a tone of natural authority. All three froze, as he had intended. "We hope to draw you out. It seem we succeed."

"Come off it!" said the man with the razor. His derisive laugh turned into a racking cough. "I *cut* you, man. Gimme yo' wallet!"

"I have only to lever . . . to—excuse, *Bitte*." Rommel reached into his pocket, and the men braced themselves. He held up his dictionary to show that it was not a weapon. "I find the correct word, just a moment." He flipped through the pages, turning the paperback book to the faint light of the nearest streetlamp. The men were confused by the dictionary. More unsettling was the white man's calmness. He even seemed to be enjoying himself in an unnatural way.

"Who you kiddin' wid dat *book!*" said the leader.

"Oh, yes. I have it, now," Rommel said eagerly. "I have only to *raise* my hand—*raise* (to lift or move upward)—and my patrol will come to the attack, you see. So, now, it is important that you understand. I am with special park patrol. They follow at a distance." He cut his eyes to one side and was rewarded by a glimpse of an automobile slowly coming around the curve in the street. The man with the razor followed his gaze. Rommel knew this was the moment. He emphatically pocketed the dictionary.

"Surrender your weapon!" This was a phrase he knew in six languages. "It will go . . . worser . . . if you be caught *mit* weapon." The razor dipped in the air, faltered, and slowly, reluctantly, was lowered.

"You ain't got—" the man argued. Rommel's arm shot up.

"*NOW!*" he boomed at the top of his lungs. The leader staggered drunkenly backward, into the shrubbery. His partners hesitated, arms held stiffly at their sides. Rommel sprinted down the slope, stumbling over rocks and unseen shrubs. He heard footsteps behind him. He staggered into the path of the oncoming automobile. It braked abruptly. The driver honked the horn in protest. It was a checker cab. The driver and a male passenger sat bewildered in the front seat.

"Wanna get killed?" the cabby yelled angrily.

"Was—robbing!" In his relief, Rommel's English failed him. "Bad mens." He pointed expressively at the top of the hill, where shadowy figures disappeared in the gloom. "Give ride?"

The cabby complained about taking two fares at the same time, robbery or no, but Rommel stood in the street negotiating until he was allowed inside the taxi. Sitting in the safety of the back seat, with the passenger staring warily at him as if *he* were a mugger, Rommel recalled Bedford Forrest's favorite surrender demand: ". . . in order to avoid the unnecessary and fruitless effusion of blood."

Especially when it is your own.

At the Essex House, an hour later, he sat in bed in his shorts and undershirt and wrote his first letter of the tour to his wife.

3 July 37

Dearest Lu,

We had splendid weather for our crossing. The food aboard ship was very good. I am afraid I put on a few extra pounds, but I will walk it off on the battlefields. Tell Manfred I saw the Statue of Liberty today and went to a baseball game.

America is not what I expected. One has a strange sensation of freedom here. It is not simply the "skyscrapers" and suspension bridges and parks and American customs. I cannot explain where it comes from, but it exists.

I seem to be having a language problem, even though I studied up on my English during the crossing. American dialect is as different from standard English as Swabian from Prussian.

I have discovered the plight of the Negro to be quite as bad as we have been told. They are even forced to turn to robbery or prostitution to survive. It never occurred to me that the unfortunate Jesse Owens incident at the Olympics in Berlin might be a source of personal embarrassment for me. Athletics mean more to Americans than we realize.

We leave for Gettysburg in the morning. That is a small town in Pennsylvania where a battle of the War Between the States took place. I am eager to get on with our business here, although I did enjoy taking some time off today to see the sights.

All for now.

As always,
Erwin

P.S. I am working to improve my English.

When his fellow officers returned from dinner, their four faces poking around the corner of the doorway with expressions ranging from amusement to annoyance, they found their lost sheep sleeping like a baby.

II

Mrs. Biggers cautiously opened the door to the O.O.D. files room. The handmade sign taped to the door read "G2-GOF," but it was still the Out of Date files room. The lieutenant could call it whatever he wanted. The ladies of the secretarial pool often referred to the long, dark room with rows upon rows of musty, unused filing cabinets as "Grant's Tomb." Reaching the end of the silent ranks of dust-covered cabinets, Mrs. Biggers turned up an aisle illuminated by a row of high windows. Lieutenant Speigner's "office" consisted of two long wooden tables set end to end in the aisle. Stacks of foreign-language newspapers, mostly German, covered both tables. The boys in the mailroom called them "Kraut confetti," and the lieutenant, who appeared each morning to collect his papers without a word, was "Lieutenant Sourkraut."

Speigner's face was buried, as usual, in a newspaper. When Mrs. Biggers loomed up beside him without warning, he lowered the paper with a snap that echoed off the ceiling like a pistol shot. The secretary pressed her hand against her ample bosom and breathed heavily.

"You startled me," she accused the young officer.

"*I* startled *you?*" He shook his head with a wry expression. "I've got to stop doing that."

"*You* have a phone call," she said in the same tone of indictment and turned on her crepe-soled heel. Speigner stared at his *Berliner Morgenpost* as if it held a clue to this unexpected summons. In the two years that he had belonged to the War Department General Staff, this was his first phone call. He was suspicious of the telephone, which allowed bad news to travel faster than nature intended. With a cunning born of mistrust he had resisted all efforts to install a phone in his filing-room office. He had used hit-and-run tactics against Physical Services with a 1919 requisition form, in quadrupli-cate, exhumed from an anonymous file. For two years this

26

archive had passed from one office to the next. Speigner confidently expected it to circulate until at least 1940, when his five-year tour of duty would be over. With tentative step and an expression of foreboding, Speigner followed the secretary into the main office, where heads turned for a glimpse of the reclusive lieutenant from Mississippi. Mrs. Biggers nodded peremptorily at a vacant desk, and Speigner eased into a swivel chair to await transfer of the call.

He tried not to stare at Brigitte, who tap-tap-tapped maddeningly on her typewriter as if there were no more important instrument in the world. He had never known a girl named Brigitte—not that he claimed to know her, although he had indulged in so many erotic fantasies about Brigitte that sometimes he thought of her as an ex-lover whom he had led to the outside limits of human passion with so many bizarre and wonderful acts, there was nothing left for them to say or do to each other. As her last name was McPherson, it presented a mysterious Gallic/Scottish combination that intrigued him. *Could it mean: 1) her mother was French; 2) her mother had a romantic temperament; 3) her father had once had a French mistress?* What should one make of French passion married to Scottish frankness? He shuddered at the possibilities.

Brigitte had just graduated from high school. Her position at G-2 as clerk/typist was her first job. She sat demurely at her machine, day after day, and gave rapt attention to each stencil she cut, whether a requisition for bathroom tissue and flyswatters or an important memo concerning the errant shipment of 300 unwanted rubber jungle ponchos. G.S.A. did not want them back, as to admit of their continued existence— quietly rotting on a quartermaster dock somewhere—was to accept blame for error. He had almost joked with her about it, to break the ice, with some line like, "Jungle ponchos and German Officers Files.—who needs 'em, ha-ha!" But she was the pet of the secretarial pool, and the tough old biddies circled their wagons whenever an officer, leering hopefully over the cookie plate at coffee break, made a run at her.

She was the vestal virgin of the typists' section, with dark, carefully combed bangs over a smooth forehead, long lashes lowered primly, oval-shaped face serene in mute concentration, her touch on the typewriter keys reverent. Yet the full breasts floated luminous and fresh under her high-collared blouse, waiting to be released.

Here was the pivot, the nub of it: he could wait. It was the
one thing in life he was good at. Practice had made him adept
at waiting. He wore the close-fitting vest of his virginity with a
diffidence which he had to believe bordered on the sublime.
After his twenty-third birthday, however, the vest had begun
to feel more like a hair shirt. As he waited for the phone to
ring, he extended his senses toward Brigitte like quivering
antennae. Was that a pulse, an electric signal, he detected?

*"She's a baby, she's seventeen for chrissakes, give her
time,"* the superego counseled.

*"She's a woman, with a woman's needs, ripe for the
taking!"* the libido crooned.

The phone rang.

"Lieutenant Maxwell Speigner," he answered.

"Speigner!" The voice was dictatorial. "About time we got
hold of you. Colonel Manchester at Staff Headquarters here.
Your report is overdue. Tell me about it."

In his two years at WDGS, Speigner had made out one
report. Although the officer in charge of his section, Major
Parham, had not requested it, Max had learned that such
documents were regularly submitted and often expected. He
had borrowed a sample report from Mrs. Biggers, had studied
it carefully to acquaint himself with style and usage, and after
several rough drafts had written of his progress since having
been assigned to G-2. With understated pride—and a con-
scious effort to keep the report concise—he had related the
facts of his German Officers Files, which listed members of the
High Command as well as outstanding cadre. Since the
National Socialist Party had come into power, the German
army had been greatly expanded. What few files G-2 possessed
were therefore badly out of date. The new GOF contained all
available news reports or publicity releases of promotions,
inspections, transfers, parades, and maneuvers, including
many photographs. The report concluded with an inventory:
two tables, a chair, twenty-seven filing cabinets transferred
from O.O.D. files, one lamp, subscriptions to thirty-two
German-language newspapers and journals using periodicals
budgets already functioning within their section. Not only had
no one subsequently mentioned the need for a second report,
but Major Parham had not acknowledged having received the
first, some fourteen months earlier. Max had naturally assumed no further reports would be required.

"Sir, what report?" he asked.

"Your *monthly* report, Lieutenant! Nobody seems to know just exactly what you're doing over there."

"Sir, Major Parham, my section chief, has a report on file."

"A report?"

"Yes sir."

"May I ask the date?"

"Yes sir. May 4, 1936."

"You've submitted only one report in a whole year?"

"Fourteen months, sir. No one requested further—"

"Do you know what this means, Lieutenant?"

No one at the War Department had ever addressed him in such an ominous tone, though he had lived in dread that someday it would happen. The tone implied a sphere of knowledge beyond his experience, a universe of regulations which hummed like a careless machine of whirring gears and slicing rotors that routinely maimed the innocent and the ignorant. It had been his policy to avoid the machine and to hope that it, in turn, would leave him alone. Now he knew that he had been living with false expectations.

"Not really, sir."

"Lieutenant, every army on this planet has a contingency for screwups like you. In Russia, they'd send you to Siberia. In France, to the Foreign Legion in the Sahara. In the U.S. of A. there is only one place for you to go. Lieutenant, your ass is headed for Mississippi."

The hollow pause that followed this remark became charged with comic relief. The "colonel's" voice had seemed somehow familiar all along. Max visualized a Cheshire-cat smile at the other end of the line. The rest of the face took shape above the grin.

"Major!" he cried with such relief that secretaries turned to stare.

"So you haven't forgotten, m'boy."

Max heard melancholy in the bluff tone. A memory flashed before him. Major Shoemaker faced him across an antique desk in the antebellum ROTC building at Ole Miss. The unhappy misfit from Indiana was running away from the magnolia conspiracy of Southern gents and belles. He wanted to give up his scholarship and go back to the steel mills of Fort

Wayne, which had been good enough for his father and grandfather before him. The major had let the cadet sit in silence for an unbearably long time before he spoke. "There is no way I will let you leave Mis'ippi, alive, without a commission." Max had not forgotten.

"What are you doing in D.C., Major?"

"I'm calling from Mis'ippi, town of Oxford, county of Lafayette. But I ought to ask the same of you. I had a devil of a time tracking you down. I thought your assignment to the Army Language School came through?"

"The great white father of personnel decreed that a German language specialist was needed at G-2. So here I am."

"And since nobody at G-2 asked for you, they don't know what to do with you?"

"Right. But I try to make myself useful just the same." Max began to tell his former professor about his G.O.F. system, but Shoemaker broke in at the earliest opportunity.

"Sounds great, m'boy, good for you. Now, I'm calling to talk you into flying down here this weekend. We got some German military coming in here. Colonel Adler in Jackson—he's ranking regular army in the Mis'ippi military district—asked me if I could line up an interpreter. The Huns don't speak good English."

"Germans? In Mississippi?" Max's interest was kindled. "What for?"

"Nathan B. Forrest, of course. What else has Mis'ippi got? The German Embassy told Adler they were touring Civil War battlefields . . ."

"The German Embassy called?"

"Yeah, they got Adler's name from the War Department. Wanted to make sure we'd have a delegation waiting to receive their people according to standard protocol and all."

"The embassy phoned," Max mused, possibilities rampant in his mind: Jodl, Guderian, Keitel? "Do you have any names?"

Shoemaker chuckled. "I knew we could count on you. I took the liberty of making your plane reservation, D.C. to Memphis, Friday."

"Major, I can't—"

"It's $28.50, round-trip fare. We'll reimburse you, of course. It's coming out of the Christmas party kitty. The cadets will have to spike their own punch next year."

"What about Eieschied?" Max's former German professor at the University of Mississippi seemed a logical choice for the temporary job of interpreter.

"Ahshad is gone. Fired."

"What for?"

"Nobody signed up for his classes. Had to happen sooner or later. You were the only student in ten years who could keep up with Ahshad's curriculum. After you graduated, the language department didn't have anything for Ahshad to do."

"Poor Eieschied." Speigner remembered indecipherable chalk marks on the blackboard, round shoulders bespeckled with a shroud of dandruff, a fragile, thin-haired head, and burning eyes behind rimless spectacles.

"We need you to talk that Deutsch for us, m'boy. How 'bout it?"

For a year and a half Speigner had lived inside the pages of the *Leipziger Volkszeitung*, *Bild Berlin*, and *Westdeutsche Zeitung*. Five days a week, every week, he had clipped, pasted, catalogued, and categorized the inexorable rise of the *Wehrmacht—Panzertruppen*, *S.S.*, *Luftwaffe*, *Pioniere*, *Nachrichtentruppen*, *Infanterie*. He had traced careers from commands on the company level to regiment, battalion, brigade, division and army. He had discovered patterns of leadership, the conservatives and the adventurers, pets and whipping boys. He had watched single careers garner fat files of clippings unto themselves alone, then vanish into thin air. He knew who wore Knight's Cross, Crossed Swords, Iron Cross and *Pour le Mérite*, the "Blue Max." Yet he had never met a German soldier face to face.

"It would be nice to see Mississippi again," he said.

"Good for you! Adler has sent a request to your company exec, through channels. I'll phone Thursday to verify your arrival time. It will be mighty fine to have you down here again. Max, I appreciate it."

"I'll do my best," Speigner said.

"You always did, m'boy."

You wouldn't let me do otherwise.

Max hung up, turning his mind toward the jewel-like campus set in the hills of northern Mississippi and the man responsible for the Dixiefication of Speigner. In Shoemaker's military history class, the roll call itself was imbued with the romance of the Confederacy: "Wilburn?" the major would say, glancing up from his roll book. "Of the Okolona Wilburns? Who was your great-grandfather, boy? I thought so! *Captain* Able Wilburn, wasn't it? Of the 18th Mississippi under General Stephen D. Lee. Big shoes to fill. You stand tall, boy." Shoemaker customarily would begin to digress about his favorite subject, Nathan Bedford Forrest, five minutes into his lecture. A superb storyteller, acting out each role in pantomime, the major sometimes seemed to be the "Wizard of the Saddle" himself, wearing olive drab in place of butternut gray, standing before the amused or enrapt or sleepy Ole Miss cadets.

Reading about Forrest, Speigner's own impression was that, like most men born to lead desperate battles, war was the best thing that could have happened to him. A self-educated planter, Forrest had devoted his energies before the war to slave trading and raising cotton on Mud Island in the Mississippi River. To Max the prewar Forrest was like a grenade wrapped in a gauzy cocoon. It was not the god who enthralled Speigner so much as the priest.

Every moment spent with Shoemaker had been an exercise in the imagination. The professor would call a cadet to the front of the class to act out a cowardly attack on General Forrest by an embittered Confederate lieutenant. The cadet had his hand stuffed into his coat pocket to illustrate the pistol fired at close range from concealment. The major demonstrated the path of the ball, which bounced off hipbone and looped around inside Forrest's back, severely wounding him. Then, gripping the embarrassed cadet against him with one hand, Shoemaker pretended to open a pocketknife with his teeth and repeatedly stab the would-be assassin. The class roared at the look of terror, not so pantomimed as real, on the cadet/villain's face as Shoemaker enthusiastically gutted him with a make-believe knife.

When the professor took his tactics class on a tour of nearby Brice's Crossroads, site of Forrest's greatest victory, his entourage swelled to more than a hundred followers. For students, teachers and townspeople as well, the annual excursion had become a local tradition. The crowd faithfully trooped up and down the somnolent farmland behind the shouting, gesticulating professor, who led them to glorious victory, year after year. Max remembered standing among that group beside the rotted remnants of the fateful wooden bridge and listening to Shoemaker recount the carnage of a hot summer's day.

"I'm gonna let you boys in on a little secret," he would say, pausing for effect. "War is not some game grown-ups play for fun. It's a man-eater. Where boys like you get to be dead long before their day. You weren't born in time for the Great War in France, but you've read about it in books and magazines and you think it was a fine and noble adventure, but I hope you never have to fight another war like it!" Again he paused. "If you do, remember that you heard it here at Brice's bridge from your old professor: war is a place that keeps three types of fellows—the heroes, the careless, and the unlucky. Which type are you?"

The crusty major had seemed a reincarnation of Forrest, forced to shun modesty for the sake of his audience. What Cadet Speigner had admired, had thirstily swallowed on the banks of Tishomingo Creek, was more than examples of a nineteenth-century general's cunning. Shoemaker spoke to his incipient respect for the human imagination.

"Major P wants to see you."

Max looked up into Mrs. Biggers' moon-shaped face. The secretary wore a characteristic expression of secret satisfaction, as if she possessed facts beyond nearly everybody's comprehension. She escorted him to the section leader's closed door, where she knocked with a little flourish, cocked her head to listen for the muted consent and ushered Max inside.

The major, to whom Speigner had spoken three times during the preceding year, was engrossed in paperwork. Parham had excellent posture. He was athletic, clean-featured, aristocratic. He glanced up at Max, nodded, then returned his eyes to his desk, sparing them both the awkwardness of prolonged eye contact.

"Nice to see you, Lieutenant. How are things going? Did the storage space work out okay for you? Have everything you need?"

"Fine, sir." Max appreciated that not much was expected of him.

"It appears that your talents are needed in . . . uh . . . Mississippi. Visiting dignitaries—under the aegis of the

German Embassy. They need an interpreter, and you were specifically requested. We're going to have to loan you out over the weekend, Lieutenant." Parham smiled genially in the direction of Max's right shoulder. He gave an impression of relief.

"Thank you, sir." For the first time since he had been at G-2, Speigner wanted attention. "Would you care to inspect my files before I go, sir?"

Parham fidgeted. "Perhaps after you return from this assignment."

"I can tell you which members of the High Command were Franco's guests on the Riviera last week!"

"That's very interesting. This request indicates you will be needed over the weekend, but I suggest that you take as much time as you require. There's no problem at this end."

"I believe I can prove that Jodl is in disfavor with the Führer currently."

"Mrs. Biggers will take care of the papers. I've already signed the order."

"News of recent maneuvers indicates increased coordination between the Luftwaffe and Panzer divisions."

"Just check with Mrs. Biggers." Parham gave Max a flat stare.

Max drew himself erect and resorted to military courtesy.

"Sir, I respectfully request that you inspect my files."

"Oh, all right," Parham said peevishly. "Five minutes is all I can spare!"

All the secretaries except Brigitte looked up in surprise at the reclusive lieutenant leading the section chief to his lair. Speigner hoped that Brigitte stared at him after he passed. The back of his neck grew warm. Parham stopped at the door and pointed to the hand-lettered sign.

"What's *gof?*" he asked skeptically.

"It's not meant to be an acronym," Max explained. "G.O.F. stands for German Officers Files. It's not official, however. I would welcome any suggestion you'd care to—"

"Let's get on with it," said Parham.

Speigner held the door open. The major entered the O.O.D. files room with precision, as if reluctant to disturb the dust of skeletons. Speigner eagerly led the way between the rows of filing cabinets. Parham sniffed the air. He might have been entering a combat zone in another century. He stared dubiously at the lonely tables set end to end under the two windows, the empty chairs, the single table lamp with its extension cord snaking along the baseboards. Max watched Parham's eyes trace its progress as it wound around furnace registers, moldings and corners and disappeared beyond the cabinets, seeking power like a vine climbing a tree for sunlight.

"Sir, the German Officers Files inventory," Max said proudly, "includes two tables, two chairs—I recently acquired this one from the duty room downstairs; they were going to throw it out, but all it needed was a brace on that leg—one lamp, twenty-seven filing cabinets—"

"Tell me about the files," Parham interrupted, in case this recital of inventory was the prelude to a request for a budget increase. Speigner considered where to begin. He had been prepared to recount the history of the G.O.F. from the day he had discovered the cranny behind the cabinets and marveled at the amount of illumination provided by the two windows, to the hours of salvaging used manila folders or rusted paper clips, to the redirection of periodical subscriptions, canceling two-score unread magazines such as *The American Rifle* or *Scouts International* and replacing them with nearly three dozen German-language newspapers and journals—all at no extra cost. Instead, he pointed to the headings taped to each filing cabinet drawer, reading them aloud and drawing out sample files for Parham to examine:

File I: "Possibility of War with Germany"

   Sub-file I-A: "Economic Conditions"
          I-B: "Pattern of Conquest by
             Intimidation"

File II: "German Strategy"

   Sub-file II-A: "Franco-Prussian War"
           II-B: "Great War"
           II-C: "Traditional German Allies"
           II-D: "Maneuvers & War Games"

File III: "Chain of Command"

Sub-file III-A: "Adolf Hitler"
　　　　III-B: "General Staff"
　　　　III-C: "Individual Officers Files"

File IV: "War Materiel"

Sub-file IV-A: "Weaponry & Armament"
　　　　IV-B: "Natural Resources"
　　　　IV-C: "Heavy Industry"
　　　　IV-D: "Science & Technology"

"Of course, the individual officers files take up most of the space," Max concluded. "I guess I'm more interested in individuals than in the big picture. I have to start with the trees to see the forest."

Parham was overwhelmed by the evidence of unbidden labor in his department, which put one in mind of a dry pump running white-hot in the desert.

"You've certainly been busy," he said.

"Thank you, sir." Max cast a glad eye over his station. He tried to see it through the unbiased eyes of his commanding officer. The G.O.F. might not be much, at this point, but it was *his*. "What do you think, sir?"

"Unreal," Parham whispered.

"Sir, in the event that the U.S. should be at war with Germany . . ."

"Yes, well, I'll keep your files in mind."

"Yes sir, thank you, sir." Speigner assumed a deferential pose, hands clasped before him. "I was wondering about the possibility of augmenting—"

"We're in the process of tightening our operation," Parham cut in briskly, "as you may or may not be aware. But to put your mind at rest, I will recommend that you continue your—activities, maintaining your unofficial status, naturally, and perhaps, if the need ever arises . . ."

"*When*, sir!"

". . . *if* and when," Parham amended, "we will of course review your system for budget eligibility." His body assumed the rigidity of a pencil, his face as inscrutable as a typewriter.

"Thank you, sir," Max said.

"You've done a fine job," the major contended, "and you deserve a nice, long trip down to—where was it?"

A remote outpost of civilization, like Kyzyl or Pango-pango.

"Mississippi, sir."

They went into the main office. Mrs. Biggers presented the temporary leave forms for Max to sign, in quadruplicate. She also had a package for him.

"Somebody unwrapped this by mistake in the mailroom," she said guardedly. "It was already open when it reached my desk." He reached for the brown paper bundle, but Mrs. Biggers was too quick for him. "It's just a book. *Infantry in Grief,* by some guy named Rommel."

III

Released from the railroad crossings of Harrisburg, the train streaked through the green hills, a black-and-silver arrow. During the six-hour trip from New York, Rommel watched America unfold in its unending variety, from the skyscrapers of Manhattan to the smokestacks of Allentown to these Pennsylvania Dutch farms partitioning the land in emerald symmetry. He marveled at this magnificent heartland and wondered at people who could take such dimensions for granted. He looked again at the faces in the crowded day coach. The five Germans, dignified in their dark suits, collars tacked neatly into place by gold tiepins, were a study in contrast with the boisterous American travelers. Black and white and yellow, Irish and African, Polish and Portuguese, Italian and Chinese, their voices rose and fell, laughing, making jokes, calling for Coca-Colas. A black family—a thin, nervous husband and a fat, cheerful wife with an indeterminate number of young children, restless as puppies—were eating a lunch of fried chicken from greasy paper sacks. The fecund aromas of chicken, the mother's heavy perfume, and the children's coltish smell of perspiration and jubilation permeated the coach.

"*Es ist zum Ersticken hier.*" Schörner's fastidious observation about the closeness of their quarters went unnoticed by the multi-lingual group of travelers. Over his *Wall Street Journal* Walther shared a disapproving nod with Ferdinand. Rommel suspected that the munitions specialist was scanning industrial news for an overview of the U.S. economy. Each to his own, he thought, and inhaled the earthy odors of America.

The conductor, dodging children in the aisle, announced, "Next stop, Gettysburg!" Rommel envisioned a series of ridges shaped like a fishhook, overlooking a wide valley. He thought of the land as sleeping, awakening to the tramp of soldiers' feet and the thunder of their caissons. He thought of two great armies creeping like blue and gray caterpillars across the hills and blundering into each other; the newly appointed Union commander, George Meade, vacillating about withdrawing right up to the moment of attack; Lee blind without his chief scout, Jeb Stuart, who was searching frantically for his commander in Maryland; and, finally, the machinery of destiny trucking men into position among boulder-strewn hills, hurling strangers into mortal intimacy with the capriciousness of summer lightning.

Gettysburg.

The train ground to a halt at Gettysburg Station. Rommel could see a line of automobiles inching forward, bumper to bumper, in the tree-shaded streets of the town. He leaned across the aisle toward a young man who had dozed for the past hour but who now was wide awake and staring intently at the commotion in the town.

"Please, you tellen me . . . why so much auto-mobilen?" he asked.

"On the Fourth? Are you kidding? It's the reenactment!" the young man exclaimed, reluctant to take his eyes away from the window. Sensing Rommel's puzzlement, he added politely, "The battle is being reenacted today by historical groups. It's going to be quite a show."

Rommel sat up in his seat with a pleasant buzz of anticipation. He was the first of the officers to step off the train, valises in either hand. Above the sightseers crowding the small station platform, the imposing figure of General Hans Boetticher, who wore a civilian suit of the same cut and color as a Wehrmacht uniform, stood out like a blue spruce among boxwoods. The military attaché at the German Embassy in Washington hurried forward to greet them. Boetticher was an old guard from the spike-helmeted days of Bismarck. He had not lost influence in the modern Wehrmacht, however. The High Command itself had bowed to the attaché's memos exalting the virtues of a U.S. battlefield tour. Rommel smiled at blue eyes sparkling above a white walrus mustache. Boetticher was in a frenzy of expectation, barely pausing for amenities before he led them to a black limousine. A chauffeur helped stow their bags in the trunk.

"*Sie sind zur rechten Zeit hier.*" Boetticher exclaimed in a youthful voice. The embassy limo smoothly joined the traffic winding through Gettysburg. "Your timing is impeccable. It is the perfect day to be here. We will go to the far end of Seminary Ridge and follow each wave of attack back this way, from the wheatfield to Cemetery Hill." The attaché took it for granted that each of them had studied the battle, although Rommel alone had done the reading prescribed in Boetticher's voluminous memos.

"We are to be on the Confederate side, Herr General?" he asked wryly. The attaché turned in the front seat, nodding his appreciation.

"The view is better from that side," he said. "Otherwise, it is every man for himself!"

As the limo reached the open spaces of the national park area, Rommel was enthralled at the sight of gray-backed soldiers clustered among the trees of Seminary Ridge. They would have been Pickett's brigade, hiding from the blistering sun but scorched anyway by the hot hours of waiting to cross the valley into the guns of Cemetery Hill. Behind the gray line, like a reserve force arrayed in uniforms of many hues, were thousands of spectators resting on their picnic blankets or lounging under holiday canopies: men, women, children, dogs, vendors, green-shirted park rangers, battle "directors" with red armbands and megaphones, camera crews mounting their equipment on camouflaged platforms among the trees.

Rommel was surprised to feel butterflies in his stomach and a strange sense of *déjà vu*, as though he were squatting on his heels among the trees, sweating under the weight of full

combat kit, cartridge box and grenades clipped to his belt,
joking with his men to steady his own nerves. He dreaded
Lee's stubborn decision to engage the enemy at all costs. It was
a nightmare Rommel shared with all field commanders: a
wasteful general order based not on fact but desire to which
the blood of one's men was in arrears. The chauffeur parked the
limo on the side of the park road overlooking the Wheat Field
and Devil's Den, and Rommel got out of the car, imagining that
he could hear Longstreet arguing with Lee.

"*General, we are in a strong position.*" *Under the bushy
eyebrows, Longstreet's eyes were somber, unblinking.* "*All we
need do is maneuver around their left and interpose our army
between the Federals and Washington. Meade will have to
attack us.*"

Lee dropped his gaze and listened to faraway sounds. The
two armies growled at each other with the bass voices of
artillery. Then he looked at Longstreet. Lee had an abiding
respect and affection for the burly forty-two-year-old Geor-
gian whom the men called "Old Pete," but the two generals
were adamantly opposed on the issue of whether to attack
here, at Gettysburg.

"No," Lee said at last. "The enemy is there." He thrust a
gloved hand toward Cemetery Ridge. "And I am going to
attack him there."

"General," Longstreet persisted. "He wishes us to attack
him. To my mind, that is the best of reasons not to do so."

"We will whip them a unit at a time," Lee said firmly. "We
attack from south to north, in echelon. I will whip the enemy
or he will whip me."

The two men locked wills in a brief, fierce struggle. Then
Longstreet turned away and got on his horse.

Boetticher led the five officers to a roped-off area. Across a
sloping valley they could see the blue-clad soldiers behind
fencerows and under trees. On their side of the hill, men in
gray were being formed into line. A man on a horse shouted
directions through a megaphone, aiming it left and right.

"The Union brigade took position on the left," Boetticher
lectured, "and advanced to line from Peach Orchard to Devil's
Den, there. Between four and five o'clock, they were attacked
by Robertson's and Benning's brigades and were pushed back
after prolonged fighting . . ."

None of the German officers noticed Rommel mingle with the tourists thronging the battlefield. He did not wish to seem disrespectful to his host, but the reenactment was about to begin and he did not want to miss the opening moments. Already a familiar lull had fallen over the valley.

He went among the spectators waiting in the shade of the trees. On a blanket a young mother changed a crying infant's diapers. Children crowded around a cold-drink stand. A man opened the door of a portable urinal, releasing a sharp stench. On vendors' tables were swords, muskets, pewter mugs, belt buckles, buttons, wooden racks of cartridges and minié balls, insignia of all kinds. Rommel picked up a powder horn with "Made in Italy" stamped on the bottom. He wandered through a Confederate encampment with authentic-looking tents and blankets and a strong smell of horse manure. He overheard a sweating Confederate private report to the officer with the megaphone:

"Fifteenth Alabama just collapsed in the heat and won't get up. They want to be the first casualties down in the ditch where the trees are."

"I don't care what they want," the man bellowed. "They got five minutes to get on line."

The private ran to report these instructions, and after a few minutes Rommel saw a company of red-faced men in gray wool tunics form up and march into the valley, singing:

> *"Oh, little Liza, little Liza Jane,*
> *Oh, little Liza, little Liza Jane!"*

A deep silence took hold. The spectators grew still. A small boy broke the spell when he cried, "I gotta pee, Mommy." Then the quiet returned. Rommel was aware of short motions—a hand waving gnats away, a meadowlark flitting from one twig to the next. Then voices rose in a yelping cry. A cloud of smoke erupted from a thicket. The clatter of muskets echoed up the hill. Blue and gray lines came together.

Brother against brother. Classmates from West Point on opposing sides. The Great War cemented the two halves of this nation back together.

Rommel began to move toward the battle. Where the rope crossed a ravine, he ducked under it and walked down the gulley toward Devil's Den. He passed near the overhanging boulders and said to himself, "It is the work of the devil, all right." He squatted on his heels and watched the gray line break into a stumbling charge and overrun the blue. A swollen brook surging through the boulders could be heard above the hollow crack of muskets. The acrid smell of black powder was intoxicating. He slipped into the brush and hurried to stay abreast of the Confederate charge.

Out of the corner of his eye he saw a green-shirted figure dodge between the trees. He ducked under a leafy branch and saw two small boys crawling ahead of him, their faces close to the ground like hounds on a scent. One of them pounced in discovery, and Rommel saw him display to his friend an empty shell casing.

"This is a restricted area, sir."

Rommel was amazed that he had not heard the ranger behind him. He looked up respectfully at a bony, long-jawed face. It was not often that he was outflanked.

"We got rules, sir," the man repeated. Rommel stood, his arms hanging limply at his sides.

"I come from Germany," he began in confusion.

"I'm from Yorktown," said the ranger, formal under the trees. "But this is still a restricted—" A ripping volley of musketry distracted him. The two men peered with equal interest into the valley where mock armies clashed. Tiny blue and gray figures struggled and fell with rifles like toothpicks.

"Simulating hand-to-hand," the ranger remarked. In the man's voice and manner Rommel discerned an enthusiast. He did not know the word *simulating*, but *hand-to-hand* was an expression he knew in seven languages.

"They say it was like Indian fighting down there, every man for hisself," the ranger said. "Privates shouting orders like they was generals. You can see 'em getting into it down there, see? On that patch of cleared ground? Mixing it up pretty good. They can get rough down there, y'know. Some of these guys—jeez, there are some crazies out there—drop popcorn kernels in with their wadding, or wood chips. Keep your head down when they pop off at close range! Guy can lose an eye out there. They ain't all playin' make-believe, y'know. Sometimes those reenactment units come up from Virginia with jugs and fire in their furnace, and the hand-to-hand gets rowdy. Run up to a guy in another color uniform and yell, 'All right, easy does it, I'm gonna pretend to swipe you with my rifle butt . . .' And *Whap!* He cold-cocks you." The ranger dug in his pocket and brought out a pouch of tobacco.

"You fought in the Great War?" Rommel asked.

"Fourth Marines," the ranger said. "At the Marne— Belleau Wood, Château-Thierry. How about you?"

"I fought in France, but I was not at the Marne."

The ranger held out his tobacco pouch. Rommel stared into it suspiciously.

"Same as baseballers?" he asked.

"Yeah, same as baseballers. You chew over there?"

Rommel shook his head. His fingers reached into the pouch.

"Whoa, not that much. Choke to death on that. That's about right. Chew it easy."

He watched the ranger tuck tobacco into his mouth and did likewise. The texture was smooth and pleasant. His eyes moistened at the sting of the juice.

"It's a sweet one," said the ranger. "Don't swaller none of the juice."

Rommel blinked as he chewed. The ranger pointed into the valley.

"They get carried away, but they wouldn't be out there if they didn't love it."

If he would share his tobacco, he does not mean to arrest me for trespassing.

"Name's Winfield Dowling." The ranger extended his hand. Rommel clicked his heels together.

"Erwin—Rilke," he said, resenting *Oberkommando Wehrmacht*.

"Rebels are past Devil's Den." Dowling indicated the gray line moving toward the rocky crest of a ridge on the east side of the valley. "They'll be going for Little Round Top next. See it sticking out, there? See 'em forming up, at the base of the hill?" Rommel thought of the awful joy of assault, of citizen soldiers—farmers, blacksmiths, schoolteachers—poised at the greatest moment of their lives. He spat as he had seen the ranger do and wiped brown juice from his chin.

"We must go . . . close," he said.

"Not supposed to."

"It is holiday, no?"

Dowling glanced in the direction of the main body of tourists, then raised his shoulders and let responsibility slide.

"There's an old trail through there," he said, "to Round Top." Chewing and spitting like brothers, they tramped through dusty woods dappled by sun and shadow. "I may not have told you," the ranger resumed speaking with stiff pride. "I'm related to Winfield Scott Hancock, who commanded the Union side here. He was my grandmother's uncle, which makes him my great . . . great-great—is it two or three greats? Anyways, we're kin."

Rommel's tongue tingled from the strong tobacco juice. He discovered it was nearly impossible not to swallow some of it.

"When the Confederates first attacked the ridge, up here on Round Top—just ahead of us—there were no Federal troops in position to oppose them," Dowling said as they hiked along. Rommel's head was bent in concentration. "But it was a different matter when they got to Little Round Top. . . ."

From the conical hill with its jutting crown of rocky ledges, Brigadier General G. K. Warren looked over the valley. Little Round Top had been recently cleared of timber and afforded a brilliant prospect of the heavy fighting in Devil's Den less than a half mile to the west. Warren, thirty-three years old, a slender New Yorker with a drooping mustache and a fashionable dark tuft of chin beard beneath his lower lip, frowned angrily as he wondered what jackass had allowed this tactically important hill, as well as the one just south of it, to go undefended. If the Rebels occupied this high ground they could enfilade the entire Union line with a few rifled guns.

"I want signalmen on the crest, in plain sight of the enemy, to keep their flags busy. I want the Rebs to think we've got a staff headquarters up here."

The army's chief engineer then sent a courier at a gallop to notify Meade of the danger to his left flank. While Warren waited for reinforcements, he directed the difficult ascent, by hand, of two artillery pieces to the rocky summit. Soon, four regiments—one each from Pennsylvania, New York, Maine, and Michigan—came trotting at the double-quick up the wooded hill. The brigadier and his staff had barely positioned these soldiers along the rocky ledge when gray uniforms could

*be seen creeping up through the woods, low to the ground like
a great flock of feeding birds.*

Rommel nodded to himself. The Confederates had delayed their flank attack too long, then attacked with insufficient
force to carry the high ground. *N. B. Forrest would have
badgered a general to let him attack and come up blazing in
the Union rear.* Stumbling over a log, he swallowed more
tobacco juice. Dowling continued his story.

*"Hold fire until they get close!" Warren shouted to his
lieutenants, who scurried off to pass the order.*

*The Confederate line had ascended about two thirds of
the way up the hill when Warren's men fired together, a
terrifying volley of muskets along with canister from the two
cannon. The gray line rolled back under the single blast, the
cries of their wounded distinct in the long pause before their
answering fire. The Rebels gathered for another desperate,
uphill charge.*

*"Don't yield an inch!" a young Union colonel shouted to
his men and fell dead with a bullet through the heart. The
Confederate surge, impelled by the hysterical keening of their
battle cry, broke like raging surf on the hillcrest, and the
Federal line ebbed and flowed against it, leaving tidal pools of
blood in the rocks. The gray line washed back down the slope
under sporadic fire from muskets which barked like seals
among the white boulders.*

Clapping and cheers broke out in the woods to his right,
and Rommel glanced irritably toward the source of this
intrusion. Concentrating on Dowling's narrative, the mock-
battle action ahead through the trees, the natural obstacles in
their path, and the tobacco juice seeping like rust from an iron
spigot through his system, he had not noticed the army of
spectators grouped on this side of the valley. Now he saw that
they were everywhere, perched on banks and outcroppings,
even in the crotches of trees. The two men were approaching
the base of Little Round Top where the reenactment had
ended, and men of both sides were mingling up and down the
hill, comparing bruises and congratulating one another for
their part in the show.

Rommel felt sick. He covertly ditched his black cud under
a dogwood tree, but the juice he had swallowed had formed a
hard lump in his stomach. He reminded himself that in France

he had fought for weeks with bowels raging, unable to eat anything but bread and water.

"Climb to the top!" he doggedly suggested. Dowling looked at his companion's greenish complexion and shook his head with a grin.

"This is as far as I go. It's back to work now. I hope the chew didn't get the best of you." They shook hands.

"Ah . . . *danke*," Rommel said. "*Ich* enjoy—" He tasted bile and left off his hypocritical affirmation of the chew. "I would like . . . if it not is re-structured?" He pointed at the steep face of Little Round Top.

"Naw, it ain't restricted now," said the ranger affably. "This is 1937, and we're all King of the Mountain! So long."

Through his binoculars, Boetticher saw a familiar figure climbing the face of Little Round Top a mile away. A man in a dark suit and a homburg leaped from boulder to boulder like a mountain goat. "*Draufgängerisch!*" Boetticher said. "A daredevil. What was it they said about Rommel at the Italian front? 'Where Rommel is, the front is'?" He passed his glasses to Schörner for confirmation of the sighting.

The stones breaking under his hands gave Rommel a feeling of satisfaction, no matter how sharp or treacherous. He had not attempted to scale a steep face since Monte Mataiur, in 1917, though this one was child's play by comparison. Pebbles and grit sifted down on the uniformed actors who stood, blue and gray together, at the base of the low, rocky bluff and stared up at the one-man assault on Little Round Top. Rommel climbed the final 25 feet hand over hand—feeling with sure instinct through the soles of his cordovan shoes for crevices to support his weight; his fingers curved into claws like grappling hooks. His shirt was wet against his back, but the nausea from the tobacco juice was gone, burned away by adrenaline. His head was clear and he experienced a deep calm. All that was lacking was live ammunition in the weapons of the blue and gray soldiers standing above. Even so, they had become a tactical objective against which he could pit his skills. He throbbed with the heat radiating from the stone. Unaware that a hush had fallen over the twin armies of actors and spectators, he crept up the last boulder and stood sweating, breathing deeply, looking over the wild, boulder-strewn valley as if it belonged to him. A low cheer rippled through the audience of costumed soldiers and people flocked on the adjacent ridge. The applause meant no more to Rommel than the chirping of feeding birds. By placing himself at hazard on the rocky bluff, he had become one with the valley where smoke still hung in blue patches. He strained across the void to meet the courageous dead and to salute them.

"It's a good thing the Johnny Rebs didn't have you on their side!"

"Mein Gott!" Rommel started, his head snapping back at the sight of a young Union lieutenant with muttonchop whiskers and a waxed mustache. For an instant it seemed as if a grinning nineteenth-century ghost had come to recruit him.

"I mean," the young actor added, "a man who can climb like that oughta be on the winning side!"

"Meinst du . . . which side do you mean?" said Rommel.

Cloaked by a majestic silence, Rommel stood alone on the Mall and gazed up at the Washington Monument. The shining obelisk framed against the sky reflected something in his soul. He thrilled to this marriage of technology and honor in the name of a great general. The Mall was deserted after midnight except for a few groundskeepers stabbing at debris with their pikes. The symmetry of the globed streetlamps seemed to exist for his eyes only.

When they had arrived in Washington, Rommel had not been ready to retire with his companions at their hotel on New York Avenue. America's secret places were waiting. His stomach growled, reminding him that he had not been able so much as to look at the she-crab soup served at a restaurant in Chevy Chase. He had not told his companions about chewing tobacco.

It had not been easy to get away from the group again, but something made him restless. He had slipped away and walked to Pennsylvania Avenue, soon drawn to the spotlighted White House where he clung to the iron fence like any other gawking tourist. The guards had watched him for a moment, then relaxed their vigilance. No one in memory had climbed the White House fences wearing a homburg.

Rommel's footsteps echoed on the empty sidewalk, his face private except for the flash of an occasional taxi's lights.

With his eyes fixed on the white dome of the Capitol, he passed the massive buildings lining the green expanse of the Mall. Turning from the Washington Monument, he saw reflected in the long pool the shimmering Doric columns of the Lincoln Memorial. He began to walk quickly toward the marble temple, drawn toward it by the sight of a great stone face which seemed to move into view as he approached from the side. He took the Memorial steps two at a time, the sound of his running feet absorbed by a glassy silence as smooth as marble. The face looked down at him, gentle, strong and sad. Rommel tilted back his homburg so he could study the statue. In the deep-set eyes he read conviction, in the forehead he read justice, in the wide mouth he saw compassion. It was a face that made a soldier feel like saluting.

Rommel moved to a huge brass tablet on one wall of the building. He began to read the words of the Gettysburg Address. At first his lips moved silently, shaping the unfamiliar English syllables; then he spoke out loud. It was easier to understand if he could hear the words. He was alone with the statue and he did not think Lincoln would mind.

"Four score and seven years ago our fathers brought forth, upon this continent, a new nation, conceived in Liberty, and dedicated to the pro . . . the pro . . ." Rommel faltered.

"Proposition," said a clear voice.

Rommel whirled, hands ready as though to ward off attack. He relaxed when he saw that the speaker was much smaller than he. Rommel guessed the boy's age at about twelve, but the face could have been sixty. It was small, brown and wizened, with a low forehead, a nose thin at the bridge but spreading like the Nile Delta at the nostrils above lips that were thick and protruding. The eyes were black and bright under a long-billed maroon cap with a single white "W" on the crown. They regarded him steadily with a mixture of irony and humor. Rommel glanced around the marble walls and two entranceways for the expected Negro gang whose presence might account for the youth's bravado, but the boy apparently was alone.

"What you doin' out here this time-a night, man?" the youth repeated. Rommel was both amused and intimidated by such authority in one so small. The youth seemed to derive a strange sustenance from the night, having appeared like some blithe spirit that inhabited the temple of Lincoln.

"*Ich frage*—ask you—same question," Rommel retorted, drawing up to his full height of five feet seven inches and staring down imperiously as if at a private with a dirty uniform.

"Say, where you come from, talkin' like dat?"

"I comin' from Germany."

"Germany? Where dat?"

"Across the Atlantic. In Europe."

"Germany. I heard of it. Germany, Germany." The boy crossed his arms, his wizened face screwed tight in concentration. "*Some*thin' happened over dere . . . somethin'—oh, yeah! Mister Hitler, he wouldn' have nothin' to do with Jesse Owens!"

Rommel turned away to cover his hesitation. He raised his eyes to the brass tablet.

". . . the proposition," he continued to read aloud, "that all men are created equal. . . ." His own face seemed to be reflected in the tablet.

"Hitler wouldn' shake Jesse's hand!" the husky voice persisted. "I seen it at the movie show."

"He was not expected to shake hands!" Rommel said irritably without taking his eyes from the inscription.

"Hey, don' tell *me*. I seen it at the movie show. He shake some othah man hand but he wouldn' shake with Jesse." The voice was flatly accusing, but there was in it also a cynical acceptance of man's shortcomings. Rommel thought of the Führer's commanding presence, the brooding eyes that did not look at you but rather consumed you, the mannerism of turning abruptly from a speaker and causing self-doubt, the sudden, titanic rages which were at the heart of Hitler's power, the rage of ancient warriors who drank their enemies' blood where they felled them and brought their victims' heads to their sons. To Rommel, such uncontrollable urges were the antithesis of civilized warfare. Men who fought from rage were as beasts—devoid of thought, courtesy, sacrifice, gallantry, nobility, honor. A seed of doubt burst secretly into flower inside Rommel, and he shut his mind to it with a terrific effort of will.

"'Now we are engaged in a great civil war,'" he resumed

reading, "'testing whether that nation, or any nation so conceived and so dedicated, can long endure . . .'"

"What yo' name?"

"Was?"

"Yo' name. What dey call you? My name Isaiah. Bet you a quahtah you cain't spell it."

"Same as in Bible?"

"Right."

"I-S-A-I-U-H."

"Wrong. I-S-A-I-A-H. You said *U*. Where my quahtah?" As Rommel dug into his pocket, the youth persisted. "You fo'got to tell me yo' name." Rommel held out a coin and elicited a grin so wide and bright, it seemed impossible that lips, however thick and strong, could contain such dental splendor.

"Rommel," he said, and stuck out his hand.

"Rommel! Funny name." Isaiah shook his hand with an even wider grin.

"Funny?"

"Yeah, funny. Ha-ha, funny."

"Isaiah say Rommel funny?"

"Hey, Isaiah from de Bible, man. Doan' be down-talkin' Isaiah."

"Rommel from *meinem Vater*."

"You don' talk American, do you? How dey talk in Germany?"

"Wir sprechen Deutsch."

Again the smile leaped across the brown face as though escaping from captivity, accompanied by a single peal of laughter like a bell in a tower. "Dat crazy. It doan' mean nothin'. You need some he'p to git through dat speech on de wall. My mama taught me to read ever' word of it. I tell you anything you wants to know fo' two bits."

"Two bits?"

"That's twenty-five cent," Isaiah carefully explained.

Rommel dug into his pocket again. Isaiah clinked his quarters together and they turned to the tablet.

"'. . . we here highly resolve that these dead shall not have died in vain; that this nation shall have a new . . .'"

"Birth!" said Isaiah.

"'. . . birth of freedom; and that this government . . .'"

Isaiah joined in and they read together, "'. . . of the people, by the people, for the people, shall not perish from the earth.'"

"Hey, man, you gettin' bettah. You jus' need some practice."

With the words of Lincoln resonating in his mind, Rommel smiled at Isaiah and thought of his young son, Manfred. The craggy stone face looked benignly down on them.

"Boy of your age should not be out of doors at this hour," Rommel said.

"Boy! Seein' as how you from Germany, I gonna overlook dat. I fast, man. Anybody dat cotches me kin have me." He paused. "You cross dat ocean on a boat?"

"Yes, a ship."

"Yeah, ship. You come up de 'Tomac?" He gestured toward the unseen river beyond the marble walls.

"No. We dock at New York."

"New York." Isaiah took off his baseball cap and scratched his head. "Where you goin'?"

"Mississippi."

"Ohhhh, dass bad." The youth took a step backward and shook his head sympathetically. "What you lookin' for in dat place?"

"I am looking for a man named Forrest."

"He yo' frien' or sump'm?" Isaiah inched closer to the open entranceway.

"He is a teacher," Rommel said.

"Well, you learn good." The boy stood poised in silhouette against the pool gleaming like platinum. "I gotta go, Rommel. See you in the movies!"

The silhouette vanished. Rommel waited for a moment, then walked to the entrance and looked in all directions. The child was gone. He regarded the statue one last time. It was so quiet he could hear his own breathing. The face seemed to be smiling. What did Lincoln know that he did not?

Whatever it is, it will cost "two bits" to find out.

He went into the summer night, swinging his thoughts south toward Mississippi and a slave trader named Forrest.

IV

Speigner watched the land fall away beneath the plane, expanding before his eyes until he could see half of Virginia from horizon to horizon. In his lap was the copy of *Infanterie greift an* (The Infantry Attacks), by Erwin Rommel. German newspaper reviews had been unstinting in their praise of the new book, apparently on its way to becoming a sensational bestseller. While the engines of the DC-3 droned steadily outside his window, Max settled himself in his seat and began to read. He became immersed in the world of two men named Rommel: one, a young lieutenant who from his first battle was clearly a born soldier; the other, a seasoned infantry instructor with the rank of major, who looked back on the exploits of the lieutenant with understated pride. The major carefully plotted each battle with maps and noted the lessons of warfare to be gleaned from his experience.

From Belgium to the Argonne to Rumania to Northern Italy, the lieutenant had led companies, platoons, squads, and on one occasion had faced the enemy alone with an empty rifle. Always, he attacked. He attacked villages, hills, fortified positions, barnyards. He lay in the mud under a drizzling rain, hungry, tired, waiting for the enemy to sleep so he could cut the wire and storm their trenches. He lay all night on freezing ground in heavy snowfall and watched the eastern sky for first light to signal the attack. Possessed of seemingly inexhaustible energy and determination, he drove himself as fiercely as he drove his men. He was the ultimate fighting machine, fearless under fire, able to sleep soundly during constant bombardment.

Major Rommel patiently charted Lieutenant Rommel's path of conquest, diagramming the terrain with affectionate care as if he owned a piece of each vanquished hillside, meadow, woods or farm. Forests, roads, villages, cultivated fields were reproduced in meticulous detail, the world trans-

52

formed into military objectives. Bold, curving arrows were the artist's single license. They cut and slashed at the static quadrants of enemy positions waiting to be taken. Men's agony, blood, terror and courage were reduced to lines of skeletal clarity by the major's fine pen.

Erwin Rommel began to emerge for Max in the repeated formula of event, illustration, and lesson. Life was combat, combat was life. Mass, movement, field of fire, deployment could be reduced to calm, neat lines on paper, but there was more to it than that. The infantry instructor apparently placed his trust in those lines—a simple unshakable faith in the physics and metaphysics of a bullet's path and an inferior force yielding to a stronger one. Rommel lived somewhere within the serene fury of those lines.

While Speigner read, the American Airlines flight landed and exchanged passengers at Charlotte, took off and crossed the Smoky Mountains enroute to Knoxville. Max paid little attention to the green ridges and valleys passing under the silver wings. He had noticed that Rommel's pen-and-ink illustrations, apart from the maps, were particularly interesting. Technically, they were the line drawings of a talented novice. Form, perspective and shading were adequate to convey image but little more. Yet Rommel's selection of images, his gothic imagination, appealed to Speigner. In a scene of surrender visualized from a short distance, German soldiers dashed into a dead forest of blasted trees in which explosions appeared like foliage among the bare limbs. The Germans were so intent on their objective they seemed not to notice French soldiers emerging from the trees with their arms upraised as if in imitation of the naked branches. Another scene revealed a line of German soldiers launching a night attack down an enemy trench. They stealthily disappeared into an open tunnel curving like a vagina in the mounded earth— an unexpected force poised to plunge into the enemy.

Contrasting drawings revealed the spirit of the mountain campaign in Italy. In one sketch, German troops moved confidently down a high road surrounded by sunny spaces. Speigner could imagine the wind cold in Rommel's face and the piercing cry of a hawk. Another sketch showed an exploded bridge sliding into a deep cleft between mountain walls. Shadings of the artist's pen created brooding faces in the rocky bluffs as though the earth itself—Italy—were yielding grudgingly to the German attack. As he turned the pages, following the indefatigable lieutenant from one successful campaign to the next, Max half expected to happen upon a devastating picture of corpses among twisted and torn machines, of refugees moving with the somnambulance of abject terror. But Rommel's images remained steadfastly the images of attack. If *Infanterie grieft an* were one's single reference, Max thought, one would have to assume that Germany had won the war.

The DC-3 began its descent near Memphis, where the sluggish brown moccasin of the Mississippi lay coiled on the green land. Speigner hurried to the conclusion of the book. What would Rommel make of it: the harsh testing of men's endurance, the courage, the cowardice, the suffering, the dying, and beyond it all—on the top of a mountain in Italy— Rommel's personal triumph, the capture of an enemy garrison for which he had been awarded the *Pour le Mérite,* Germany's highest decoration for valor. What ultimate lesson would the infantry instructor pass on to his dedicated students, to serve them in peace as in war? Max read the final paragraph:

> In the east, west and south are to be found the final resting places of those German soldiers who, for home and country, followed the path of duty to the bitter end. They are a constant reminder to us who remain behind and to our future generations that we must not fail them when it becomes a question of making sacrifices for Germany.

Must not fail.

Max leaned back in his seat and tried to conjure up an image of Erwin Rommel's face, put his photographic memory to work, sorted through mental stacks of German newspaper clippings. Where had he seen the face? Announcement of staged maneuvers in Bavaria, a group of officers wearing fatigues and the expectant expression of combat veterans? Appointment to the *Kriegsschule,* somber and proud mug shot? *Jugend?* The *Jugend!* He had seen it in the *Morgenpost:* two men, posing side by side but in a subtle way distinct and separate, eyes just slanted in opposite directions—Baldur von

Schirach, aristocratic young leader of over five million Hitler
Youth, and Erwin Rommel, newly attached *Wehrmacht* liaison
for the *Jugend*. It had been a recent appointment, five months
before, in February. Speigner remembered having speculated,
at his private table beneath the file room's single window, on
the probable collision between the professional soldier and the
arrogant Von Schirach. It would be interesting to know how
soon the mismatched pair had crossed swords. In his mind's
eye he magnified the picture of Rommel's face, imagining the
dots separating as he brought his glass close, recalling the
smooth, ascetic cheeks, the firm mouth, the hooded eyes. This
was the major, doing his duty even if it meant sleeping with
politicians; and this was the lieutenant, the *Draufgänger*
waiting patiently for the call to the front.

The plane landed. Speigner closed the book and joined
the shuffling line of departing passengers. Outside the small
terminal he took a taxi to downtown Memphis, where he
bought a bus ticket to Oxford. An hour later he occupied a seat
aboard a Greyhound, which pulled out of the depot and
headed south along the bluffs past Victorian-style homes
weathered and peeling from river mists, past filling stations,
pawnshops, garages, junkyards, and shanty towns clustered on
the banks of swampy tributaries. Max slid back his window.
Honeysuckle bloomed everywhere—on trees, fences, barns,
rusted hulks of abandoned automobiles or farm machinery.
Ever since his first crossing of the state line below Memphis,
as a college freshman in 1932, this rife perfume had been for
Speigner the odor of Mississippi. He was coming home.

Soon the bus paused to take on a passenger in the sleepy
town square of Hernando, where the marble statue of a
Confederate soldier reminded Max that Bedford Forrest had
lived in Hernando before the Civil War.

The Wizard.

Max's impression of Forrest was that of a stout, country-
bred, near-illiterate, slave-trading yeoman who discovered
that war suited him. The Forrest of the war resembled the
Forrest of before the war as a butterfly resembled a caterpillar
or a wasp its larvae. There would have been no manual on
tactics, ghost-written or otherwise, by *this* soldier. Max
remembered several famous dispatches by Forrest, which
Shoemaker had often quoted in his lectures as examples of the

cavalryman's ingenuousness. Announcing the capture of Fort Pillow, in 1862, with its garrison of black Union troops, Forrest was alleged to have written:

> *We busted the fort at ninerclock and scatered the niggers. The men is still a cillanem in the woods.*

Later, referring to the disposition of prisoners taken, the general (then a colonel) wrote:

> *Them as was cotch with spoons and brestpins and sich, was cilld, and the rest of the lot was pay rold and told to git.*

Max's favorite, however, was Forrest's hastily scrawled reply on the back of an importunate soldier's third request for a furlough:

> *I told you twist Goddammit know.*

To Shoemaker, the Wizard's lack of education was perfectly balanced by common sense and cunning. "He had a Ph.D. in horsemanship and local terrain," the major would tell the cadets. "His mind was uncluttered by the baggage of an education we deem a necessity. Force him to parse a sentence—can anyone in the class parse a sentence?—and he loses the gift of finding a ford at floodtime. Hell, Sherlock Holmes believed the sun revolved around the earth, but he spoke a dozen languages and was an expert in chemistry, botany, world weaponry from day one, and he played a fair violin. It's a give and take, boys. The age of specialization began long before the twentieth century. Forrest read trail like an Indian, smelled enemy miles away, knew every spring and sweet-grass meadow and defensible hill from Memphis to Montgomery. It was God's blessing no schoolmarm ever knocked the rough off him."

Speigner thought of his former ROTC instructor with his passionate love of history and of the benign beauty of the university campus waiting in Oxford. The miles of clay hills passed slowly as anticipation began to build. His days there seemed like a dream. Two faces remained steadfast in his memory, Eieschied and Shoemaker, two teachers who had made all the difference. Because of their patience, sly humor, and unwavering encouragement, he had grown to love the school which had at first seemed so remote. The brick buildings framed by white lattice-work were like women's faces behind lace veils. There were immense green lawns and spring flowers named jonquil and narcissus. It had taken him a year to gain admittance into the stratified campus society. As a freshman scholarship student who cleared tables in the cafeteria, the closest he had come to the lush coeds with syrupy accents and fluttering white hands that shaped their thoughts in the air was across the aisle in class. He surreptitiously smelled their just-bathed scent and watched the sunlight catch in their hair.

As a sophomore he organized a dance band in which he played a bass fiddle borrowed from the school symphony. He had joined a fraternity and discovered that the planters' sons he had envied as they drove down sorority row in white linen suits and sleek convertibles were nearly as poor as he. Their inheritance, hundreds of acres of rich delta land, was being sold a piece at a time to pay for one suit and one semester's tuition every six months. The convertibles were actually few and far between. Max had found his niche at Ole Miss in the Sigma Alpha Epsilon lodge, where his fraternity brothers affectionately dubbed him "Sherman" Speigner, the Yankee scourge who had slipped behind the lines to pillage and despoil.

The Greyhound entered Oxford on a tree-shaded street that wound past the university. Max pulled the emergency-stop cord and got off the bus at the northern entrance of the school grounds. With his valise in one hand and his copy of Rommel's *Attack* in the other, he leisurely walked up the long hill to sorority row. In the late afternoon, the white façades of the Greek-revival style houses on his left seemed to bathe in the rosy glow of the present, while on his right the columned houses stared morosely out of an intractable, shadowy past.

The campus was nearly deserted during the summer session. Few students could be seen walking across the quadrangles and lawns baked apple green by the July heat. On the front steps of a nearby sorority house three girls sipping Coca-Colas through straws ceased their animated chatter as Max approached. They leaned toward one another with a giggle, their eyes sliding liquidly toward the tall soldier in his khaki uniform.

A Pandora's box of memories rushed at him so strong that he almost turned up the sorority walk to meet his coffee date. He read the Greek letters over the door, Chi Omega, and remembered a balmy night in 1934.

Her name was Alice. She was a willowy, brown-eyed strawberry blonde, slender, of medium height, with a delicate, fine-boned face and hair as smooth as cornsilk. Her lips were small, well-shaped and slightly pouting. He thought immoderately about those lips. She had been a campus sensation her freshman year, voted "K.A. Rose," yearbook "Campus Cutie," a princess in the homecoming court. Her datebook was filled weeks in advance with deadly precision. In her sophomore year, her career took an indefinable pause. She was still lush, still beautiful, but the Chi-O phone seldom rang for her. A campus mystery had occurred. Alice was entangled in a malaise known as Sophomore Slump. "Too much too soon," the seers said and turned away.

Max, himself a sophomore wise in college ways, noted this circumstance with interest. The former cafeteria worker, whose eyes had devoured the beauty while she deliberated between fruit cocktail or tossed salad, phoned the fallen star. Her hopeful "Hello" gave him courage. He was not so rash as to ask for a Friday or Saturday but for a Wednesday date—known on campus as a "casual"—to listen to records or perhaps play a few hands of bridge if another couple appeared to make up a foursome. A year ago, he knew, she would have said, "Max, I'd love to but I have plans for that evening." In her distress, she said, "I'd love to."

Wearing starched shirt and perfectly creased trousers, hair slicked and pomaded, after-shave lotion still on his cheeks, Max nervously sat on the French provincial sofa in the Chi-O parlor and waited for Alice. Even for a casual, one could expect to wait at least ten minutes. Perfection could not be achieved slapdash. He was content.

"You're Max Speigner." The contralto voice did not belong to Alice. He turned and looked into a pleasant, square-jawed face. He stood. He recognized Myrtle, a campus matchmaker. With heavy hips and lank hair, Myrtle had been born to be a blind date, of the type categorized as "great sense of humor, lovely clothes, fantastic dancer, whiz at bridge, knows everybody, can be trusted to keep a secret." It was in this last category that Myrtle had made her mark. She approached Speigner with the level gaze and somber eagerness of a valued messenger.

"Alice will be down in a minute," Myrtle said. "She's looking forward to going out with you. She remembers you from a pledge swap—we looked you up in the annual—but Max . . ." Her husky voice rose to almost soprano pitch, and the revealing pause told Speigner to pay attention. ". . . Alice is feeling a little low this week, so be patient with her." Again the pause, the brown eyes willing him to understand. Thickly, as though moving through a slough of molasses toward a lantern on the levee, Max struggled to a meeting of minds. Alice was having her period. Myrtle could see that her communiqué had been decoded. With a look of benediction she turned to go, but issued a warning: "Sometimes she faints."

In Myrtle's talcumed wake, Max gripped the sofa. All he knew about menstruation was that it had its season. Since puberty, he had preferred to dwell not on the reality of female organs but on their possibilities. Before he had time to unravel Myrtle's augury, Alice appeared. She wore a radiant smile but kept part of herself removed, as though at a distance of three or four feet, to judge her effect. He leaped up.

"Hello, Max, so nice to see you," she said, extending her hand. "Well, I'm ready!"

She does not look sick.

When they entered the SAE house, Max found that the living room was empty. He glanced about hopefully for the distraction of other voices, other bodies. Someone had left the radio playing. Speigner recognized the domestic babble of "Fibber McGee and Molly." Alice smiled and excused herself to go to the powder room. He tried not to think about what she was doing and dawdled in front of the cold fireplace. The lonely room mocked him with a smell of vanished parties, stale cigarettes and spilled beer. He turned off the radio. Alice's footsteps echoed in the hall. The Victrola was their only option.

"Our record collection is scratched, but we have them all," he said. "Spin a few platters?"

"Swell," she said, gripping her purse.

They entered the informal living room, also called the "smoker," which was used for dancing and occasionally for rumored, legendary fornications. Speigner fumbled to turn on a table lamp. The corners of the room sullenly resisted the light. He felt that he was seeing its bare essence for the first time. Overstuffed leather sofas occupied their side of the room; the other side had purposely been left unfurnished—for dancing—except for the frat "library," which consisted of a single glass case containing several dozen untouched volumes. The case had always remained locked—it was an SAE tradition—and the fraternity annually voted the least popular member "librarian," relieving the tedium of weekly meetings by calling for a library report. No one had ever tried to find the key to the case. Its contents could be examined only by peering through the glass. The abandoned volumes stood as mute trophies to the lost alumnus who had donated them. Once, finding himself alone in the room, Max had examined the contents of the library. The case contained Lord Chesterfield's *Letters*, Ovid's *Art of Love*, a complete set of *Rover Brothers* in leather, Dicken's *Great Expectations*, and selected volumes of *The Confederate Record*. He felt like apologizing to Alice for the bookcase, which seemed to wait in place in stodgy, unreconstructed hope. He turned to the record rack in the Victrola cabinet and selected "Mood Indigo," by Duke Ellington.

"Let's start with the Duke, okay?" he said to Alice. She nodded indifferently and he turned on the record player. They waited for the machine to warm up. He put the record on. The wail of saxophones relaxed them and they sat on the sofa. Alice opened her purse and rummaged in it. Speigner avoided noticing what was inside. She took out a pack of Lucky Strikes, extracted a cigarette using fingernails as precise as tweezers, tapped it lightly on the package, and held it stiffly between index and middle fingers, elbow cupped in her free hand. The whole procedure took only a matter of seconds, but Max was enchanted by its artfulness. He could have watched her hands repeat the motions for hours. She was waiting for a light. He groped in his pocket for matches. Ellington's trombones shifted into "Blue Moon."

"Actually, I like Jimmy Dorsey's arrangement better," he

said, holding the flaring match inside his cupped palm. She sucked greedily at the flame. Her red lips taut on the white cylinder made his hand shake. He blew out the match. "But we only have Ellington," he added. They shared a stoic smile. They sat together, wreathed by smoke and an indigo mood. Max's attention returned to the old bookcase. He silently implored it to give up a conversational subject, his first choice being Ovid. He felt warm pressure at his side and, without moving his body, ascertained that Alice was cuddling up to him. Her head rested against his shoulder; her eyes were closed, her breathing soft and regular. He felt her thigh against his and wondered at that fine warmth, which made him remember a story from his youth in Fort Wayne:

A farm boy had a religious-minded girlfriend who repeatedly rejected his advances. One night, parked in a cornfield in his truck, the girl suddenly laid her hand on his shoulder and appeared to fall asleep. When he tried to awaken her, she stubbornly refused to open her eyes. He was beginning to become irritated, when a mournful snore signaled him to proceed. He undressed her, careful not to disturb her slumber, and enjoyed prolonged sexual union. She never woke up although she moaned and smiled in her sleep. After he had dressed her, using the same elaborate care, she opened her eyes, sat up, stretched, and apologized for "drifting off." This happy arrangement was often repeated, the boy whistling hymns to help his lover become drowsy. One night on their way to a basketball game he wheeled the truck into the cornfield, stamped on the brakes, glanced imperiously at his pocket watch and said, "We got ten minutes. Go to sleep."

Max looked down at Alice, his mind rife with possibilities. The record ended. The needle rasped back and forth, the grating sound magnified by the Victrola's speaker. Alice did not stir. He saw that her cigarette had nearly burned down to her fingers. He reached across her clumsily with his free hand and removed the butt, flipping it into an ashtray on the coffee table. His right shoulder jiggled her head. She opened her eyes and sat up. He appraised her blank stare and said, "Are you okay?"

"I'd love a Coke," she said with a drowsy smile. They sat apart, facing each other formally as though on opposite sides of a receiving line.

"Sure thing," he said. "Back in a jiffy."

He walked to the kitchen, now empty, its counters clean but smelling of meatloaf. With a troubled expression, he fished in a water cooler beside the commercial-sized refrigerator for two bottles, dropped a dime into a cigar box marked "Cokes 5¢—Pay Up!" and returned to the informal living room. He could hear thumps through the ceiling overhead. Some of the brothers were doing calisthenics in the hall upstairs. A muffled voice called, "Pipe down, we're tryin' to study in here!" Alice accepted her Coca-Cola gratefully. She offered a cigarette to Max, and the ritual of exchange seemed to bring them closer. They put another record on—"Night and Day" by Bing Crosby. The mellow baritone was comfortably familiar, and they returned to the sofa with the assurance of old friends. They settled themselves, pleasantly occupied with the business of listening to Bing, sipping from the ice-cold bottles sweating in their hands, and flipping their ashes in turn into the ashtray. She crossed her legs with a sigh of silk, and he was compelled to dream again. He watched her purse her lips against the bottle and tilt her head to drink the dark, bubbling liquid. She bent to set her bottle on the floor and her dress hiked up. Max saw the pearly thigh gleaming under the brown band of her garter.

I wouldn't ask for much, he prayed, heart thumping. *Just light petting.*

To steady himself he leaned forward to go through the motions of tapping his ash. Without a sound she fell limply away from him. Her left hand flew up and the lit end of her cigarette embedded itself in his upper lip. The pain was blinding. He gave a muffled scream and grabbed at the cigarette, vehemently stepping on it as if it were a hornet. His drink had spilled in his lap, and he jerked the bottle away before it all poured out. Gasping, he looked at Alice while Bind Crosby sang, ". . . whether near to me or far, no matter, darling, where you are, I think of you . . ." Her rounded hip and gartered thigh were thrust up invitingly, as though in compensation for his discomfort. The pain in his lip had somewhat subsided, and he thought of the not unrelated fact that in many parts of Africa the maiden bride brought to her wedding night an embroidered pillow on which to rest her forehead.

With a burnt lip there would be no kissing, only sudden, overpowering passion. I would take her like a bitch in heat, from behind.

He pressed the cold bottle against his upper lip and remembered Myrtle's words of caution: "Sometimes she faints." He had not wanted to think of it before, because that would have meant giving up. His lip was numb against the frigid glass.

It may never be worth it, but tonight is not the night I find out.

Alice sat up and looked around. She seemed surprised to see him. "Less dance," she mumbled.

"You are ill," he said.

"I feel fine," she argued sleepily. "I fell like *dancin'*, boy!" She stood and slowly pirouetted to demonstrate her restored health.

"I better take you home." Speigner turned suspiciously on the sofa and watched her walk to the Victrola to answer its rasping summons.

"Too early!" she cried. "How about 'All of Me,' by Benny Goodman! It's number three on my all-time favorites." She shook the record out of its cover, placed it on the turntable, turned up the volume and as the music began, danced toward him with one palm outstretched, the other pressing an invisible partner against her neat, well-defined breasts.

Sophomore Slump has deranged her.

He dubiously approached Alice, raising his hand to hers. They began to move to the music. Her trim body pressed against him, thighs blending with his. Her breasts moved against him with a slow insistence, back and forth, back and forth. She thrust herself more urgently against him and he buried his face in her hair, inhaling deeply. As if she could not bear the weight of his face on her head, she abruptly slid down his body like a rag doll.

"Don't!" He groped to catch her before she slumped to the floor. He grappled with her dead weight, arms encircling her tiny waist. His head bobbed like a madman's as he dragged her toward the sofa.

"Good God, Sherman! What the hell are you doin'!"

Speigner turned like a hunted animal. One of his fraternity brothers stood in the open doorway with a horrified expression, his hand shielding his girlfriend's face. Still clutching Alice, Max gave a stifled cry for help.

"Gimme a hand!" he cried hoarsely. "She passed out again!"

They carried Alice's limp body to the leather sofa where they laid her out like a corpse. Speigner took the hem of her dress between thumb and forefinger and chastely pulled it down. The new girl, a petite blonde whom Max vaguely recognized as one of Alice's sorority sisters, approached the unconscious figure in a matter-of-fact way. She pushed the two young men aside.

"She'll be awright," said the blonde. "She does this every once in awhile."

Every twenty-eight days, and tonight's the night.

The blonde patted Alice's hand and called her name. After a moment the long eyelids began to bat—coquettishly, Max observed, even in semiconsciousness, testimony to years of practice. Alice smiled.

"Hey, Martha," she said. "I ditn' know you were here, too!" Max was disturbed that neither female seemed to admit that something very, very wrong was going on. The record, "All of Me," ended, and the needle jerked back and forth. Infuriated by the sound, Max strode to the Victrola and snatched the needle arm up, then switched the machine off.

"Don' do that!" Alice cried. "Th' party's just gettin' started."

"The party's over," he said firmly, one hand resting on the Victrola. "I'm taking you home."

"I'm stayin'," Alice cried. She sat like a small child, legs straight in front of her, arms crossed, hugging herself, lower lip pushed out. Max wondered if the pout was part of her regular repertoire, if, in fact, *anything* about Alice was spontaneous and unrehearsed outside of the faints.

"You're going," he said.

"Oh, Max, she'll be just fine." Martha slid an arm protectively around Alice's shoulders. "This happens—"

"—once a month!" he cried.

Both females assumed identical bland expressions, presenting a unified defensive front. Speigner knew that somehow he had gone too far, had done the unmentionable, and blame was being shifted in his direction. He struggled to reverse the trend.

"How can you pretend nothing has happened? Look at me!" He pointed to his upper lip, where a pearly blister had risen, and to his pants, wet and sticky where the soft drink had spilled. "I'm not used to this!"

The girls beamed meaningful looks at Max's fraternity brother, who sighed and turned a placating smile to Speigner.

Life at Ole Miss is a series of messengers bearing small demands.

"It's gonna be awright, Max," the boy said. "Don't worry 'bout it."

He looked at their smooth, unfathomable faces. Grouped expectantly—the two girls on the sofa, the boy standing behind them—they seemed to blend together like white Mississippi jonquils that had popped up beside one another with no object except to bloom under the sun in a jonquil conspiracy. He drew himself militarily erect.

"Do I take it," he said elaborately, "that *you* are accepting responsibility for Alice?" His friend's head twisted on the axis of his neck and sank a fraction of an inch. His expression—half doubtful, half knowing—said, "It's a shame you cain't trust a Yankee to do the right thing."

"I reckon so," the boy said warily.

Without a word, Max gave Alice and Martha a curt bow and left the informal living room. Their open-mouthed astonishment filled him with satisfaction. But as he walked back to his dormitory, alone in the spring night, he suffered doubts. There would be, he realized, repercussions. The next day at lunch in the SAE dining room, Martha's escort leaned over the salmon croquettes and said, "Sherman, your ass is grass at the Chi-O house."

Later, in the privacy of Major Shoemaker's office, he recounted the story, asking his professor "Do I have to fight the war all over again?"

"Now you know, m'boy," the major said with a twinkle in his eye; "it's still going on."

But he loved Ole Miss. The name itself was wonderfully archaic. On the plantations, with their two- or three-generation tier of white inhabitants, the slaves referred to the planter's wife as "Young Miss," while his mother—who acted as nurse, lay minister in charge of weddings and funerals, and choir director for singings on Sunday afternoons—was called

"Ole Miss." Max's personal frame of reference was that he had known a typical Young Miss in Alice, while in him she had known a slave from Indiana.

Coeds with books in their arms turned to stare at the young lieutenant who was laughing out loud, all by himself. As he turned down Faculty Row, Max thought of all the Alices he had known at Ole Miss, the tantalizing sweetness of their smiles, the veiled promise of their glances, the soft reluctance with which they yielded themselves to the Mississippi rhythms. Life unfolded as everyone expected. It was a point of honor for Ole Miss coeds to marry no later than June after graduation. *His* Alice, then, would have now been married for thirteen months. Now she was doubtless basking somewhere on the sunny side of the menstrual cycle, the willowy figure ripe with child but fashionably so. Wreathed in a pastel rainbow of maternity dresses, smoldering with robust good health and unforgiving resentment of this indignity with which Nature had punished her, Alice was lending her beauty to some Delta lawn party, church picnic, barbecue, fish fry or wedding reception. In some green corner of the floodplain between Memphis and Vicksburg she was swinging in a glider, deflecting the July heat with an oriental fan which she waved back and forth, back and forth. Her vigilance of a husband's wandering eye would be distracted by the kick of a tiny planter's foot next to her heart.

And if, after a lifetime of supervising with a critical eye the training of future generations of Chi Omegas, having ascended now to the role life had intended for her from the start—Ole Miss herself—if she should turn in her glider at some Delta lawn party in, say, 1986, and see standing beside her a white-haired relic of their college days in Oxford, he was certain that the fan would cease its undulations and she would say, in a voice containing an artful echo of youth, "You left me at the SAE house to get home the best way I could, you Yankee son of a bitch, but come sit down."

V

Speigner remembered the Roof Garden of the Robert E. Lee Hotel from his college days, when dancers swayed through a mist of cigarette smoke to "Darkness on the Delta" by Sammy Kaye and his Orchestra. Campus beauties whom Max had thought as delicate as the white magnolia blossoms which turned brown at the slightest touch stood on tables to see and be seen, rosy-cheeked and guffawing, clutching Dixie cups of bourbon and Coke. The Rebels might have lost to the Crimson Tide by three touchdowns, but the party went on just the same. Now the ballroom, with its polished parquet floors, bandstand, linen-covered tables in orderly rows against the walls, was empty except for three army officers in civilian clothes and two Negro bellhops. Colonel Adler strode briskly across the floor to meet them.

"Damn a dry state!" Adler fumed, shaking hands with a punishing grip. Major Shoemaker introduced his former student as "our language man from Washington," but the effect was lost on the colonel, a practical man who took things one at a time.

"The bellhops were supposed to get the booze," Adler continued, waving his hand in dismissal at the blacks, who stood apologetically behind a table with glasses, ice, water, setups—everything but liquor. "They say that their supply man is in jail. Fine time to let us know about it! Hell, any teenager or little old lady in Mississippi can buy a bottle. Somebody's going to have to step out and find some, quick. *My* regular place is across the Pearl River, in Rankin County. No time to get there and back before then. Nicholson and Petrey"—he introduced the two reservists who had joined them, looking concerned about the logistics problem—"are from out of town." Adler paused. Max looked at their faces. There were two colonels, a major, and a captain. Everyone seemed to be looking at the lieutenant.

67

"How about the bus station?" Max said.

Speigner walked west on Capitol Street, with Colonel Adler's five-dollar bill in his pocket and instructions to buy "one bourbon, one scotch—Old Charter and Johnny Walker, if they have it."

Inertia as palpable as the odor of grease and cigar smoke filled the Greyhound Bus Station. Two black teenagers played cards in a booth. At the grill counter a white waitress of indeterminate age poised quizzically over a crossword puzzle, pencil in one hand, cigarette in the other. Max tentatively leaned against a stool and waited for her to finish printing a word. She frowned and began to erase what she had written.

"What kin I do ya?" she said without raising her eyes.

"I need some . . . uh . . ." The pause was a signal demanding her immediate attention. Her eyes flicked over him. She waited for him to declare himself.

"I used to be able," he said, "to get something to drink in here." Although Max's midwestern accent had been rounded and softened by his four years in Mississippi, his clear enunciation still marked him as an outsider.

"We got coffee, milk, o.j., Coke, and ice tea," she said with a shrug. Max did not reply but waited for their eyes to reach an understanding.

"Ruby!" she yelled over her shoulder. A perspiring black face hovered in a door behind the counter. "Man to see you." The waitress concentrated on her puzzle, dismissing him. From the kitchen a woman emerged, or rather ballooned, from the door, her immense body startling beneath a small, well-shaped face. She mopped her brow with a rag and gave Max a sorrowful look as if having passed him a guilty secret.

"What'll it be?" she said.

"One Old Charter, one Johnny Walker," he said.

She stared past him and frowned. He resisted an impulse to look over his shoulder.

"Five-twenty," she said at last. At first he did not understand what might be some kind of kitchen code. "Two-fifty for the Charter, two-seb-ty for the Johnny Walkah." He gave her the colonel's crisp bill and fished in his pocket for twenty cents. She turned massively and disappeared into the grease smoke. After a moment she poked her head out the door. She seemed more cheerful with only her face showing.

"Go to the men's room," she said. "They brings it to the window. Five minute."

The men's room smelled of a war between urine and chlorine. A thin trail of cigar smoke rose undisturbed from a stall. A man's shoes partly obscured by trouser folds were visible underneath the closed door. The cracked mirror over the rust-stained lavatory gave Max's face a narrow, fugitive quality. He moved to the open window overlooking an alley, but no one was in sight. A low grunt came from the stall like a note of warning. As the seconds extended into minutes, Max began to worry about the identity of the man-in-the-stall. He envisioned a newspaper heading, "LIEUTENANT JAILED FOR VIOLATING STATE LIQUOR LAWS," then toyed with its appearance in the *Berlin Morgenpost*: "LEUTNANT INHAFTIERT WEGEN ÜBERTRETUNG DES ALKOHOLVERBOTS." In German it took on the gravity of a felony. Suspicion emanated from the stall like a bodily odor.

He went to the lavatory and made a show of washing his hands. There were no paper towels, so he returned to the window holding his hands in the air. He wondered if delivery would be completed before his hands were dry. On the wall beside the window among the penciled graffiti of scatalogical verse, homosexual invitations accompanied by phone numbers, and lonely declarations of penis size, printed clearly in ink was "William Faulkner loves Temple Drake." *People do read books in Mississippi*. Max forgot about the man-in-the-stall and thought about the literary-wag-of-the-urinal. Perhaps it was a newspaperman, bored with waiting for a late bus from New Orleans, or a schoolmaster from some small town like Learned, Mississippi, whiling away the anxious moments before his rendezvous with a star pupil, a would-be poet for whom he entertained the highest expectations.

A car pulled up to the window. Max looked down into a woman's unsmiling face. She pushed back a damp strand of hair and said wearily, "One Chartah, one Johnny Walkah?"

"Yes," Max said. Behind him a toilet flush. He held out his hands for the brown paper bag. There was no time to waste.

Erwin Rommel was the last man to step into the elevator. An old Negro operator, his cap pushed far back on his balding head, swiveled his eyes at the Germans and waited for instructions. Rommel stood next to him. "Roof Garden, please," Rommel said. The operator reached out with a long arm to close an accordionlike arrangement of folding steel bands through which the inner walls of the elevator shaft could be seen as they ascended slowly.

"Wie lange wird diese Angelegenheit dauern?" Model was impatient about their meeting with the Americans.

"Not long at all, Herr Oberst," Hanke replied diplomatically.

"Who is our host?" Model continued to speak German.

"A Colonel Adler," said Hanke.

"I only wish that Boetticher were less fascinated with the nineteenth century." Model directed his remark to Rommel. "How much more useful it would have been to have visited industrial sites in Pennsylvania. The American assembly line is a modern art form."

Rommel spoke without turning around. "We are in Mississippi. Why not make the most of it?"

"We are in Mississippi," Model said laconically, "because *you* got Boetticher stirred up over Bedford Forrest. I thought he would *never* quit talking about him. Forrest, Forrest, Forrest."

"I'm glad we're here," Rommel growled. "I don't give a shit about the assembly line." The elevator stopped at the top floor. The operator expertly matched up the floor levels and pulled the folding gate open.

"Watch yo' step, gentlemens," he said.

Rommel and Krüger led the way across a hall through double doors that opened onto the ballroom. The Germans advanced on their hosts in a loose box formation, with Schörner and Hanke on each flank and Model lagging behind in the middle. Their footsteps echoed on the polished floor. The American officers met them in the middle of the room. The bellhops watched with mild interest.

"Willkommen, willkommen!" said Adler, using one quarter of his German, the remainder consisting of *danke schön, jawohl,* and *Achtung!* It would now occur to Adler that the Germans might naturally assume he was fluent in their language and break out in a rash of katzenjammer gibberish.

Rommel, however, had seen an expression similar to Adler's half dread on many American faces during the past week, usually after the speakers had asked hopefully, "*Sprechen Sie* English?" So he promptly replied, "Thank you very much," to their host's evident relief. Introductions were attempted and names exchanged in some confusion, which suited Rommel fine. He was occasionally having trouble remembering "Rilke." Now the conversation, not healthy from the start, appeared headed for an early demise. The Americans sneaked worried glances at the bar-table.

"Your state Capitol?" Hanke, the public relations man, asked. Adler led the group closer to the modern glass windows of the Roof Garden for an unobstructed view. The Capitol dome burned copper-bright in the sunset. This prospect, however interesting, received more attention than it deserved. The Germans, whose corduroy summer suits were more suitable for Bavaria than Mississippi, were warm. Ceiling fans circulated the humid air.

- "Did you have a good trip?" Adler spoke very distinctly.

"Yes, good." Rommel was amused at the American reliance on the word *good*. He had stopped counting the times he had heard it. Did the colonel mean *sicher* (safe), *ereignislos* (uneventful), *erbaulich* (edifying)? Schörner contended that this continual use of *good* stemmed from the Puritan influence on American philosophy. But then the Schörner/Model influence was having its own effect on their group. One should not, he admonished himself, analyze one's hosts. He turned to the young captain, who seemed ill at ease. Rommel mentally rehearsed the English sentence before he spoke. "Do you have a command, Captain?"

"Yessir, a CCC battalion."

"CCC?"

"Civilian Conservation Corps, sir."

Rommel struggled with the unfamiliar word "conservation." Hanke translated, "*Erhaltung*. Roosevelt. New Deal."

"That's it," the young captain said happily. "We put people back to work."

"*Bürgerwehr?*" Rommel asked him through Hanke, who searched for a closer meaning than *militia*.

"The CCC, is it paramilitary?" Hanke said. Adler, Shoemaker, and the other two Americans appeared relieved that a conversation was at last taking shape.

"No sir, we supervise a work force engaged in reforestation, soil conservation, road building." The captain warmed to his favorite subject. "I just wish we *could* give 'em a little bit of military trainin'. We got 'em in barracks, in uniform. If we could drill 'em . . . it's a real waste. For example," his voice became confidential, "during formation when we lower the flag, we cain't even give the order, 'Attention!' Too military! We have to say, 'Stand fast.' A little drillin' would do those boys a lot of good. I mean, they're gettin' paid a dollar a day, which is more than a private in Uncle Sam's army gets!"

Rommel had caught the words *barracks*, *drill*, and *attention*. Hanke summed up, in German. "The captain supervises civilian conservation work, but is not authorized to conduct military training." Rommel nodded sympathetically. Von Schirach had summarily rejected his similar plan to send bachelor officers to the *Jugend* summer camps to train the Hitler Youth.

The Americans kept glancing toward the double doors, where they expected Speigner to appear any moment.

"We have some liquor coming," Adler said. The Germans stared at him, groping for the connection between conservation and alcohol, as well as for the unfamiliar compound *liquorkomming*.

"So the CCC, it gives work and feeds the poor?" Rommel asked encouragingly.

"Yessir. Our allocated ration is just under fifteen cents per diem, but we feed 'em three good meals on that." The captain grinned. "I cut corners here and there and saved up three hundred dollars for Easter Sunday. We splurged and put on an all-day buffet for the men and their families. We started servin' dinner at eleven A.M., and they were still folks eatin' at seven P.M. I mean, we fed 'em *good*."

"He is speaking of his accomplishments as mess officer," Hanke said dryly. Before Rommel could respond, Max walked briskly through the door with sack in hand.

"Here's the booze!" Adler cried.

Max was slightly winded, having hurried up the stairs rather than wait for the elevator. He saw all eyes turn to him as he took the bottles directly to the bellhops.

"Bar's open, gentlemen," Adler cheerfully announced. "You have a choice, scotch or bourbon!" On firmer ground now, the colonel took the visitors' orders for drinks. The group moved closer to the bar-table. Model and Krüger asked for scotch; Schörner and Hanke opted for bourbon. Rommel ordered a Coca-Cola. Shoemaker waited until drinks were handed round before introducing his protégé to the Germans.

"Here's our linguist, gentlemen," he said proudly. "Lieutenant Maxwell Speigner." Max experienced a tremor of expectation as he shook hands with the Germans. He thought he recognized at least one of them from a newspaper photograph, an article about an appointment? Some technological advancement? His mind raced: armament—the *Abteilung für technische Fragen!* He was about to shake the hand of Walter Model, head of that institution. If memory served, Model was also highly respected by Hitler and Goebbels and was fully accepted by the Nazi party. Max paid particular attention to the names as he was introduced: Rilke, Kleist, Spitzweg, Hauptmann, and . . . Meitner. These were illustrious names of German *artists* and *scientists!* Yet he was positive he was gripping the hand of the Wehrmacht's foremost developer of modern weapons, Walther Model.

They are traveling under assumed names. Why? Who are the others?

"Es freut mich, Sie kennenzulernen," he told Model with a congenial smile.

The man beside him, Rilke, was also familiar. Over the rim of his bourbon and water, Speigner studied the gray-blue eyes, the clean jaw-line and forceful nose.

"How do you like America thus far, Oberst Rilke?" he asked Rommel.

"Very much. Your German is quite good. Where did you learn it?"

"Thank you, Herr Oberst. My family is German. At college my major subjects were American history and German literature. I have kept up my German by reading German books and newspapers."

"Who are your favorite authors?" asked Hanke, who had been following the conversation. Such a question would never have occurred to Rommel.

"For the classics, Goethe and Schiller," Max answered with a bookworm's self-consciousness. "Among contemporary authors, Mann, Hesse, and of course, Kafka. I am an admirer also of Rainer Maria Rilke's verse." He pointedly addressed Rommel. "Any relation?"

Rommel did not enjoy reading poetry, and had not expected to meet an American familiar with Rilke's work. His preparatory reading had been of Civil War battles, not literature. "Not that I know of," he said and sipped his Coca-Cola to forestall any further questions along that line. He sensed Hanke's hidden sigh of relief beside him.

"Ah well, *that* Rilke was Austrian, anyway." Max continued, aware now that the rest of the visitors were listening. "Most recently, I have enjoyed reading *Infanterie greift an*, by Erwin Rommel. You have read it as well?"

Except for Rommel, who was a paradigm of detachment, the Germans became tense in subtle ways: a momentary cessation of breath, a shifting of weight from one foot to the other, a casual sideways glance. For all their patina of urbane confidence, they were shaken. Speigner felt five pairs of eyes boring into him.

"I am familiar with that title," Rommel said.

"When you return to Germany, Herr Oberst," Max said, "you really should obtain a copy. I recommend it most highly. *Infanterie greift an* is a classic text on tactics! I predict that it soon will be taught at military academies throughout the world. West Point should adopt it as soon as it is translated into English."

"Perhaps you would consider translating this work into English, Lieutenant?" Hanke interjected.

"You allow me too much credit as a linguist, sir," Max said with a deferential wave of his hand. "My Swabian is not up to par."

Rommel started, but immediately regained control of himself. He silently cursed the OKW for this game of false identities. The die, however, was cast, and he would play it as it lay. He sensed that Speigner, too, was on guard, and for a few seconds he and the lieutenant faced each other as adversaries, pleasant expressions frozen in place with the civility of filigreed saber guards.

"Swabian?" Rommel inquired indifferently.

How can an American lieutenant know of my background? Who is he?

Rommel! This could be Rommel himself. Who else would react so strongly to that shot in the dark!

"I understand Rommel is from Württemberg," Max

explained. "Not that he uses his native dialect in his book, of course. My little joke."

Hanke forced a wry expression. The Americans, who had been content to sip their drinks quietly while the "linguist" entertained their guests, were watching faces and body English with a casual awareness. They sensed that something lively had happened, and they regarded Speigner narrowly.

"Let us in on the joke, Max," said the major.

"They invited me to translate a new manual on tactics, but I said my command of idiom was too weak."

"Uh-huh." Shoemaker turned to Hanke amiably. "Don't let Speigner pull your leg. These G-Two fellows can get frisky if you don't keep the lid on 'em."

"G-Two?" Hanke said politely. "What branch, may I ask?" Rommel's gaze was so strong, Max could almost feel his cheek burning.

"Cartography," Speigner lied.

"I hear you have an interest in Nathan Bedford Forrest," the major changed the subject and tinkled the ice in his glass expectantly.

"Do you know . . . the Battle of Brice's . . . Cross-roads?" Rommel said immediately. He was relieved that someone had initiated this subject, though he would have been happy to talk about anything if it would put an end to this role-playing. *Let the Gestapo play games. There are more important things in the world.*

"I know it well," said Shoemaker without false modesty.

"We want to . . . visit . . ." Rommel looked at Hanke for assistance.

". . . the battle site tomorrow," Hanke finished the sentence.

"It's located near Oxford, up our way," Shoemaker said. "I take my students on a tour out there every year." Max could not discern whether the Germans failed to note or ignored altogether the major's veiled invitation. Rommel turned to Speigner.

"Would you please ask the major if he would favor us with a story about Forrest?" The hooded eyes were guileless, the peacemaking gesture straightforward, with the certitude of command. Max responded in the spirit Rommel valued most in a junior officer: he obeyed immediately and translated the request.

"Have you ever heard about the Battle of Streight's Raid?" Shoemaker asked, lifting his bushy eyebrows. His manner had been transformed from listener to storyteller. The fire of the past was kindled in his eyes. The officers, no longer German or American but fellow military men, unconsciously moved into place around Shoemaker so that all could see his face. Rommel stood in the center of the group, and the major focused on him as though staring into the flame of a campfire.

"It was April of 1863 when an Indiana colonel, Abel Streight, presented Union General Rosecrans with a bold plan to strike into the heart of the Confederacy, cut railroad and supply lines, destroy arsenals, bridges and foundries in General Bragg's rear, below Chattanooga. The objective was Rome, Georgia. . . ." The major paused for Max to translate.

"Der Plan der Union war, die Konföderation ins Innerste zu treffen." Max could see by the Germans' expressions that they had understood much of Shoemaker's narrative, and he limited his translation to the salient facts to allow the major's tale to flow unimpeded.

Rommel perceived with spiritual clarity the flat bleak landscape of northern Alabama, the fallow fields raw with the stubble of last year's cotton on either side of the muddy road. The Confederate column advanced east into the wet dawn at a steady trot. A vast, hospitable silence received the temporary sounds of their intrusion, the rattle of harness and saber, clanking of caissons, drumming of hooves against earth. Rommel yearned toward that nineteenth-century silence divested of clattering machines, the profound hush before a great cavalry charge when one distinctly hears birds or insects, a brook, dogs barking, a man's whisper, horses breathing—not the airplane droning incessantly, truck gears clashing, panzer engines idling; only the land itself, poised to allow man his moment.

At the head of the moving column, leaning forward in the saddle, the collar of his greatcoat turned up against the rain, drops sparkling in his chin beard, sensing the enemy rear guard before him like a hawk tasting the air, was Forrest.

He rode at the head of a handpicked force of two cavalry regiments and a small battery of eight howitzers, about 1,200 men in all, hardened veterans who he knew would stand with him in the hottest fight. Before leaving Tuscumbia at 1 A.M.

that day, Forrest had personally supervised all details: ammunition properly distributed, horses shod, three days' rations cooked for the men, and two days' ration of corn for the horses. Though tired and wet from seven hours of riding in a drizzling rain, Forrest was in excellent spirits. The chase was on, and he knew his game. Reports from scouts and from local residents along the march told him that the Federal raiding party ahead consisted of some 1,500 cavalry mounted on mules, including two companies of Union Alabama cavalry serving as guides. The enemy was about twenty-five miles ahead, moving due east. Having reached the town of Moulton at noon, Forrest ordered saddles off and stock fed. The men rested and ate in an open field near town.

Bedford warmed his hands over a campfire and half listened to the sounds of soldiers fortifying themselves for battle, voices murmuring quietly, local townsmen hawking hot food and blankets, a cobbler's hammer tacking a boot, flames crackling, somewhere a banjo. His spirit drank in these refrains of the march while he focused his powers of concentration on the enemy, who even now was putting distance between them. Soon he gave the order "Mount up!" And the rumble of grousing voices fell on his ear like a deep duet by cello and string bass.

Is there anything finer than marching against the enemy at the head of one's soldiers?

They rode all afternoon and into the night. By midnight Forrest's advance party, a scouting company led by his brother, Captain Willie Forrest, had reached the base of Sand Mountain, a flat plateau rising some 2,000 feet and extending about sixty miles across north-central Alabama. The Union cavalry was ascending the western face of the mountain up a narrow, twisting road which led through a pass called Day's Gap. Willie Forrest's men captured a vedette posted in the woods before the sentry had a chance to give the alarm. Not far ahead was the enemy rear guard of Alabama Unionists, who had not yet left the campfires to follow the main party up the zigzag road.

Born in Württemberg in 1893 . . . no, 1891. That would make him about forty-six. Looks young for his age, very fit. Has a history of athletics, skiing, cycling.

At dawn the Confederate scouts attacked and began a skirmishing action. Hearing the cheery sound of small arms fire popping nearby, General Forrest ordered two regimental commanders, Biffles and Starnes, to make a flanking movement and ascend to the plateau crest through another gap to the north. With about 1,000 of his column having closed up at the base of Sand Mountain, Forrest gave the order to follow the skirmishing scouts and Union rear guard up the winding road. He could feel in his bones the enemy creeping up the mountain pass only five miles away.

We know the enemy's strength, but he does not know that he enjoys a three to two numerical superiority. Yet he also possesses the advantage of foraging new mounts from farms along his route. By the time we arrive, there is no fresh stock left for us. The enemy is well aware that the broken terrain of this plateau is better suited for defensive purposes and allows him to lay ambushes to delay us. We must not let him trick us into time-consuming flanking movements. Our only course is to pursue and harry, run him to ground.

Colonel Abel D. Streight stood holding his mule's reins and looked down the mountain road. The Rebel commander, whoever he was—he hoped with all his might that it was Forrest—would of course have sent a flanking movement through another pass. If he positioned his men here, on the crest of the plateau, and rained fire down on the pursuing enemy, that flanking force would slip up behind him. Streight gave the command to hurry forward, and he led the way to select a strong position to defend. Soon he found the perfect terrain: a U-shaped ridge not easily flanked, with an impassable marsh to the left and a precipitous ravine to the right. He ordered his infantry to dismount and dig in along the ridge. His command included his own regiment, the 51st Indiana, the 73rd Indiana under Colonel Gilbert Hathaway; the 3rd Ohio, Colonel Orris Lawson; the 8th Illinois, Lieutenant Colonel Andrew Rogers; and two companies of Union Alabama cavalry under Captain D. D. Smith. In the center of their position, two 12-pound howitzers were concealed with cut brush. Streight lit a cigar and waited.

Commissioned second lieutenant in 1910, entered active combat service in 1914, captured Italian position on Monte Mataiur and was awarded Pour le Mérite, *the "Blue Max."*

High, yelping voices and the bark of pistols echoed off the surrounding ridges. Soon the clattering of mules' hooves could be heard, and the Union rear guard broke from the woods below the Federal position with the Rebel scouts in hot pursuit, firing pistols and rifles from the saddle. As the rear guard disappeared over the top of the ridge, the line of Union troops rose up and delivered a volley at close range. The scouts melted away under the deafening blast. Horses and men screamed, lost in the gray cloud billowing down the slope. The Confederates retreated under sporadic fire to the cover of the woods below, leaving half their number killed or wounded on the field. Willie Forrest's thighbone was crushed by a minié ball. While an aide cut away his pants leg to staunch the bleeding, Forrest dispatched a rider to report back to the main party and passed out.

It is a standoff. The enemy field of fire is too hot. Wait them out. Time is on our side. They must move on, soon. The longer we hold them, the better. If they remain past dark, we have an even chance with a night attack. Let the men rest and wait for Biffles and Starnes to come in on the northern flank.

Bedford Forrest stood under a pine tree and looked up the ridge, admiring the Federal position. Even with his blood boiling to attack, beard trembling for imminent retribution, he appreciated the enemy's choice of terrain. Up there on the ridge was a man worth fighting. Forrest's staff—Roddey, Julian, Edmondson—stood grouped tensely around him, awaiting his command.

"That ridge's a bear," he said to no one in particular. He glanced at the ambulance wagons being filled with the wounded. "Is William going to lose his leg?" he asked his chief surgeon, J. B. Cowan.

"The bone is crushed through," Dr. Cowan spoke up in his crisp, efficient way. "I can set it, but he will be on crutches for three months."

The general shook his head angrily, as though horseflies buzzed around him. It was an intolerable inconvenience not having his favorite brother by his side. They would attack in the usual manner, at both flanks and in the center simultaneously. Bedford gave the order and watched his staff mount up and hurry back to their regiments. It was 8:30 on a cool, clear April morning.

1929, infantry instructor at Dresden Infantry School; 1933, promoted major, assigned command of rifle battalion at

Goslar; 1935, promoted lieutenant colonel, instructor at Potsdam Kriegsschule.

Streight could see the lines forming up in the woods below, the gray coats bunching at the edge of the trees, sprouting like mushrooms on the flanks. He gave the order to hold fire and let them get close. When the attack came, the roar of voices growing in volume like boulders leaping uphill, he saw that the center line had dismounted and was running low to the ground in good order, while the mounted cavalry leaped and snorted up the ridge on either flank. When the graycoats were within a hundred yards, the entire Union force answered with a terrible volley, firing their repeating Sharps carbines without ceasing for two minutes while the howitzers boomed through their brush cover. The Confederate line was driven back in some confusion. They had regrouped halfway down the ridge and were beginning to return fire when Streight ordered his bugler to sound the charge.

The bluecoats swarmed howling down the ridge on the heels of the retreating Confederates. Forrest bellowed at his lieutenants, furious at the disorderly and indignant retreat. He gestured with his saber like a symphony director in a world gone out of tune. Men in gray slipped through the trees and vines, bullets nipping the leaves around them. Forrest was forced to join the rout momentarily. Looking over his shoulder, he was dismayed to see two artillery pieces being overrun, caissons upset as horses reared madly, entangled in traces of harness.

"*Warum hat er nicht bis zum Einbruch der Nacht gewartet?*"

Speigner translated Rommel's question for Shoemaker, who, thrown off his rhythm, asked for a fresh drink. The major's patient explanation reminded Max of a hundred yesterdays in the ROTC building at Ole Miss.

"Forrest couldn't afford to wait until dark," he told Rommel through Speigner. "He couldn't take the risk of them slipping off with a token force left behind to man the ridge. Besides, they shot his little brother, and the Wizard was pissed off."

"Goddamn your eyes, where are my guns you little bastid?" Forrest shouted into the red face of a young battery commander braced before him. Bedford sat on a log, feet spread wide apart, looking up at the lieutenant. The rest of the staff found a stirrup that needed mending or remembered that they had forgotten to write a letter home. "Who gave a greenhead son of a bitch like you command of those guns? I'll have his stripes. A lady's sewing circle could have done a better job of keeping those animals straight in the traces and pulled those guns out. You shit-a-britches, you farted away my guns. I'll not forgive you for it in a thousand years. You think we hauled those guns 'way up here so they could be taken in a skirmish like that? If I ever lay eyes on you again, my dog will eat your ears for his supper. Git!"

Now that the sacrificial lamb had done its job, the rest of the staff approached the lion to make their reports: thirty Confederate dead and over twice that number wounded. Biffles and Starnes had not yet rejoined the main party. Forrest ordered the troops to assemble before him. He stood on top of the log to address them.

"There will be no horse soldiers," he said, his eyes searing them. "Without guns, we have no need for horses. Every man will dismount and hitch his horse to a tree. We will attack again." He drew his saber and stabbed the air above his head. "We will retake those guns or let every man perish in the attempt, by God!"

Like Forrest, Rommel's standard frontal assault tactic, as shown in his book, was penetration in depth. Break through, divide and conquer.

A thousand graycoats crept through the woods to the clearing beneath the ridge. With a death-rattling yell they surged up the hill, defying the enemy's guns. Forrest, in the front line climbing at a rugged pace, was surprised that the enemy fire was so light. It ceased altogether before they reached the top, and his misgivings were realized with the sight of a small Union rear guard disappearing over the next ridge on their mules. All that was left behind was an open-air "hospital" of about a hundred dead and wounded, Federal and Confederate alike. Forrest first moved among the Confederate dead, kneeling by the still figures, whose enemies had laid them out in perfectly dressed lines as though for one last inspection, and covered their faces with pieces of rags or towels, blankets or flour sacks or shirts. The general uncovered every face, recognizing many and speaking their names under trees feathery with leaf buds. Bluejays attacked a squirrel in a dogwood tree, and pink petals floated to the ground.

We are burdened with the responsibility of human life.

Then he went among the Union wounded, where bleeding men were soon sitting and standing to get a glimpse of Forrest himself. "Who is your commanding officer?" Bedford asked a private with a bandaged head and a cheerful countenance. "Colonel Abel Streight of the Fifty-first Indiana," the private said. "He's a fighting man, General."

"Indeed he is that," Forrest quietly replied. The two precious artillery pieces had been recaptured but were found to have been spiked. Streight liked to hit and run.

Thirty minutes later Bedford was riding hard at the head of a column diminished in size by half. His secret vexation was that the enemy might veer north and double back toward the Tennessee River. "Men," he had shouted to his column as soon as it had formed up, "we will pursue him day and night from here on out. I want you to fire at anything blue you see, and keep up the chase." Biffles and Starnes had come up at last, from the left flank, and Forrest had ordered Roddey and Julian to return to occupy a large Union force on the Mississippi-Alabama border. He also had detached Edmondson's 11th Tennessee regiment to march east toward Somerville in a line parallel with Streight to prevent an escape in that direction. Forrest retained only his escort companies, Captain Forrest's scouts, and Biffles and Starnes' regiments, less than half the enemy force ahead of them.

Now we know the enemy. He is in a hurry to get to his objective. He can be beaten with an inferior force.

At Crooked Creek, some ten miles south of Day's Gap, the 4th Tennessee regiment caught up with the Union rear guard and sharp skirmishing broke out. As the rest of the Confederate column reinforced the advance party, Streight reluctantly ordered his troopers into battle line on a ridge called Hog Mountain. Through his glasses he could see in the fading light before the gathering dusk a tall, bearded figure riding among the troops moving their horses forward at a steady walk. "By God, it's him," Streight exclaimed to himself and sent an order to his battery commander to train the mountain howitzers on the bearded officer.

Quail calls from the ridge were answered by buglers sounding the charge below. The dark trees erupted in volley after volley. Streight pressed his eye to the telescope as puffs of smoke blossomed close to the bearded rider. Forrest's horse fell, but he jumped clear. Streight watched him run to the nearest cavalryman and take his mount from him. The Confederate charge had been repulsed by the concentrated downhill fire. Streight saw Forrest's horse fall again. This time, the bearded one fell heavily to the ground but bounced to his feet as though made of rubber, commandeering another mount, galloping up and down the line, rallying his men. Against the dark ground his saber flashed like a torch of silver.

He moves like a demigod, erect in the saddle behind the flowing mane. His gold braid shines as he raises his arm in command, so that the men around him seem to catch fire from his spark. He pulls them burning behind him to attack again.

Darkness fell and each side searched for the other, their alternating flashes winking like fireflies seeking mates in the fragrant spring night. About 10 P.M. Streight ordered his regiments to slip away, one by one. Several miles east of Hog Mountain he positioned the 73rd Indiana in a thicket to ambush the pursuing Rebel scouts. The Federal troopers lay hidden in leaf shadow at the edge of a clearing. Hooves thudded into soft ground as the head of the Confederate column passed the ambushers unsuspecting. With the line of Rebel troopers outlined against the stars, the Federals opened fire. Forrest's men broke to the right and left under the hail of bullets. Bedford appeared among them, his mount snorting and stamping, wheeling so that Forrest constantly was turning his face to his troopers and repeating a single command, "Keep after them!" Staring into the black, broken landscape ahead, he sensed that the main Union force was not far away and dispatched a runner to order one of the regiments to make a flanking movement while he led a frontal assault. Streight's mule holders were thus surprised by the charge on their flank, and abandoned some thirty wagons and teams to the triumphant Confederates who sang out in the night.

A laying on of hands, feeling for the enemy. What was it the Sudwest Presse *said about Rommel? That he had "Fingerspitzengefühl," a sixth sense in his fingertips.*

Streight's raiders kept up their march, their rear guard

continually attacked and harried by Forrest's scouts until about 2 A.M., when Bedford gave the order to dismount and rest for a few hours. Many troopers barely loosened the cinches on their horses before falling to the ground and sleeping instantly, so exhausted were they from forty-eight hours of riding and eighteen hours of fighting. Forrest removed his boots and received reports which showed he had gotten the best of the night skirmish, losing only six killed or wounded to some fifty Union soldiers found on the field.

While the Confederates slept, Streight's slower, mule-mounted infantry pushed on. At dawn they descended the eastern slope of Sand Mountain into a prosperous valley of corn and cotton fields near Blountsville. A large crowd of farmers and townspeople had gathered around the Blountsville square. Girls and boys were dressed in holiday green. Hand-painted signs proclaimed "May Day." A string band played merrily. Faces turned in alarm, however, and the music stopped as the mule train with bluecoated riders trotted up Main Street in a brisk, proprietorial manner. The Union troopers surrounded the square and eagerly confiscated the fresh mules and horses which providence had concentrated there in large numbers.

"You're feeding the Lightning Brigade, madam," a Federal soldier told a horrified farmer's wife, whose cakes and pies had been scooped up from her table and quickly devoured.

"I hope you choke on it!" the lady cried and hid her face in her apron.

Streight ignored the mayor's pleas for leniency and ordered the local commissary burned to deny Forrest supplies. Glancing over his shoulder at Sand Mountain looming behind him, he decided to lighten his train and proceed only with pack mules. The empty wagons were grouped together in a field near the village and set on fire. The raiders then rode east on the Gadsden road, many of them reeling in the saddle from the exhaustion of nearly three straight days of riding and fighting.

Relieved cheering burst from the townspeople as Forrest's scouts galloped up in time to exchange fire with Streight's vanishing rear guard. With the help of a village bucket brigade—men, women, and children in May Day green rushing with wooden tubs and buckets from a stream in the meadow to the burning supply wagons—the scouts extinguished the fires and saved a pile of discarded rations stored in boxes. They found few mules or horses in Blountsville, however, other than the footsore, blown animals left behind by the Union raiders.

Forrest galloped up at the head of his escort and was immediately surrounded by an adoring throng of Alabamians. The mayor begged the general to address the company: "This is a May Day to end all May Days, General Forrest!"

Bedford bowed to gentlemen and ladies and, speaking from the saddle, said boldly: "It is a pleasure to be here in fair Blountsville and an honor to defend it. I only regret that my men and I cannot tarry to enjoy your hospitality. The enemy will pay for cutting our visit short. I bid you farewell. God bless and keep you. Scouts, move out. Press their rear guard!"

"Interesierte Forrest sick für Politik?"

Shoemaker was nonplussed at Rommel's unexpected question. Max looked askance at the wiry German colonel. Throughout the major's narrative, Rommel's gray-blue eyes had fastened on Shoemaker's animated features, following every expression, every gesture. When his gaze flicked to the translator, Max appeared artlessly engrossed in the story's flow, a conduit across which Forrest and his cavalry clattered. Speigner completely ignored the other Germans, who variously displayed polite interest or—as in Model's case—barely suppressed boredom. The American officers seemed relieved that the "social" was going smoothly and that Shoemaker had things well in hand.

The bourbon was almost gone.

"I can't say whether Forrest was interested in politics or not," Shoemaker answered, "but as a natural leader, he was a first-class speechmaker and a civic leader in Memphis before and after the war. Where was I?"

Rommel is not a member of the Nazi party, is nonpolitical but probably holds career Wehrmacht officer's trust in Hitler to free Germany from the shackles of Versailles.

Ten miles from Blountsville, Streight's force reached a rocky ford on the Black Warrior River. While the rear guard skirmished with the Rebel scouts, the main body crossed and set up their howitzers for covering fire from the eastern bluff of the river. Streight stood on the edge of the bluff and watched some of Forrest's scouts retrieve canisters of hardtack loaded

on two mules that had drowned. The Confederates ripped
open the cans and held up pieces of hardtack for the Federal
soldiers to see, eating it in exaggerated pantomine to prove
that it had not become soft. Streight had not been so lucky
with his ammunition, however, much of which had accidentally gotten wet.

That quote in the Badisches Tagblatt, *in reference to the
legend of Rommel swimming the Piave in December 1917?
"Where Rommel is, the front is."*

An hour later the Confederate cavalry had forded the
river, Forrest having personally supervised all details to
ensure that the ammunition remained safe and dry. He then
called for his favorite horse, King Philip, an iron-gray stallion
eleven years old but with its master's fighting spirit. In battle it
charged the enemy with ears laid back and teeth snapping.
Forrest expanded his escort to 150, shouting, "Let's catch us
some mules!" King Philip stretched out in a long gallop at the
head of the flying column. They soon caught the Federal rear
guard, and Forrest rode in front, exchanging pistol fire with
the rear guard at every bend in the trail. His blood was up and
he wore a fixed expression of fierce joy. Whenever the enemy
skirmishers held a strong temporary position with an imposing
field of fire, Bedford would leave the road in a flanking
movement, which encouraged the Federals to mount their
mules and fall back. At the sight of their general and his
famous iron-gray horse jumping ditches and fencerows, the
powerful combination suspended as one—for every man,
forever in memory—the 150-man escort roared, and Forrest
raised his hat to them in midstride.

God help us all, it can be fun sometimes.

At a flat gallop they rode behind Forrest, reckless of
further ambush, into the Black Creek bottom. They could see
the distant rear guard trotting to safety across the wooden
bridge. A single vedette had been posted halfway between the
Rebel party and the bridge. King Philip reached out in a
magnificent, rhythmic stride and pulled away from the rest.
Pistol in hand, crouched low in the saddle, his face a mask of
savage jubilation, Bedford closed in on the vedette, who was
riding for the bridge as fast as his mule would allow. Ahead of
them, orange flames began to lick across the bridge, feeding on
coal oil. Seeing his escape cut off, the sentry began to rein in.
Forrest fired a warning shot over his head, and the soldier

threw down his carbine and raised his hands in surrender. "Dismount and stand down!" the general shouted and glanced angrily at the flames now devouring the bridge. High banks rose on either side of the sluggish creek. Because of these bluffs, Forrest knew, the stream was considered unfordable for miles in either direction. A howitzer boomed a single note of defiance from the opposite bluffs, sending up a geyser of dirt on the Confederate side of the bridge as if to say, "We have won."

This is the turning point. This is our challenge.

Streight gave the order to push on, promising his officers that the exhausted men could rest when they reached Gadsden. By his estimation, burning the bridge had gained for them nearly a day's lead on the Confederates. Half sleeping, half waking in the saddle, he was nevertheless seized by holiday spirit and bit off the end of a fresh cheroot in celebration.

Forrest stood chafing with disappointment on the west bluff of the creek. It suited his mood to dare the occasional sniper's bullet buzzing overhead. He could not be still, and while waiting for the rest of his column to close up mounted King Philip to reconnoiter the area for himself. Not far from the bridge he discovered a farmhouse, a plain wooden dwelling sheltered by a large hickory tree and guarded by a snarling pack of mongrel dogs. Forrest dismounted gingerly, escorted by the mastiffs with bared fangs. "Hello the house!" he called.

The front door parted an inch and a woman said, "Leave us be." The dogs seemed to take their mistress's tone of alarm as a signal to increase their growling. The largest of them nipped bravely at Bedford's heels.

"I am a Confederate soldier, ma'am. No harm will come to you. I'd be obliged if you would call off your dogs." The door opened. A woman in shawl and apron hesitantly appeared on the porch. Wisps of hair sprang out from the severely knotted braids at the back of her head. Her face bore the strain of poverty, manual labor and sorrow. Forrest softened to that face, which was like thousands he had seen in the streets and countryside of Tennessee, Mississippi and Alabama.

"We heard shootin'," she said in a tone of accusation.

"Union raiders burned the bridge yonder," Bedford

replied. "We are looking for another ford. Do you know of a crossing?"

"I am the Widow Sansom," she announced, taking charge of the conversation. Forrest respected her manners. He noticed the faces of two girls framed in the doorway behind her.

"My name is Forrest, ma'am." He added a little bow to the introductions.

"My son, Luther, and my brother, Edward, are serving in the 19th Alabama Infantry," she said.

"Mighty fine," he said.

"My second son, Mark, is with a Georgia regiment."

"You have given a good deal. More than most."

"Mark is young to be a soldier. Just sixteen. We tried to turn him, but he wouldn't listen. Had to up and enlist." She stared past Forrest, lost in private defeat. He waited patiently for her to come back. "There's an old, dilapidated bridge, 'bout two miles thataway." She pointed south with a small gesture of dismissal. "It's rotten clear through." Forrest glanced over his shoulder. His men had repaired many a country bridge with timbers and fence railings for night crossings behind enemy lines. "Ain't no roads or trails to it," she added, as if reading his thoughts. "Mostly marsh and swamp down there."

"You be General Forrest?" A teenaged girl stepped shyly out on the porch. Below her cotton dress, one bare foot stood on top of the other. Forrest looked into clear blue eyes above freckled cheeks.

"I am him," he said.

"My daughter, Emma," the widow said proudly, reminding Forrest of another world, another time.

"I know a place to cross," said the girl. Bedford's eyes widened. "There's an old ford near our farm. I seen cows cross by theirselves. If I had me a horse I could show you."

"No time for that, missy!" he exclaimed, jumping off the porch and swinging up on King Philip with his arm outstretched to her. "Get up behind me!"

"Emma!" the mother cried as the girl bounded into the yard among the roiling mass of barking dogs. She clutched the general's arm. He pulled her up on the horse, her bare legs white against the iron-gray flanks.

"Madam, be assured of your daughter's safety." Bedford touched spurs to King Philip, and as they galloped toward the creek sniper fire followed them along the bank. The widow sat on her porch steps, face in her hands.

"Down yonder," the girl said in Bedford's ear. She rode with her arms around his waist, and smiling. They dismounted and she led him through a thicket so dense that they crawled along a deer trail to the water's edge. A shallow indentation in the bank showed where cattle had crossed, though not recently. Forrest waded into the stream and found a shallow ledge extending from bank to bank.

"The boys call it 'Lost Ford'," Emma said.

"I thank you missy," said the general.

Riding back across an open field near the Sansom house, they ran another gauntlet of sniper fire. Forrest signaled to the main road for a courier. As Emma slid off the big gray, her mother and sister emerged from hiding in a storm cellar under the house. The widow approached with mouth puckered and Bedford said to Emma, "I think I'd rather take my chances with that sniper over there, missy." She looked up at him radiantly, her brown hair tousled over her forehead. "You said 'If I had me a horse,' didn't you?" Forrest said. "I thought so. My courier will bring you a pretty mare, missy, with my compliments. And one more thing: how about sending me a lock of your hair—address it to 'General Forrest, Tupelo, Mississippi.'" He saluted and turned to go, feeling the mother's disapprobation from across the yard.

"Wait a minute!" Emma cried, and disappeared into the house, her bare feet silent on the porch and quick as a cat. She returned in an instant with quill and inkwell and a piece of paper. "Could I have your autograph?" she said. Forrest smiled, reached for the paper, wrote with a flourish, and galloped away to join his men. Emma stared with a silly grin at the inscription:

Hed Quaters in Sadle
May 2 1863

My highest regardes to miss Ema Sanson for hir Gallant conduct while my posse was skirmishing with the Federals across Black Creek near Gadesden Allabama.

N.B. Forrest
Brig Genl Comding N. Ala—

They crossed Black Creek within the hour. The ammunition was carried over by hand. The artillery and empty caissons were pulled across with ropes. Forrest immediately dispatched his scouts forward to harry Streight while the rest of the Confederate train forded the creek.

"Keep the skeer on 'em!" he yelled.

Pursuit, swift and unrelenting. Pursue them to the edge.

Streight ignored ladies' millinery and sundries, and pointed instead to the blankets and pillows in household goods. He stood in the dusty aisle of a dry-goods store in Gadsden, supervising the confiscation of materials prior to destruction of the facility. The men could sleep at last, if only for a few hours, and they deserved to be as comfortable as possible. He turned with a frown at the heated voices breaking in on this ordinary and thus relaxing duty.

"Confederate scouts coming at full gallop west of town, sir!" a picket breathlessly reported. Streight grabbed a handful of corsets and flung them angrily to the ceiling. One of them draped on the picket, who was already full of dread that the commander would vent his ire on the carrier of bad news. He did not so much as brush away the corset which hung over his cap like a visor. His eyes were alarmed behind the flimsy barrier. Streight fixed him with a red-rimmed look of transparent rage.

"So the devil has found a ford, damn him!"

Streight glanced through the door which opened onto the Gadsden court square, where at high noon sleeping blue-coated soldiers lay as still as corpses on the courthouse lawn, not one head stirring. The dark doorframe composed the picture as though for a painting, a caricature of the deep and lasting sleep. They had been on the move without ceasing for three days, and now he had the responsibility of stealing their rest away from them. They were good men and true, but Abel was afraid they might for the first time refuse to obey his orders. For the first time, the colonel decorated by Sherman for valor and distinction in the western Tennessee campaign began to consider the possibility of defeat. His thoughts turned compulsively to the railroad bridge waiting unmolested at Rome some forty miles away. On impulse he sent for Captain Milton Russell, one of his best officers, and dispatched him with 200 well-mounted men to ride at full speed to Rome and secure the bridge until the main Federal force could arrive. Then he went out to awaken his men.

They arose and, moving as somnambulists, mounted their mules. As the train plodded eastward, Streight rode up and down the line, thanking and congratulating and cajoling. Waking them had been a victory in itself, but now he worried that sleep would be harder to fight than Bedford Forrest. He began to scrutinize the terrain for a place to make a stand.

Arriving at Gadsden, Forrest put out the commissary fires and listened to local citizens tell of the 200-man detail that had set out at a brisk trot on the road to Rome. He immediately sent a local courier to beat Streight's special force to Rome and rally the local militia to hold the bridge. His scouts soon reported that the main Union force had been observed forming into battle line at Blount's Plantation, fifteen miles east of Gadsden. Forrest stood in the street with the fading sun at his back, staring at the darkening eastern horizon, smelling a fight. The energy welling up in Bedford radiated through his officers, who stood anxiously about him and watched his lips for the order to advance.

Follow the line of thrust. Advance, advance, advance.

They went forward to meet the enemy. Their scouting party drove Streight's rear guard back, and Forrest, eager for the battle to begin, ordered a sudden attack before all his units were in battle position. This attack was repulsed by concentrated heavy fire from the momentarily wakeful Federals dug in at Blount's Plantation. Forrest had his men fall back to a ridge near the edge of the plantation and massed his formation for a consolidated assault.

Streight's men fell asleep with their weapons cradled against their bodies. Worse, the skirmish had proved that much of the ammunition was still wet and unfit. As darkness fell, Streight decided to deny Forrest a frontal assault. He ordered his men to fall back, unobserved if possible, and to set up an ambush in a thickly wooded area east of the Blount Plantation. Forrest's pickets, however, were quick to report the quiet withdrawal.

We own them. They belong to us.

"The son of a bitch plans another ambuscade." Bedford laughed. "He repeats hisself." It was a simple matter to feign a flanking movement with part of a regiment to force the

Federals out of position. With darkness his ally, Forrest ordered a single company to "Jest devil 'em all night long" and allowed the rest of his force to get a good night's sleep, eat their rations in leisure, and gather their strength for the final battle.

The time has arrived as we knew it would. Constant pursuit is the mother of victory. Spread thy legs, little mother, and push.

Now began a living nightmare for Abel Streight and his raiders. Staring hopelessly into an unforgiving night, they bounced on mules that shuffled stiffly on tender hooves. At the Cedar Bluff ferry on the Chattooga River, where Russell's 200 men had crossed earlier that day, Streight discovered that no guard had been posted and civilians had hidden the ferry boats. His Alabama Unionist guides advised him to turn northward toward the Gaylesville bridge, six miles upstream. The raiders entered a forest where timber had been cut for a pig iron furnace at nearby Round Mountain. Following a trail of cuttings as the path of least resistance, Streight's sleep-walkers came upon the smelting plant and were set, grumbling, to wreck it. Yet the trails of choppings leading away from the furnace became a horrific maze, a labyrinth with blind walls of dark trees in which the column twisted and doubled back on itself, the troopers leveling their weapons momentarily on their fellow soldiers stumbling like heavy-footed ghosts among invisible tree stumps. Daylight harshly introduced them to the drawn, pale faces of the familiar strangers riding beside them. They staggered to the river and, up stream, to the bridge, which Streight ordered burned behind them. At 9 A.M. they reached the Lawrence Plantation, some five miles from the Georgia line. Their column had begun to inch forward at so painfully slow a pace that Streight was forced to make his final choice: stand and fight to the end. He deployed his force in a defensive line and ordered rations distributed. Men fell asleep with unchewed hardtack in their mouths. A picket galloped up to the Lawrence house on a lathered mule.

"Sir!" he cried to the grim-faced Streight, who sat rocking on the front porch like an old man. "Skirmishing hot on this side of the river. The graybacks done drove in our rear guard. They be right behind me."

Moving at dawn, Forrest's rested troopers had ridden in five hours the twenty miles the Federals had wandered all night and all morning. The Confederates had swum their horses across the Chattooga and pulled two artillery pieces submerged through the water on the sandy bottom. Forrest was cheerful and eager to engage the enemy, discounting as of little importance the fact that he was outnumbered and outgunned more than two to one.

Bring us to them. We glitter in the sunlight on a dancing stallion.

At the sound of cannon and small arms fire, Streight's men left their fires and tottered into position. Many fell asleep over their weapons as they awaited the attack.

Confidence blazed from Bedford like the sun on his saber. Looking down from a low ridge, he watched with a ballet master's pride the dance begin. Biffles' regiment was deployed on the right, McLemore's on the left. From a stand of timber in the center, Forrest's escort made a show of charging. The general was alert to the sluggish Federal response to this feint. Although he could not know it, Streight's men were dozing off over their gunsights.

"Cease fire and maintain positions," he told his runners, who galloped off with the new order. Bedford then had his aide draft a message. Hand thrust carelessly in his pocket he dictated, "As your gallant fight has entitled you to the treatment of brave men, I now offer you the opportunity to surrender your force and to avoid the further effusion of blood. You have my assurance that your men will be treated humanely as prisoners of war. Should my demand be refused, I cannot be responsible for the fate of your command. N.B. Forrest, Brig. General, Commanding."

Captain Henry Pointer, of Bedford's staff, was sent under a flag of truce to parley with the Union commander. Streight read the message, handed it to his chief of staff to read, deliberated for a moment, and made what Forrest would regard as a fatal gesture. "I must speak with Forrest himself," he told Pointer. Squirrels argued overhead as Bedford received Streight's request.

Shed sweat, not blood.

"Have the two artillery pieces brung up here to that clearing yonder on the crest," Forrest ordered before riding out to meet with Streight. "Haul the guns through the clearing without stopping until I return. Circle over the ridge and back around through the trees so the Yankees see the guns only when they cross that clearing. Don't let 'em stop."

Look at Rommel's face. He is still the young lieutenant burning like a star on the summit of Mataiur. Always the snap decision, always goaded by the spur of the moment.

The two officers met in a newly plowed field, the ripe smell of the fresh earth enveloping them, Forrest on horseback and Streight on his mule. Men of both sides strained to see. Union soldiers woke up their sleeping comrades to watch their colonel meet the devil himself. The adversaries faced each other with the intense, restrained curiosity of soldiers who at last are able to shape into flesh and bone the human will against which each has fought and grappled at a distance.

"General, you have gall," Streight said. "My men are well dug in. We can repulse any assault you make."

"We'll be sorry to oblige you," Forrest said without rancor. He observed the dark circles under the colonel's eyes. "I will permit your officers to retain their side arms and personal property, of course."

"How many men have you," Streight's eyes shifted to catch some movement on the ridge behind Forrest. He could make out batteries being pulled into position.

"Enough," Bedford replied in the tone of a man who does not need to boast, "to run over you in thirty minutes. And a column of fresh troops between you and Rome." Streight seemed to deliberate, his eyes fastened on the ridge.

"Name of God!" he suddenly exclaimed. "How many guns have you got?" Bedford paused before answering, and Streight added, "There's fifteen I've counted already!"

"I reckon that's all that's kept up with us," Forrest said. His horse stamped impatiently and he reined it in.

"I must see my officers." Streight's statement was more a request than a demand.

"Suit yourself," Forrest said indifferently. "It will soon be over, one way or the other." The two men turned away from each other and rode back toward their respective lines.

Streight called a meeting of his officers. He leaned against the hollow trunk of a dead elm tree, his tunic unbuttoned, his expression hovering between defiance and futility. As his staff gathered around him, a courier arrived with a report from Russell.

"Cap'n Russell reports the Oostanaula bridge well defended by militia waiting in hiding," the young courier gasped. "Cap'n Russell says the whole town of Rome is armed against us. Cap'n Russell sent a sortie against the bridge to test their defenses and was driven back by heavy fire. Cap'n Russel is therefore withdrawing and heading this way to join up with you, sir."

Streight dismissed the messenger and addressed his officers: "The enemy outnumbers us three to one," he said, making a great effort to disguise his own weariness. "He has a good deal of artillery, more than I would have guessed. His troops appear fresh and spoiling for a fight. Our men are worn out, ammunition is low and much of it wet." He did not look at the officer who had been in charge of the Black Warrior crossing, but the man studied the ground. "The enemy may have another force between us and Rome. We can make a fight of it here, but I want a vote. Now, all for standing fast?" Not a hand was raised, the officers glancing around for confirmation but avoiding each other's eyes. "All for surrendering?" Every man except Streight raised his hand. Abel turned to his aide, who was transcribing the minutes of the meeting. "The record will show a unanimous vote for surrender by the staff. It has been my fight all the way through, but this is not my surrender."

The moment Forrest was informed of the surrender, he directed Streight to have his men stack arms and march into a hollow between the lines, where his smaller force could surround them. Streight counted the Rebel cavalry who stalked with self-conscious dignity around the rim of the small valley. "The majority of their force remains on our flanks and in our rear," he told his officers with utter conviction. Then he addressed his men, shouting his thanks over the silent hollow filled with blue, commending them for their gallant service to their country, and calling for three cheers for the Union. With leg thrown carelessly over the pommel of his saddle, Forrest listened to this enthusiastic, forlorn display. Then he saw that his troopers were all watching him for his reaction. They were his boys, and they would do anything he asked of them. He merely raised his hand, and they responded with a high, boyish cheer as though from a single throat that would never grow old, a hosanna to the man on the iron-gray horse.

To know it once is enough. That is our secret.

"I'm sorry the story outlasted the booze," Shoemaker said, not sorry at all.

"Forrest liked the . . . odds him . . . *gegen*, against?" Rommel was reluctant for the story to end. His Coke was warm in his hand. Soft lighting had been turned on in the ballroom. Outside the wide glass windows, blue globes of streetlights were satellites around the silver moon of the Capitol dome. Taillights of cars of late Saturday shoppers were moving lines of red disappearing in the dark streets.

"That made it a fair fight," Shoemaker replied with a bourbony grin.

"*Das war ein gerechter Kampf,*" Max repeated. No one glanced at him, as his voice had become an echo of the professor's narrative. Ice rattled in glasses and feet shuffled on the polished floor. The Americans drained their highballs with the satisfaction of hosts who had discharged their duty. The meeting had turned out to be more than fellow professionals brought momentarily together by ancient protocol. Because of Shoemaker's storytelling and Speigner's translation they were men bound in a common appreciation of soldiering. Max, however, noted that not all of the visitors were as spellbound as Rommel. Model, for example, was looking at his watch. Hanke, the public relations expert, took the hint.

"Well, gentlemen, we have enjoyed . . ." the Nazi publicist began.

"In *diesem* bat-tle of . . . Sand Mountain," Rommel interjected, determined that what he perceived as a lecture be permitted to reach its fitting conclusion, a summation of facts and lessons, "*Forrest verfolgte einen Feind* . . ." He glanced at Max for help.

"Pursued an enemy . . ." Speigner translated, relieved that the Germans were not leaving just yet. His eyes met Shoemaker's and made silent claim. Unless some overture was made soon, their tenuous connection with the Germans would be broken. The visitors would never accede to an invitation from a representative of G-2.

"*Die Zeit war auf Forrests Seite.*" Rommel addressed Shoemaker to confirm his own assessment. Max followed with a translation.

"Time was Forrest's ally . . . He perceived instantly that

it was not in the enemy's best interest to stand and fight. Because he was a 'general of the saddle' and led from the front, he could make immediate decisions based on firsthand knowledge. Also he could personally supervise river crossings and make sure the ammunition did not get wet. Three things strike me as all-important."

"And I was enjoying my holiday from the *Kriegsschule*," Schörner, an instructor at the War College, moaned, entertaining Model and Krüger.

"What are those three important factors, Herr Rilke?" Krüger burlesqued interest, but Rommel would not be distracted.

"First, when Forrest perceived that the enemy could not stop short of his objective, he sent back half his force to serve where they were most needed." Rommel paused for Max to translate for the Americans. "Next, he refused to accept another's assessment of the river as being unfordable, and found a crossing through his own initiative. Last, he was sure enough of his enemy's plan to take time to rest his men. Sleep, or lack of it for the enemy, was also Forrest's ally."

"What about tricking the Union colonel into surrending to an inferior force?" asked Krüger, genuinely interested now. "I rather liked that part myself. Reminded me of someone I know."

Rommel grinned in acknowledgment. "Icing on the cake," he told his friend, the cavalryman. "His men were rested. They would have won anyhow, and he knew it." Shoemaker nodded his appreciation of Rilke's appraisal.

"Now *we* would teach our hosts the history of America, ha-ha," Model said in English, chuckling humorlessly. He clicked his heels together and addressed Adler. "Thank you very much for your kind hospitality." Four other pairs of heels snapped curtly together. The Americans tensed and stood a bit straighter, secretly envious of men to whom elaborate forms of courtesy came as naturally as breathing.

"It has been our pleasure," Adler told Model with a tone of genial formality which marked them as fellow administrators. "Where do you go from here?"

Model consulted briefly with Hanke. "Brice's Cross-roads," he said. "It is north of here, I believe."

"We happen to be going in that same general direction,"

Shoemaker said. "I would be glad to show you around the old battlefield at Brice's Crossroads, if you like." Max felt his body stiffen with anticipation, and he willed himself to relax.

"We would not wish to impose . . ." Hanke began, glancing at Model's impassive face.

"It is *nicht weit* out of *Ihrem* way?" Rommel exclaimed. He felt Model glaring at him and relished it.

"Only an hour or so," Shoemaker replied offhandedly. "Nothing like walking the actual terrain, eh, Herr Rilke? And Speigner will be with me, so we'd have an interpreter." He glanced at Max.

"*Das wäre eine Ehre für mich.* I would be honored." Max bowed gravely.

"What good fortune!" Rommel said and turned to Model with an innocent grin.

"I suggest we meet out front of the hotel in the morning," said Shoemaker. "Say, eight o'clock? You have a car?"

"Yes, an Oldsmobile rental car," Hanke replied, forgetting Model's disapproval.

"Very good," said the major, taking a step backward, so that the group began to break apart and move toward the elevators.

"Yes, Oldsmobile is good car," said Hanke.

"It's no Mercedes Benz, ha-ha!" said Adler. They shook hands all around once more.

"Thank you very much," Rommel said to Max, the hooded eyes friendly. "Until tomorrow, then?"

"Tomorrow," Max said with an eager smile.

"See you after breakfast!" Shoemaker called, as the Germans walked to the elevators.

"Those guys are no slouches," Adler observed.

"General staff, I betcha," Nicholson chimed in.

"Let's hear it for our word-man from D.C.!" Shoemaker cried. "He's not bad on finding liquor, either."

Max did not hear. He was staring intently at the closing elevator doors.

Why the assumed names?

The black elevator operator locked the inner door in place and started the electric motor for the descent. Model's displeasure filled the cramped space like murky water in an aquarium. He addressed Rommel over his shoulder. "That young one, Speigner, works with their military intelligence, Herr Rilke, or did you not notice?"

"Discussing Bedford Forrest is not exactly swapping state secrets," Rommel retorted.

"Forrest! I have heard enough about Forrest to last me a lifetime."

"The man was an artist." Rommel shrugged. "One could do worse than pay attention."

"I have your guarantee on that?" Model persisted.

"Walther, you have too little appreciation for art," Rommel said, as they reached the first floor. "I suggest that you take up the violin."

"Watch yo' step, gentlemens," said the operator.

VI

The drumming of the hooves drowned out all but thought, a constant, rolling wave of sound under the perfect silence of a starlit sky. The road ahead was slick with moisture, but the rains had stopped and Bedford sensed that the June day would be clear and hot. Happiness surged through him with a fiery warmth and he stood in his stirrups, turning to Rucker who rode behind him.

"Good ol' Sol," he shouted. "He'll do our work fer us t'day!"

"What?" The colonel lashed his mount's withers and moved up abreast of Forrest, who rode as always at the head of his escort.

"The sun," Bedford yelled across the wet road rushing beneath them, "is goin' to make it hot as hell!" He grinned from ear to ear, his chin beard sticking straight out like a dark, inverted horn. As soon as their scouts had reported that the Union force was moving south on the Guntown road toward Tupelo, Forrest had been in a frenzy to ride. He had ordered his scattered units to converge quickly, throughout the night,

on the spot he had carefully chosen as his battleground: Brice's Crossroads.

At their temporary headquarters in Booneville, Rucker earlier had argued with his commander, "We're too spread out. How will we get enough men massed at the Crossroads in time?" Rucker was incredulous. Forrest's 4,200-man force was spread over twenty-five miles. It violated all accepted tactics to initiate a battle with one's command divided.

"My troopers have not failed me yet," Bedford had said, his gray-blue eyes uncompromising. Soon, Rucker knew, those eyes would begin to glitter with battle yearning. "That narrow road across the marsh north of Brice's Gin will slow the enemy down. The high ground where we'll fight is thick with woods, and they will not know our inferior strength. Their cavalry should reach the crossroads three hours ahead of the infantry." He spoke more rapidly as he strapped on his saber. "We should lay into their cavalry—we kin whup 'em in an even fight—and when their infantry comes on the run fer five miles to support the whupped cavalry, ol' Sol is goin' to do our work fer us! Sir, you will move yo' brigade up as quickly as possible. I will go ahead with Lyon and the escort and open the fight."

Rucker glanced at the forty-two-year-old general riding hard beside him. The Wizard of the Saddle was bent forward, leaning into the night, his shoulders rolling with his mount's rhythm, his eyes searching the black horizon under its starry curtain. Muddy water droplets from the pounding hooves whirled past his face like glistening bullets from an unseen enemy.

"I hope you're right!" Rucker shouted.

Crouched in his stirrups above the surging animal, Bedford gave Rucker an enigmatic smile, reached into his breast pocket and, by way of reply, held up his good luck charm between thumb and forefinger—the minié ball surgeons had removed from close to his spine after Shiloh.

It was a magnificent victory in a war that was lost, Rommel thought. He and his German companions listened to Speigner translate Shoemaker's enthusiastic narrative beside the burned-out shell of the old Brice house. Two brick chimneys, scorched black and trailing wisteria vines, were all that remained of the antebellum mansion. Debris from Fourth of July picnickers—empty soda bottles, cardboard cups, wax paper fluttering in a faint breeze—littered the bare ground around a single stone monument. To the northwest they could see the swampy bottom cut by the sluggish, tree-shrouded creek called Tishomingo. To the east the land rolled away in gentle undulations, offering mute testimony to Forrest's genius.

Shoemaker showed them how Forrest had moved in swiftly from the east and checked the Union cavalry near the hilly crossroads. The muddy road below, with its fateful, narrow bridge, seemed to have been devised by nature and man working in concert for a classic military purpose, awaiting only Forrest's will. It was there, under a relentless sun, that the Federal infantry would lose the battle before they fired the first bullet.

Farmland now softened the aspect of the terrain. Cultivated fields lush with corn, sorghum and cotton stretched between wooded ravines. Cows grazed in green meadows bright under the noon sun. A hawk circled lazily above a farmhouse where chickens pecked unceasing and dogs lay panting on their sides under a lone shade tree. Yet for Rommel the ground trembled from the trampling of hooves and the rumble of caissons. The battle pulsed in his fingertips. He smelled gunpowder and wisteria.

A quarter mile away, small arms fire popped and snapped briskly like green twigs burning in a campfire. Bedford assumed that Lyon's regiment, advancing west on the Baldwyn road, had run into the Federal scouts. He rose in his stirrups, enjoying the warm, fresh breath of a summer dawn against his face. He was thinking of Lyon and the decision the colonel should make, willing him, across the thickets where foxes lay and thrushes called, to throw out cavalry companies on either side of the road, dismount the rest of his brigade, and advance at double-quick until engaged by the enemy. The boom-and-thump of Union cannon disturbed the cloudless day. Bedford whipped off his coat and rolled up his sleeves. Hovering loosely around him, men jumped to his orders like puppets on a string.

"Tell Bell and Buford to move up fast with all they've got!" he shouted at his staff major. "And forward Morton's battery at a gallop." The major bolted into his saddle and spurred his mount into the woods to the southeast. Seized by afterthought,

Bedford grabbed a sergeant's arm. "Barteau is comin' behind us. I want him to take the Second Tennessee around the northern flank, gain the Federal rear, and destroy their supply train."

Forrest was playing for time, Rommel thought, tying up the enemy and waiting for his guns to come up. He planned it in three stages: holding attack, main attack, pursuit. Simple, clean, elegant.

Twisting through thick scrub oak and blackjack, vines and briars, Forrest led his escort company cross-country and emerged behind Lyon's regiment. He saw, with satisfaction, that they were advancing up the long slope surmounted by the two-story Brice house, the green roof of which was just visible over the treetops. Men in gray fired, reloaded, slipped forward to the next cover, tree or hedge or fence, creeping forward inexorably against the retreating Federal skirmishers. Bedford dismounted and, walking upright, advanced behind them, saber in hand, fiercely oblivious to the bullets that sang past him. A minié ball whacked into a soldier not two feet from Forrest, and the man fell, nodding, as if his skepticism regarding his own immortality had at last been substantiated. At the edge of a large cleared field Bedford could see the Union cavalry. They had dismounted and formed into battle line in a dense blackjack thicket on the western edge of the field, about a half mile east of the crossroads. He listened to their batteries with the critical ear of a maestro appraising the bass section and ascertained that the enemy had four guns in firing position.

"I want Lyon to lay these fences down," he told a smooth-faced lieutenant with eyes like brown marbles. "We goin' to simulate charges up and down the line."

"Forrest used these piecemeal charges," Shoemaker pointed across a pasture where cattle grazed, "to disguise the fact that his forces were badly outnumbered."

The seven men—two Americans and five Germans—walked east on the gravel road to Baldwyn and looked out over the terrain where Forrest had ordered the feints. The sagging, rusty barbed-wire fences which now separated woods and field had a temporary look, as though the farmer expected soldiers to come presently and lay them down for another charge. In deference to the July heat, the Germans carried their coats folded over arms or slung across shoulders. Occasionally a pickup truck would clatter past and they would retreat across the roadside ditch to keep from being bombarded by stones scattering like shot from the moving wheels.

Max kept pace with Shoemaker's narrative—condensing, surprising himself with idiom learned in childhood and now used as easily as if he spoke German every day. His attention was divided between the major's face and that of Rommel. Whether Shoemaker was more inspired than usual, or whether it was the fire of imagination burning in Rommel's eyes, Max came alive to the battleground as never before. As an ROTC student following his professor up and down the storied landscape, he had allowed distractions, the jokes of classmates, wildflowers, small animals flushed out of hiding, to obscure Shoemaker's account of Forrest's tactics. The fact, too, that men had bled and died here had struck him as more important than the nuts and bolts of how it had happened. He had been too busy learning to be haunted to pay attention to details. Now the plan revealed itself, tailored to the terrain like glove on hand. Speigner felt a weird rush of respect for the bluff, violent, ballsy, obscene cavalryman who fell on his enemy at this place with such care and frenzy, who bowed the land itself to his hand and struck a blow with it, who seemed now to be grinning across the pasture and all eternity. Speigner realized that Rommel also was smiling at him, whimsical and carefree.

"*Nennen Sie das* 'Dog Trot'?" Rommel indicated the unpainted wooden frame dwelling they were passing. The roof sagged in the middle over an open hallway. There were cracks in the walls wide enough to see through. In the yard, chickens pecked with metronomic regularity and scruffy orange-and-black mastiffs growled without venturing from the shade under their tree. In a dilapidated barn a young man wiped a motorcycle with an oily rag. The machine gleamed amid its dismal surroundings like a silver nugget in a gravel pit. The man looked at them with a blank stare. Near the barn a middle-aged woman in a blue cotton dress slung wet laundry over a clothesline.

During their drive northward from Jackson, Rommel had become fascinated with such shanties and the peasants who inhabited them. The barrenness of Mississippi's red clay hills and dirt roads and rickety wooden bridges appealed to him. He had become a connoisseur of crossroads hamlets with a single general store, where men in overalls whittled wooden sticks with pocketknives and dogs slept in the middle of the road, where cultivated fields lapped up to the walls of sharecroppers' cabins as if the landowners were loath to spare a few yards of ground for lawn or garden. The unending poverty, painful to the eye, was somehow ennobling, as if the land, Mississippi, had struck a balance—depriving its people of material possessions on one hand while sustaining them with a tenacious pride in family, friends and self on the other. Rommel felt that he was beginning to understand the source of Forrest's genius, which defied fate itself, and of his men's undying loyalty.

"Mississippi was wounded by the Great Depression?" he added. Shoemaker was alert to Max's translation. Rommel was charmed by the major's reply.

"The Depression barely made a ripple in Reconstruction," Shoemaker said through Max. "Banks and stores still doing business on the barter system can scarcely be affected by the devaluation of the dollar."

"Could you please tell us," Model interrupted, obviously impatient with this digression and addressing Shoemaker carefully in English, "the general opinion of Forrest's . . . potential—whether he would have . . . ummmm . . . benefitted from formal military training at West Point?" Rommel was irritated by the weapons expert's lack of appreciation.

"It is a matter of speculation," Shoemaker answered pedantically, "whether the conventional methods imparted by a West Point education could have made him a more effective leader in the field, but perhaps he would have started out with better ideas of military discipline and the science of war—"

"No, no!" Rommel cried, surprising Max with the force of his emotion. "Do not tie him down with mundane realities. Let him fly! He is a bird of prey, high above, that sees everything at once. He is a wild thing of great beauty and courage. He cannot be regulated or have any curb put on his spirit. He is the air itself. *He must not be denied.*"

Rommel had stopped in the road, glaring at them with his coat slung over his shoulder. The Germans were embarrassed at their colleague's outburst. Max and Shoemaker, however, exchanged delighted glances. The major tactfully resumed his narrative, although he now directed his remarks to Rommel, in the habitual manner of the professor who tends to address his lecture to his brightest student while ignoring the rest.

"Forrest's three piecemeal charges," he said, drawing his audience down the road after him, "disguised the fact that his forces were badly outnumbered. But in the dense, brush-screened line, the Union cavalry commander, Brigadier-General B. H. Grierson, could not tell what size forces confronted him, and he failed to note that—for the time being—his horse artillery was unopposed. In fact, Grierson fell for Forrest's feint, and he sent a courier pounding back to Sturgis."

Brigadier General Samuel D. Sturgis glanced up from his hand-drawn map. The courier quivered at attention as straight as an arrow. "Where!" Sturgis demanded. "Show me." He thrust the map under the soldier's flushed face, but the courier merely turned and pointed at a distant ridge.

"Brice's Crossroads, sir! Up on that hill yonder."

Sturgis looked from the map to the marshlands steaming in the rising sun below them. His handsome column—250 new wagons loaded with a twenty-day supply of food and ammunition, twenty-two guns of various calibers, and a dozen modern ambulances outfitted with the best medical supplies—labored across the narrow, muddy causeway flung along the bottom-land like a crumpled brown ribbon against bright green cloth. The day had begun splendidly, with a letup in the infernal Rebel rain, and his troops were well rested and in high spirits. The brigadier was glad that the enemy had been found, but the terrain disturbed him.

"I'll ride ahead and see the situation for myself," he told the courier. "Instruct Colonel McMillen to keep the infantry proceeding as rapidly as possible without distressing the troops."

Sturgis spurred his horse through the long line of wagons and caissons and men. The stocky ex-Indian fighter maintained a calm expression and politely tipped his hat to his soldiers. A West Point graduate in the same class with George McClellan and Stonewall Jackson, he would be forty-two on the morrow, the same age as Forrest. Grierson had promised him the Rebel general's hair for a birthday present. But now Grierson was reporting his division heavily engaged with a superior enemy force; he believed he had an advantageous position that could be held if infantry were brought up promptly.

Sturgis's thoughts were interrupted by shouts and curses. He saw artillery and ambulances jamming the road. He circled the stalled vehicles, helping a flustered lieutenant restore order, and soon found the cause of the problem: a narrow wooden bridge spanning a swollen creek which surged to the very lip of its banks. The structure was barely wide enough for a single line of traffic. Wagons and artillery had ground to a halt. "Clear that bridge so the infantry can get through!" he commanded, then swam the creek on his horse and galloped up the road ascending the ridge. At the crossroads he found, to his surprise, the cavalry dismounted and fighting in confusion. The wooded terrain was overgrown too thickly to mount a cavalry charge, and temporary breastworks of logs and fence rails appeared through the trees as if strewn helter-skelter by a massive storm. Union soldiers lay behind this cover and returned the steady enemy fire in desultory fashion, every man for himself. Sturgis looked around, scowling, for his division commanders.

Colonel George E. Waring, Jr., was the first officer to report to him. "I'll have to fall back unless I receive some support soon," Waring cried. Hatless and red-faced, the young colonel galloped back to his beleaguered division immediately. Colonel E. F. Winslow was more pessimistic, saluting dourly and saying, "We may have to be relieved, General." At last Grierson rode up. Sturgis's foreboding was lightened by the sight of his cavalry leader looking as confident as ever. The young brigadier's report, however, belied his appearance.

"The Rebels are present in large numbers!" Grierson shouted to be heard above the cannon and clatter of riflery. "They have double lines of skirmishers and heavy supports. Our troopers have succeeded in holding their own and repulsing with great slaughter three distinct and desperate charges." Grierson unknowingly referred to Forrest's feints. "I am afraid, however, that I cannot hold long unless reinforced. Will you bring McMillen up, now, please?"

Sturgis glanced apprehensively at the sun blazing in a cobalt sky. The air hung in leaden layers, not a breeze stirring.

He called for a courier and dictated an order: "To Colonel McMillen—make all haste in bringing up your three brigades. S. D. Sturgis." The soldier saluted and galloped down the hill to the creek. Sturgis stared, brooding, at the Union breastworks clustered against the trees like driftwood among pilings. He called for another courier. "To Colonel McMillen," he dictated a more emphatic order: "Lose no time in coming up. Sturgis." Shading his eyes with his hand, he peered up at the sun again, his expression tense with concentration, as if conjuring a benign presence.

A half mile down the long slope east of the crossroads, Forrest's eyes flashed with fierce approval. He had just received word that Bell's brigade, with 2,787 men the largest in his command, had arrived at last. "I want Bell to straddle the Guntown road with our left flank," he told the young courier panting for breath. "I'll be conferrin' with him directly. Move!" He gave the runner a friendly shove to start him on his way, turning to the ubiquitous staff couriers who buzzed around him like gnats everywhere he went. He had only to raise his hand and a captain instantly reined in at his side. "Tell Buford he's in command on the right. That includes Lyon's, Rucker's, and Johnson's brigades. Now, where's Morton!" Listening unconsciously to the intermittent rifle fire of skirmishers and snipers, he went to look for his batteries. An aide led him to a clearing behind a stand of scrub oaks. As they rode through the trees his men rose up one by one, cheering him. In a festive mood, he doffed his cap to them. "We whupped the Yank cavalry," he yelled. "Now we'll whup their infantry. Ol' Sol is doin' our work fer us."

Morton saluted his chief. The young artillerist was smiling and eager. His men stood at attention by their guns, every eye on Forrest.

"Morton, here you are!" Bedford said without dismounting. "I want you to double-shot four of your guns with canister, and when you hear the bugle sound the charge, advance with the front rank and keep pace with it. Ketch their countercharge in enfilade. The Yankees will be surprised." His eyes twinkled at Morton's open-mouthed astonishment.

"Charge? With my guns?" Morton could not help gaping. "Unprotected? In the front rank?"

"Why, Lieutenant," Bedford said good naturedly. "Artil-

lery is meant to be captured." He wheeled his horse, and without a backward glance trotted away to confer with Bell. Morton stood with mouth open. As was their habit whenever a fuse was lit, his gunners tucked their chins and braced themselves for an explosion.

Forrest was sailing high and alone, Rommel thought, to put artillery in the front rank. He was riding the high currents.

To get a better view, Sturgis climbed into a pear tree in the backyard of the Brice home. At the upstairs windows of the house, the frightened and angry faces of the Brice family watched the Union commander raise his binoculars and peer down the ridge at his infantry trotting uphill with rifles slanted before them. He could see men dropping out in the heat. Those in the front rank now reaching the crest near the crossroads were red-faced and gasping, their uniforms stained with sweat.

"Everything is going to the devil as fast as it can," McMillen complained, looking up at Sturgis's austere face surrounded by pale green globes of fruit. "Grierson's cavalry is withdrawing in disorder, General. My infantry is having to fight through them to occupy the positions they are vacating. The heat is killing us. If the Rebels mount a concerted attack, we will be in a bad way."

"Keep them coming," Sturgis said stiffly. Sweat beads popped out on his forehead and, one by one, rolled down his cheeks. It was 1 P.M. McMillen whirled irritably and hurried away to try to bring some order to the Federal line, where his sun-ravaged men were stumbling and falling in the overgrown thickets, creeping gratefully under whatever shade they could find.

Forrest's coat was folded over the pommel of his saddle. Sunlight turned his shirt to gold as he spurred his big sorrel through the trees. His dismounted troopers looked up from where they lay behind trees and fence rails, and saw the saber in his hand. His color was up and his eyes were burning.

"Get up, men!" Forrest shouted, and they rose like sleepwalkers at the sound of his voice. "I have ordered Bell to charge on the left. When you hear his guns, every man must charge, and we will give them hell. This is a fight to the death for victory."

Repeating his message to each unit he encountered,

Forrest rode to the left, where he expected the stiffest enemy resistance. His line formed a wide semicircle, almost enveloping the shorter but stronger semicircle of Federal troops. His strategy was for the two outside brigades, left and right, to pinch down toward the center in a movement intended to converge simultaneously at the Union middle and break through of its own momentum.

Forrest abruptly reined in and listened. Silence had fallen over the battlefield, a suspension of sound and movement penetrated only by the twittering of birds and the fanciful clank of a cowbell. Forrest rose up in his stirrups and attended to the silence. Every part of him was alert—eyes slanted, head cocked, shoulders rigid, hands poised over the reins.

Rommel understood: Forrest was born knowing when to strike.

"Forward!" Forrest rode among Bell's 7th Tennessee Brigade as the bugle sounded. "You're the pride of Tennessee!" he called to them, cajolingly, as they moved out of the trees. "You're the bravest and the best." From a thousand voices a Rebel yell gathered momentum, propelling the gray line into the open field, the mad yelping answered presently by a roar from the blue line across the clearing. Men of Illinois, Indiana and Minnesota returned a galling fire and rose to mount a furious counterattack.

The Federal charge broke the dismounted Tennessee cavalry, whole companies staggering toward the rear. Unaccustomed to infantry withdrawal, many men walked backward, as if it were no disgrace to retreat while facing the enemy. His face brick red, Forrest charged into the breach filling with bluecoats, firing his pistol until it was out of bullets, then unsheathing his curved saber of Damascus steel and slashing left and right without distinction to uniform. His own soldiers quailed from the whirring blade. From his horse he could see Union cannon smoke blossoming on the left flank with no accompanying sound. He saw Wilson's men fall in enfilade at the same time the boom of the guns reached him, as though the sound were made by the combined impact of their bodies. The center had to hold or all was lost.

"Goddammit, turn and fight!" he cried at the Tennesseans, wheeling his sorrel to cut off their retreat. "Turn or I'll shoot you myself! Remember your pride, Tennessee. You,

trooper, git back in line, goddamn you. You the bravest and th' best! I'll blow yo' head off, sir. Turn! Fight!"

If soldiers lose their nerve and break, the commander must take vigorous action, using his personal weapons if necessary.

Forrest went forward, at first alone, then saw to his delight a hatless, towheaded private walking with musket at the ready beside the general's horse. The boy could not have been older than sixteen.

"See this man!" Forrest bellowed at the troops cowering behind him. "Give me a hunnerd more like him'n I'll whup the damn Yankees myself." Men began to fall in, singly, then whole companies were moving back into line. Forrest beamed at the private.

"See what you done? You're a good'un, son," he shouted. "Where you from?"

"Collierville," the boy cried morosely, "but I cain't go back, now. I stole my grandpap's horse to jine up with you, and they done shot it out from under me. I'd as soon git kilt as face my grandpappy."

"Oh," said Forrest and turned back to the fight.

With his escort company from the 7th Brigade, Forrest led a countercharge. The lines surged together in a riptide of clashing bayonets. Bedford's men fired revolvers into enemy soldiers at point-blank range, and the Federals began to fall back.

"Ein Maschinengewehr hätte ein ganzes Regiment zurückschlagen können," Model sniffed. Rommel, who was shielding his eyes against the sun, jerked his arm down as if it had been stuck with a pin. The party had turned and was now headed uphill, on the attack.

"One machine gun could have repelled an entire regiment," Max translated Model's remark for Shoemaker.

"I wish they'd never invented the thing!" he growled under his breath. Rommel grinned at his host. They understood each other. Yet Shoemaker was not satisfied. He began to digress—primarily for Model's edification—on the devastating effect on tactics caused by the advent of the machine gun. Rommel caught Max's eye and drew him off to one side, leaving Shoemaker's audience to pick up stray cognates as best they could.

"Können wir dieses Motorrad leihen oder mieten?" Rommel pointed to the barn and the young farmer's silver machine.

"Können Sie es fahren?" Max was intrigued with the colonel's boyish notion of renting the motorcycle.

"Jawohl, Herr Leutnant!"

They walked past the growling dogs, who followed them to the barn along with the stares of the men standing in the road. The young man, towheaded and about nineteen, called off his dogs and stood wiping his hands with oily rags as if they also needed polishing. His dark eyes regarded them with suspicion.

"How do!" It was a voice of the clay hills, suspicious and singsong.

"That's a good-looking motorcycle," Max said, smiling and nodding at the machine. "Do you think we could rent it for a short ride?" There was no change in the farmer's expression, no sign even that he had heard. "We're from the university at Oxford," Speigner added. Prior experience with Brice's natives had taught him that they regarded battlefield tourists as lunatics, harmless but worth keeping an eye on, especially Yankees. Max hoped to achieve a bit of respectability with the reference to Ole Miss. The farmer spat and leaned a hand firmly on the handlebars.

"Brand-new." He spat again, for emphasis.

"Nicht zu vermieten." Speigner said to Rommel, who had been unable to understand the provincial accent. The boy's forehead wrinkled at the sound of a foreign language.

"What's that?" he exclaimed, his eyes widening.

"German," Max said. "This gentleman has come all the way to Mississippi to study Nathan Bedford Forrest."

"Oh," said the farmer self-consciously. "I'm kin to Forrest. On my daddy's mama's side." He let the remark hang between them, self-explanatory. Rommel reached into his pocket and took out some folded currency. He peeled off a five-dollar bill.

"It . . . is enough?" he said quietly but with a peremptory tone of command. The way he offered the bill to the farmer was less a request than an order. An oily hand reached out, and the crisp bill disappeared into a pocket.

"This here's a Harley," the boy said, speaking distinctly for the foreigner's benefit. "You know Harley? They got Harleys over there in . . . where you come from? Here's the clutch.

You know the clutch? Works like this? Okay. Here's the
throttle. Okay? Now, you know how to drive one of these
thangs?" By way of reply, Rommel pulled his homburg on
tighter, but the farmer would not allow him to start the engine.
He set the ignition himself and stamped the starter pedal.
When the engine roared to life, exhaust fumes boiling around
the barn, he smiled with the pride of ownership, revealing
yellowed teeth. Then his face was narrowed by concern. "You
take good keer of it, now."

The other Germans and Shoemaker gaped as Rommel and
Speigner came rumbling out of the farmyard and turned east
toward Baldwyn. Max held on to Rommel's waist as he
experimented with the gears, stopping and starting again,
becoming familiar with the action. The young farmer loped
down the road behind his beloved machine. They retraced
Forrest's path, following the Old Carrollville Road across the
Baldwyn Road. Max found himself remembering Shoemaker's
lectures as if reading from notes. They turned off the main road
onto a country lane and entered a pasture. Rommel stopped on
a knoll, engine idling.

Max said, speaking in German, "I thought Forrest was a
slave-trading adventurer, a pirate on land like Quantrill or
Jesse James. After today, I am not so sure." Rommel twisted to
glance back at him.

"It is the warrior we remember. That is important." He
nodded up the slope, toward the main battle site where the
others were now walking. "You must visualize the battle as it
was. It is not merely history. It is *alive*. *There* is the Seventh
Tennessee, firing and reloading. See, behind that fence they
lay down! Here comes the bugler, riding up the line, sounding
the charge. And we are Forrest. We must rally our troops to
fight their best."

They looked up the slope where Forrest's men had made
their final, triumphant charge. Rommel revved the engine.
Max felt the colonel shaking, and at first he thought it was
caused by vibrations from the engine, then realized Rommel
was laughing. With a burst of power they were off, bouncing
across the grass through a small herd of grazing cattle which
danced out of their way as nimbly as deer.

"We advance!" Rommel shouted. "Where is Morton's
battery?"

"Over there!"

Max could visualize, almost as though the motorcycle had blasted them into another plane of existence, the four guns being rolled by hand to within sixty yards of the Federal line. The bluecoats rose to mount a countercharge where a corn patch now stood. Morton, desperate to avoid being captured, had his gunners run beside the cannon holding cut branches over it in a futile attempt at camouflage. The muzzles of the guns protruded obscenely through the shaking stalks. Rommel revved the motorcycle engine and burst through the corn as Morton's guns unleashed their deadly hail of canister, enfilading the Union line running toward them. Entire squads vanished, dissolved in the gray cloud swooping up to embrace them. On either side of Rommel and Max, a roaring gray line charged up the hill, and Morton's guns rolled with them.

"Artillery leading the charge!" Rommel cried. "Like armor!"

"Barteau's regiment was hitting the right flank about now!" Max yelled into Rommel's ear. "He had his bugler gallop up and down the line, sounding the charge at different points to create the illusion of greater force. Waring and Winslow were compelled to order their cavalry to shift left to meet this attack in their rear."

"Weakening the Union center," Rommel cried joyfully, "at the moment that the Confederate pincer bit down." The young farmer charged across the field toward them, waving his arms in distress. Rommel deftly slipped down into a drainage ditch and accelerated away from their pursuer in a shower of watery bullets.

"Now we are with Barteau," he yelled back to Speigner. "We must envelope the right flank. Deceive. Move quickly. Behind these trees. Down this path." They were following a cow trail which wound over a ridge. Max could see Tishomingo Creek coiled like a cottonmouth in the sunny valley below. "*There* is the Federal rear," Rommel cried. "They turn and are devastated by what they see—*us!*"

"*We've routed them!*" Forrest screamed exultantly above the ripping of gunfire and the cries of men and animals. He spurred his sorrel into a gallop and cleanly leaped the hedge surrounding the yard of the Brice house. Ladies stood on an upstairs balcony and waved handkerchiefs at him.

The blue line had begun to diminish, subtly at first, like water seeping under a dam. Men drifted toward the rear, one by one. "We cannot keep them in place!" McMillen cried at Sturgis. Seeing their companions flee, other soldiers dropped their heads, as if this small gesture somehow made them invisible, and slipped away. The line wavered, sank in on itself, then collapsed with a rush. Union troopers threw away their weapons and surged past the crossroads, swept shoulder-to-shoulder toward the deadly funnel of the railless bridge across Tishomingo Creek. Sturgis had made the tactical error of bringing his supply train across to the east side of the bridge, and the abandoned wagons blocked the avalanche of panicked men. The ground trembled under their feet.

Morton's batteries, increased by the capture of four Federal guns, had reached the ridge above and, firing low, as fast as the gunners could reload, ravaged the confused, milling mass of infantry, cavalry, and artillerymen huddling together in the bottom. "Keep it hot!" Morton yelled. He could see that a wagon had overturned on the bridge, blocking the indiscriminate mass of caissons and ambulances and supply wagons. Hundreds of troopers were leaping into the creek, swimming or wading neck-deep to the opposite side. Officers swinging their sabers at their own men formed a few dozen into a ragged rear guard on the west bank of the rain-swollen stream. But the whooping and whistling Rebels pouring down from the crossroads were so close that the rear guard broke and ran before a position could be established. Only the abandoned wagons could slow the victorious Confederates.

"Lookee here, boys!" a private shouted, standing on a wagon seat and spilling a hamper of biscuits over his head. "Fresh hardtack and nice, thin side bacon!"

Max told the story of the fateful convergence at the bridge as he had heard Shoemaker tell it on numerous occasions. Rommel had stopped the motorcycle on the cow path twisting with bovine logic through the scrub oaks. Speigner squatted on the ground beside the machine. Rommel still straddled the leather seat, hands gripping the black handles while the engine idled like a great heartbeat. They watched the brown creek flow past the place where the original wooden bridge had long ago rotted and caved in. A few pilings which dimpled the otherwise smooth surface of the water were all that remained, but the present did not intrude on Rommel's inner vision of panicked swimmers thrashing forlornly beside the bridge crowded with useless wagons and caissons. A hundred yards south of them the new highway spanned the creek on a modern bridge with steel girders.

Speigner noticed that part of a low bluff behind them had recently given way, leaving a red clay scar some fifty feet long in the leafy hillside. His feet had begun to sink into the soft dirt, and he shifted his weight to keep from sinking farther. As he looked down at his shoes, he saw a small object embedded in the ground. He dug it out with his fingers and began to scrape off the clay caked around it. Rommel watched him with growing interest. The shape that emerged was conical, with the hollow base of a minié ball. Like a gold miner lusting over a dirt-encrusted nugget, Speigner feverishly wiped the bullet against his trousers, careless of the red streaks it made. Rommel bent over Max's shoulder. The engine's thump-thump-thump was like the pulse of the earth. It was as if Speigner were wiping away the years, revealing a secret long forgotten. The minié ball emerged, still perfectly formed, its patina of clay drying to a yellowish tint before their eyes, as though time had suddenly reversed itself and speeded up the oxidation of the metal.

"It has two grooves," Max said, not stopping to wonder when Shoemaker had buried such hitherto irrelevant facts in his memory. "So it must be the .58-caliber Federal minié ball. The .577 Confederate minié ball had three grooves."

"Perhaps a Union soldier was firing at Forrest," Rommel suggested, his eyes riveted to the small yellow sphere.

"Well, they missed." Max held his treasure between thumb and forefinger. He saw the gray-blue eyes searching the ground for another relic.

"Here," Max said immediately, extending the prize. "It is yours."

"Oh, no, I could not." Rommel shook his head.

"I have found dozens," Speigner lied. "They are everywhere." He remembered his fellow cadets exclaiming gleefully over similar finds and how he had regarded such souvenirs as so much junk. He dropped the minié ball into Erwin's hand. Rommel rotated the bullet between his fingertips, feeling each tiny pore and scratch in its antique surface, its grooves flattened and pitted by corrosion.

"*Danke schön*," he said, his eyes priestly. "I will take many memories of America home with me, and I will have *this* to remind me."

"I hope it brings you good luck," Max said. "Think of it as a gift from Bedford Forrest to Erwin . . . Rilke."

The gray-blue eyes did not flicker, but Max saw in them a silent laughter, as though Rommel were saying, "Yes, I am Rommel, but you must allow me this little subterfuge which is not of my choosing. What difference do names make, when men know each other in their hearts?"

Speigner heard footsteps in the woods above them, and as he turned to look, so did Rommel. The young farmer was about fifty yards away and closing fast. He ran with his fist held high before him, like a standard bearer without his flag. His face was brick-red.

"Oh shit!" Rommel cried, depositing the minié ball in his shirt pocket. "Let's go! I am going to have my five dollars' worth."

Max swung his leg over the machine and threw his arms around Rommel. They rambled through the trees, bumping over fallen branches and roots, and emerging from the woods on a dangerously steep incline. Below them, arranged in a scholarly circle around a stone monument commemorating the Confederate victory, were Shoemaker and the four Germans. Max wondered if the major was about to deliver his "War is a place that keeps three types of fellows forever" speech. They stared at the motorcycle blasting down the grassy slope. The spinning wheels threw a geyser of gravel over the historical group as Speigner and Rommel sped past them across the bridge.

"Keep the skeer on 'em!" Forrest shouted to his soldiers, laughing at their cheeks bulging with Yankee biscuits. "Heave those wagons—and that dead horse, there—off the bridge into the creek. And keep after 'em!"

Past the long causeway, some two miles northwest of the main battlefield, McMillen rallied several companies and made one last stand which enabled many of the Union troops to escape on foot. But Morton's batteries found them and broke up this small pocket of resistance.

As the long shadows merged into darkness, the Union train floundered in a nightmare of abandoned vehicles and dying animals. Within three miles of Stubbs's farm, site of the previous night's bivouac, the retreat slithered and ground to a near standstill in the muck of the Hatchie River bottom. Sturgis sat on the front porch of the Stubbs house and blankly regarded the horror of defeat. He realized someone had spoken to him and awaited his reply. He raised his eyes to the face of Colonel Edward Bouton, whose Negro brigade was relatively fresh, having served as train guard.

"For God's sake, General," Bouton repeated. "Don't let us give up so."

"What can we do?" Sturgis felt as if he were speaking to the sultry air, the drooping trees. The memory of the scorching sun mocked him in the rising half-moon.

"Give us ammunition and we'll hold Forrest on the east side of the bottom whilst the guns and wagons make it to solid ground."

"I have no ammunition," Sturgis muttered. Bouton bent to catch the low voice. "If I did, Forrest has got it by now. If Mister Forrest will let me alone, I will let him alone. You have done all you could and more than was expected." He raised his eyes awkwardly to Bouton's stern face. "Now all you can do is save yourselves."

Bedford spurred his mount glistening with water up the riverbank and turned a wildly impatient eye on the Confederate troopers lagging behind him. He was operating on sheer nervous energy, having been continually in the saddle for thirty-six straight hours; yet he trembled with the fierce excitement of the hunt. Pursuit was the game. The night would pass all too quickly. As soon as his escort caught up with him, he wheeled his fresh mount—his third of the day—and galloped into the velvet darkness, pistol in hand. He reined in at a creek where a company of Rebel cavalry had stopped to listen to night voices. The could hear a Federal rear guard close ahead.

"What's the trouble?" Bedford demanded, his mount turning and stamping.

"General, there's a strong rear guard a few rods in front of us," a private called.

Forrest took a small piece of candle from his pocket, lit it, and held it over his head. His men stared aghast at their chief's bravado, expecting a bullet to smash into him at any second. Bedford waded his horse into the creek.

"What is that?" He held his candle toward a shape looming out of the water.

"A wagon," replied the private.

"And that?"

"A caisson." The cavalrymen were urging their mounts into the water behind their commander.

Forrest dug in his heels and plunged ahead into the creek, shouting recklessly, "Come on! In a rout like this, ten men are equal to a thousand. They will not stop to fight."

In the flooded bottom, they could see black and white Union soldiers perched close together on floating logs like chickens on a roost. The advance guard stared at them curiously, then kept going after Forrest, leaving the Federals to be picked up by those following in the rear. Soon, Bedford's triumphal procession was lighted by the surrealistic glare of burning wagons. Reeling in his saddle from fatigue, Forrest had energy left for one tantrum over this destruction of property which he considered now belonged to him. He yelled at the Confederate cavalry pausing like sightseers to watch the flames.

"Don't you see the damned Yankees are burning my wagons! Get off your horses and throw the burning beds off!"

Rommel made Speigner hold his hat and opened the throttle wide. Max watched over his shoulder as the speedometer needle climbed to 60, 65, 70, 75. The motorcycle thundered over the straight gravel road crossing the Hatchie River bottom. The Stubbs house still stood on a hill rising out of the alluvial plain lush with green cotton fields.

"That's the place, the Stubbs house!" Speigner shouted into Rommel's ear and he backed off the throttle. He coasted up the hill and let gravity brake the motorcycle. At the summit he turned and stopped. No cars or trucks were visible in either direction. Their dust cloud reluctantly drifted over the fields.

"That did not frighten you, I hope," he told Max, who had been scared witless but also exhilarated by the burst of sheer speed. "Pursuit is strange music. It gets into one's blood." Rommel's mouth curved downward in a sad smile. "Once it gets hold of you, you must let it run its course. Ah, well . . . it has been a wonderful time here. Too bad . . ." He shook his head, then pushed off and drove sedately back to the Tishomingo bridge where their group waited, standing apart from the angry young farmer.

The youth stared bullets at the riders. Model and Schörner, representing the farmer's cheering section, smirked. As soon as Rommel braked to a halt and switched off the engine, the young man leaped to the assault.

"Look at it! All covered with dirt an' mud an' all. You ruint it. You got to pay fer a new one. It's ruint. I'll sue!" His fists were clenched, as though he had a speedier remedy in mind. Unruffled, Rommel held out a reassuring hand and, with his other, reached into his pocket. Max watched him peel a five off his roll. The young farmer took a deep breath and exhaled slowly, eyes never leaving Rommel's hands.

"*Die* machine *ist nicht* hurt," Rommel said, speaking slowly and carefully. "Only a bit of dirt, perhaps? Zis should pay . . . to have it . . . cleaned?" He peeled off another five and handed it to the farmer, who shuffled the bills nervously, then slid them into his pocket. He hesitated, seeming to wait for some means of restoring his dignity after having let his anger be bought. Rommel perfectly appreciated his situation.

"You said . . . kin to Forrest?" he asked politely.

"Yeah, that's right." The youth's voice was sullen at first, then warmed to the subject. "It was a great-great uncle, or sump'm, on my daddy's mama's side. He warn't but a kid, 'bout fifteen when it all happened. He heard the fuss and fetched his daddy's shotgun to try an' git into the fight. Didn't git there in time fer the battle, but saw the Yankees retreatin' fast as they could. He hid under a wooden bridge and watched them pass over above him. He could tell they wasn't plannin' to stop fer nothin'. So he waited till 'bout all of 'em were past and held up his gun near the boards and popped off. Blew one of 'em suckers' balls off!" The mouth stretched wide, baring yellowed teeth and pink gums. Revealing his ancestor's treachery seemed somehow to have appeased him, and he straddled his motorcycle. With casual expertise he kicked the starter pedal and revved the engine, listening to its reassuring roar. In afterthought, he backed off to idling speed and looked at his foreign customer. Rommel had understood only bits and pieces of the youth's story, but the meanness of it was apparent in the cruelty of the farmer's smile.

"One more thang," said the boy. "Far as I'm concerned, we won the fuckin' war. Yankees just wouldn't admit it!"

He revved the engine, exhaust fumes swirling in their faces; then he released the clutch and spewed gravel as the machine stormed up the road. They watched the motorcycle disappear over the hilltop in an angry cloud of dust.

"Tell me, Max," Rommel asked wryly, "was he retreating or attacking?"

VII

Erwin Rommel went for the violin. He had kept his eye on it throughout the wedding reception, and now the compulsion to make music overwhelmed him. He drifted around the edge of the crowd toward the pecan tree with softly lit oriental lanterns hanging like night flowers from its branches. The five-piece orchestra had at last taken a short break and laid their instruments on folding chairs under the tree. He did not stop to consider what inspired him, whether moonlight or champagne, the layered perfume of gardenia and wisteria, or perhaps what Schörner and Hanke had begun to call his *"Mississippi Wahnsinn,"* Mississippi madness. He knew only that a soldier must exploit the terrain. Tucking the instrument under his chin without bothering to re-tune it, he turned his back on the chatter of guests and began to play *Liebestraum,* which with *O Tannenbaum* and *Deutschland Über Alles* rounded out his repertoire.

A hush descended on the two hundred or so men, women and children assembled on the lawn of Oxford's most stately antebellum home. People stopped whatever they were doing—congratulating bride and groom, eating, drinking, gossiping, laughing—as the timeless refrain rose above the player's labored scratches and squeaks to blend with the honeyed night and the cicadas' song. Standing beside Major and Mrs. Shoemaker, Max craned his neck to see the soloist. Rommel played with his back to the crowd, his shoulders stiff with a musician's ardor, his entire being bent on coaxing the song out of the unwilling instrument. Glancing aside, Speigner saw

Schörner and Hanke shaking their heads as if to say, "What next?" Then the father of the bride gallantly offered his hand to his daughter and to the delight of the party began a slow, graceful waltz on the dew-wet grass. Rommel, hearing the soft stir and patter of gloved applause, turned, saw the dancers, and knew that his moment had arrived. He played for father and daughter with all his might. He was a gypsy miscast as a soldier, and his business was romance. When the song ended, Rommel bowed self-consciously to a spontaneous burst of applause, trying not to grin. With an artist's instinct for curtain time, he replaced the violin on the folding chair and started to slip quietly into the shadows.

"You're one of our *Ger*-man visitors!" A husky female voice slid up and down a half octave. A pair of eyes under dark lashes scorched him with a blue flame. Heavy perfume besieged his senses. She was exactly his height, red-haired, with sharp features, a full mouth, and a décolletage that vigorously claimed his attention. "May I address you as *colonel?*" She accentuated her request by leaning toward him in a pelvic slouch and holding out a fresh glass of champagne. He accepted the glass, struggling with the word "kunnel."

"*Wie wissen Sie*—how . . . know you . . . zis?"

"News travels fast in Oxford. I never knew a soldier who played the violin. Hidden talents, Colonel . . ." She cradled her glass against her shoulder languidly. "What would you like to know about Nathan Bedford Forrest?"

"*Wie* . . . how know?"

"Major Shoemaker took you all over the old battlefield at Brice's Crossroads, didn't he? I happen to be distantly related to General Forrest, on my mother's side." Rommel grinned.

"Have *all* folk of Mississippi kinship mit Forrest?"

"Honey, except for the Delta Chinese, everybody in Mississippi is kin to nearly everybody, including colored people, Jews, Eyetalians, and Indians. I don't think your Mister A-dolph would approve of us at all."

"So Forrest *ist Ihr* kinsman?" Rommel said, avoiding the subject of Hitler.

"Have you ever heard the story about how Forrest met his wife? They got stuck in a creek and . . ."

"Stuck?"

"Oh, you naughty!" She pushed teasingly at his chest. "I

mean the *wag*-on. Her wagon was stuck and he *res*-cued her and her friend and carried them to shore. It was love at first sight. Like they say, he got there firstest with the mostest. Do you subscribe to that theory, Colonel?" She nuzzled her champagne glass against her cheek, supporting her elbow with one hand and rubbing it slowly in a narcissistic caress.

What manner of woman is this?

The soldier who had faced three Frenchmen alone with an empty rifle at Varenness glanced around for reinforcements. He caught sight of a small man with dark hair and a trim moustache standing nearby at the edge of the crowd, almost in the shrubbery. He was puffing on a pipe with a curved stem as he watched the festivities, aloof without appearing self-conscious. There was no glass in his hand, but Rommel saw him take a half-pint bottle from his hip pocket and drink from it, then replace it in his pocket. People who passed close to him spoke to him only if he spoke first. Otherwise, they merely nodded or waved to him, as though they understood that his role was to observe and theirs to perform. The redhead followed Rommel's stare.

"That's Bill Faulkner, our Most Famous Person. Maybe you've read his books? I'll introduce you to him, but don't expect him to be very sociable. I 'magine he'd rather be out at deer camp doin' some serious drinkin', but our host, Dr. Cullen, is a friend of his."

"He is . . . writer?"

"You never heard of William Faulkner? Oh, I'm gonna *love* introducin' you to him! There's been so much pub-licity over his book *Sanctuary* that he prob'ly expects every livin' soul to have some strong opinion of the 'corncob man.'"

"What man is this?"

"It's in the book, this scene where—you haven't read it, but . . . I can see where they prob'ly don't wanta translate it into German . . . But anyway, there's this scene in a barn where a girl from a good fam'ly, a judge's daughtah, who the author seems to think was *ask*-in' for it, is cruelly attacked with a . . . you know . . . corncob."

"I do not know . . . corncob."

"Oh, you know, an ear of corn?" She laid her hand lightly on his arm, as though to guide him.

"Ear?" He pointed at his own ear.

"Of corn." With hands and fingers she shaped an object in the air before them. "It's about this long and this big around. *No!* Look what you got me *do*-in'! We need us some more *bub*-bly—thank you, waitah!" She grabbed a full glass of champagne from a passing tray. "Let me pour you a little from my glass, now. Officer-an' a-gentleman cain't refuse, now. Billy Faulkner has got a strange sense of *sanctuary*, I can tell you that. Bet you cain't guess where Temple Drake wound up."

"Temple?" Rommel did not want the refill, but found himself draining his glass at a gulp.

"Ha-ha, it was no temple. That *is* a quaint name for a nympho, isn't it? Uh-oh, there you go again. How do you get me to *say* such things! What I meant was, she wound up in Memphis in a . . . you know . . . house of ill re-*pute*. I do a whole lotta shoppin' in Memphis, but I only drove down Gayoso and Mulberry streets once—on a dare. Memphis *is* diff'rent after *daarrrrk*. That blues on Beale Street. Just throw yo' cares to the wind!"

The look she gave him was universal. Rommel, who had never considered himself a prudish man and tolerated any extreme of barracks talk among his subordinates, caught the eye of William Faulkner. He was astonished to see a smile appear beneath the mustache. She laid a lingering palm on his shoulder, as if to fix him in place while she looked to see what held his interest.

"Oh, all right. If I'm gonna introduce you to Bill, it'll be a big help to know yo' name. Mine's Mary Kathryn Woodall."

"Erwin Rilke, madame." His bow brought a smile to her lips.

"Come on," she said affably, slipping her arm through his. "I've en-*joyed* talkin' with you, Colonel." As they approached Faulkner, the writer studiedly looked away from them. Rommel noted that they were about the same height. He guessed the author's age at thirty-six, though Faulkner was actually thirty-nine, six years younger than Erwin. Close up, he also saw that Faulkner wore rough khaki work pants and muddy boots beneath an impeccable dinner jacket and black bow tie.

"Hello, Bill Faulkner. I'd like you to meet Colonel Rilke, who has come all the way from Germany to chase Nathan Bedford Forrest around! You two should have a lot in common, with you bein' a famous World War pilot and all." Faulkner shook Rommel's hand and bowed stiffly, then puffed on his pipe without saying a word. "I think I'll go powder my nose," she said and suddenly was gone, leaving in her wake a silence stronger than the party murmur and the drone of cicadas.

"I understand you are . . . writer." From Rommel's limited experience with writers they seemed a conceited, garrulous, argumentative lot who expected an inordinate amount of esteem for their calling. He was therefore surprised that Faulkner did not immediately lay claim to the title.

"I am a farmer," said the writer. "Between harvest and planting I write," the farmer added. The pipe went back into the mouth. They stood with the shrubbery touching the hems of their coats and watched the party commotion with twin disinterest. To Speigner, who saw them from across the softly lit lawn, they looked like two old friends, fishing partners perhaps, who were accustomed to unhurried conversation while their eyes followed the motion of lures through the water. Max overheard two matrons exchange stage whispers over their champagne:

"Who is that with Billy Faulkner?"

"Some German."

"Isn't that the one that played the fiddle?"

"Yes, wasn't he terrible?"

"Oh, but he was cute to join in like that."

He had recognized Faulkner at once. During Max's student days at Ole Miss the author, with his mysterious comings and goings on campus, had been idolized by the serious students.

"The lady said you . . . were flier in war," Rommel said, trying another tack.

"I trained in the RAF." Faulkner clenched his pipe between his teeth. World War I had ended before he could finish flight training in Toronto, thus denying him the combat experience he had yearned for. People in Oxford, however, knew only that he had joined the RAF.

"You airmen have war too easy."

Faulkner took the pipe out of his mouth. His dark eyes regarded Rommel with a subtle appreciation. "So?" he said.

"Yes," Rommel continued, encouraged by the writer's sudden interest. "For you, the war was . . . *de luxe* affair.

You have . . . bestest mess, billet in *châteaux*, while us infantry we eat from cans, sleep on ground. For us, hot bath mean everything—what luxury! *Guter Schlaf* . . . sleep in . . . *richtigen Bett* . . . real bed, ah!" Rommel's eyebrows arched merrily.

Beneath the trim mustache a smile came and went. "You forget, Herr Rilke, that the combat flier assumes he is already, in effect, a dead man. He therefore regards his accommodations or amenities as most temporary and, under the circumstances, takes them for granted."

"You do not then say the flier . . . *beneidet*—" Rommel pulled out his pocket dictionary and guardedly flipped through it until he found the word. ". . . *envies* the infantryman?"

"No sir, I do not say." Faulkner gave him a cheerfully competitive stare as one fighting man to another. They shared a soundless chuckle, and the brief silence that followed was not uncomfortable. "I hear your group is interested in Bedford Forrest." Faulkner relit his pipe.

"It would seem everyman knows what our business." Rommel's bantering tone implied a question.

"This is a small town. It is of more than passing interest that some German officers in civilian clothes come here to study Nathan Bedford Forrest. By the way, the Union army pursued him for four years without appreciable success. I hope you have better luck." The writer spoke low and fast in a soft voice, and Rommel frowned with the concentration of translating by ear.

"Thank you," he said lamely. "We been to Brice's Crossroads today." He glanced at the faces in the crowd, searching for Speigner to come to his aid. His eyes met those of the young lieutenant, and Rommel gestured for Max to approach him.

"My family played a small part in that victory," Faulkner said proudly. "When the Union force passed through Ripley, not far from the Crossroads, my great-grandmother had a conversation with one of General Grierson's staff officers, a Colonel DeWitt Thomas. Told him Forrest rode at the head of 28,000 cavalry. Fact being, of course, that he had less than 5,000. The Yankees' belief in being outnumbered led to their rout that day. If they had known they had two-to-one superiority, they would have taken the time to set up a

defensive battle on terrain to their advantage." A victorious
cloud of smoke emerged from the briarwood pipe. Rommel,
however, had understood very little of the story. At that
moment Max joined them, shaking hands with Faulkner and
telling him they had once met, by chance, outside the Ole
Miss post office. Rommel was aware of Speigner's obvious
veneration for the author and the way that Faulkner, in turn,
accepted the respect in a natural way. Rommel asked Faulkner
to repeat his story, and Max adroitly translated it.

"Say, now that we have an interpreter," Faulkner said
after a moment of deliberation, "let's slip this party. You've
come to Mississippi seeking examples of military excellence. I
have something to show you."

Max relayed the invitation which Rommel was glad to
accept, though he cast a lingering glance at the violin now
being reclaimed by its owner. As the orchestra began to play
and dancing couples filled the open space in the lawn, the
three of them walked through a shadowy path in the shrubbery
unobserved by Hanke and Schörner.

"Rilke," Faulkner mused, steering his Ford Phaeton with
one hand, his pipe suspended in the other. "There's a German
poet by that name, isn't there?" Max, seated in the back seat,
noted that they were headed in the direction of the university.

"No relation." Rommel spoke curtly to forestall any talk of
Rilke. He had grown to despise the name. Max looked at the
strong German face profiled against the dashboard lights. He
felt almost positive that this officer was Erwin Rommel, and he
watched Faulkner closely to see if the author was aware of any
tension. The writer seemed merely concerned with their
destination, however, and the subject was dropped as they
turned off Fraternity Drive onto a dirt road leading into the
woods south of the campus. The old Phaeton came to a
grinding halt before a concrete and brick wall fringed with
cedars.

"Here we are!" Faulkner said. They got out of the car into
a night whine of insects so strong it seemed to vibrate through
one's body. A bottle cap rasped against glass, and William
offered Erwin the whiskey. He looked on approvingly as
Rommel gamely took a pull at the bottle and breathed deeply
through open mouth to cool his fiery throat. He had never
tasted liquor like it, sweet and very strong. He passed the

bottle to Max, who drank and passed it to Faulkner, who drank
and pocketed the bottle with care. Their eyes had adjusted to
the darkness, and they looked at the open ground enclosed by
the low wall. At the center of the clearing, moonlight shone on
a solitary stone obelisk some seven or eight feet tall. "What do
you reckon this place is?" Faulkner said.

"Soldiers buried here."

No one had ever had to tell Rommel when he was
standing in a military cemetery. He could feel in his marrow an
ache of death and loss. Faulkner led them into the clearing and
approached the obelisk.

"You can't see them now, but graves are laid out in rows
up and down this place." Faulkner's voice was so musical he
seemed almost to sing an incantation. "Grass got high and one
day the president of the United Daughters of the Confederacy
hired a man to clean up the cemetery. Man was efficient, took
up all the wooden markers and stacked them up so he could
cut the grass. Man couldn't read. So now we just have the one
marker."

Rommel listened somberly to Spiegner's translation, then
said, "Perhaps it is just as well."

With the moonlight at their backs they could make out
raised lettering on a bronze plaque attached to the marble
pillar. Faulkner read the inscription at the top as if he knew it
by heart:

> "Here rest more than 700 soldiers who died on the
> campus of the University of Mississippi when the
> buildings were used as a war hospital, 1862–65; most
> of them Confederates wounded at Shiloh; a few
> Federals of Grant's army; a few Confederates of
> Forrest's cavalry; even their names, save these,
> known but to God."

The sibilant voice had a proprietorial tone, and Max wondered
if Faulkner had had a hand in composing the inscription. A
crest emblazoned above the epitaph identified the sponsors:
"Mississippi Division—U.D.C.—*Deo Vindice*." The monument looked relatively new, polished slab gleaming.

"The Yankees had a name for combat," Faulkner said.
"They called it the 'elephant,' told green recruits marching to

their first battle, 'Come with us to meet the elephant.'" He put his hand out to feel the list of names engraved on the plaque. "J. W. Allen, Company C, 41st Tennessee." His fingers traced the raised lettering as though reading Braille. "The names of brigades are interesting," he told Rommel. "Here's 'Pointe Coupée Artillery,' and 'Whitfield's Texas Legion,' 'Blythe's Battalion.'" Rommel, too, felt the letters with his hand, leaning closer to the plaque as he found a name he recognized.

"Forrest . . . Cavalry," he said, a catch of enthusiasm in his voice. "Company E. The soldier was . . . W. M. Copeland." He added hesitantly, as if it was none of his business, "It is good that they rest here at a university, where the young, the future generation, will be reminded of their sacrifice. They must not be allowed to forget."

Faulkner digested this in silence. Max hovered between them like a moth between fireflies.

"Of 78,000 Mississippians," the writer said, "who fought in the War Between the States, over one third were killed, died either from wounds or disease. In 1866, one fifth of all state revenues were appropriated for supplying artificial limbs for those lost in war. I can envision the long line of amputees queuing up at the Jackson Depot to receive the state's bounty of crate upon crate of wooden legs and feet and straps and pegs and hooks! Do you reckon," he looked back at the bronzed list, "these were the lucky ones?"

The lucky ones are the strong ones.

Rommel thought of his regimental motto in 1914: "Faithful—Unto Death." He remembered leading his rifle battalion in an assault on Monte Mataiur in 1917. They had scaled sheer rock cliffs and lain all night covered by snowfall in sub-zero weather. At first light they attacked, capturing hundreds of Italian prisoners. When Rommel reached the summit of Mataiur he had ordered a sergeant to fire three flares, one white and three green, to signal his triumph to the German army below. There had never been a more beautiful sight than the brave arc of the colored lights drifting down through swirling mists to the river winding at the foot of the mountains. To Faulkner he made no comment.

"The men buried here were wounded at Shiloh," Faulkner said. "Have you been up to that battlefield yet?"

"No. Our main interest in Mississippi is Forrest."

"Well, Forrest was at Shiloh too. His role was not as grand as some he performed elsewhere, but there are lessons to be learned from him at Shiloh." He spoke to Speigner in an aside. "What's the German for *lost cause?*"

"*Verlorene Sache,*" Max said reluctantly. The author's face was in shadow, though the moon turned his hair silver.

"Were you at Amiens?" Faulkner suddenly changed the subject. In the dark Rommel frowned.

"No, I was not. I was fighting in Italy then."

Faulkner turned his face slightly, and the moon caught the aquiline nose. "I went there twelve years ago, seven years after the war had ended. I was taking a walking tour of France. Where that last big push took place, the battlefield now looks as if a cyclone had passed over it. Trees reduced to stumps. Along the main roads farmers have piled unexploded shells and wire and bones that their plows have turned up. Walking along, you see these things at first hand. Children jerking with rickets from lack of food. Farmers plowing fields with live shells buried in the ground, expecting to be blown to kingdom come any second. I think the French are heroic."

It depends whether one fought with the French or against them. The German people have seen their share of destruction.

Faulkner held out the bottle. Mosquitoes whined around their heads while the whiskey passed from hand to hand. Alcohol meant nothing to Rommel, and he had little taste for strong whiskey. Yet he sensed that to this strange writer, drinking proved something. The bourbon was almost as smooth as schnapps. Rommel drank and handed the bottle to Faulkner, who turned it up and drained the last swallow.

"Bottle's empty," Faulkner said. "Time to go to the house. Will you join me?"

Rommel hesitated. "It is growing late. We have a plane to catch tomorrow." Something told him, however, that the author, who knew Mississippi, knew something of war, and knew Forrest, was just warming up to him. The fabled sixth sense which warned him of the enemy's presence now told him that the night held a revelation. "But, well—*jawohl*. Thank you very much."

They started walking back toward the car, their footsteps deadened by a cushion of cedar needles. Faulkner suddenly said, "If Hitler starts another war, it will exhaust the earth, like Napoleon did in 1800!" Rommel stopped. The moon hid behind branches. Faulkner stood so close that his voice seemed to come from within Rommel. "When the last shell has been fired through the last barrel and they have fought a little longer with sticks and stones, exhaustion will bring a hundred years of peace like the hundred years between Waterloo in 1814 and the first Marne battle of 1914."

Max chose not to translate Faulkner's remarks. He was not ready for the evening to end. Rommel, too, remained silent, though he had understood much of what the writer said, especially the reference to the Führer.

No one wishes for peace more ardently than the soldier.

"Napoleon," Faulkner continued, "thought actions were important; Joseph Conrad thought emotions were important; John Brown thought beliefs were important. Where do you stand on that, Herr Oberst?" Max translated the epigram, identifying John Brown for Rommel as the leader of an armed insurrection protesting slavery.

"I have always been an admirer of Napoleon," Rommel said.

"Let's go to the house," said Faulkner.

Rommel approved of the "Private Yard PLEASE Do Not Enter" sign that reflected the Phaeton's headlights at the entrance to Faulkner's driveway. He was not familiar with the word "yard," however, and suspected it meant *home* in Mississippi. Along with the writer's bearing and wit, his eloquence about war and the past, here was tangible proof of his celebrity. As a published author himself, with a new book that had sold out two printings in a month, Rommel, warmed by the unfamiliar bourbon and the humid July night, was seized by a secret longing to identify himself to Faulkner as more than a mere colonel, but as a fellow *writer*. He smiled wanly in the dark and let the impulse pass.

They entered a curving, needle-strewn drive lined by cedars. On the left they passed a huge magnolia, its heavy branches sweeping dramatically to the ground; on the right, downstairs windows aglow with golden light, the antebellum house rose with quiet dignity among the lush trees. As Faulkner drove under a porte cochere on the west side of the house, Rommel saw a white-railed fence and beyond it a barn bleached stark white by the full moon. He was curious about the house and what it would reveal about Faulkner.

Max craned his neck to see inside the windows. Like many university students he had strolled self-consciously past the author's property, hoping to catch a glimpse of Faulkner—perhaps playing croquet or lolling on his veranda, drink in hand or, best of all, musing over pad and pencil, his thoughts contagious to anyone who laid eyes on him at that moment. The house could barely be seen behind winding drive and trees, however, and Max would never have entertained the thought of walking up to the door and knocking.

"Welcome to Rowan Oak." Faulkner led the way to the front door framed by Doric columns and an ornamental balcony. They entered a hallway, and Faulkner ushered them into his book-lined study. Taking off his dinner jacket and bow tie, he invited them to make themselves comfortable. Rommel preferred to leave his coat on, though he did loosen the buttons in deference to the heat. He sat perfectly straight on a sofa facing an empty fireplace. Faulkner went into an adjacent room, and they heard a rattle of metal coat hangers. "I'm takin' orders for drinks," he said. Rommel hesitantly asked for coffee. "We keep a pot goin' from six in the mawnin' until midnight, and—" Faulkner glanced at his wristwatch, "you beat the deadline by five minutes." The author left the room to fix the drinks. Max and Rommel looked at the loaded bookshelves crowding two walls and at the paintings, including one of a white-bearded Confederate officer.

"I have always wished I had more time to read," Rommel said lamely.

Max went to find Faulkner under the pretext of helping him fix the drinks. He wandered through the parlor, gazing at grand piano and French provincial furniture like a pilgrim at his shrine. In the dining room he counted how many guests the table would seat: twelve. He glanced out the French doors at a private veranda surrounded by a dark garden. He dallied beside china cabinet and sideboard set with antique silver service and candelabra. Faulkner was in a narrow room between kitchen and dining room opening an ice tray. His back was turned to Max, who examined names and numbers written in a small, neat hand on the plaster wall next to a telephone: Gath. Reed—2324, Chester McL—724, Bama—B-80964, Billy Ross—207, Kate—963, Jack—5-4704, Louise—1518.

Speigner half expected to see "Temple" with a Memphis number. He saw Faulkner watching him over his shoulder.

"Is there anything I can do to help?" Max said quickly.

"Long as you're here," said Faulkner, "you can pour Herr Rilke a cup of coffee." He indicated a coffeepot steaming on an electric stove. A cup and saucer had been set out on the counter. "How do you take yo' whiskey, with or without water?"

"With, please. I hope we are not disturbing you at this hour."

"Nobody to disturb but us mice. My wife and daughter have gone to bed upstairs." As Faulkner spoke he poured bourbon over the ice from two bottles: Four Roses in one glass, Jack Daniel's in the other. Max poured the coffee and watched Faulkner add water from the kitchen faucet to the glass of Four Roses and bring it to him. "Is that the way you like it?" The writer opened a cabinet and got out a small tray on which to serve Rommel his coffee. "I'm glad you two happened along," he told Max. "I'm rather enjoyin' this Rilke fellow, even if he is a Hun. I reckon the RAF did a good job of indoctrinatin' me, because my impression of the German race has been fattish, blond people who composed music once and painted pictures but now cain't seem to win a bicycle race with dignity. But Rilke seems different, don't he."

Speigner deliberated for a second, then decided to tell Faulkner about Rommel. At the time, he supposed himself the worst security leak at G-2. In later years he would come to believe this was the pivotal moment in his career. While Faulkner listened intently, Max poured out the facts of his connection with Shoemaker, the files he had started at G-2, Rommel's war record and his book on tactics which had made him a rising star in Hitler's Reich.

"Anything you can learn about Rommel through your conversation with him would be of immense assistance to the government," he concluded. Reciting the facts had taken only a minute or so.

The author drew himself up to his full height of five feet, five inches. His brown eyes fixed Speigner where he stood. He held out his glass to Max in a solemn toast. "Count me in, Lieutenant," he said sternly. "Do anything I can to help unseat the Austrian paperhanger."

In the study Rommel was examining the painting of the white-bearded Confederate officer, who bore a family resemblance to Faulkner. The writer bowed and presented the coffee on the tray.

"My mother painted that picture of my great-grandfather," Faulkner explained and paused for Max to translate. "He commanded the Mississippi Partisan Rangers under Forrest." Rommel glanced up with lively curiosity. "At the annual reunions of the old veterans I can remember hearing them tell us boys stories on my grandfather's front gallery."

"Your ancestor serve under Forrest?" Rommel asked as they resumed their seats.

"My great-grandfather," Faulkner pointed at the painting with his glass, "fought at Manassas and later in Mississippi and Tennessee. When Partisan Ranger units were disbanded he resigned his commission. His most notable contribution to the war effort, I reckon, was as a civilian engaged in private business. While he and his body servant, Nathan, were traveling to Memphis in 1864 with goods for sale, they precipitated Forrest's great raid into Memphis."

"*Bitte,*" Rommel asked Speigner after he had finished translating Faulkner's remarks, "*Artikel zum Verkauf . . . heisst das Schwartzer Markt?*" Max glanced uncertainly at Faulkner, who lit his pipe impassively. The crackling of flame in bowl seemed inordinately loud in the still room.

"He didn't run the blockade for charity," Faulkner said. "As an officer and a gentleman, he naturally understood the primary purpose of war which is the acquisition of property and money." As Speigner translated, Rommel sat on the edge of the sofa, back straight and stomach tight.

"*Man kämpft, um sein Vaterland zu verteidigen,*" he said.

"One fights to defend his homeland," Max repeated dully.

Faulkner set his glass down, tucked his fingers into his shirtfront in the old-fashioned tradition, and began to quote:

> "Forth from its scabbard pure and bright,
>   Flashed the sword of Lee!
> Far in the front of the deadly fight
> High o'er the brave in the cause of Right
> Its stainless sheen like a beacon light
>   Led us to Victory."

Rommel stared at the writer as if he were crazy, then looked to Speigner both for explanation and confirmation.

"*Das Schwert von Lee,*" was all Max would say.

"Please ask Herr Faulkner to continue his story about running the blockade," Rommel said.

"Glad to," said Faulkner and took up his glass. "My great-grandfather and his servant, Nate, had encountered a Federal patrol around midnight and moved into the woods to avoid being picked up. Nate's mule was covered with pots and pans, sacks of sundries piled and tied on it like an Arab in the night. While the Federal patrol was passing by, Nate dozed off on his mule. Mule bolted and Nate charged the Federal picket, scattered pots and pans in all directions, would have gotten away—Yankees were so astonished at bein' attacked by a black on a mule armed with pots and pans—but tried to jump a barbed-wire fence and got tangled up. Federals captured him. Wouldn't talk to them. Shined their lanterns on him, made him out to be a walking Rebel commissary, lieutenant sent courier to warn Memphis garrison of Rebel forces in the area. When Forrest heard that Federal pickets had been alerted, he was forced to order an attack before all his forces were in position, thus achievin' total surprise and creatin' havoc throughout the city. At the Gayoso Hotel, Yankee generals climbed out upstairs windows in their nightshirts while Forrest's scouts rode their mounts into the hotel lobby and captured the uniforms left behind. Since generals cain't make war without their uniforms, a détente was temporarily in effect until Forrest returned their clothes under a flag of truce. My great-grandfather was thus indirectly responsible for puttin' things into their proper perspective and strikin' a blow for civilization."

Faulkner relit his pipe. Rommel set his cup and saucer on the coffee table. He tugged at the lapels of his coat.

Uniforms do not make the soldier!

Rommel had seen men in combat fighting with the clothes literally blown from their bodies. He regarded Faulkner narrowly. Although Rommel's contact with writers and intellectuals had been limited to observing *Biergarten* debates between radicals, communists, and opponents of the Weimar Republic, he gave them their due for their brilliant command of the language. Yet he was suspicious of their unpredictability and high-flying motives. They seemed trapped, as did this American author in his armchair, in a confused world of siren songs Rommel felt blessed not to hear. Faulkner's dark-eyed, penetrating look, instead of being glazed by the alcohol he had consumed, seemed to blaze the brighter for it. From his experience of appraising men's characters and abilities, Rommel knew this was a man to be respected. Yet he wondered if there was anything useful to be learned from William Faulkner.

"Do you play tennis?" Faulkner said.

"Tennis?" Rommel replied, startled. "*Nicht* . . . since I was boy."

"Like ridin' a bicycle—you never forget. I have a court behind the stables," Faulkner added with the pride of ownership.

"You wish to play tennis with me?" Rommel said, amazed. *Is this some exotic Mississippi custom? In Pamplona men get drunk before running with the bulls, but that is Spain. Surely he is too drunk to play tennis!*

"I'd be much obliged," Faulkner said.

"At this hour?"

"Won't hurt us to work up a sweat." Faulkner stood up. "Besides, it'll be in the interest of our respective alliances." His brown eyes sparkled. "I'll play for the vineyards of Burgundy and the Maginot Line. You play for the munitions industry and the Hitler-Mussolini pact. We'll have an international competition."

With Max at his heels Rommel awkwardly followed his host into the hallway, where Faulkner dug in a dark closet for racquets, balls, towels, and water bottle. Rommel wondered if he could still hit a tennis ball and make it go where he wanted. Faulkner apologized for not having proper playing costumes for them on such short notice.

They went outside and crossed the yard, wetting their shoes in the dew. Behind the stables, in a moon-blanched clearing, a tennis net cleanly divided a rectangle of cropped grass into equal halves. Faulkner dramatically flipped a switch at the base of one of the poles, and the court became brilliantly illuminated by outdoor lighting. The writer smiled beneath his mustache. From the trees bordering the court came a bird's confused morning call. Rommel saw that the court was marked off neatly with lime. Dull brown patches in each backcourt indicated recent use, most of it near the respective baselines. He guessed this meant Faulkner rarely played the net.

Writer offered soldier his choice of racquets. The players took the court. Max crouched beside the net on the sideline, happy to serve as ball boy. They began to warm up, hitting short strokes from backcourt with the chopping or swatting motions of self-taught players. Neither could sustain a rally of more than three shots without hitting into the net or the trees. Rommel was enjoying the unexpected exercise, breathing deeply. He whacked a forehand shot with gusto, and the ball ricocheted off a tree limb. Speigner retrieved it and tossed it to Faulkner, whose hair and narrow forehead already gleamed with perspiration. Max was amazed that the author could hit the ball at all, given the amount of alcohol he had imbibed. Crouched at the baseline, racquet held straight in front of him, Faulkner attacked each return with economy of motion and managed to place his shots within reach of his rusty opponent. Rommel soon began to get his rhythm, however, and when they were able to sustain a rally of a dozen shots, Faulkner caught the ball, signaling that play would begin.

"Have you ever read Mann's *The Magic Mountain?*" Faulkner asked; Max translated from squatting position, surprising Rommel, who was familiar with the German author's name, but not his work. He shook his head. "I wonder how long it will be before Hitler deports Mann," Faulkner mused. "First service to the visitor. House rule."

Rommel double-faulted into the net. "Love-fifteen," Max called as he scooped up the balls and tossed them to the colonel. Rommel's next serve was deep but in bounds. Faulkner's backhand return was too hard, over the baseline. "Fifteen all," said Speigner. Faulkner's crosscourt return of the next serve made the score 15–30. Max lumbered about in the bushes and found the ball. On the next serve the players enjoyed a prolonged baseline rally, and Rommel began to appreciate his opponent's stamina and daring crosscourt slices. Anticipating just such a shot, he rushed the net and deflected the ball to win the point. Faulkner took off his low boots and socks. His return of serve, however, was into the net, and he stood rubbing his bare feet determinedly against the wet grass as Max called, "Forty-thirty!" They started another rally,

Faulkner scrambling dexterously to meet each shot. Rommel rushed the net again, and Faulkner lobbed over him for the point. "Deuce!" They exchanged baseline shots after the ensuing service, until Rommel saw his chance and rushed the net again, only to have the writer lob neatly over him and win the point. "Advantage out!"

He likes that lob. Feign rush and drop back quickly. His backhand is weak. Hit sharply to backhand and rush net. Press him.

With the return of service, they sparred with careful baseline shots, waiting for an opening. Rommel hit a hard shot to the writer's backhand and rushed, then doubled back to catch the expected lob. Faulkner, however, surprised him by rushing the net to catch his short return in the air and put it away with a deadly volley.

"Game, Faulkner!" said Max.

"Forrest shot a Negro on his plantation after the war," Faulkner said. "Acquitted. Excuse me one minute."

"Forrest hat nach dem Krieg einen Neger auf seiner Plantage erschossen, wurde aber freigesprochen," Max translated. Faulkner could be heard retching in the trees. Rommel thoughtfully removed his shoes and socks.

"What does he mean by this?" he whispered.

"I do not know," Speigner said.

Faulkner returned, gray-faced but clear of eye. He poured a handful of water, rinsed his face and toweled off.

"Forrest was the first Grand Wizard of the Ku Klux Klan," he told Rommel through Max. "Do you know the Ku Klux Klan? Something like your Brownshirts."

Rommel was on guard. Like most *Wehrmacht* officers, he had despised the bullies of Ernst Röhm's *Sturmabteilung*.

"After the war . . . Christian night riders who intended to . . . purify the South of all outside influences?" Rommel said warily.

"Brotherly love and burning crosses. My serve."

The rhythm of their first game was quickly reestablished. Rommel rushed the net, or feigned a rush to anticipate the lob. Faulkner prowled the baseline, content to stay back and select his shots. Max hustled errant balls back into play, translating an occasional remark when necessary as he crawled over the grass, feeling for the ball with his hands.

"Forrest was a great speechmaker," Faulkner was saying
between games. "Main reason the Ku Klux Klan needed him.
Mankind's curse, all the evil and grief of this world, stems from
the fact that man talks, in the sense of one man speaking to a
captive audience. Except for that, and its concomitants of
communication—radio and newspaper—there would have
been no Hitler or Mussolini."

"I am not political," Rommel said impassively. "I am a
soldier."

He went into a defensive crouch awaiting Faulkner's
serve. After an exchange of shots he feigned a rush and
dropped back, expecting the lob. Instead, Faulkner hit a
passing shot that caught Rommel going away, his back to the
net.

"As a soldier, then, you'll agree with me that Hitler is
more dangerous than Mussolini because all Il Duce has had to
work with are Italians, who are more interested in eating,
drinking and fornicating than in war." Faulkner spoke over the
water bottle. "This man of yours has got you, the Germans, to
work with."

"I do not understand what is dangerous," Rommel said,
hitting his open palm nervously with the strings of his racquet,
impatient for an end to such talk. "The Führer has rebuilt our
country, stabilized the economy, brought us together, restored
national pride."

Max translated while crawling in the grass searching for
the ball.

"All I can say is, you Germans have to believe well in
yourselves," Faulkner swung his racquet high, poised before
the serve, "to endure Hitler and wait out his folly. Ready?"

From Max's crouching position beside the net, the match
was a game of cat and mouse. Rommel rushed or feigned a
rush without a discernible pattern, always pressing, attacking.
Faulkner seemed to have an uncanny ability to anticipate
Rommel's next move. The author's white shirt clung moistly to
his chest, shoulders and back. His hair dripped with sweat.
Max listened to the ping of the ball, the buzzing of insects
around the lights overhead, the drone of cicadas and disturbed
cries of awakened birds. He wished it would never end.

With the score tied at six games apiece, Faulkner
proposed a means of breaking the tie: whoever was the first to

earn four points with alternating serves would win the set. He insisted that Rommel take first serve. Writer and soldier faced each other from opposite sides of the court. On the sidelines Max tensed, every muscle coiled tight as if he were playing. Each man held his service, and with the score tied at 3–3, Rommel set himself to deliver the winning serve. Faulkner crouched, racquet held before him like a two-handed sword. The first serve was too hard, and Max cried, "Back!" The second serve, to Faulkner's backhand, was more softly hit, and the writer drove Rommel deep with a strong return. As he raced to get into position for a return, Rommel saw Faulkner out of the corner of his eye moving quickly to the net, and he stroked upward to lob the ball past the author. But the lob was not deep enough. Faulkner waited for it, racquet pointed at the sky. Swinging with precision, he hit an overhead smash that was too hard for Rommel to handle. He approached Faulkner at midcourt with his hand outstretched.

"Very good," he said in English, comfortable with the familiar sway of emotions after being fairly beaten. They shook hands and smiled, pleasantly weary, their sweating skin cool in the night air. They knelt on the grass and toweled off, passing the water bottle back and forth. A half mile away, the Oxford clock struck one o'clock in the courthouse belfry, reminding the sleeping town that moonlit time was passing.

"I recall a joke from the RAF," Faulkner said amiably. "A British ace has just returned from a tour of duty at the front. A ladies' club invites him to speak to their group. They want to hear about a dogfight from the horse's mouth. He is embarrassed at first, but pretty soon warms up to it." Faulkner imitated a British accent. "'I spot the fokkers before they see me, and climb above 'em,' he says. 'I dive with one of the fokkers in my sights. I am just about to fire when bullets rip through the cockpit, and I see fokkers to the left of me, fokkers to the right of me, and fokkers on my tail . . .' The president of the club gently interrupts him. 'Excuse me, Leftenant,' she says. 'For the sake of fuller understanding, let us explain to our audience that the Fokker is an aircraft of German manufacture.' 'Oh, no ma'am,' says the pilot, 'those fokkers were Messerschmitts.'"

Faulkner bent over, snorting and patting his thighs repeatedly. Max laughed out loud, then remembered his translation. He glanced at Rommel, wondering if the colonel would consider it worth translating. He saw that writer and soldier were enjoying his indecision. They shook with soundless laughter.

"It is Anglo-Saxon, no?" Rommel said to Faulkner.

"*Jawohl, Herr Oberst, jawohl,*" said the writer. After a moment he added, "Say, let's drive up to Shiloh."

"*Bitte?*" Rommel stared in surprise. "*Meinen Sie, jetzt*— now?"

"The battlefield is about a two hours' drive from here. If we hurry, the ghosts will still be up!"

"I *schätze* . . . appreciate your *Angebot*," he glanced at Max, who supplied the word *offer*, "yet tomorrow . . ."

"Herr Oberst," Faulkner said sternly, "if your intention is to catch Forrest, you must pursue him through the night." Max translated, watching Rommel hopefully. Rommel's impassive expression began to crack, first the smile wrinkles forming around the eyes, and then a twitch at the corners of his mouth.

"No one sleeps in Mississippi!" he said with a shrug.

"Leastaways, none of us ghosts," said Faulkner.

VIII

"Let's reconnoiter the terrain," Faulkner said from the back seat of the Phaeton, clearly in command. With Speigner at the wheel and Rommel riding shotgun, Faulkner's partisan rangers rolled through the still streets of Corinth, some eighty miles northeast of Oxford. The time was 3 A.M., and Faulkner was out of bourbon. "Circle the block!" he added. "The taxi stand is bound to be near the bus station. Not a taxi stand in Mis'ippi don't sell bootleg whiskey."

Rommel watched the deserted alleyways between buildings apprehensively. At any moment he expected to see the headlights of a police car flash on. He shifted on the hard seat of the Ford. It would never have occurred to him that anyone, anyplace, needed to purchase illegal alcohol in the middle of the night, much less that he would be an accountable party to such misadventure. If he were caught, Model and Schörner would dine out for a week in Berlin with the story: "We missed our plane because Erwin was imprisoned in Mississippi. Guess what for!" Searching night streets for black marketeers was like spying behind enemy lines out of uniform. If captured, one had no choice but to keep quiet and take his medicine. In regular combat at least a man knew exactly where he stood. Rommel perceived that his Rilke passport might be confiscated and checked out, causing embarrassment for the Reich and ruining his career. His deep-seated reservations about writers and intellectuals had now been irrevocably confirmed. *They are all mad.*

To Max these were enchanted streets, the Phaeton his magic carpet. If it suited Faulkner, Max would have driven to the moon. His single concern was that the writer might pass out and leave them without a guide to Shiloh.

"That's it! Let me out."

Speigner stopped the car in an alley behind a café whose sign announced: "BUS STOP—EAT." Rommel cautiously opened the door to let the writer out. Faulkner tucked in his shirt, pulled on his jacket, and approached a small outbuilding which leaned against the back of the café. On its door was a hand-painted sign, "Willies Cab You Call We Haul." Faulkner rapped on the door. A light was turned on inside. It seeped richly under the doorsill, then washed over him as the door was partially opened, turning his face to gold. Rommel watched with sunken cheeks. Faulkner was speaking to someone behind the door. A black man's face peered out at the Ford and its occupants, then disappeared, drawing Faulkner inside like an omnipotent puppeteer. To Rommel, minutes passed like hours. Then Faulkner reappeared, clutching a brown paper bag.

"I'm ready for Shiloh," he said. "Let's go."

Max backed the Ford out of the alley and drove to Main Street. Paper rustled in the back seat. "Three dollars and fifty cents for a fifth of Four Roses!" Faulkner's soft voice was indignant. "Told them it was highway robbery. Told them I could get it in Memphis for half the price. Told me, 'Go on to Memphis, then.'"

"Please keep the bottle out of sight, Mr. Faulkner," said

Max as they stopped at an intersection. He was looking in his rearview mirror. "We have company."

To Rommel's horror a police car eased up beside them with engine purring. He blinked rapidly as a light pierced the Phaeton, flashing from face to face and stopping on Rommel. He sat nearest to the police, only a few feet away. His window was open.

"Whatchew boys doin'?" drawled a high-pitched voice behind the spotlight. Rommel looked straight ahead, isolated by the terrible glare, his face burning on the exposed side and cold on the other. Max spoke for them.

"We're from the university, officer. The history department, at Oxford. Is this the road to Shiloh?"

They waited out a dubious silence. The high voice said, "*His*-try?" Rommel sat quite still, debating whether he looked professorial. He had lectured at the *Kriegsschule* at Potsdam, but true academicians wore pince-nez and had bad posture. He sank in on himself and tried to look dowdy. A match flared in the back seat and Faulkner's pipe tobacco wafted out for the authorities' inspection. Professors smoked pipes. The tobacco crisped and burned with the sweet smell of propriety.

"Mighty early to try and see the battlefield," said the voice pitched now at a higher level, moving up from suspicion of alley prowlers to distrust of ivy-wall inhabitants. "Easy to git lost in them back roads."

"We'll be careful, officer," Max said with a blend of respect and obedience.

"What kinda team're the Rebels gonna have this time?" The voice was still testing. The university football team had been called "the Flood" when Max had been a student there but had recently acquired the new name *Rebels*. Luckily, Max had listened to the broadcast of the 1936 Orange Bowl game, in which Catholic University had defeated Ole Miss. He therefore remembered the name of a single top player.

"We still have Bruiser!" he said, praying that the All-American tackle Bruiser Kinard had not yet graduated. The spotlight was switched off. Rommel's right cheek felt wonderfully cool in the soothing darkness.

"You boys be keerful." The squad car eased across the intersection and parked beside the curb. Max waved as he drove slowly past the police.

"Goddamned *po*-lice," Faulkner grumbled. "Mindin' everybody's bizness but the criminals'." Paper rustled and a bottle cap was unscrewed. "Here's to law and order."

During the final twenty miles of their journey, Rommel soon forgot about the bootleg crisis as he listened to Faulkner sketch the outlines of the great battle: the arena itself, a four-mile square around a country chapel called Shiloh after the ancient Hebrew word for "peace," bounded by the Tennessee River to the east and two creeks north and south; the even strength of the opposing sides at the beginning of the battle, about 40,000 each; Albert Sidney Johnston's personal reasons for attacking Ulysses S. Grant—his desire to vindicate himself in the eyes of the South—and his famous line—"I would attack if they were a million."

Rommel was enrapt with a wistful understanding of the forces sweeping soldiers into battle. He turned and rested his forearm on top of the seat to watch Faulkner's animated features, barely illuminated by the glow of dashboard lights. Faulkner told of new Confederate recruits so green that they learned the manual of arms as they marched to battle; torrential rains that turned the roads below Shiloh into shin-deep mud wallows and wrought havoc with the Rebel marching orders; graybacks in their ill-matched, homemade uniforms, firing off their weapons regiment by regiment, ostensibly to test their powder though more a celebration of the sun coming out at last and of being alive. In doing so, however, they unwittingly destroyed their one tactical advantage of surprise.

"It rains on us all," Rommel said quietly. He remembered Forrest waiting on the high ground at Brice's Crossroads while the Federals struggled through the swampy bottomland below.

"There's Lick Creek!" Faulkner exclaimed. Max stopped the car in the road so Rommel could see the thin ribbon of water shining through the trees. "Ol' Bedford had been ordered to guard the right flank south of the creek, but he couldn't stand bein' left out of the fight. Ordered his regiment to cross over and went to find a general who would accommodate him with an order to charge." The Phaeton's headlights revealed a fork in the road ahead. "Take your left," commanded Faulkner.

The car wound through a corridor of trees bordering a

narrow dirt road. "They had been fighting all day," Faulkner continued. "Battle started on its own, not surprisingly, with thousands of armed soldiers having listened to each other's bugles across the hollows all night. When they happened into each other and opened fire, Beauregard was at that very moment trying his damnedest to persuade Johnston to break off and withdraw. At sixes and sevens, both sides, all day and from there on out. Fought among themselves nearly as hard as they fought the enemy. Federals broke and ran under the first big charge, but reformed on a ridge and gave a good account of themselves. They paved the fields below with Confederate dead and wounded, and successive waves could run a hundred yards without once touching ground. Stop the car. We're here." Still translating for Rommel, Max obeyed.

They got out and stretched stiff joints. A faint breeze stirred a cool, raw smell of freshly plowed earth, and a dog barked far away. Before them in the dark, Rommel discerned an orderliness about the woods, an unusual symmetry.

"Peach orchard," Faulkner explained, sniffing the air. "Smell the ghosts?" Now Rommel could make out the rows of small, well-shaped trees. "Federals posted a strong body of infantry in there. Johnston himself led a second charge that broke them, but he was mortally wounded. Bled to death. Bullet cut a femoral artery in his leg and his boot filled with blood. Trees were in blossom then," he added.

Max had translated as far as the boot filled with blood when subtle movement caught their eye. Holding their breath in concentration, they peered into the dark grove. A spectral shape rose and stood very still in the gloom, its form speckled by moonlight filtering through the peach branches.

"Deer!" Faulkner snorted. He sucked on his unlit pipe noisily and dug in his pocket for matches.

"Too bad . . . rifle . . . we do not have!" Rommel's teeth gleamed in the dark. Faulkner took his pipe out of his mouth in surprise.

"What! A doe?" His soft voice was edged with stern disapproval.

"Oh, yes, I did not . . . see," Rommel apologized and shoved his hands into his pockets as if to express his nonviolent intentions. Faulkner lit his pipe without haste, his match flaring briefly against the night.

"Forrest found himself a general, but he couldn't extract an order to charge." Faulkner gestured with his pipe, sketching sudden red lines in the dark.

Forrest reined in his mount, which grew more and more restive with the snapping of musketry off to the left and the boom of cannon and vibrations of shells exploding on impact up and down the line. The sun was high overhead in a clear sky. Bedford took off his coat, folding it over the pommel of his saddle.

"My men cain't stay put under this fire, General," he repeated stubbornly. Cheatham shifted in his saddle and looked out over the rolling wooded hills where smoke hung in patches and men crept alertly through the trees. He was surrounded by his staff, who were keenly interested in the cavalry colonel they had heard so much about. Forrest struggled to keep his temper in check.

"If you want to make a charge, go ahead," Cheatham said at last, still without looking at him. "But I will not order you to do so."

"We kin either move forward or move back." Bedford managed to keep his voice calm. "But we'll be blown to bits if we stay still." As he spoke, his men were squinting into the sky, sighting on cannon balls rising near the river and deftly moving their horses to create empty places for the balls to land.

"You are not under my command, Colonel," Cheatham said and fixed his eye on Forrest for emphasis. "You are free to charge, as far as I am concerned, but you must take the responsibility."

"Charge under my own orders?"

"That is correct," said Cheatham. Forrest saluted and wheeled his horse, touched spurs to flanks, and galloped back to his men without wasting any more valuable time. The troopers saw that Bedford had drawn his saber. They gave a cheer and brought their mounts into line. Forrest led them through a stand of dense timber and emerged at the edge of a vast open field. They advanced toward a grove of peach trees in the opposite corner, blossoms waving like tiny pink flags above two Federal batteries and a regiment of infantry. Smoke billowed up through the pink flowers as the gunners began to feel for their range. Forrest rode at the center of the column,

signaling his bugler to sound a flanking movement that swung the column left or right and zigzagged away from the exploding shells. The precise maneuver was marred by a direct hit, which instantly killed two troopers and four horses and splattered the rest of them with blood. They were near enough to the grove to charge, now, and Forrest raised his saber, then brought it forward with a lethal shining.

Rommel was sure the charge would be successful—if for no other reason, because of the jaunty way Faulkner goose-stepped across the field, jerking his knees high to lift his brogans clear of the wet grass. The writer seemed to list to one side, however, and Rommel realized that the weight of the bottle in his pocket made Faulkner's seersucker jacket sag out of shape. Max blundered over hidden logs or into grassy potholes the others had avoided. He was too busy to watch his step, hovering close behind Faulkner, trying to understand the sibilant voice and keep up with his translation for Rommel. He wished they appreciated the difficulty of walking in the woods at night while mentally scrounging for declensions and cognates, but he was determined not to have to ask Faulkner to repeat himself.

"Forrest led the charge himself, standing up in his stirrups and slashing at anything within reach. They overran the Federal guns right through here, and when Forrest looked back, Cheatham's regiments were running up behind him to take possession of the captured pieces."

The three men walked in shadow between the rows of peach trees. Rommel felt, as always, a humbling respect for ground bought with blood. Underfoot was a bed of trampled grass where the deer had slept. Through the trees moonlight glistened on still water.

"Off to the left, there, is the Sunken Road, where Prentiss's Minnesotans dug in and held the Confederate charge long enough for the Federal reinforcements to land under the bluffs. You know, on April the sixth, 1862, this was the highest-priced real estate in America. Behind the sunken road was that small pond, see it? The wounded from both sides crawled to it and in it and drank from it and washed themselves in it and turned it red with their blood."

They stood at the verge of Bloody Pond. The bullfrog chorus fell temporarily silent at their intrusion. Rommel listened to Faulkner describe Bedford Forrest walking his horse around the pond, seeing broken creatures lapping at the water's edge, no longer soldiers or even men but sucklings in blue and gray. Rommel knew the tragedy of war. He had experienced the agony of the wounded. He had been hit himself, once seriously, during the Great War. Not long ago his young son, Manfred, had asked him what war was like, and by way of reply Rommel had snatched up pencil and paper and sketched a nightmare of destruction—machines blasted to pieces, dead horses and men with legs and arms poised like sticks in the air. He resented the writer's implication that he could be insensitive to the devastation of war.

"Forrest had a saying," Faulkner continued. "War means fighting and fighting means killing."

"Yes," said Rommel.

A single bullfrog defiantly resumed his jarring song, and a hundred of his fellows joined him in full voice. Faulkner offered Rommel the bottle, but he refused with a shake of his head. "When the sun strikes the water," Faulkner said, "it looks just as red as it can be." He drank and carefully replaced the bottle in his pocket.

"*Das Wasser sieht in der Sonne rot aus.*" Max glanced at Rommel, who made no sign that he had heard.

"Down toward the river are the Indian mounds Forrest climbed with his scouts to see Buell's reinforcements come up the river from Savannah."

Faulkner found a logging trail through the woods. His soft voice became one with the night sounds of insects and birds and the rustlings of dewdrops and falling branches and animals feeding. He told Rommel of the end of the first day. The Confederates had gained possession of most of the terrain around Pittsburg Landing, although successive charges by Bedford's cavalry and infantry units failed to dislodge the Federal guns defending the bluffs above the river.

Instantly understanding that this failure was crucial, Rommel experienced a pang of concern for Forrest. He listened for the final, triumphant salvo from the bluffs and the rattle of saber and harness as the Confederates retreated to the Union campsites they had overrun earlier.

Wounded lay everywhere, Faulkner said, gesturing right and left, blue and gray together. They screamed or wept or prayed or sang hymns or exchanged names with their neighbor and inquired where his home was before dying under the stars. Around the campfires, the living rolled in their blankets and tried to get some rest before daybreak. They became accustomed to the night voices calling for water, a constant drone blending with the cicadas' whine which, toward dawn, gradually ceased. Faulkner pointed to a square hillock looming over the shining river.

"There's the mound. Come on! Forrest and his scouts climbed it to see the Federal troops debarking from the steamboats. I'm goin' to put my bottle in the crotch of this tree, here. Speigner, when we come back down, would you please remind me where I left it?"

Breath frosty against the crisp night air, Forrest and his scouts scrambled up the steep slope dressed in blue overcoats captured from the Federals. They grabbed on to vines and pine saplings, hoisting themselves to the top of the 20-foot-high mound. The lead scout showed Bedford what he had discovered. A half mile downstream, troops moved by torchlight down wide gangplanks to the muddy bank, where they formed into companies and marched up a teamsters' road cut into the bluff. Boats were lined up behind one another, waiting to disgorge their human cargo, great paddle wheels churning the water white to hold their stationary position against the strong river current.

Forrest was horrified by the mass of men skulking under the shelter of the bluffs. Thousands of deserters clustered like dark rows of seabirds blown off course by a hurricane and nesting forlornly on this sandy bank far from home. Debarking troops passed right by the campfires and blanket hovels of these skulkers. No one seemed to have the time to drive them back into battle. Forrest could see dozens of tiny figures thrashing in the river near the steamboats, trying to climb aboard. Boatmen wielding long poles pushed them back into the water.

"I'd shoot the cowardly sons of bitches," Bedford muttered under his breath. *"Officer oughta find the time to set a good example."*

Side by side, Rommel and Faulkner stared at the silver band of water flowing powerfully below the high bank. To the east the land lay silent, open to the sky. Rommel found it easy to imagine the turbulent wake of the steamboats, men disembarking, skulkers flailing the water, gunboats upstream lobbing an occasional shell into the Rebel camp.

"*Ich denke, dass ich sie sehe,*" Rommel said.

"I think I see them," Max said.

"That's the ticket," said Faulkner.

Forrest slithered down the steep path and mounted his horse. It was clear that he had to organize a night attack, but where were the generals' headquarters? Johnston was dead, and Bragg and Beauregard were someplace on the west flank. Bedford set out to find Brigadier General James Chalmers, whose Mississippi brigade was positioned close by.

On the way down the side of the mound behind Forrest, Rommel's right foot caught in a vine and he fell. Faulkner and Max helped the colonel to his feet and he brushed himself off indignantly, refusing to admit that his ankle hurt. He had broken it at the age of sixteen. Max remembered the writer's bottle and they retraced their steps up the logging trail. After a hundred yards Faulkner turned onto a cow path. Rommel, disguising a limp, brought up the rear. He slapped a mosquito against his neck and felt a telltale wetness.

A scream made Forrest's horse shy off the path. He reined in and looked down on a man lying on the ground. The horse had almost stepped on him. The soldier lifted his head and showed Bedford a haunted face.

"*Where's the ambulance?*" *he asked hoarsely.*

"*I don't know,*" *said Forrest.* "*Are you with Chalmers's brigade?*"

"*I'm hit.*"

"*Can you tell me where Chalmers's brigade is at?*"

"*Have you got a drink on you?*"

"*We got to mount a night attack,*" *Bedford persisted. He hated to waste the time jawing with a private, even if he was wounded, but he also felt guilty about passing the man by. There was no help for it.* "*I got to find Chalmers.*"

"*My name is Horace McGee.*"

"*I'll send somebody for you.*" *Bedford guided his mount carefully around the prone figure.*

"*I cain't wait,*" *the man said and nestled his head in the leaves sleepily.*

Not far ahead a picket challenged Forrest from behind a

pine tree. "Who goes!" *The colonel identified himself and asked directions to Chalmers's headquarters. The sentry shrugged.* "Mebbe thataway," *he said, pointing west. Soon Forrest came into the large field where his cavalry had charged the peach orchard. Tents and glowing embers of campfires were scattered helter-skelter across the field as if men had dropped down in midcharge and made their beds. He urged his mount slowly among the small camps and after a while found a sergeant who knew where Chalmers slept.*

Bedford stood holding his horse while an aide reluctantly awakened the general. Chalmers, younger than Forrest by several years, emerged sleepily from his tent, fully dressed but rumpled and ashen with fatigue. The aide quickly produced two camp stools, and the officers sat face to face.

Rommel stood in the open field leaning his weight on his good ankle, rubbing the welts on his neck and wrists. The terrain looked different when one's own troops occupied it. Those undulations of ground, fencerows and blackberry thickets which during attack seemed virginal and wild now took on a domestic appearance, comfortably filled out with tents and campfires and the smell of coffee in the air.

"Buell's Army of the Ohio has landed," Forrest said urgently. "I seen 'em myself, down by the river. It behooves us to attack tonight. I can—"

"We all need our rest for the battle tomorrow," Chalmers interrupted Bedford, and yawned.

"Ain't goin' to do us no good to sleep just so's we kin git whupped all to hell tomorrow!" Bedford's color was up. His chin beard quivered in frustration and anger. "Buell's here! Boats unloadin' a new regiment ever' hour. We must attack tonight!"

Chalmers came fully awake. "Are you certain it is Buell?"

"My scouts got close enough to hear the new troops tellin' the Yankee skulkers that the Army of the Ohio had come to do their work for 'em. I seen 'em. It's Buell, all right."

"That's very bad," Chalmers said resignedly. The tone of his voice made Bedford tremble with impatience.

"Fact remains," Chalmers lectured in a schoolmarmish tone, "my men have fought the day long and need rest badly, Colonel Forrest. An attack is out of the question."

"They're no tireder than my troopers!" Bedford cried,

leaping to his feet and glaring down at Chalmers, a West Point man, who remained unperturbed. "We kin put the skeer on the Yankees tonight with half a division. Give me half yo' division! Let me call for volunteers, right now. I'll drive them batteries off the bluff, and all them skulkers beneath the cliffs will stampede the boats like a herd of spooked cattle." His face had turned brick red and he sweated profusely. In the heat of battle he was almost carefree by comparison.

"Even if I had fresh troops, I'd have to have an attack order in writing from Corps Headquarters," Chalmers said forcefully. "I won't send in an entire division on my own responsibility. You find Bragg or Beauregard or Polk and let me know what they say."

Towering over the youthful brigadier, Forrest shook his finger in Chalmers's face, hot enough to kill him. "If we wait till mawnin', we'll be whupped to hell!"

Chalmers yawned again, shaking his head sleepily. Forrest turned away to keep from slapping him and mounted his horse. Telling himself there were other generals in the woods, he spurred his mount through the tall timber. Rain began to drift through the pines and cooled Bedford's cheeks.

Mosquitoes were biting Rommel through the back of his shirt. He noticed that Faulkner did not appear to be affected by them. He strained to scratch his back and the writer stopped to sympathize. "If it ain't mosquitoes, it's somethin' else," he said. Immediately Rommel's pants leg caught in blackberry thorns and he heard the cloth rip as he tried to jerk it loose. Faulkner bent to help free him.

"Berries are ripe," Faulkner felt for Rommel's hand and made him form a cup with his fingers to receive several soft, wet berries. Rommel hesitated, unsure what to do with them. He watched the author pop one into his mouth. Rommel tried a small one. The tart sweetness flooded over his tongue. "Something to wash 'em down with?" Faulkner asked, holding the bottle out. Rommel took a fiery gulp. He licked blackberry juice and bourbon from his lips.

"The general staff envied Forrest his tactical genius," he prompted Faulkner. "And also his successful, unorthodox methods, did they not?" He waited for Max to translate. "It is not difficult to understand why they would refuse him his night attack."

"Where were we?" said Faulkner.

Forrest poked his head into the tent of Brigadier Marcus J. Wright, of Polk's I Corps. "What the hell!" cried the general, who was composing by candlelight a tender letter to his wife and children.

"We got to attack tonight," Bedford exclaimed. "Buell is comin' upriver in strength. Their reinforcements will run over us in the mawnin', but we kin throw 'em back in the river if we attack at once!"

"What is the source of your information?" Wright asked testily.

"I seen 'em, goddammit!"

"Don't curse at me, sir!"

"Ever' second we be talkin', a Ohio man steps ashore. They'll whup us to hell in the mawnin'."

"I'll stay put until daylight." Wright sniffed. "It would take all night to muster my division out, anyway."

Forrest tore away in a frenzy, crying, "See you in hell!"

"Good night to you too, sir," said Wright and yanked the tent flap shut.

Forrest turned his collar up against the rain, which had begun to come down in earnest. Even his horse seemed to be against him as it gingerly climbed in and out of ravines, resisting reins and spur, balking before a fallen log looming darkly ahead so that Bedford at first mistook it for a dead man. Voices of the wounded could be heard whispering, and once or twice Forrest thought he saw a face or a hand held out to him. He refused to stop for them, saying over and over to the silent trees, "Got to attack tonight. They'll whup us like hell in the mawnin'."

". . . *werden uns am frühen Morgen besiegen*," Max repeated. Rommel's ankle was very tender and swelling. Although he could barely put weight on it, he did not complain as he limped after his guide.

Bedford emerged from the woods into another clearing filled with tents. Campfires sizzled in the downpour. A picket pointed out the corps headquarters of General John C. Breckinridge, who only a year before had been Vice-President of the United States. Forrest pushed into the tent of this personage with no more preamble than he would have given a sergeant. The general squinted from his cot into the golden light of a lantern held by his aide-de-camp.

"My command is being held in reserve," he told Bedford wearily. "I cannot assume the authority to order another general attack." He saw the cavalryman's anxiety and added, "We have won, man. They won't push us off the ground we hold now."

"Wait and see, General," Forrest snapped. "They'll be fresh tomorrow. Buell's boys won't be like those skulkin' rascals we routed today, not countin' Prentiss's Minnesotans, who put up a hell of a fight. We'll be whupped good tomorrow, General."

"Try Beauregard or Polk," Breckinridge said, waving his hand in dismissal and pulling his blanket around his chin.

"I cain't find 'em!" Forrest exclaimed with a boy's pent-up outrage, his voice high-pitched on the verge of breaking.

"Well, Hardee then," Breckinridge offered from beneath his blanket. "He's camping just north of my corps."

Lanterns of stretcher bearers bobbed deliberately among the dripping trees. Forrest paid them no more attention than fireflies. He resisted a strong impulse to gallop back to his own regiment and order them to attack at once, without support. He told himself that if anyone would listen, General Hardee would. Time was passing quickly, and every minute was in the Federals' favor. The dark overcoat, saturated with moisture, hung on him like a dead weight. Hardee was his last chance.

A small captain hopped out of a lean-to of cut branches draped over a fallen tree. He blocked the entrance to Hardee's tent. Forrest struggled with the little man, who gripped his arms like a terrier. Bedford stepped back, his hand on the hilt of his sword. The tent flap was pushed aside. Hardee's adjutant appeared, drawing the cord around his dressing gown. Forrest stared in disbelief at the man's carpet slippers. The adjutant, a colonel, was tall, middle-aged, with delicate white hands. Wrinkled lips and sunken cheeks sagged over missing false teeth.

"May I helth you," he lisped. Forrest struggled to keep from tearing the robe and nightshirt off the man's back.

"I got to see Hardee!" he said.

"Impothible, Colonel. The general hath retired for the night and cannot be dithturbed. Perhath I can helth you?"

Bedford breathed through his nose, teeth clenched. "I got an urgent repo't Hardee has got to hear."

"What ith it?" The adjutant stifled a yawn.

"Buell is landin' the goddamned Army of the Ohio right now. If we don't attack tonight, they'll whup us like hell tomorrow!"

"Muth you curth?" The adjutant cocked an imperious eyebrow. "General Beauregarth headquarterth ith thure to have that informathon available, and they know whath beth. Their orderth are to attack at dawn." He smothered another yawn, patting his barren lips. "On behalf of General Hardee I thank you for your vigilanth, Colonel, and bid you good night and good fortune."

He had done his best. Wet to the skin, he stood in the drizzle resigned to the fact that Buell's army had mostly come ashore by now. They would be in position soon, before a night attack could be mounted. There was nothing to do but try to get some rest in the few hours remaining before daybreak. Yet, like a small boy determined to get in the last word, he spoke above the sound of water dripping steadily off the canvas. "They'll whup us like hell."

"And they did, too," said Faulkner, puffing on his pipe. "Forrest did all he could. Was up at five, skirmishin' all day, fell back under massive infantry assault and cannonade. Furious at the number of Confederate stragglers, especially after havin' seen the Yankee skulkers under the bluff. Railed and cursed and rode his horse into them, slapped at them with the flat of his sword and threatened them with firin' squads and hangin'. It was not the kind of work he admired."

Faulkner suddenly noticed that Rommel was limping, and he insisted that they return to the car at once. Rommel accepted another sip from the bottle and the writer's arm to lean on.

"You would like us to understand that Forrest had feet of clay," he said as he hobbled by the author's side, "like the rest of us, eh?" Faulkner listened thoughtfully to Max's translation.

"Oh, he was not like the rest of us." He made a small gesture of dismissal with his pipe. "Any more than Gulliver resembled the Lilliputians. There is a final chapter to this story. It happened right down the road."

Max started the Ford's engine and turned the car around, nearly getting stuck in the process. As before, Faulkner sat in the back and Rommel in the front passenger's seat. The writer directed Speigner to drive until they passed the roughhewn Shiloh Church and to turn left on the road to Monterey. After a few miles they crossed a wooden bridge over a small stream. Faulkner asked Max to stop the car.

"Breckinridge was in charge of covering the Confederate withdrawal," Faulkner began. "He reinforced Forrest's regiment with a company of Texas Rangers and a Kentucky cavalry squadron. Forrest was ordered to fight a rearguard action with these 800 against a smartly advancing line of infantry and cavalry under the command of none other than William Tecumseh Sherman himself. Outnumbered five to one, the Wizard laid his ears back and waited for 'em to come on."

Slapping his gloves restlessly against his thigh, Forrest watched the wagonloads of wounded rattle past. After the long, frustrating night and the following day of defeat every part of him cried out for retribution. Below the low ridge where he waited for the enemy was a sluggish stream and swampy bottom called Fallen Timbers, site of a logging operation before the war. He watched Sherman's force advancing in perfect textbook order, a line of skirmishers in front protected by cavalry on each flank with a solid brigade marching behind, neatly formed up in battle columns. He was about to order his cavalry to dismount and prepare to defend the ridge when his eye seized on a weakness. The line of skirmishers was breaking up as they entered the log-strewn bottom. Disorganized pockets of blue-clad troops had become dispersed among the thickets of cane and bramble that had sprung up around the felled trees.

"We kin git the bulge on 'em," he whispered happily. He glanced down his line of cavalry. Every face was turned to him. His saber seemed to leap out of its scabbard. He held it above his head, transfixing them in a moment when they lived forever. Then he brought it down.

"Charge!" he bellowed and dug in his spurs.

The Confederate cavalry surged into the broken blue line and delivered a volley with shotguns and pistols at close range. Several dozen skirmishers fell at once, killed or wounded, and the rest scattered wildly or threw down their rifles and raised their hands. Behind them the Federal cavalry, surprised by the sudden charge, broke at full gallop through their infantry support, firing their carbines in the air. Still yelling "Charge!"

*at the top of his lungs, Forrest drove through the skirmishers,
gained the solid ground above the bottomland, and burning
the air with his saber rode like wildfire at the heels of the
Union cavalry. It was as if nature, having endured interminably sluggish, humid days, erupted in storm, cleansing the
earth.*

"Forrest had a problem," Faulkner said. "He had outstripped his own cavalry and was out there all alone, one man
charging a full brigade. The Federals recognized him and
swarmed around him, yelling, 'Get Forrest! Kill him! Stick
him! Knock him off!' The Wizard had overplayed his hand."

*Forrest's horse whirled in a tight circle, lunging and
kicking at the enemy soldiers closing in on all sides. He hacked
first on one side then the other, trying to clear a path of escape.
A soldier bolder than the rest leaped into the circle and danced
with the horse. Forrest felt the barrel of the man's rifle punch
him in the back like a horsefly, and he swatted at it with his
saber. He did not hear the weapon discharge, nor did he feel
the ball enter his body. It was as though a blast of hot wind
had blown him sideways, off his saddle. One hand still gripped
the pommel, and with a massive effort he regained his seat.
The Union soldiers froze around him to see the imminent fall of
greatness. Forrest stared into the frenzied eyes of a little
corporal. Without pause Forrest reached down and grabbed
him by the collar, swung him up with one hand, and suspended
him against his back as a shield.*

"Let me be, sir!" *the small man screamed, his midwestern
accent intact even in terror.*

*Slashing right and left Bedford broke free of the gauntlet
and galloped back toward his own lines. His horse, belly shot,
trailed ropes of blood which slapped the ground and left a
track of red.*

"Turn me loose!" *cried the tiny prisoner as he flapped
against Forrest's broad back.* "I'll go home to Illinois."

*As soon as he perceived that he was out of rifle range,
Bedford released his grip and the corporal tumbled to the
ground, wounded not by bullets but by legend. He lifted up his
face where he lay sprawled and watched the Rebel colonel ride
back to his own lines. Bedford refused to slump in pain even as
his men ran to help him.*

"Had a ball lodged next to his spine," Faulkner concluded. "By all the odds, they should have finished him then and there. Surgeon removed the ball later." He rapped his pipe against his open palm. "Died in Memphis after the war at the fairly early age of fifty-six. Anybody ready for the corn gourd?" He held out the paper sack with the bottle in it. Rommel shook his head and watched the writer drink, unwilling for the story to end.

"Would you like to hear Forrest's final address to his troops?" Faulkner said moistly, screwing the bottle cap back on. "It was his surrender notice, issued in Gainesville, Alabama, May 5, 1865. My grandfather read it to me and my brothers so often I have it by heart." Faulkner began to quote from memory, pausing between sentences to allow Speigner to translate.

"Soldiers: By an agreement made between Lieutenant-General Taylor, commanding the Department of Alabama, Mississippi, and east Louisiana, and Major-General Canby, commanding United States forces, the troops of this department have been surrendered.

"I do not think it proper or necessary, at this time, to refer to the causes which have reduced us to this extremity; nor is it now a matter of material consequence to us how such results were brought about. That we are *beaten* is a self-evident fact, and further resistance on our part would be justly regarded as the very height of folly and rashness.

"The armies of Generals Lee and Johnston having surrendered, you are the last of all the troops of the Confederate States army, east of the Mississippi River, to lay down your arms.

"The cause for which you have so long and so manfully struggled, and for which you have braved dangers, endured privations and sufferings, and made so many sacrifices, is to-day hopeless. The Government which we sought to establish and perpetuate is at an end. Reason dictates and humanity demands that no more blood be shed. Fully realizing and feeling that such is the case, it is your duty and mine to lay down our arms—submit to the 'powers that be'—and to aid in restoring peace and establishing law and order throughout the land. . . .

"I have never, on the field of battle, sent you where I was unwilling to go myself; nor would I now advise you to a course which I felt myself unwilling to pursue. You have been good soldiers; you can be good citizens. Obey the laws, preserve your honor, and the Government to which you have surrendered can afford to be, and will be, magnanimous."

"So!" Faulkner relit his pipe, sucking the flame into the glowing bowl.

"There is no greater dilemma," Rommel said after a while, "than telling soldiers victorious in battle that their government has surrendered."

"You know how Forrest felt."

"*Ja.*"

"He had no choice."

"*Das ist richtig.*"

"Herr Oberst, will there ever be a more intrepid commander of cavalry?" Faulkner's eyes gleamed in the dark.

Rommel pondered the unexpected question. He thought of Forrest charging, his saber lit like a silver torch, or standing silent on the Indian mound, his silhouette dark against the moonlit surge of the river, or taking the ditch on King Philip and raising his hat to his cheering soldiers in midleap just for the hell of it. He thought also of flares fired from a mountain summit, one white and three green, drifting through the mist. What was it he felt? Envy? Challenge? Warning? Faulkner was watching him closely, pipe between clenched teeth. Without a word Rommel reached for the bourbon.

IX

"Last stop!" Faulkner parked his Ford beside the Confederate monument in front of the Lafayette County courthouse.

The three of them got out of the car. The Oxford square was quiet at 9:30 on Sunday morning. Birds sang in the oaks surrounding the white courthouse. Two boys pedaled past on their bicycles, pursued by a barking dog. Rommel leaned on a pair of crutches, his swollen ankle firmly taped, and looked up at the marble statue. Upon arriving in town Faulkner had insisted they stop at the local hospital and have a nurse "fix Herr Oberst up." Some aspirin and a cup of coffee had done wonders for Rommel, whose stamina had never before been tested by a combination of alcohol and a night march with a writer. His ankle throbbed, his pants were torn and studded with cockleburs, his shoes were caked with mud, there was dried blood on his collar and wrists. Yet he could not remember when he felt more in tune with the world.

Faulkner appeared little the worse for wear. He wore the burs in his khaki trousers and stickweed in his seersucker jacket as carelessly as any country squire home from his fields.

Max was on his last legs. Months behind a desk in Washington had not prepared him for a four-mile hike in the woods and a 180-mile drive, roundtrip, on mostly unpaved roads. His eyes were red-rimmed and shadowed, his clothes sodden and disheveled. He thought longingly of a soft bed and pleasant dreams of people who conversed in the same language. He would be happy if he never heard another umlaut or modal auxiliary.

"Most Confederate monuments," Faulkner told them, "the soldier stares *northward* in defiance. As you can see, our man is contemplating a swift withdrawal or a trip to New Orleans."

Rommel squinted up the shaft. At the summit an infantryman rested his rifle on its butt and surveyed a changing world through stone eyes. Rommel was reminded of military statues in Germany with their spiked helmets and epaulettes. He read the inscription engraved on the front of the statue.

"In Memory of the Patriotism of the Confederate Soldiers of Lafayette County, Mississippi—They Gave Their Lives in a Just and Holy Cause—Erected 1907."

Moving around the statue, he read another inscription at the rear: "The Sons of Veterans United in This Justification of Their Fathers' Faith." He turned to Max and repeated the unfamiliar word, "Justification?"

Max summoned up his mental reserves. "*Rechtfertigung.*"

"Think he's got *Rechtfertigung* on his mind?" Faulkner said, gesturing at the statue above them.

"Politicians start wars, and *he* fights them," Rommel said, his eyes on the stone soldier. "On his mind is *Stolz, seine Pflicht getan zu haben.*"

"Satisfaction in having done his duty," Max said.

"Herr Oberst," Faulkner said after a silent pause, "I've got to ask you, what are you *really* doin' in the sovereign state of Mississippi?"

Rommel thought for a moment. He put his hand into his pocket and felt the minié ball Max had given him. He thought of battlefields bristling with sweet berries and sharp thorns. "I was interested in Forrest's *Geheimnis . . .*"

"His secret," Max mumbled.

"And you found something else?" Faulkner said alertly.

"Something." Rommel smiled. "*Etwas.*"

"And this '*etwas*' should prove useful on the battlefield?"

"Everything does not have to have a use, does it? That is also something I found here. I have you and Herr Leutnant to thank for that." He paused, looking beyond them. "My colleagues, however, do not seem to have shared my experience." Faulkner and Speigner saw a patrol car stop beside the Phaeton, followed by the Germans' rented Oldsmobile. The sheriff, a large man in a vested suit, approached them in a dignified manner. Model, Schörner, Hanke and Krüger got out of the Olds. They eyed Rommel's ragged, cockleburred trousers, taped ankle, and crutches.

"Mornin', Bill," said Sheriff Roberts.

"Mawnin', Ike!" Faulkner replied.

"I have some gentlemen here who have been vitally interested in yo' whereabouts since around five-thirty A.M." Roberts glanced at the bottle sticking out of the writer's coat pocket but declined to comment on it.

"I apologize for the inconvenience, Ike," Faulkner said.

"No problem. I told 'em there was no need of puttin' out an A.P.B. Then we got a call from the hospital that you were back in town . . ." the sheriff looked at Rommel's ankle, ". . . a bit the worse for wear."

"*Was ist los?*" Model demanded.

"We took one more battlefield tour," Rommel said quietly. He felt like a schoolboy caught playing in puddles by the truant officer.

"*Die ganze Nacht!*" Walther was indignant.

"When will I be in Mississippi again?" Rommel said.

"Yes, but *all night!* Why did you not tell us where you were going?"

"All right, Walther. The truth is, we were drinking." Rommel grinned at Krüger, who alone among the Germans seemed to appreciate the whimsy of it all.

"You look like you spent the night in a barnyard," Model said doggedly.

"*Bitte,* we are on holiday, no?"

"What happened to your leg?"

"*Ich bin hingefallen,*" Rommel said.

"Herr *Rilke,*" Model retorted, "remember who you are!"

"That is something," Rommel replied, a sharp edge in his voice, "that has been on my mind."

Model glanced at the Americans, especially the G-2 lieutenant. Hanke crossed his arms, signaling that they break off this squabble in the public square. Rommel smiled at the Nazi press man. He had become a drinker of bourbon, a discoverer of minié balls and blackberries, an explorer of Mississippi's hidden places. It seemed natural to be defending himself in the sunlight beside a Confederate monument. Turning to Faulkner he held out his hand, American style. The writer clicked his muddy heels together and bowed from the waist, then shook hands.

"Most grateful *für ihren Beistand und ihre Gastfreundschaft,*" Rommel said, inclining his head.

"Assistance and hospitality," Max repeated.

"I will practice up on my tennis, in case we meet again," Rommel continued. "And I must be sure to buy a duty-free bottle of bourbon on board ship to take to my wife. I will tell her it tastes like Mississippi."

"*Auf Wiedersehen, Herr* . . . Rilke." Faulkner's eyes twinkled. Rommel could not resist meeting them in kind.

"Our plane departs from Memphis this afternoon," Model said coldly.

"Just coming!" Rommel turned to Max, who reluctantly took his hand. The moment for saying goodbyes had slipped up unawares, and Speigner was not ready. "I would have learned nothing if it had not been for you." The blue-gray eyes embraced Max. "I will not forget my American tutor. Thank you . . . my friend." Max was stunned. No words came, in either language. He realized he was pumping Rommel's hand up and down, and he released it awkwardly. "I believe we will meet again someday," Rommel added. "Perhaps you will visit Germany? If you do, you must look me up."

Rommel turned and swung on his crutches to the Oldsmobile. As he maneuvered himself into the back seat, he looked back at Speigner and Faulkner. They were incredibly familiar, like childhood friends—Faulkner in his seersucker jacket that still sagged out of shape, his khaki trousers too short so that the brogans seemed outsized, like a clown's shoes; Max with his pale scholar's face, lanky torso bent forward inquiringly at the waist, eyes squinting into the sunlight. Hanke started the engine and backed the Olds away from the curb.

"I need to ask a favor," Faulkner said, diverting Max's attention from the departing automobile. "I have a little gift I'd like you to take to the Colonial Hotel before Herr Rilke, or Rommel, leaves Oxford." Sheriff Roberts tipped his hat and gave "Bill" an affectionate pat on the shoulder. Faulkner resumed his place behind the steering wheel for the drive to Rowan Oak. He skillfully negotiated the winding driveway between the cedars and parked beside the front gallery. Max followed him inside, and Faulkner told him to have a seat in the study while he busied himself in the adjacent "office."

Max eased his tired body into an overstuffed armchair and leaned back luxuriously. Too much had happened in the past forty-eight hours to assimilate it at once. He would be sifting through memories for weeks to come.

"May I help you?"

Max sat bolt upright. An elegant, small face looked down at him with curiosity and amusement. Something about the lady made him rise to his feet instantly. She wore a flowing pink kimono which accentuated her delicate features. Her beauty seemed to derive more from her graceful carriage and the way she inclined her head toward him with a hint of a smile than from any single physical attribute.

"I am Estelle Faulkner," she said, extending her hand. Max carefully accepted it and introduced himself, glancing pointedly in the direction of the office. Mrs. Faulkner seemed unperturbed at discovering a strange, unkempt man sitting in her house on a Sunday morning. Speigner was relieved to hear paper rustling in the other room.

"Mr. Faulkner and I have been to visit the battlefield at Shiloh," he said.

"Yes, Bill loves history," she said.

"He is wrapping a gift for a man who accompanied us to Shiloh." Max hoped he made sense.

"Would you like a cup of coffee?" she said.

Faulkner walked into the library, relieving Speigner of his obligation to justify his presence. "I'm sendin' the lieutenant, here, back to town with a gift for a German officer name of either Rilke or Rommel." In his hand was a small package wrapped in newspaper and tied with string. "They're leavin' for Memphis to catch a plane, so he don't have time for coffee, thank you."

Estelle gave her husband a knowing glance and said, "Nice to meet you, Mr. Speigner. Come back any time." She glided from the room with a grace that seemed Oriental. The men went out on the gallery. Faulkner stared thoughtfully over his well-tended brick walks and flowering shrubs and trimmed hedges.

"You asked for my opinion of Rommel. Still interested?"

"Very much so."

"Well, here it is. I believe we will be at war with the Huns directly. I can't say when, but the way Hitler is goin' it won't be long. When we do, look for Rommel to be in the thick of it. I judge him to be watchful, perceptive . . . keeps his own counsel, speaks only when he has something to say. Methodical like all Germans, lines up his ducks . . . I'd guess that he prepares his tactics with great attention to detail. Has dignity but is flexible, with a sense of humor. You saw him take his shoes off during our tennis match? Competitive to the nth degree. A battler. As an enemy his most dangerous quality, I believe, would be his ability to adapt and to use what he has learned. He has a reverence for the past and also a strong sense of the pathos of war, which means he has sensibility, which means he is continually at war with himself and no doubt with commanders who have less imagination than he. I sense that he is an ambitious man. Remember that defensive phrase he kept usin'—'I am not political, I am a soldier'? In war he would make the deadliest of enemies. If I don't miss my guess, we will all be hearin' from Erwin Rommel again in a big way."

Faulkner abruptly walked to the car. Max followed slowly, trying to record every word the writer had told him. Faulkner started the engine, then turned to Speigner.

"One more thing," he said. "I hate the goddamned Huns but I like Rommel."

They drove in silence to the square. Faulkner stopped the Ford at the Colonial Hotel. Max noticed that the Oldsmobile was gone. They shook hands.

"Much obliged to you for deliverin' that package," Faulkner said. "In fact I'm much obliged to you, period!"

Max's face suddenly became unhinged by deference. "It has been an honor and a privilege . . ." he began. Faulkner glanced painfully at Speigner's angular face.

"Those words are too big for me!" He waved away Max's formality. "Just remember what my wife said. Come back any time, glad to see you. *Auf Wiedersehen*, Lieutenant."

Speigner stood on the sidewalk and watched the Phaeton drive away. He had spent so much time in it, had become so intimate with its creaks and rattles, fumes and road noise leaking through rust holes in the floorboard, that he felt unalterably deprived by its absence. With a feeling of regret he entered the hotel. The desk clerk informed him that the "German party" had checked out a few minutes before. Max immediately telephoned Shoemaker and asked if they could leave for Memphis earlier than planned. He explained that although his return flight to Washington did not depart until 4:00 P.M., he wanted to catch Rommel before the New York flight took off. The major soon came to pick up Max and return briefly to his home where Speigner hastily packed his things and said goodbye to Mrs. Shoemaker.

They arrived at the Memphis airport in something less than two and a half hours, after a hard drive over the unpaved roads of northern Mississippi. Shoemaker dropped Max off at the entrance and doubled back to the parking area. Speigner hurried through the tiny terminal to the departure gates at the rear of the building. He looked for the five Germans, but they were nowhere to be seen. Through the plate-glass windows he glimpsed a man on crutches standing in line to board an American Airlines DC-3. He pushed through the gate, flashing his own ticket to the attendant as if he were a late arrival. Heat from the tarmac blasted his face. The aircraft's engines turned over and the giant props revolved lazily, then exploded into hypnotic spheres of motion. Passengers were ascending a portable ramp. Rommel stood at the end of the line, apparently waiting so no one would be delayed while he negotiated the steep steps. The other Germans had already boarded. Rommel smiled when he saw Max.

"I wanted to say goodbye again, Herr Oberst," Max shouted in German. A stewardess turned to stare. Speigner produced the package wrapped in newspaper. "Mr. Faulkner sent you a going-away present. He said to tell you, 'Good luck!'"

"Thank him very much for me," Rommel shouted in Max's ear. "I hope this is one of his books. It feels like a book. I am interested in reading his works. Thank you, Max. I say again, it has been a pleasure meeting you."

"One thing else," Max shouted. "Would you consider signing this book? It would be a great honor." The book he took out of his briefcase was *Infanterie greift an*. Rommel looked at it solemnly, then raised his eyes to Max's face, blinking against the wash of the propellers. He was distracted by movement in the cabin door above them. Model appeared, flushed and impatient, gesturing for him to hurry up and board. Rommel set his jaw and reached for the book.

"Perhaps the *author* would not mind if I took the liberty of signing it," he yelled. "'From one admirer of Bedford Forrest to another'?" He held a pen poised above the flyleaf.

"Oh, no, Herr Oberst," Max cried. "You misunderstand. It is not for me. It is for Mr. Faulkner."

Rommel stared at Speigner for a long moment, his eyes opaque. Then he scribbled brusquely on the open page, snapped the volume shut, and thrust it into Max's hands. Max drew himself erect and saluted. A smile tugged at the corner of Rommel's mouth as he turned away and struggled up the boarding ramp. Max felt a tap on the shoulder. A flight attendant had come to escort him back into the terminal. Rommel had reached the top of the ramp.

"Good luck, Herr Oberst!" Max yelled as loudly as he could. Rommel heard him, reached in his pocket and held up the minié ball. Then he disappeared into the aircraft.

Inside the terminal building, Max watched the DC-3 taxi to the end of the runway and wheel about for takeoff. It swept down the strip of pavement. Its silver body seemed to stretch, to attenuate into a thin creature of the air. Max opened the book. On the endpaper was written in a bold, wandering hand:

"*Für* William Faulkner—*Beste Wünsche*, Erwin Rommel."

Rommel was seated across the aisle from Model. Disapproval leaked from the weapons expert like oil from an experimental flak gun. It was hard duty to endure Model's carping all the way to New York.

"I understand that authors have large, not to say monstrous, egos," Model said, leaning across the aisle, "but I trust that the book you were signing on the runway did not happen to be your own?"

"You may assume," Rommel replied, flipping through a magazine, "that whatever I sign is my responsibility, not yours."

"I see," Model said ironically. "First we waste our time endlessly and, I might add, redundantly, touring American Civil War battlefields. Next we violate security because of authorial magnanimity! I do not know which is worse. Everyone except you has been bored stiff all week. I blame Boetticher for this and his addiction to the archaic? He would have us dressed in knight's armor if he could. There were so many important things to do in America . . ."

". . . Such as genuflecting to Henry Ford!" Rommel whispered fiercely. Other passengers up and down the aisle turned their heads at the machine-gun-like bursts of German conversation. "My feelings on that subject, Herr Oberst, are well known. However, there is a great deal more to waging war than the application of machines. You must be blind, Walther. Could you not sense the energy of this country, its resolve, its admiration—no, affection!—for its military heroes? How many people did we meet who claimed kinship with Forrest? The glorious past is not dead for Americans. It lives as a part of their everyday existence. This profound sense of tradition gives them great strength and makes them formidable. I, for one, hope I do not have to fight them." He leaned back in his seat. Model glanced about, aware that people were watching. There might be German speakers among the American passengers. He, too, settled back with a sigh.

Rommel could not concentrate on the magazine. He returned it to the rack on the seat in front of him. Remembering the package Max had given him, he reached into his pocket and took it out, untied the string, unfolded the newspaper wrapping. Instinct made him fold the paper up so that the contents were not visible to prying eyes across the aisle. He looked at the cover of the book. The title was *The Sound and the Fury*. He opened to the title page. Printed in a fine hand almost as small as text type was an inscription:

To Erwin Rommel,
Best wishes,
William Faulkner
9 July '37—Oxford

Looking at the inscription Rommel remembered the author's handsome face in the gloom of the Phaeton's back seat, pipe clenched in his teeth, as Faulkner waited for a reply to his question: *Will there ever be a more intrepid commander of cavalry?* Rommel watched the green flatlands growing ever wider as the aircraft gained altitude. The brown band of the Mississippi River came into view, wandering the yielding earth with prehistoric claim. He was gripped by a sense of premonition which thrilled and terrified him at once. He rested his head against the seat and gazed down at America unfolding for him, on this summer Sunday of 1937, a vast, innocent, unending land rolling toward the sea.

II
Der Lehrer

X

Her perfume was maddening, an invocation of magnolias. What was there, Max wondered, about being in a dark motion picture theater with a woman that put the olfactory sense into overtime? Compensation for the dim light? The intimacy of the darkness, which seemed to wrap the layered scent around them like a fragrant chrysalis?

Brigitte's head rested lightly on his shoulder as she collapsed in giggles at the Three Stooges' antics. His shoulder glowed where her head touched him. He reached for her hand. Their fingers interlaced with a gentle insistence, like lovers in miniature. Since Brigitte had broken off her engagement to another man, Speigner and his secretary at G-2 had been dating all summer. Tonight—Monday, September 1, 1941—was a Labor Day he hoped to prove worthy of its name. Her fingers coiled tighter across his knuckles. She had an unexpected strength, did Brigitte, he thought lazily.

"Isn't she *beau*-tiful!" the secretary whispered. Max focused his attention on the preview of coming attractions. On the screen, actress Irene Dunne, larger than life and wearing a manicured expression of concern emphasized by perfect eyebrows and meticulously painted lips, paused on cue for Robert Montgomery's embrace and the graphics' announcement: *"Unfinished Business,"* with a narrator's baritone voice:

"Together for the first time—Dunne and Montgomery in youthful romance and Park Avenue escapades, a magic holiday!" He glanced down at Brigitte's profile, luminous in the reflected glow of the screen. Her oval face seemed hypnotized, long lashes unblinking.

Speigner mentally rehearsed his drill: a languorous kiss or two during the movie, a hand draped casually over her shoulder to brush the breast and encounter the nipple hardening in its cloistered cell of brassiere and sweater, the

171

thigh-to-thigh bus ride home to his apartment in Forest Heights, where he would ask her to come up for strawberry shortcake. (He knew she had a sweet tooth. He had watched her wolf down cookies at coffee break and lick the crumbs with a greedy pink tongue.) Then they would sit on his sofa and turn nature loose. He had discovered at long last that it was as simple as that. Yet as he came closer to the sexual watershed of his existence, he found himself in no great hurry.

"Beginning Wednesday, September 10," screamed new graphics, "two gay and spicy comedies: Danielle Darrieux is *The Virgin Bride!*" A shapely starlet fled across the screen pursued by an eager young male who might have been the bridegroom. "'Only a cad would ask for his money back on such a dish,' says Walter Winchell!"

"Walter is a man who knows what he likes," Speigner whispered in Brigitte's ear, allowing his lips to graze the orifice and watching her lashes close drowsily.

"*School for Husbands,* starring Rex Harrison," the preview graphics continued. "'Just plain naughty!' says the N.Y. *Daily News*. The frothy and frivolous double-feature bill begins Saturday, Sept. 13 at The Plaza. Don't miss it!"

Speigner detached his hand from Brigitte's hot grasp and casually put his right arm around her. They cuddled in a silvery aura of romance, pleasantly distracted by the rooster's crow announcing the dawn of Movietone News. Just as casually, Brigitte rested her palm on Max's thigh. The warmth of her hand penetrated to his thighbone and spread like a heating coil from his coccyx to his cervical vertebrae.

"Hitler Spends War Anniversary at Eastern Front," announced the graphics. A staccato voice accompanied footage of Hitler surrounded by generals outside a tent. "Heavy camouflage hides Nazi headquarters from Soviet aircraft. The Reichsführer voiced hope, as the second anniversary of the war approaches, that the Axis powers will emerge victorious. Recent progress in the Russian campaign has bolstered German confidence. Premier Mussolini's recent five-day visit with Adolf Hitler along the German-Russian front resulted in a four-point program of the 'European New Order' . . ."

Max moved his arm to give Brigitte's neck an affectionate hug, as though to protect her from the new Axis Pact; then he allowed his hand to drape possessively beside her full breasts. She was wearing a white cotton blouse under a wool sweater unbuttoned so as to frame the bust in the flickering light.

"RAF 'BOMBS' HOLLAND WITH WILHELMINA'S TEA!"

Airmen emptied sacks through bomb bays, scattering thousands of tea bags like wind spores over the flatlands. This was the kind of war-can-be-fun news that was designed to make popcorn taste better. Max felt a vague reluctance to join in the audience's enjoyment of the news feature. He had often wondered how he would react in combat. Compiling German newspaper clippings and statistics seemed boyish by comparison, like collecting enemy helmets or insignia. Yet the possibility of his actual involvement in the war seemed remote. Newspapers and newsreels were doubtless as close as he would get to it. His hand continued to rest alongside Brigitte's right breast.

The nipple is already hard.

Brigitte's slow intake of breath made her breast rise and fall against the side of his hand. He brought all his senses to bear on the rigid secret he had discovered.

"During recent raids over the Netherlands, British fliers dropped seventy-five thousand two-ounce packages of tea in celebration of Queen Wilhelmina's birthday."

The regal person herself appeared on some balcony waving to her subjects in absentia. Brigitte had closed her eyes again. She leaned against him affectionately and her elbow brushed against his groin. He immediately had an erection which supported her arm like a natural armrest. Brigitte moved her elbow back and forth.

O gentle O elegant elbow.

"The tea was a gift of the Netherlands Indies. Each package was wrapped in orange paper, the color of the Netherlands House of Orange."

With the desperate gratitude of Wilhelmina's most loyal subject Speigner watched the tea bags billow over the tulip fields.

O lovely O gracious elbow.

Brigitte's eyes opened in a sleepy squint and her arm moved slightly as if directing the rudder of a sailboat for two across a wondrous sea. He stretched his thumb out to find her nipple and galvanize them together with an irresistible current. It had a flat, button-hard shape. He stroked it for a few seconds, waiting impatiently for her response, before he realized it *was* a button inside the folds of her sweater.

"In the Middle East, the newly formed British Eighth Army gets a new commander—General Alan Cunningham, shown here with Sir Claude Auchinleck, Allied Commander-in-Chief in Cairo."

Two British officers, one tall, one short, stood in the desert wearing identical mustaches and purposeful expressions. They also squinted, much like Brigitte, into the desert sun.

Her elbow moved back and forth with a lazy assurance which surprised and delighted him. They clung together, riding the slow swells of passion. His arm squeezed her neck, his hand shaped itself to her wondrous breast. She steered him toward a forgetful harbor. Their eyes focused on a home port beyond the movie screen.

"Cunningham's mission: defeat Erwin Rommel, the Desert Fox!"

Rommel stood against a background of foamy, slate-gray water. More menacing than Max remembered, he wore a panzer cap and the curiously transsexual knee-length leather coat of the general staff. The camera drew back to reveal him standing beside a tank that had been driven to the edge of the English Channel. Waves lapped against the treads.

"The commander of the Afrika Korps is reported to be near Tobruk, gathering his panzer forces for a fall offensive."

Speigner tore his eyes away from Rommel to glance momentarily at Brigitte, who with parted lips and closed eyes kept up her stroking oblivious to the images on the screen. Max took his hand away from her breast and laid a staying hand on her industrious arm. Brigitte froze, then hastily withdrew her elbow and sat very still. While aware of hard-earned opportunity slipping from his grasp, Max became increasingly concerned with the audience's reaction to Rommel. He sensed in the rapt faces around him an American reverence for success, a numb adoration for the warrior. Rommel smiled and waved, probably at the cameraman's direction, and for an instant Max remembered him straddling the rented motorcycle at Brice's Crossroads with the same stiff, fleeting grin. It

made Speigner want to stand up and shout, "I know this man."
Then the famous face closed into a mask of self-assurance.

I have met the enemy, and he is a star.

Max had the distinct feeling that his fellow moviegoers
were prepared to grant Rommel a divine license to wage war.
He was striking at present and future enemies not on desert
flats but in movie houses from Georgetown to Cairo. He
possessed a weapon stronger than the Damascus steel of
Bedford Forrest's saber.

*History demands that Forrest receive equal time. Reroll
the cameras. Forrest reins in his iron-gray mount at the verge
of rain-swollen Tishomingo Creek; brown water eddies around
the wheel of a submerged wagon beneath the ruined bridge.
Forrest exhorts his troops: "Keep the skeer on 'em!" Camera
pulls in tight for a close-up of the ruggedly handsome face, a
smiling shell disguising a seething core of daring.*

He could not laugh it off. The audience's electric
response to Rommel lingered on people's faces as a kind of
alert expectation, even as Movietone News ended and was
replaced by the credits and theme music of the feature film,
How Green Was My Valley. Why was Rommel any different
from a dozen other up-and-coming German generals, heroes of
Poland and France such as Guderian, Paulus, Manstein, or
Schörner? What quality in him made audiences respond in this
way? This was a different Rommel from the relaxed tourist Max
had met in Mississippi. Rommel was rolling again. He had an
awesome effect on his troops, more now than in the Great War.
He was their general-of-the-saddle, leading from the front.
Somehow this muscularity of command had been captured in
the brief newsfilm.

Max turned his attention back to Brigitte. He discovered
that it was too late to take up where he had left off. They sat
apart like a married couple with unspoken tensions. Brigitte
had wholly committed herself to the emotional film about a
Welsh mining family. Her face, framed by dark bangs and
curled wings of hair, became solemn. She assumed sentiment
like the shawl Maureen O'Hara clasped around her shoulders.
Max settled back but found it difficult to concentrate on the
film. He kept seeing Rommel at the edge of the Channel, with
foam hissing around his boots and the cry of sea gulls on the
wind. When the movie ended and the lights came up, he was

surprised to see that Brigitte's eyes were red from weeping. He shyly offered her his handkerchief, but she refused with a tart shake of her head much like O'Hara's Celtic independence. They merged their identities with the crowd surging toward the exits. Outside, they went to the corner bus stop and stood near the curb.

"It was a beautiful movie," Brigitte said.

"I'm glad you enjoyed it," he said.

"It was real sad the way their family broke up."

"It really was." He did not remember the story. "Want to come by my place for strawberry shortcake?" His voice sounded redundant, an echo from another, randy existence.

"I guess." There was a jaunty cast to her chin as if to show that she and Maureen could not be taken lightly.

On the bus they sat side by side, watching the familiar sights along Wisconsin Avenue. Max tried to piece together the threads of his seduction—strawberry shortcake, soft radio music, overstuffed sofa with fluffy pillows—but it was not easy.

They got off at his bus stop in Chevy Chase. She held his arm as they walked to his apartment building. They did not talk at all. He noticed that the evening was unseasonably cool, but to have mentioned the weather would have been to kiss his chances away. He concentrated on strawberries.

Having quietly negotiated the hallway past his landlady's door, they climbed the three flights to his apartment. He fumbled with his keys and unlocked the door. Other than being short of breath, Brigitte did not seem uncomfortable. It occurred to him that she might have done this before. His gray cat, Amma, danced to meet him, but recoiled in jealous horror when he ushered Brigitte inside. Amma retreated to the kitchenette at the far end of the single room that combined dining and living area. His bedroom was a 9×9-foot cubicle off to one side. The cat bounded to the counter beside the kitchen sink and began to patrol back and forth. Except for Speigner's landlady, Mrs. Tasco, no other female had come between him and the cat. He helped Brigitte with her coat and offered her a seat on the sofa, unobtrusively turning on the radio.

"I didn't know you hadda cat," Brigitte said, browsing through a *Saturday Evening Post*. "What's its name?"

"Brigitte," he lied. "I hope you don't mind."

"That's cute," she said with a toothy grin. Max looked

proudly at his pet, receiving a disdainful yellow glance in return. He went to the refrigerator.

He had never had a cat before Amma. As a boy he had owned a succession of dogs. The cat had simply appeared one spring night on the fire escape outside his window, and he had let her in. He loved the cat's fierce solemnity. The supercilious V of her mouth was an inflexible standard on which he could always rely. They shared a vigorous domesticity that centered around eating and defecating. He no longer noticed the odor of her sandbox in the bathroom.

He opened the icebox, humming in harmony with music from the radio, Harry James playing "Blue Moon." He stopped humming. Inside the icebox next to the cupcakes, strawberries, and half pint of cream was a slice of cheesecake wrapped in wax paper. Mrs. T. had been there. A sweet surprise was her style. His landlady, who was either divorced or widowed, he had never ascertained which, left him pieces of pie or cake to let him know he was on her mind. Mrs. Tasco was short and stocky, with two noisy sons. When she had started bringing him desserts, he relied on their age difference—about ten years—as a buffer zone, but Mrs. Tasco took such obstacles in stride, piepan in hand. She continually implored Max to call her "Maria," but he had settled on the informal "Mrs. T" as a less familiar alternative. He wished she did not feel so free about entering his apartment, but if she had to come, it was just as well while he was out.

As Amma paced the counter, he made a small production of preparing the strawberry shortcake. It was, after all, the featured attraction. He whipped cream and sugar with an eggbeater, doled berries and topping onto the cupcakes, and in a moment of inspiration placed a strawberry on top of each mount of whipped cream. They stared at him like bright red nipples. He gave the leftover cream to Amma and served the dessert to Brigitte with a lascivious grin. The song on the radio was "Temptation," by Jimmy Dorsey.

"Ummmm," Brigitte said. She held her spoon delicately between her thick fingers.

He had been so preoccupied with more salient parts of Brigitte's body that he had overlooked her hands. They were square, strong, with blunt-ended fingers and powerful thumbs: hands to grind corn and beat it into flat cakes; hands to crush dark wine from ripe grapes; hands to dip a newborn infant in an icy mountain stream and bring it howling into life. Clever hands to guide him, stroke his back, grip his buttocks; hands strong enough to be gentle, to smooth the storm. Strawberry seeds crunched between his teeth. She finished eating before he did.

"What's your favorite car?" Brigitte picked up the *Post* and flipped selectively from one ad to the next.

"De Soto." Max chose a manufacturer at random.

"Mine's Packard." Liquid contentment made her voice silky.

"There's a good serial in that issue." He stared at her hands. "It's by C.S. Forester."

"Serials take such a long time to read," she complained. "What's your favorite watch?"

"Hamilton."

"Mine's Elgin."

He was relieved to hear the broadcaster announce "That Old Feeling," by Ethel Waters. "Want to dance?" he asked.

"I guess," she said.

They got up and went to the center of the room. Amma watched them with eyes that were slits.

"Jeepers creepers, wotta shave," she said, when their cheeks touched. "Mennen," she explained against his ear. He did not reply, hoping to discourage further such conversation.

They moved to the music. Her body relaxed possessively against him. The cat leaped without a sound to the top of the counter and curled up with her back to them. Before the song ended they kissed, still swaying to the music. Brigitte's mouth parted lusciously. She tasted like strawberries and cream. The song ended, leaving them holding each other as if they had no other means of support. The broadcaster announced a request: "The Yellow Rose of Texas."

They returned to the sofa holding each other's arms, as if trapping the mood between them. She sat in an experienced way, leaning back and pressing his right arm behind her. They kissed to the bouncy rhythm of "The Yellow Rose." He let his free hand play delicately over her shoulder and drift down her bicep, so that his forearm lay against her breasts. She giggled, irritating him. She had not giggled in the movie theater. The kissing evolved into an exploratory phase. Their tongues met while the music urged them to seek new frontiers. Brigitte pulled back coquettishly and took his sliding hand out of action by intertwining her fingers with his. He was encouraged by her flushed face.

"You have nice hands." She placed her palm against his. Their hands were a mismatch, her broad fingers against his slender ones. "You have the hands of a surgeon," she added, "or an artist."

He kissed her hard, and to his surprise she opened up and enveloped him with her arms, her lips, pulling him down on top of her and arching herself against him while her tongue slashed and searched. His hand cupped her breast and she moaned. He heard the cat hit the floor. Brigitte opened her eyes, and he was startled by the look of desire she gave him. He had anticipated her passion to be juicy and energetic, like her robust body, but also contained in a secretarial way. Here, instead, was a thin-lipped, glittery-eyed, ravenous intensity. As he slid his hand toward her thrusting pelvis, he was both thrilled and intimidated by this discovery, which he accepted as one of life's mysteries.

A tapping on the door made them freeze. Max recognized the coy manner of knocking. The cat, Amma, responded at once by running to the door and sniffing at the crack. Max stood unsteadily and went to turn the radio down.

"I know who it is," he whispered. Brigitte had begun to smooth her hair and mussed clothing. "I'll get rid of her, don't worry."

He opened the door wide enough for one eye to see through. Mrs. Tasco's anxious smile was replaced by the germ of suspicion. Her eyes darted at the opening to see into the apartment behind him.

"Did you find your—?" she said.

"Yes, thank you," he said. "Very thoughtful of you."

"This being a holiday, I thought you might enjoy—" Her lips clamped shut. He noticed that she had a wispy black mustache sprouting at the corners of her mouth. Squinting suspiciously, she resembled a long-haired Charlie Chan. "May I speak with you for a moment in the hall?"

He squeezed through the door and quickly closed it behind him. He was aware that his shirt had come untucked. Mrs. T averted her eyes as he stuffed it under his belt. The cat had slipped through the door and now twined in and out of Mrs. T's legs. He had never seen the animal so much as acknowledge his landlady's existence. It was two against one.

"Do-you-have-a-guest-you-know-my-rules!" said Mrs. T in a single breath. She pinched her blue housecoat against her throat as if it were about to spring open.

"Let me explain . . ."

"What's to explain? You got a girl in there."

"My cousin, Brigitte—"

"Cousin-schmuzzin. I'm very disappointed. You disappoint me. I never expected you to disappoint me, you know?"

Max heard Amma begin to purr. He braced himself. "Would you care to come inside and meet Brigitte?"

"Oh!" A look of horror passed over Mrs. T's broad features. He might have mentioned a surprise audit by the IRS. "No, that won't be necessary." She regained her composure. "I do have my rules, you know."

"You were so nice to bring the cheesecake." He tried a flanking movement. "I really appreciate it."

"Forget it." She frowned in an effort to regain the initiative. "You put me in a helluva fix." Amma was going like a small dynamo underfoot.

"Please don't be distressed. Brigitte is from out of town. She just popped by for a short visit to bring me news of the family." He amazed himself. He actually had begun to enjoy the conversation in a perverse way.

"Yeah? Well, I suppose . . . but I got my other tenants to consider, unnerstan'? Rules're rules, you know?"

"Are you sure you won't come in?" he said expansively.

"Too late for visitin'!" Mrs. T muttered, retreating toward the stairwell. She turned at the top of the stairs. Her hand rested dramatically on the banister, the housecoat falling open to reveal flower-print pajamas. "You disappoint me."

"I'm awfully sorry," he intoned richly, his voice echoing upstairs and down for other tenants to hear if they chose to listen. "I promise never to disappoint you again!" His words drove her down the stairs, slippers flapping abjectly against the steps.

The flush of victory faded, however, when he returned to his apartment. Brigitte was standing over the sink, washing the dessert plates and drying them to a high gloss. Amma leaped upon the counter to resume patrolling her territory, and Brigitte gave the cat a patronizing smile. He was at a loss: he would never have a better opportunity with Brigitte, but Mrs. T was waiting downstairs with her eye on the clock and her ear to the door. Brigitte gracefully resolved the dilemma by announcing that it was getting late and tomorrow was a working day. He accepted her suggestion with mixed feelings of relief and regret. In leaving the building, he made more noise than necessary, feeling like a traitor to love. He insisted on seeing Brigitte home, even though it meant a long bus ride to and from her parents' home in Bethesda. They made the trip in awkward silence. When he escorted her to her door, she offered him her hand and told him she'd had a nice time. Her civil tone of voice grated on his nerves all the way home. It was her secretarial voice, polite and accommodating, without a hint of passion.

Major Parham was hovering near the door to Max's office when he arrived at work the next morning. Max thought Parham was going to say something about his being five minutes late. The major had the constipated look he wore when something upset him.

"They liked our memo!" Parham laid a hand briefly on Speigner's arm. Max became violently alert. It was the first time his section chief had ever touched him. "They want us to fly to Cairo!" Parham spoke with such force that spittle flew with the word "Cairo."

Our memo?

"Who liked it?" Max said.

"The intelligence section at General Headquarters, Middle East. The *British* liked it. We're getting a commendation!"

"That memo was sent over a year ago, before the Germans invaded France," Speigner said in some confusion. "You mean the British have noticed it now, when it's no use to them?"

"It's plenty useful. They're fighting Rommel in North Africa. They need everything on him they can get." Parham crowed, "We may know a few things about him they don't!"

"I'd better refresh my memory about that memo." Max moved away toward his office door. Parham followed him with a deferential manner that was unnerving.

Speigner now had an office and title of his own, the benefit of having been "discovered" by the War Department shortly after Hitler's invasion of Poland. His German Officers Files had immediately proved of practical value to a G-2 Department scrambling to assemble information about the German war machine. Parham had been thrilled by the high efficiency ratings his section had received almost overnight as a result, and he hovered around Speigner like a proud father. All out-of-date files had been transferred to a warehouse in Alexandria and the O.O.D. files room converted for Max's new section. His hand-printed sign taped to the door had been replaced by an official title painted on the glass: GERMAN MILITARY FILES. He now directed a full-time staff of three (representing a budget increase of 2500%). He had experienced the growing pains of bureaucracy (inventory controls, personnel reports, budget analysis: a 2500% increase in paperwork) with the irritability of a teenager with swollen joints. Control of his files now had to be shared with Parham, who seemed to be forever pawing through them with a proprietorial hand.

"A whole drawer just for one colonel?" Parham had questioned, having found in his initial inventory in 1939 the extensive files on Rommel.

"He's worth it!" Max had retorted and refused to elaborate.

Max slowed as he passed Brigitte's desk, and Parham stepped on his heels. She sat studiously before her typewriter, lining up a triplicate set of forms with their carbons. She wore glasses for typing. Her blue sweater was securely buttoned over a high-collared blouse. Was he back to ground level with her? Would he ever see that lovely, severe, unsmiling face contorted into a desperate mask of desire again?

"'He will strike deep and fast where he is least expected,'" Parham quoted authoritatively.

"What!" Max said.

"'. . . He will rely on audacity, courage, and the element of complete surprise to break through and cause havoc and confusion,'" Parham continued. "Our memo," he added, seeing the lieutenant's perplexed expression. Max turned to his files secretary, Ruth.

"Would you pull that memo I—we—did on Rommel?" he said. "It's dated March something, 1940." The secretary glanced in some embarrassment at Parham, who clamped the folder containing the memo under his arm.

"They want us to leave right away," said the major. "I'm having the orders cut and verified. We are to be special liaison attached to the American Embassy, Cairo." Parham lowered his voice. "This means promotions for us, Speigner."

"I need to go over the memo, if you don't mind." Max stared pointedly at the folder Parham held. "My memory is a bit fuzzy on what . . . we wrote."

"Yes of course, certainly." The major handed him the folder with an indulgent smile. "Let's talk later. Free for lunch?" The last time Parham had invited him to lunch was the Monday in 1939, nearly two years ago, when the Assistant Director of War Planning had commended Parham's section on its innovative German Officers Files.

"Let me check my schedule and get back to you," Max said.

The world had gone haywire. It was weird to control his section chief like this. Parham left him with a solemn nod of discretion, bobbing on his toes as he left Max's office.

As Speigner settled in behind his desk with the half-forgotten memo, he recalled the circumstances of its composition. In early 1940, while others at G-2 had been concerned with the greater significance of German innovations in modern warfare—mechanization, rapid deployment, coordination of air and ground attack—Speigner, though aware of these new techniques, kept to his growing files. Others could worry about Nazi war power. He was sublimely concerned only with the comings and goings, promotions and maneuvers and appointments, psychology and development of the German officer cadre, and with Rommel in particular.

As a German invasion of Western Europe grew imminent, however, Max had begun to turn his mind toward a practical exposition of his theories. What would Rommel *do* when the attack came? What would his role be? Max collected all that he knew of German military tactics, superimposed what he knew of Rommel's character and traits—Rommel's hometown newspaper in Württemberg had informed him of Rommel's new assignment to command of the 7th Panzer Division—and seasoned it all with Rommel's fascination with Nathan Bedford Forrest. What Max had compiled was a kind of amalgam of personalities, Rommel's and Forrest's, and it took on a life of its own, so that he came to believe in it.

When he had taken the completed intelligence report to Parham, the major had succinctly dismissed it as, "interesting but irrelevant." Undaunted, Max requested permission to send it through channels to the British War Office. Though it had been a matter of supreme indifference to Parham, he had approved the request. Now it was the major's hastily scrawled signature underneath Speigner's that gave Parham such cause for rejoicing. Max reread the memo with a mixture of dubiousness and curiosity.

TO: Department of Intelligence   Mar. 15, 1940
      War Ministry, London   War Department
                                   Washington, D.C.

FROM: U.S. Army Intelligence
         G-2, Section 25D

RE: Assessment assault tactics of
     Oberst Erwin Rommel, commanding
     officer, 7th Panzer Div.

Col. Erwin Rommel—*Pour le Mérite*, Knight's Cross—commanding 7th Panzer Division can be expected to play a key role in a German invasion of Western Europe. There are three important reasons why Rommel stands apart from other division commanders: 1) rapid appreciation of a tactical possibility; 2) rapid organization of his troops to confront it; 3) personal leadership at the critical point.

1) It is expected that Rommel will break through and penetrate far behind enemy lines. He will strike deep and fast where he is least expected. Such penetration will be the result of exploiting a weak link in the Allied line and bursting through with concentrated force, or a flanking movement around static defensive positions. In either case, Rommel will not expose his troops to unnecessary danger, but will rely on skill and daring to achieve his objectives. He will rely on audacity, courage, and the element of complete surprise to break through and cause havoc and confusion. What seems unreal and extraordinarily inventive to his enemies will be

standard operating procedure for Rommel. Once he gets his enemy on the run, he will not stop until he runs him to ground and obtains his surrender.

2) His troops will be well trained; their hallmark will be efficiency and poise under fire. Their nature is to be aggressive and always to seize the initiative. Rommel expects more of his men than the average commander does. He drives them as hard as he drives himself. Because of his example, leading as he does from the front, his troops will do anything he asks of them. The esprit de corps of Rommel's division will typically be greater than most, because his men become imbued with their commander's sense of purpose and identity. They will have a deep, competitive pride in their ability to achieve more than their fellow divisions. They doubtless will emerge from their first major campaign with a distinctive name that will set them apart from other units.

3) In placing his division headquarters at the front of his column, Rommel is able to issue orders quickly, without time-consuming encoding of radio reports back and forth from a rear command post. He thus is in a position to exploit openings decisively, where other commanders would be too late. Personally fearless under fire, Rommel displays absolute physical courage. He also exhibits a seemingly super-human stamina during battle. He will go as long as it takes, on a few hours' sleep and little food. He typically waxes stronger as the battle progresses.

Conclusion: Erwin Rommel is a fire-eating cav-alryman in the tradition of a Nathan Bedford Forrest. He has a finely honed instinct to break out unexpect-edly and then turn in his enemy's rear to counter-attack. Whereas in conventional, positional warfare he might lack composure in a "set battle," he will prove virtually unstoppable in a highly mobile, running battle. He is the pure warrior, the General of the Saddle of modern times: ceaselessly spurring his men into action, changing plans on a moment's notice, always advancing, penetrating, relentlessly pursuing. He will keep coming until the last drop of gasoline in his tanks.

Lt. Maxwell Speigner
(Research Specialist)
Maj. George Parham
(C.O., Sect. 25d, G-2)

For something that was written before the invasion of France, he thought with cautious pride, it was not too bad. Yet the British had apparently ignored it—and why shouldn't they?—until long afterward. Who had found it? Some clerk cleaning out unsolicited materials from dead-letter files? Who was responsible for inviting him and Parham—*Parham!*—to come to Cairo, and what could he tell them about Rommel that they did not already know? The British were in the thick of it, whereas he knew absolutely nothing except what he read in the newspapers. His tools of war were a reading lamp, scissors, and a glue pot. It was true that he had enjoyed a limited success with his Wehrmacht personnel files. It had been fun to see business booming at his small corner of the War Department. But he did not claim to be anything other than what he was: a competent clip-and-paste man. If his business was soldiering, it was a hybrid variety. He knew that he was in for the duration. He believed that it was only a matter of time before America was drawn into the war. Yet his feelings on the subject were ambivalent. He refused to involve himself in the greater questions of morality and conscience and duty. If Uncle Sam was asking him to shoulder his scissors and glue pot, cross an ocean and set up his vendor's stand of facts and figures, he would do what he was told. If the Brits needed a paper soldier, he stood ready to serve. It would save everybody a lot of time and effort, however, if they merely requested photostats of his file on Rommel.

His desk phone rang twice, punctuating his doubts. He picked up the receiver. "Speigner."

"Watkins, State Department," said a bland male voice. "I'm calling in regard to the information we received from our embassy in Cairo. We phoned about it earlier this morning. We have booked you on a clipper flight out of New York tomorrow. I know that is impossibly short notice, but I hope you can adapt?"

Max thought immediately of Amma and who would feed her. He had an impulse to ask this Watkins if he could adapt *his* schedule to feed Amma and change her sandbox.

"Wednesday? Tomorrow?" he said. "I can try, but you'll have to check Major Parham out. I can't speak for him."

"Who?"

"Major Parham, my section chief."

"How did his name come up?"

"He's the one who told me about this . . . news. If you phoned earlier, he must have taken the call. He told me *we* were going to Egypt together."

"Your major jumped to conclusions." Watkins's laconic tone implied that he had many other important duties to perform before lunch. "The message we received was that the British want *you* to brief them on Rumpel or Rondell—"

"Rommel."

"Yes, whoever. Anyway, this was a priority request at the *highest levels* . . ." Watkins's voice rose a half octave and grew momentarily profound. ". . . and orders have been processed through G-2 Headquarters. The orders do *not* include Major Parham."

"Why me?" Max said thoughtfully. "They could requisition all pertinent materials on file here."

"My records show that their embassy requested your personnel file some time ago. Their invitation, if you will, made reference to the fact that you are the only man on this side who has actually met Rumming personally. That seems to have made a big impression on them . . . I can't help being curious. Who *is* this person?"

"His name is *Rommel*. He's the German general kicking British tails all over the desert. Don't you read the papers? But back to Parham—he really has his heart set on going."

"Sorry. He's out."

"Well, would you mind phoning him and telling him?"

"I'll be glad to talk with him if he phones *me*," Watkins said officiously, "but it would be superfluous to call a person to inform him of orders that do not exist."

"Then it's all right with you if I suggest that he phone you?"

"Certainly, but I may be out of the office the rest of today. At any rate, your reservation is set. The connecting train trip to New York leaves Washington late tonight—there was nothing that could be done about that. Sorry. Your orders and names of contact persons at our embassy in Cairo are being sent to you by messenger this morning."

"Wait! How long will the British want me to stay?"

"I suppose as long as you're useful to them. Well, good luck and . . . cheerio, Lieutenant!" Watkins hung up. Max sat very still as the reality of what was happening began to sink in.

Cairo.

The man at State had said his train left D.C. that night and his plane the next day. There were only a few hours to get things squared away in the office and to hurry home to pack. Max stood up, partly in a state of shock and partly exhilarated. He assembled his secretarial staff and told them of his assignment, hoping it was regret he saw in Brigitte's eyes. Although there were fewer German-language newspapers and magazines to scan, due to wartime censorship, there was much more military news to catalog. He reviewed goals and priorities to keep in mind during his absence, and told them he had every confidence in them.

As they stood around him—tall Ruth, ample Ethel, luscious Brigitte—nervous about his departure but sharing in his achievement, he perceived the dimensions of his command for the first time. Here were *his* troops. They wore lipstick and nylons, they smelled of starch and toilet water, but they carried on the fight. In a rush of sentiment he shook their hands, beginning with Brigitte.

"I don't know how long the British will need me," he told her, "but I'll be back before you know it." He could tell she was beginning to appreciate the drama of his unexpected leave-taking, because her bosom rose and she squeezed his fingers in her big hand. He found himself turning in some relief to confront Ethel.

"Don't let the forms pile up while I'm gone. Just fill them out like you always do and get Major Parham to sign them in my place."

Then Ruth, his right arm—quiet, efficient Ruth, who knew as much about his research section as anyone—looked him in the eye and said, "Be like Forrest."

"What?" he said.

"You know, think like Forrest. It they want you to help them figure Rommel out, all you have to do is think like Forrest."

"Ruth," he said, "if *you* believe that theory, it must be true." He regarded her for a long moment with mixed feelings of amusement and wonder. Then he added, "Please pull all related files on Rommel and I'll select what I need to take with me."

He went into the section office and saw Parham across the open room, talking with Mrs. Biggers. He loitered beside a row of filing cabinets until he saw Parham leave the office. Then he approached Mrs. Biggers's desk. The head secretary wore a look of doom that seemed to be directed at him.

"Yes?" said Mrs. Biggers.

Speigner drew on years of Biggers-watching to surmise what the problem must be. The one thing that Mrs. Biggers despised more than anything was change in office routine. Speigner was responsible for Parham's apparent assignment abroad and therefore was a threat to office harmony. Mrs. Biggers's narrow gaze told him that he was the enemy. He leaned confidentially over her desk.

"I need to leave a message for Major Parham," he said.

"Don't we all!" she countered, snatching a pencil and holding it poised like a dagger above her notepad.

"Please tell him I just received a call from State. They inform me that the orders are for me to go to Cairo alone. Major Parham has not been included in the assignment."

Mrs. Biggers looked up in unconcealed joy at such bounteous news. At the War Department, glad tidings like these were so rare as to set her eyes swimming.

"Apparently," he added, providing salve for the major's ego, "the British want someone who has met General Rommel personally." He waited for her to write this postscript, anticipating having to spell *Rommel* for her. To his dismay she glanced up, saw someone behind him, and put her pencil down with a gesture of finality.

"You can tell the major," she said sweetly, "yourself." Max spun as if being attacked from the rear. Parham approached him bubbling with enthusiasm.

"I've been trying to find out if Egypt has a tropical climate," he told Max. He wore an expression of hilarity. "Do *you* know? I've called home to get my wife to press my whites for me. We don't have much time, you know. Do the British wear pith helmets over there? I've still got mine from the Canal Zone in twenty-eight, if I can find where the hell it is!"

"Could we step into your office for a minute?" Max said somberly. Parham led him inside the adjacent room. Max closed the door behind them.

"I just got a phone call from State," he said. "They have booked a train to New York tonight to connect with a flight tomorrow."

"That's short notice, by God," Parham said eagerly. "The Brits are in one hell of a hurry to find out what we know about Rommel, aren't they? Well, I can make the train if you can!" Speigner's courage began to fail him. He cast about for some means of breaking the news.

"I think I can," he said, "but I may need your help."

"You and me both, pal!" Speigner winced as if his C.O. had hurled an obscenity at him. "Just ask for it, you got it."

"I know this sounds absurd," he said tentatively, "but I need someone to look after my cat."

"Your cat?" Parham's grayish eyes turned opaque. Max rushed ahead.

"You know how people get attached to their pets. I'd worry about her, and it might affect my performance . . . over there. I would ask my landlady to do it, but she's not very favorably inclined toward me just now. I was wondering if you would mind sending someone over every couple of days to put fresh food and water out for her, maybe change her sandbox every other week. I leave a window cracked for her to go in and out. She jumps from the sill to the fire escape. She'll do fine with very little attention. She's quite self-sufficient."

They stared at each other in a moment of dire understanding.

"*You're* going to Cairo," the major said, "and you want *me* to feed your goddamned cat."

"I'll do my best on behalf of our section," Max said hopefully.

"I don't believe it," said the major.

Someone knocked on the door. A messenger carrying a leather pouch delivered a manila envelope to Speigner. Max glanced at the orders and handed them to Parham, who read them at arm's length as if the papers were contaminated.

"They want you," he said in an awful tone of accusation. With his arm outstretched, thrusting the papers back to Max, he looked like a parody of the Uncle Sam recruiting posters.

Speigner took a step back, came to attention, and briskly saluted. Parham did not return the salute. Max hesitated in the doorway, deliberated about telling the major something, and decided it had to be said.

"Her name is Amma," he said.

"Who?" said Parham.

"My cat."

XI

Rommel stood amid camel thorn and desert rocks the size of grapefruit and watched the enemy milling about, unsuspecting, on their beaten track. Sweat stained the armpits, back and chest of his khaki tunic with its red collar insignia embroidered with the gold leaf of a *General der Panzertruppen* and its cuff brassard with the single word AFRIKA. He had waited a long time for this moment. Never before had he held such a grudge toward his fellow creatures, an angry vendetta in which destruction of the enemy had become an obsession. Nothing less than obliteration by holocaust would satisfy his craving for revenge. As was his custom, he personally supervised all details of the operation, none too insignificant for his inspection. When all was in readiness, he ignited the gasoline by tossing a lit taper at the target. It erupted in a searing blast of flame. The enemy was trapped, scrambling in vain to avoid being broiled alive. Rommel rubbed his hands at the hissing sound of their cries. There was no escape.

"Flies you can get used to," he called to Schmidt, his aide, above the withering roar of the flames. "Fleas and lice are bad, but at least you can purge them once a week with a bath. But bedbugs are the filthiest creatures on the face of the earth. They get you when you are down and out."

Rommel had lived with the harsh extremes of the desert

for nearly seven months—116-degree heat of the day dropping over eighty degrees to freezing temperatures as soon as the sun disappeared over the horizon; infestations of flies; sandstorms that shut out the sun and made day into night; sand that fouled tank carburetors and jammed cannon turrets; fine grit that permeated one's very pores and made the inside of one's underwear like sandpaper; the recurring diarrhea which Rommel called "Bedford's Tennessee Two-Step"—yet none of these constant discomforts aroused the general's ire more than the bedbug. Rommel needed very little sleep. He could fall asleep instantly on bare ground, sitting upright in a moving jeep over rough terrain, or in the midst of heavy bombardment. In the bedbugs of Cyrenaica, however, he had come to know sleepless nights which hollowed out his eyes and interrupted his recovery from a long bout of jaundice.

"We got them all this time, Herr General!" Schmidt cried. Rommel grinned at his aide's enthusiasm as he watched the iron bed frame blackening in the dying flames.

"Just give me three days without bedbugs," he replied. "I will be a new man." He realized he was unconsciously scratching the welts on one leg by rubbing them with the heel of his canvas boot. He willed himself to leave the proud flesh alone so it could heal. Sores festered quickly in the desert heat. Rommel stared at the paint curling as the flames licked up the remaining petrol and thought instead of his quartermaster's complaints about wasting precious fuel on training maneuvers, much less on bedbugs. Well, it was the quartermaster's job—not an enviable one—to hoard fuel, just as it was his job to keep the troops sharp, especially during this long and frustrating lull in the fighting. The quartermaster's attitude was understandable. At the end of the summer *Panzergruppe* had received only a third of the troop replacements and a seventh of the supplies that were needed. In addition to successful British raids on German naval convoys, Operation Barbarossa on the Russian front had overriding priority where supplies were concerned. Rommel remembered a recent letter to his wife, Lucie, in which he had ironically written, "For the moment, we're only stepchildren. . . ."

"When the bed frame cools off," he told Schmidt, "have it cleaned and find me a few extra blankets to make a pallet. No more mattresses for me, straw or otherwise. At least a blanket can be shaken out and put in the sun every morning."

Turning abruptly, Rommel almost stepped on one of the live chickens his men had bought from local Arabs as a gift for their commander. The birds, frightened away by the flaming gasoline, had begun to peck their way back underfoot. He walked toward his headquarters—a low, rust-streaked building situated on a barren slope overlooking Gambut in northeastern Libya. In the distance tiers of square white houses shimmered in the morning heat against the purple Mediterranean. Winding along a nearby ridge like a shining serpent was the Via Balbia coastal highway built by the Italians, Libya's single tarmac-surfaced highway. Rommel had selected Gambut as his headquarters because it was located midway between the besieged British fortress at Tobruk and German positions guarding the mountain passes on the Egyptian frontier. Although the Italians had assigned him the Prefettúra building at Beda Littoria, some 200 miles to the rear, he had soon left the gorgeous scenery and well-stocked mess halls to set up his headquarters close to the front.

"When is Bombastico coming?" Rommel asked Schmidt. He ignored a panzergrenadier sentry who snapped to attention with weapons held up in salute. Under the thin shade of a canvas lean-to beside the building a motorcycle courier looked up alertly, greasy rag poised over his gleaming machine. His face was strangely pale around the eyes where his goggles had kept out sun and sand.

"Oh-nine-thirty!" Schmidt replied. He detailed an orderly to clean the bed frame and followed his commander inside. In the small ante-room a sergeant manning the radio console stood at attention as Rommel disappeared into his office. It was a large room sparsely furnished with a desk and several chairs in one corner and dominated by a flat worktable in the center of the room on which stood a scale model of Tobruk. He frowned at the red lines marking the hidden tunnelways spreading like veins from the walled fortress to connect a series of concrete bunkers buried in the sand. Beyond them lay a network of tank-trap ditches and barbed-wire barriers. The model had been constructed from the Italians' original blueprints of the fort which they had remembered to show Rommel *after* his attack in April had failed. He thought of the German army cemetery outside Tobruk, and how many times during the summer he had stopped there to read the names on the markers.

A corporal emerged from the adjacent room to report that Rommel's quarters had been fumigated and furniture other than the bed had been put back where it belonged. He waved in acknowledgment and, with the ubiquitous Schmidt at his heels, went to inspect the fumigation. The furnishings could almost be counted on the fingers of one hand: a wooden chest of drawers on which stood a framed photograph of Lucie and Manfred along with a clear glass jar containing three different colors of desert sand; a straight-backed chair; a bedside table with gooseneck lamp and two books. Powdered insecticide sprinkled around the corners of the room gave off a faint, piquant odor. He stepped on a dying bedbug with a satisfying crunch.

"What are you reading?" Schmidt remarked. Lately Rommel had noticed that the aide grasped at any topic that would entertain him, however briefly. He was well aware that many of his staff shared the opinion that he had become obsessed with Tobruk, the only prize that so far had eluded him.

"Did you ever hear of an American novelist named Faulkner? No? Well, I have been trying to read one of his novels, in English. It is slow going. I have to use my dictionary every sentence or so. Do you know, for example, the word 'ineluctable'? By God, now *I* do." Schmidt picked up the book, noting with interest the inscription on the title page.

"*The Sound and the Fury,*" he read aloud. "What is it about?"

"An American family struggling to survive, but no harder than I am struggling to understand the author. One chapter is told through the point of view of an imbecile, Benjy, a grown man with the mind of a two-year-old. Having dealt with the Italians for six months, I am familiar with this point of view." He made the remark with a straight face, but hearing Schmidt's delighted chuckle he broke out in a wide grin and added, "I must say, after Bombastico, Benjy is a great improvement."

His thoughts turned to the imminent arrival of the Italian commander. General Ettore Bastico had replaced General Gariboldi as head of all Axis forces in North Africa. Nominally he was Rommel's superior with final authority on all joint offensives. Rommel had come to like the square, blunt-spoken Gariboldi, but Bastico was a bird of a different feather.

"Bastico is argumentative, jealous, spiteful, and a liability!" Rommel said explosively. The smile faded from Schmidt's face. "The Italian soldier can be trained to fight, but the Italian officers are too indecisive and unstable for combat. I am stuck with a command of two-thirds Italian troops to one-third German. Let Berlin send Kesselring out here. They will soon see what I am up against!"

Schmidt placed the novel on the bedside table with exquisite care, as if closing the lid on a Pandora's box. Rommel glared at the book cover where the author's name appeared and remembered his words to Faulkner in Mississippi: "I am not political. I am a soldier."

What luxury to be able to separate war and politics.

Such neat partitioning was a relic of the ancient past, like perfect halves of a fossilized shell in a petrified forest. From the day he arrived in Africa he had been forced to play politics with Rome and Berlin. After his first attack on Tobruk had failed and he had pulled back to his present position awaiting supplies, he had found it expedient to make scapegoats of the Italians. When British raids from Malta created a supply crisis, he had asked Berlin to allow him to appropriate all available shipments for his own troops, calling the Italians "useless mouths" and blaming his chronic supply shortages on "Italian treachery." His latest conflict with *Comando Suprèmo* revolved around his new plan to attack Tobruk. Bastico, wary of a British counterattack or flanking movement during the assault on the fortress, refused to commit some of his troops to Rommel's intended deployment. Rommel had promptly gone over Bastico's head by sending his chief of staff, General Gause, to Rome for a final ruling that Hitler and Mussolini were firmly agreed to make the capture of Tobruk their first priority in North Africa. Furthermore, Rommel had invited one of Mussolini's close companions, a Major Melchiori, to visit Panzergruppe Afrika as his guest.

Bombastico no doubt saw red when he heard about Gause's end run to Rome. He will come sniffing around during Melchiori's visit. That is all right. If Bombastico wants a row, that is exactly what he will get.

Rommel glanced at his watch. The time was 0915. He had about thirty minutes before his guests arrived. The Italians were always late. He returned to his office and stood under a large map of Russia mounted on balsa wood and hanging on the wall over his desk. Varicolored pins bristled in a broken line across the surface of the map from top to bottom. Rommel casually resumed one of his favorite pastimes: charting his rival generals' progress as they stormed through Russia in Operation Barbarossa.

"Let us see how they are using *my* petrol these days," he mused. "We will move Manstein up around Leningrad. He is about one victory away from promotion to colonel general. Down here, Pannwitz's cossacks are crossing the Bug at Brest Litovsk. Give him a Knight's Cross, thank you very much. Guderian takes Smolensk there . . . now he can smell Moscow. That ought to be good for oak leaves on his Iron Cross at the very least. What have they got that we do not, Schmidt?" His eyes strayed to the scale model of Tobruk on the table. The lieutenant kept his eyes glued to the map. "Petrol, ammunition, rations, spare parts—that's what! Do you know what our troops call the unidentifiable tinned meat the Italians distribute? *Alter Mann.* They joke of elderly Italian gentlemen, peasant and aristocrat, giving all for the war effort. It is probably horsemeat. The British have Canadian bacon, canned milk, corned beef, tinned butter. Well, we are going shopping for some of it tomorrow. That reminds me—when Melchiori arrives, be sure to have cameras rolling."

"We are low on film, Herr General."

"Did I say anything about *loading* the cameras?" Rommel slanted his eyes at his aide. "Let us put on a good show for Il Duce. See to it."

Schmidt snapped his heels together and went to organize the greeting party. Left alone, Rommel was drawn back to the table in the center of the room. He stood with legs braced apart as though in a desert sandstorm and stared morosely at the intricate pattern of defenses.

Tobruk.

He was haunted by the memory of a flip remark he had made months ago to the High Command Chief of Staff, General Franz Halder, who in response to Rommel's request for two additional panzer corps had tartly inquired how he would *supply* them even if Hitler could spare them. "That is quite immaterial to me," Rommel had snapped. "That is your pigeon." The inescapable facts were that the Afrika Korps needed 24,000 tons of materiel each month for basic daily use, plus another 20,000 to stockpile for offensives, the Luftwaffe 9,000, the Italians 63,000 tons for military and civilian use, or so they claimed, and yet the port facilities at Tripoli could handle only 45,000 tons per month. The supply situation was like bedbugs: ceaseless frustration and mental agony. What was it Faulkner had said at Shiloh? "If it were not mosquitoes it would be something else"? But the writer had spoken ungrammatically: "If it ain't mosquitoes . . ." Strange affectation for a man of letters.

That happened a lifetime ago.

Tobruk lay before him in its defiant symmetry, as thorny and unyielding as a porcupine at bay. He thought of his optimistic arrival in Tripoli in February, how proud he had been of his panzers rumbling on parade through the palm-lined boulevards. He had torn a leaf from Bedford Forrest's book and instructed them to circle the parade route three times, so that the Arabs spying for the British would report a much stronger force.

Rommel impulsively entered his bedroom and opened the top drawer to his bureau. He rifled through an open wooden box containing various medals, ribbons, collar insignia, brassards. In the bottom of the box lay the minié ball, its rough, oxidized surface whitish-tan and slightly dusty to the touch. He turned it in his fingers, thinking of a Harley-Davidson and a young American lieutenant holding on behind him. He tucked the good-luck charm into the breast pocket of his tunic and went out to meet Mussolini's boy.

The Italian motorcade arrived in a fine frenzy of motorcycles, armored cars bristling with antiaircraft weapons and a single, sleek Ferrari touring car. As they slowed, their dust trail caught them so that they pulled up to Rommel's staff HQ in a dramatic dust storm. The motorcycles wheeled smartly in pairs to a stop, engines growling powerfully. Rommel waited with his interpreter, Leutnant Armbruster, standing slightly behind him. As he had expected, Bastico had accompanied the courtier from Rome. He smiled to himself. Bastico probably would not let him be alone with Melchiori for three minutes unless they went into combat together, which was exactly what he planned to do.

The Axis commander sat stiffly in the open touring car.

His light blue uniform with shining gold braid was covered by a fine patina of dust, giving him a battle-wizened appearance. Rommel absently scratched one calf with the heel of his desert boot. He consciously warned himself not to slip up and call the man *Bomb*astico to his face, out of habit. As the Italian officers got out of the car Rommel stepped forward, his palm raised in the Axis salute. Bastico merely waved his gold-knobbed baton, but the young major, Melchiori, snapped to attention and gave a stiff-armed salute. He was tall and lean with an aristocratic bearing, a wide, clear forehead above heavy eyebrows, searching dark eyes and the aquiline nose that proclaimed him one of Old Rome's own. He wore an exquisitely cut khaki uniform and a jaunty Italian bush hat tilted to one side. Rommel approved of the major's enthusiasm, his military bearing, and the bright red feather in his hatband.

I am not political, Mr. Faulkner. I am a soldier.

Rommel nodded at Schmidt and a squad of photographers began focusing and shooting. Their equipment included a whirring motion picture camera mounted on a tripod. Rommel's heels came together. He greeted Bastico, according to protocol, then spoke warmly to Melchiori.

"*Benvenuto, Maggióre. Sono felíce che Lei sia arrivato.*" Rommel's pronunciation was awkward, but his words of welcome caused white teeth to gleam under the major's trim mustache. Melchiori seemed impressed that Rommel paid no attention to a fly crawling on his tanned, leathery neck. The Roman continually brushed away the pesky flies which were everywhere, especially around one's eyes. Rommel read the thoughts which crawled like invisible flies inside Bastico's dark glasses.

Bombastico is boiling at having been outflanked last week when Gause obtained Mussolini's blessing for the German plan to attack Tobruk, but custom dictates that he keep his feelings in check.

"I trust you left *Il Duce* in a good health and spirits," Rommel said in German. Wilfried Armbruster sidled forward, cooing a translation to Melchiori in sibilant Italian. Armbruster, who had inherited his Italian-born mother's language and dark good looks, had a talent for mimicry as well. In translating, he used the exact same body gestures and tone of voice of each speaker, creating a parody of the attitudes and dispositions of both sides, a habit that was often irritating, sometimes embarrassing, but generally amusing. Melchiori responded in a burst of Italian, which Armbruster translated in the same heartfelt manner.

"Il Duce sends his greetings and warm regards, Herr General. I wish also to express my gratitude for your kind invitation. I am very glad to be here."

Melchiori gracefully inclined his head and moved back a degree or so to offer Bastico an opportunity to say whatever he wished to say. Glancing about, Bastico saw Rommel's pet chickens pecking in the sand.

"Lei prende a coltivazione in suo tempo libero, Generale?"

"Taking up farming in your spare time, General?" Armbruster demanded and stuck his jaw out.

"These are my mascots," Rommel said, "Churchill and Stalin. A bit stringy now, but I am fattening them up for the kill." Armbruster translated with an edge. Bastico maintained an insectlike fixity of expression. Rommel rubbed his hands together. "Well, first we shall inspect the troops and then I have a small entertainment planned, a gazelle hunt, Afrika Korps style."

Bastico stared indifferently over the barren hills but Melchiori cried "Splendido!" and clapped his gloved hands with elegant enthusiasm.

Knowing his guests' penchant for correctness of attire, Rommel had Schmidt show them to their quarters. Twenty minutes later they emerged wearing crisply starched fatigues, boots polished to a high gloss, and gray helmets. Rommel's single affectation was his cap with his famous Perspex goggles, which he had confiscated from a captured British outpost during his first campaign in April. He wore short-sleeved shirt and pants in concession to the scorching September heat. With Armbruster helpfully making small talk in Italian, Rommel led his guests to a waiting Kübelwagen displaying black, red and white command flags on both front fenders.

As they drove east along a desert track roughly parallel to the Via Balbia, Rommel pointed out the camouflaged supply dumps and tank repair shops and retooling factories built in the sides of escarpments. They stopped and went inside one of the noisy workshops where hundreds of German technicians were busy rebuilding tank treads and refurbishing antitank weapons. Amid the clamor and whine of high-speed electric motors, Rommel deliberately pointed out to his guests the reconditioning of Italian guns abandoned during the winter retreat, which the Germans had rescued from the desert where they had lain rusting for months. Armbruster practically had to shout in Bastico's face to be heard over the shrieking machinery. Rommel continued to lecture on the economy of reclaiming weapons and how they provided welcome additional firepower to his siege line around Tobruk. Bastico edged toward the exit.

Their motorcycle escort raised the dust of an ancient camel trail. They passed near German and Italian road gangs stripped to the waist and attacking a construction job. Melchiori sat up excitedly at the rat-a-tat-tat of jackhammers and occasional blast of explosives clearing a path through the dunes. He asked whether they were approaching the front lines. With a straight face, Rommel explained that the construction crews were building a new bypass road around Tobruk. He leaned over and instructed the driver to turn off the track and drive south into the desert a mile or so to an outpost manned by an Italian machine-gun company.

"*Ecco il frónte, Maggióre,*" he said, stepping out of the car. The outpost consisted of a series of foxholes with sandbag walls around mounted machine guns. Makeshift tarpaulins had been rigged for shade. When the soldiers saw the general staff insignia, they scrambled to fall in. But when they realized that Bastico and Melchiori were accompanied by Rommel himself, they broke ranks and swarmed around the car, cheering and waving their caps. Rommel grinned in embarrassment and— shaking hand after hand, pretending to admire a few captured British revolvers and automatic carbines—tried to direct the soldiers' attention to their important guests, to no avail. After a minute of this Bastico suggested to the company commander that he order his men back into ranks. Melchiori was staring with undisguised admiration at Rommel, who saluted the Italian soldiers and got back into the car as if nothing out of the ordinary had taken place, which in fact was the case. He did not, however, look at Bastico.

Rommel now directed the driver to head east across open desert. The motorcycles thundered ahead, and the powerful

Kübelwagen bumped across a dry wadi, or riverbed, its oversized, underinflated tires barely spinning in the soft sand. The farther into the desert they went, the better Rommel began to feel. The sun beat down on them in waves and he had to mop the sweat away from his eyes, but he was in the field where he belonged. In the distance he heard a sound dear to his heart, almost restful and somehow serene, the rhythmic thump of panzer and antitank cannon firing in gunnery skills practice. He strained to spot the first dust trail on the shimmering horizon, rising like gossamer wings behind the dark, beetle-like body of a panzer.

He owned this desert. This treeless landscape dotted with brown patches of camel thorn was his private battleground, the perfect arena for *Panzerkampfwagen*. In this lunar landscape it was destruction of the enemy's machines, armament, and supply lines that mattered, not territory won or lost. Here in northeastern Libya, the country shelved upward from the sea in a series of plateaus which rose abruptly in 100-foot bluffs. Outcroppings and rift valleys rippled diagonally across the successive escarpments, creating ideal hiding places for tanks and men. It was a stark land which lent itself to tactical planning. Rommel dreamed about it every night, between bedbug attacks.

"*Cosa c'è?*" Melchiori was interested in the training maneuvers in progress just ahead of them. They had come within a quarter mile of a swarm of dust trails clustering in the blue sky over tanks, trucks and half-tracks moving in patterns across the desert.

"See the line of panzers, there," Rommel explained, "working with the self-propelled eighty-eights?" He paused for Armbruster to translate. "See that Panzer Two matching up with the antitank machine, advancing together? And the armored trucks towing the eighty-eight guns behind those Panzer Fours? It's a concept I designed, to drill artillery and armor to work together, to bring the self-propelled artillery into the front line where the enemy does not expect them and let the heavier eighty-eight do the job. From my experience in the Battle of France, I knew our Panzer Twos and Threes with their 3.7 centimeter guns were ineffective against the Matildas with their heavy armor. Radio intercepts show that the British think we have mounted eighty-eights on our panzers. They think our equipment is superior to theirs. This maneuver has worked out very well."

"Where did you get such an idea," Armbruster translated the major's question in the same admiring tone, "to bring artillery into the front ranks?"

"You would be surprised," Rommel said and watched his beloved panzers move rapaciously across the desert.

The next stop on the tour was a staging area where the 21st Panzer Division had been placed on battle alert. A tank company awaited their inspection. A dozen or so panzers loomed under camouflage nets like elephants trying to make themselves invisible under a canopy of leaves. Bastico elected to stay in the car while Rommel showed off his men and machines. Melchiori was enchanted by the sun-bleached veteran crewmen with their red-veined eyes, hair matted and tangled and their sleeves rolled up to go to work. They regarded his fresh, clean fatigues with the combat soldier's peculiar combination of indifference and tolerance.

Rommel was at home with them, joking with an enterprising sergeant who wore a small fly net over his helmet about the ingenuity of the African fly in penetrating enemy defenses. Then he scrambled aboard a Panzer IV and motioned for Melchiori to follow him. The metal was hot to the touch. The Roman gingerly climbed to the open turret with Armbruster on his heels. Rommel lowered himself into the tank, feeling automatically with his feet to fold down the tank commander's seat.

"The Panzer Kampfwagen Four weighs twenty tons," he recited with military charm, "is over eighteen feet in length, has a frontal armor plating twenty millimeters thick. It has a top speed of twenty-six miles per hour and a range of about one hundred twenty-five highway or sixty cross-country miles on a full load of fuel." Without waiting for Armbruster to translate this information he added, *"Mi segua, per favore,"* and disappeared into the tank. Melchiori followed warily. The cramped interior of the panzer was rank with the smell of gasoline, gun oil, and sweat.

The major writhed into the uncomfortably snug sitting space of the tank commander. Beneath him in the gunner's seat on the other side of the cannon breech sat Rommel, perfectly at home. His trained eyes assessed by reflex the shells packed in tight, shining rows against the rounded metal contours. He counted eighty, the correct number. But he noted with disapproval that the glass gunsight was clouded with a thin film of dust. Someone had gotten careless. There was no room for error, however minor. Through the battle sight he saw Bastico looking bored in the back seat of the car, reaching for a cigarette. With his eyes glued to the sight, Rommel's hand found the turret crank and he turned it rapidly on its well-oiled gears so that the gun began to swing in the direction of the car. Outside the tank, everyone except Bastico took notice that General Rommel was playing with the *Kampfwagenkanone*.

"Give him the headset," Rommel called up to Armbruster, who was peering down through the open hatch, his face silhouetted against a circle of brilliant blue sky. The aide unhooked the tank commander's intercom set and placed it on Melchiori's head. "Look in your battle sight," Rommel's voice reverberated through the earphones. "*Là sua veduta di battaglia.* It's the periscope lens right in front of you. Will you identify your target, please, *il suo bersaglio.*"

Melchiori grinned. "*Generale Bastico,*" he said.

Rommel had swiveled the turret so that the gun was even with the passenger seat of the car. Now he worked the elevation crank to lower the cannon so that it pointed straight at the Italian. Outside the tank the panzermen stifled their laughter. Bastico took a deep drag on his cigarette, refusing to turn and stare into the gun barrel with its ominous blast deflector.

"*Distánza . . .*" Rommel searched his modest Italian vocabulary for the word for *range*. "*Ordine?*"

"*Otto metri.*"

"Load UP! Fire when ready, *a suo comando.*"

"*Fucila!*" said Melchiori.

"Bang, you are dead," said Rommel.

The headphones vibrated with their laughter.

"Very close quarters in a panzer," Melchiori observed. Over the intercom Rommel caught the phrase *quartieri chiusi*.

"*Molto chiusi,*" he agreed, although he found that the space neatly accommodated his medium-sized frame.

"*E molto caldo,*" the major complained. Sweat had begun to pour off him.

"*Cento venti gradi* Fahrenheit," Rommel said pleasantly.

A temperature of 150 degrees inside a tank was commonplace in the desert heat. He was barely perspiring, even though it was hotter in the gunner's seat, with less ventilation.

"The bad thing about tanks is getting trapped inside," the Roman said. "Can the crew escape if they take a direct hit?" Rommel slid back to look up at Armbruster for a translation.

"If they are not too badly injured," Rommel replied prosaically, not using the intercom any longer, "and if the shells or fuel do not explode." Suddenly he tired of his public relations role. He tried to keep the impatience out of his voice. There were a thousand things he could be doing instead of playing host to a civilian-soldier from Il Duce's court.

Politics.

"And if it does . . . ?" Melchiori persisted. Rommel shrugged.

"The Tommies call it 'brewing up,' " he said. The grim battlefield idiom silenced the major. Rommel changed the subject. "How would you like to take a ride in our panzers tomorrow?"

"*Naturali, Generale!*" Melchiori exclaimed. "*Dovè a?*"

"Egypt," Rommel said. He felt quite at home to be lying on his back in the bowels of a tank and talking to two faces framed by an open hatchway. "There will be a raid on British supply dumps by the 21st Panzer Division with the code name 'Midsummer Night's Dream.' " He omitted the fact that the sortie was being staged primarily for Melchiori's benefit. The major began to tremble with anticipation.

"Panzer battle on the Egyptian front!" Melchiori hummed to himself.

Rommel suggested they climb out of the tank. The searing 105-degree heat outside seemed cool by comparison. The company commander joined them. Rommel casually leaned his hand on the tank track and felt something he did not like. He yanked at the heavy combat treads. "Stretch of dead track here," he brusquely told the young captain. "Loose wedge nut. Have someone pull it till it hollers. And somebody forgot to clean his gunsight!" The captain's tan cheeks flushed and he frowned in embarrassment. Like a desert cousin to a chameleon, Rommel changed his colors and amiably addressed the panzermen assembled alertly around them.

"Who is ready to go shopping for groceries in Egypt?" he

shouted. The soldiers cheered and raised their fists. "I hear the Tommies have a surplus of bacon and canned milk. Shall we relieve them of their storage problem?" The men cheered wildly. Rommel escorted Melchiori back to the car where Bastico waited, evidently unmoved by the demonstration. Melchiori watched his host expectantly to see if he would repeat the announcement of the raid into Egypt. Rommel, however, looked out over the desert as if he had forgotten about it. The courtier from Rome, *molto sensitivo* to what men left unsaid, declined to mention the raid to Bastico.

"My men have arranged a gazelle hunt," Rommel said instead. "I am told it is quite an exciting affair." Rommel himself had little time for such pursuits.

As they drove southwest toward the prescribed hunting area he explained to his guests that the Arabs had introduced his junior officers to the pleasures of the gazelle hunt. Those enterprising young officers had since refined the art. Reconnaissance planes returning from their missions would note the position of any herds they saw; then a pack of motorcyclists would tear off into the trackless desert, circle the herd and drive the animals back like so many motorized "beaters" toward jeeps or powerful touring cars. The hunters then gave chase to the gazelles, which could reach speeds upward of forty miles per hour, and fired from moving vehicles with automatic carbines or light machine guns.

"The livers of these gazelles are said to be a great delicacy," Rommel concluded. With his sensitive stomach, he had rarely been tempted to taste the wild game that appeared occasionally at the officers' mess. His eyes restlessly roamed the horizon as they approached a motorcycle squadron waiting for them in the middle of nowhere. The squadron leader reported that a herd had been spotted some ten miles to the south. With a nod of his head Rommel sent the squadron screaming over the sand to find them.

They sat on folding chairs beside the car. Rommel invited Melchiori to fire off a clip or two and get the feel of the submachine gun. The major handled the .30-caliber weapon as if it were an heirloom. A sergeant showed him how to fire it braced against the hip, and Melchiori sprayed several bursts into the sand with an expression of brutal determination. The gunfire was flat and staccato, echoless in the open desert.

Rommel trained a pair of binoculars in the opposite direction
from that of the hunt.

"Take a note," he told Armbruster. "Re: Heavy weapons
company, one-oh-eighth infantry. Batteries incorrectly positioned. Too close together. Camouflage needs improving."
Armbruster wrote the order on a pad he kept in his breast
pocket. The general dictated random observations like these
every few minutes, all day long.

From the distance motorcycles hummed like angry flies.
As the sound grew louder, the drivers of the open cars started
their engines. Melchiori took a kneeling position in the back
seat and gripped his weapon fiercely. Rommel restrained a
smile. He had his doubts whether the major could hit his
target. He hoped Melchiori would simply point his weapon
away from the cars. Their spotter standing on top of a small
dune signaled that the gazelles were turning; the drivers took
off in pursuit, tires kicking up sand geysers. Through the haze
shimmering liquidly over the desert, they could see the herd
flitting over the undulating surface like flying fish over the
ocean, their hooves lightly dusting the earth's surface like
wings flicking foam off the tops of waves. The cars accelerated
in tandem, one slightly behind and to the side of the other to
escape its dust and provide its gunner with a clear line of fire.
Bastico held his weapon languidly and regarded the racing
herd as if it were so much dust weed. The gazelles began to
shear away from the cars until a daring cyclist, bouncing in
short flights over gentle undulations in the sand, almost as
graceful as the animals but with a tearing, predatory whine,
flanked them and drove them back parallel to the moving
vehicles.

"*Ora!*" Armbruster cried. Melchiori half stood, with knee
resting on the back seat and leg braced against the driver's
seat, and fired half a magazine load. The bullets sprayed a
dusty pattern short of the bounding animals. The gazelles
surged ahead, separating to avoid a rocky outcropping and
splitting into two groups on the other side like the fork of a
leaping brown river. Rommel divided his attention between
the action and the surrounding terrain. He watched for
protective cover as a pilot stays vigilant for emergency landing
space. Suddenly he turned and looked up above the dust that
was billowing behind them as if it were a living thing bent on

devouring the sky. The car gained on the nearest group of fleeing animals. Melchiori let go another half clip and screamed.

"*Un doppio!*"

Two gazelles had fallen, twisted objects flopping in the sand. Rommel continued to stare at the sky as the drivers brought the cars around and came to a stop near the downed animals. Beside him, Melchiori was struggling to restrain his hunter's pride. Rommel glanced at the gazelles.

"They are does!" he said disapprovingly, and then he heard the plane he had sensed beyond his range of vision. "Make for that wadi!" he shouted to the driver. "*Mach schon!*" He could tell by sound that the aircraft had gone into a dive. It was a British Hurricane beginning a strafing run. Melchiori turned with an aggreived expression.

"*Miei antilopi!*"

"Enemy aircraft," Rommel shouted, signaling the driver of the other car to follow them. "Sit, major! *Sièdite!*" The motorcycles nimbly dodged the big cars skidding around, then raced like mechanical offspring to catch their parents.

"*Dovê?*" Melchiori craned his neck in every direction.

"*Là!*" Armbruster pointed behind them. A solitary plane came out of a banked turn and as it leveled off in its run became lost behind their dust trail.

"There's a crossing place," Rommel shouted over the driver's shoulder. "Drive into the wadi and snug up against the near bank." A trail of sand geysers spurted up near the cars with an accompanying whine of bullets. Then the plane roared overhead, climbing for altitude to make another turn. One of the motorcycles collapsed behind them, the helmeted driver sprawled inert on the rocky ground. The cars slowed to take the crest of the bank. They could see the Hurricane turning lazily about a quarter of a mile away. As it straightened out, winking flashes in its wings translated into bullets eating a line across the desert toward them. The cars jolted down the sloping bank and skidded into the dry riverbed where their rear tires began to spin. The opposite bank erupted in ricocheting bullets.

Rommel got a memorable glimpse of the second car, where Bastico had disappeared from view. He chuckled. Melchiori, frantically jacking a fresh clip into his machine gun, looked up at him in amazement. The rear tires caught, and the cars moved sluggishly under the protection of the overhanging bank. In less than a second the Hurricane thundered over them. Melchiori valiantly fired off a clip at the vanishing fighter plane, causing Rommel to duck for the first time. Having missed them in the open, the plane did not turn again. The pilot obviously had decided they were not worth the fuel to try to flush them out of hiding.

Rommel listened to the comforting sound of the plane's engine fading away. Compared to the past weeks of begging for supplies, haggling with the Italians and the OKW, fighting the tedium of inaction and interminable waiting for a decisive battle, the attack by the British aircraft was like a cool breeze in a crowded room. Being at hazard put Rommel in a good mood. In his breast pocket he felt a spot of warmth. His minié ball had absorbed the desert heat and seemed to pulsate like a tiny heart.

The cars drove up out of the wadi. The officers were glad to find that the motorcyclist who had fallen was unhurt. His machine had merely overturned when he hit a large rock. Rommel ordered the recce squadron to continue the hunt as though nothing had happened. Major Melchiori seemed reassured and impressed by his host's calm control. Bastico, however, watched the sky periodically for the rest of the hunt, during which they bagged another gazelle. After stretching the carcasses of the once-beautiful animals across the hoods of the cars and tying them fast, they stopped to rest for a while before they started back to Gambut.

Swabbing his throat with his handkerchief, Bastico observed that it was past lunchtime. They were standing together beside the cars. Rommel looked at Armbruster. It had not occurred to him that his guests would have to be fed. He himself was a bit thirsty, now that he stopped to think about it. He took his aide aside and said, "We will have lunch—tea and sandwiches."

"Herr General?" Armbruster was distraught.

"Yes?"

"You issued no orders concerning lunch in the field. I believe lunch was to be ready at HQ."

"HQ is twenty miles away. You must have *something*."

Rommel followed Armbruster around to the trunk of the

car, where they found a field ration kit. The aide opened it. They found a full canteen of water and three pieces of stale bread.

"This bread is quite old, General."

"Is it edible?"

"I cannot say, sir."

"Is it mildewed?"

"I don't think so."

"Bring it and the water. We are all soldiers here."

"We've had a little setback in regard to lunch," Rommel reported to his guests. He rubbed his hands together with uncharacteristic deference, then clasped them resolutely behind his back. "It seems they were expecting us for lunch back at HQ. We'll have to make do on bread and water, and save our appetites for the delicious gazelle livers at dinner tonight, eh?"

Armbruster, his jaw set, brought out a folding map table on which he placed the canteen and the three slices of dark bread. The heat had curled them into the shape of tulips. Bastico would not look at them, but Melchiori was fascinated. Rommel gave his guests a deprecatory smile. Seeing his commander's embarrassment, Armbruster slumped against the fender in defeat. Bastico turned his back and dabbed at his throat with his handkerchief.

Melchiori approached the luncheon. He had killed gazelles with a machine gun, survived a British strafing attack, and now there was Rommel's bread. The dark whorls looked as if they had lain decomposing in the car's trunk for weeks. Melchiori picked one up and with stoic indifference sank his teeth into it. With difficulty he tore off a small piece and attacked it with all the strength in his jaws. The others tried not to watch him chew. His eyes shone with effort. At Rommel's insistence Bastico helped himself to some water from the canteen. Instead of drinking it he poured a little onto his handkerchief and bathed his face and neck with the wet cloth.

"Have you heard the one about the British RAF pilot?" Rommel said. His hopeful expression made his face appear lopsided. Armbruster glanced up in horror.

"*Avete sentito l'anèddoto dal pilòta RAF?*" Armbruster repeated dutifully. Melchiori squared his shoulders. Bastico took a deep breath.

"This RAF chap—an ace, *asso*, you know—is home on offical leave," Rommel began. "And a Hausfrauen club asks him to give a lecture, *un leziöne*. They want to get the 'true picture' about what it's like in the 'wild blue yonder.' So he tells them about this 'dogfight.' No, not an actual *combattimento di cani*—you are familiar with the English idiom? So the pilot says, 'The Fokkers are below me at eight o'clock, and I get them—these Fokkers—in my sights, *mia veduta*, but before I can fire on them I see Fokkers to the left! Fokkers to the right! Everywhere nothing but Fokkers!'"

Bastico's face was a mask of indifference. Melchiori wore a fixed smile.

"So the president of the Hausfrauen stands up and says, 'I must explain what a Fokker is, so our members will not be distressed.' So she says, 'A Fokker is an aircraft of German manufacture.' And he says—the pilot—he says, 'What do you say! Those fighters were not—heh-heh—*Fokkers*, they were—heh-heh-heh—Messer—ha-ha—Messer—hee-hee-hee—Messerschmitts!'" Rommel wiped away a tear.

"*Molto comico*," said Melchiori. He took a tearing bite of the bread and chewed the plug. They listened to him chewing. Bastico wrung out his handkerchief, folded it, and put it in his pocket.

"It was a British joke from the Great War," Rommel explained. "I heard it in America, actually." Armbruster was fiercely attentive, as if recording the minutes of a war planning session.

That night, after a dinner of gazelle livers served with a delicious wine sauce, Rommel treated his guests to a showing of the film *Victory in the West*, a documentary about the Battle of France. Bastico declined the opportunity, observing that he had found "one propaganda film to be quite like all the rest." Since his own Ghost Division had participated in the filming, Rommel himself had supervised the staged maneuvers recreating the crossing of the Somme and the capture of French colonial troops. It was with a critical eye that he watched the film with Melchiori in the briefing room of his staff HQ.

"Here we are, breaking out of a small bridgehead on the south bank of the Somme." Rommel raised his voice to be heard above the film narration. "And now capturing a French village. Look at those black African colonials roll their eyes in surrender! We had to film it twice because they hammed it up so . . . And this is the *Flächenmarsch* or Formation Drive I designed for cross-country attack. You see, it is an entire division complete with support units, moving across open countryside in a box formation with panzers at front and sides, rifle battalions in the center, and Jagdpanzer and recce units to the rear."

If the cameraman had used a wider angle, there, more of the division would have been in the picture. Where are the command panzers? Perhaps higher elevation, or even shots from low-flying aircraft would have done the job. Wasn't seeing it from the eye of the camera. Back to the front for us.

He could not help reliving the beauty and excitement of it, the panzers rolling across the open fields bordered by wildflowers, smashing through overgrown hedgerows and flushing deer out of thickets like mice, penetrating the virginal French farmland with the stunning speed for which panzer-armees had been created, achieving total surprise with an unsuspecting enemy who was simply amazed to find Rommel knocking at the back door.

Now it is clear what the director intended: a single infantry column is used to depict an army advancing. It's the faces he is really interested in, the young, strong German soldiers, clean-cut and determined: the indomitable soul of the Reich. And in sharp contrast, enemy troops are shown as dispirited captives with no resistance left in them. And the music: he uses comical music to transform a heavy British Matilda into a child's plaything, whereas resolute musical themes create the illusion that our panzers lumbering toward the camera are invincible. Simple but very effective.

He glanced at Melchiori to see how the Roman was reacting to the film. Melchiori's handsome face revealed the innocent delight of a schoolboy. His guest was enjoying his visit to the "front": hunting wild game, wine at dinner, a reasonably good bed, and cinema to cap it off. Rommel was reminded why he had never liked aristocrats. Life was all berries and cream for them. He thought of Mississippi blackberries. They would doubtless encounter some enemy resistance in Egypt tomorrow. It was going to be interesting to see how Il Duce's man reacted to it. The prospect was cheering, and Rommel joined Melchiori in applauding a victorious scene depicting General Witzleben giving orders to attack the Maginot Line.

"The panzer divisions of Generals Kleist, Guderian, Höpner and Hoth have an especially important part to play," the narrator commented on a scene showing tank divisions on the march.

Yes, they follow me.

"Generals Pock and von Küchler review their troops," the narration continued. "The Iron Cross and Sturm medals are the well-earned decorations for the men who now for five weeks marched, fought, and attacked."

"Victory," Rommel quoted an old army cliché, "can boast of many fathers, but defeat is an orphan."

An orderly approached Rommel in the darkened room and whispered the news that a sealed pouch had arrived from Reconnaissance. He asked Melchiori to excuse him and went to his office with a sense of anticipation. An extraordinary stroke of luck had occurred recently: Italian spies inside the U.S. Embassy in Rome had copied the State Department's top-secret "Black Code" ciphers. For the past two weeks Rommel had become addicted to the nightly transmissions of messages sent from the U.S. Embassy in Cairo to Washington, intercepted by listening posts along the Egyptian frontier, personally decoded by his intelligence chief, von Mellenthin, and flown to him daily. Of primary interest to him were the reports of a Colonel Bonner Fellers, the American military attaché, whose keen assessments of British military activity gave Rommel a marvelous advantage. Although the information contained few details as to troop positioning or strength, it served as a bird's-eye view of Allied planning: where they expected the Germans to attack, when the British began to stockpile supplies for a coming offensive, the state of their equipment, the morale of their troops. Rommel shared these "little fellers," as he privately called these decoded telegrams, with no one. His staff were aware of them and were curious about them, but he kept them strictly to himself.

He closed the door to his office, seated himself at his desk and opened the leather pouch. The message was contained in a plain envelope marked: *"Für General Rommel—nur für seine*

Augen." Holding the message under his desk lamp, he began to read:

STRICTLY CONFIDENTIAL: FOR THE SECRETARY AND UNDERSECRETARY

Egypt
To: State
From: Fellers

Date: Sept 12, 1941
Time: 3:00 P.M.
Tel # 12
Confidential file

Germans are strengthening siege lines around Tobruk. Aerial reconnaissance indicates training exercises intensified, which suggests that the Nazis are building up to attack soon.

Why do they think of us all as Nazis? It is a misconception created and kept alive by the Allied propagandists.

The attack had doubtless been delayed by diverting of materiel to the Russian front. The general opinion at GHQ-Middle East is that Rommel will attack as soon as he has enough supplies, and the British have stepped up their monitoring of convoy routes in the Mediterranean.

A note concerning Rommel's use of deception: British forces manning Tobruk fortress report that they recently discovered that the German observation posts, which they periodically shelled, were actually dummy towers with uniformed dummy soldiers hoisted up and down by rope. After wasting much ammunition shelling these phony towers, the British decided to let them stand, since it is impossible to tell the fake ones from the real ones.

Ha-ha-ha-ha-ha-ha-ha.

Lt. Maxwell Speigner has reported for duty as special military intelligence liaison at invitation of GHQ.
FELLERSXXXXXXXXXXXXXXXXXXXXXXXXXXXXXXX

Rommel remembered Speigner's face, earnest and angular and thoughtful—the fair, Aryan face of a poet or a teacher or an artist. It was an unusual sensation, for although he had not thought of Speigner in a long time the memory of his face, of his voice speaking that precise, textbook German, was so resilient that it seemed to have been at the edge of his consciousness waiting to be recalled. Was it yesterday that the two of them had tramped the hills and woods of Mississippi together?

What brought Max to North Africa? What did it mean "special military intelligence liaison"? What could the British want of him?

Rommel was not a superstitious man, but there was a sense of destiny about this young man's reappearance in his life, no matter how obliquely, and the completing of a triangle that stretched from Mississippi to Cairo to Tobruk. In spite of himself Rommel felt a thrill as if he had seen a ghost. His hand involuntarily went to his breast pocket where he felt the familiar shape of the minié ball, smooth and hard under the fabric of his shirt.

XII

The Sunderland BOAC Flying-Boat took off at dawn with foam sizzling under its fuselage. Speigner looked down at Khartoum and the shining V where the White and Blue Niles conjoined. The plane completed its ascending circle toward the north. The passenger compartment was crowded with British and Free French soldiers, newspaper correspondents and a sprinkling of dark-skinned Africans wearing colorful robes. Max was the lone American. No one spoke to the person next to him. They had come a long way together across Africa, and the journey had been exhausting.

He had left New York on Wednesday of the past week, flying by PanAm Clipper to Bermuda, then Puerto Rico, where they had stayed overnight; on to Belem, Brazil, where the mighty Amazon emptied into the Atlantic. On Sunday—he remembered the church bells of Natal—the Clipper had headed east across the open Atlantic to the nearest city on the African coast, Bathurst, British Gambia. Monday afternoon they landed in Lagos, Nigeria, and for the flight across central Africa they had switched to a BOAC Lockheed Lodestar. Max's memory of the flight across the sandy, desolate wastes of Chad and the Sudan was a monotonous dream colored in beige and tan. During stops in Fort-Lamy and El Djenein, his throat ached from the searing dust and he could not stop the roaring of aircraft engines in his head, even while he slept in a Free French barracks overnight.

Now the journey was almost complete. They would reach Cairo by late afternoon. He watched through the tiny porthole beside his seat as the Flying Boat left the westward-winding Nile and flew over the pale Nubian Desert. The Nile came back into view, and they landed on the river at Wadi Halfa, where the aircraft took on fuel for the final leg of the trip. High above the desert again, Max dozed on and off until whispers among the passengers woke him. He looked out the window. Curving across the tan plain was the compact green valley of the lower Nile. The river itself was like a bluish garden snake lying serene and fertile amid geometrical fields of green, brown and gray. The desert bounded either side of this ribbon of life like an ocean of sand crashing against a verdant coastline. He could make out white triangles of sails on the river. He felt that he was staring at the beginning of time, which flowed across the centuries and showed man the way from the womb to the grave.

Then there were the pyramids, basking in the sunlit valley like golden dice cast by the gods. And very soon there was Cairo, divided by the Nile at its center, with tall white buildings like cliffs along the riverbanks sloping away into a spidery mass of ocher-colored buildings with flat roofs, domed mosques, shining minarets pointing at the sky, markets, slums, cemeteries, tent cities and garbage dumps spilling into the desert on all sides. Steadily losing altitude, the Flying Boat circled the city and made its landing approach. The river, which had seemed too narrow and crowded with boats for a plane to land, grew wider and comfortably spacious as they descended. They landed smoothly and taxied toward a wharf.

The passengers disembarked onto a floating barge connected by a gangplank to the pier. Max took a long breath of warm, moist air. He smelled gasoline and bread baking and a woman's perfume. The engine roar in his inner ear was suddenly replaced by the deep, diffuse voice of the city: bleating of automobile horns, grinding of heavy machinery, human laughter, angry shouts, and a single, trumpeting note from the past cutting through the intrusion of internal combustion—the bray of an ass.

As he walked toward the line of taxis inching along the street adjacent to the piers, Speigner felt as awkward as a crab on land, walking sideways and possessed of esoteric crab knowledge no good to anyone but himself.

Someone was pulling at his luggage. Gripping the handles more securely, he stared down at small boys trying to pull the suitcases out of his hands. Two ragged urchins with ancient eyes screeched. "Helpee, okay? Baksheesh, okay?" At first he thought they were crying, "Help me!" He would have liked to help them—or rather, to let them carry his bags—but it was as if he were being attacked by ordinarily timid animals made ferocious by starvation. He was certain that if he let go of his suitcases he would never see them again.

The afternoon sun hid temporarily behind tall buildings, and as he came into the long shadows he spotted an empty taxi. With both bags pulled outward on either side of him like wings, he made for it. The driver burst out of the car and swiped at the children with the back of his hand, growling a curse in Arabic, and they vanished in the crowd. The driver put Max's luggage in the taxi.

"Welcome to Cairo," he said, staring hard at Max's uniform, adding, *"Bienvenue? . . . Benvenuto?"*

Max realized that, in a city overflowing with British, Australian, Indian, and South African troops, the man was not familiar with an American uniform. *Benvenuto!* Did the driver expect the Italians to return so soon? He grinned. Presumably the Egyptian had a *Willkommen* on the tip of his tongue, on the off chance that Rommel was ahead of schedule.

"The American Embassy, please." Speigner saw the driver's eyes light up with understanding.

Max rode in the front passenger seat. The taxi, an old Austin, sagged and swayed precariously as it joined a dusty race uptown among vehicles unevenly matched for speed: cars, buses, bicycles, motorcycles, carts, asses loaded with bundles and driven by old men wielding sticks. Balked by the slower-moving conveyances and constantly maneuvering for an opening, every driver seemed to be loudly protesting his right of way. Horns hooted, dogs barked, goats whinnied and dark men cursed. Shoulder-to-shoulder tides of humanity flowed along both sides of the street like a human waterfall running uphill and down at once. A golden light filled the air, transmuting modern Cairo into the ancient Egypt of biblical legend. Speigner could imagine Bedouin caravans, slaves under the whip, overbred pharaohs posing on their Nile barges, the Israelites on their epic journey. He heard stringed instruments, flutes, horns, the blare of radios, even a snatch of ragtime on a tinny piano. The naked odor of old mankind assailed his nostrils. Here were the human organs at work— sweat, urine, feces—and human appetites for food, wine, tobacco, and all manner of things. Beggars in rags and fellahin wearing long galabiehs mingled with merchants in Western suits and the British hussars dominating street corners with their size and health. Max thought he recognized the cherry-colored slacks of the "Desert Rats"—the 7th Armored Division, which had liberated Egypt from the Italians but had fallen on hard times since Rommel's arrival in Cyrenaica.

"Who are they?" Max pointed at soldiers wearing insignia he had never seen. "What army?"

"Indian," the driver said, adding, "the Fourth Indian Division." The taxi had stopped for a traffic light, and one of the Indians surprised Speigner by leaning over and saluting him through the open window.

As they moved on he caught unexpected glimpses of the dark Nile through alleyways. Overhead, solitary faces stared from a maze of balconies above the street. They passed a bus so overloaded with passengers hanging to its sides that it tipped and swayed drunkenly; also a rickety *gharry* or horse-drawn cab full of Australian soldiers wearing bush hats and singing "Waltzing Matilda." The pedestrians—street vendors, Bedouins, veiled women carrying naked children, each bent solely to his or her own task or destination—paid no attention to the singing Aussies. Above the rooftops a minaret rose gracefully to proclaim the mosque where a muezzin sang the call to prayer: *Allahu Akbar, Allahu Akbar.* The mournful litany was like a call to Max to come over, Occidental to Oriental. His uniform seemed too tight, as if he had been born to wear burnous and tarboosh.

"Pay no attention!" the driver said with sudden intuition. "The Moslems face Mecca and cry for mercy five times a day. They need more forgiveness than the rest of us. No alcohol, no pork, zakat tax, recite the el-fatha, fast of Ramadan, watch over shoulder in case angel appears all day. Who needs it! I Coptic, Christian, you see, much better. Why complicate life? We cross over to Gezira, now, much quieter there. You see."

A complicated place, Cairo, I see.

They turned back in the direction of the Nile. The cabby explained, as they crossed a bridge crowded with slow traffic, that the American Embassy was located on the river island of Gezira. Under the bridge Max saw the single sail of a *felucca.* Houseboats lined the banks of the river. On the island the grinding roar of downtown Cairo receded behind them. Through the open window Speigner saw birds circling and heard the shouts of children at play. Olive trees lined cool boulevards. The official residences of Gezira had gardens and courtyards surrounded by high walls with ornate wooden or iron gates. The American Embassy had the added distinction of two U.S. Marines guarding its entrance. The driver stopped the cab at the curb.

"The fare is one hundred piasters," he said. Seeing Speigner hesitate, he added, "eighty lire, one pound British, or four dollars."

Cairo stands ready to serve many masters.

Max paid in piasters, having obtained the foreign currency at the War Department bursar's office. He thanked the driver and set his luggage on the pavement, identifying himself to a guard. The marine phoned the embassy desk and relayed instructions for Speigner to report to a Captain Carminelli.

Max waited in a high-ceilinged foyer with polished floors and arches around the doors and windows. The oriental mood of the room was breached by a voice with a Brooklyn accent.

"Speigner? I'm Carminelli. How ya doing?"

The aide's demeanor was casual in comparison with his impeccable dress and grooming. His starched khaki uniform was spotless. He shook Speigner's hand while bending down to pick up one of his suitcases.

"No, Captain, I can manage okay," he apologized to the top of Carminelli's head. The captain had thick curly black hair.

"No trouble," Carminelli said. "I'll show you to your quarters." He smiled to put Speigner at ease. "You'll bunk with me for the time being. I'm Benners's aide. C'mon over to the annex and drop off your things."

Max followed the captain to the rear of the building, crossed a small courtyard, and entered a less imposing building with brick walls and wooden floors. Carminelli moved quickly and with an athlete's grace. He led Max up a flight of stairs, taking them two at a stride, and ushered him into a sparsely furnished room with two single beds. A slow fan circulated the warm air. On a closet door were pinups of Dorothy Lamour and Betty Grable. Through a window came the smell of curry.

"You report to Colonel Benners at oh-nine-hundred tomorrow," said the muscular captain. "In the meantime, how's about drinks at Shepheard's?"

"Do you know if anyone at British intelligence has sent instructions for me?" Speigner said.

"To the front already!" Carminelli grinned. "You a baseball fan? Let's have a drink and talk baseball. It's gonna be a great series, the Yankees and the Dodgers. Relax. We take our time around here. You'll see Benners tomorrow, British intelligence the day after that, and the D.D.M.I. the week after, if you got information they need."

"A week!"

"Nobody rushes into anything in Egypt except maybe Rommel. Say, you're the Rommel man, aren't you? Who knows, maybe the Limeys will see you right away. Grapevine has it you got some kinda crystal ball with an angle on Rommel. Hey, don't expect the Limeys to admit the Americans got something they ain't, not even Sherman tanks. Getting a bully-for-you outa them is like milking wine from a goat. All the same, the word is out on you, Lieutenant. Now, how 'bout that drink?"

Speigner did not know how to respond to the captain's half-mocking, half-flattering tone. He came to attention.

"Drinks and baseball," he said. "Reporting for duty, sir."

They took an embassy staff car, and Max observed that Carminelli drove the way he climbed stairs—competitively. He blew the horn as if it were a 3.7-mm cannon, blasting the other cars aside and continually accelerating through minute gaps in the traffic. They crossed a bridge to the eastern bank of the Nile and headed south along the river. Night had fallen and the lights of Cairo were reflected in the still surface of the water. Palm trees exploded against the purple Nile in black silhouette. Their strange shape made Max think of war.

"How are the British doing?" he asked.

"They've had the shit kicked out of them, and they're just hanging on while they build up a supply base." The captain did not take his eyes from the road. "The only objective Rommel hasn't taken on his side of the wire is Tobruk, and it may go any day now. Rommel don't waste time." Carminelli slacked off the accelerator and coasted. "We all keep track of the papers that got to be burned in case he breaks through. We go through fire drill once a week. The Limeys are grabbing at straws. You wouldn't be here if they weren't. No offense, kiddo, but you got your work cut out for you." He glanced at Max. "You got something they don't?"

Max tried to sense the desert waiting just beyond the lights glittering in the great river. It was easier to remember his growing correspondence with magazine dealers in Geneva and Lisbon to acquire German newspapers no longer available direct from his Berlin distributors. His feeling of accomplishment at getting around Nazi censorship had been positively swashbuckling. It was easier to remember Brigitte at her typewriter fumbling with a button on her blouse, or Mrs. Tasco checking her oven to see if the cheesecake was rising, or Amma sitting on the sill wondering where he had gone.

What had Ruth said? Be like Forrest?

"I don't know," he said.

Carminelli found a parking space near Shepheard's Hotel and the two officers strolled up the sidewalk past street vendors and burnous-clad dragomans touting guided tours of Old Cairo. So many uniformed military personnel hurried in and out of the hotel entrance that Max could imagine it under siege. Inside, the foyer was crowded with people, mostly Egyptian men, but the lounge was less crowded except for the Long Bar along the far end of the large room. It was packed two deep with British, Australian, Indian and South African officers, with a sprinkling of Polish and Free French. Max and Carminelli's American uniforms did not attract much attention among such variety. Carminelli grabbed a just vacated seat and waved for the attention of Joe the Bartender.

"Watch this," he told Max. "Joe never forgets a face. It's his trademark."

A white-jacketed man with heavy gold rings on his fingers approached them with deference and aplomb. Joe was short and stocky with close-cropped, wavy hair and a wide smile.

"Captain Carminelli!" Joe touched his forehead in military salute. "Bourbon, I believe."

"Right you are, Joe," Carminelli said, pleased. "Tonight, make us something special to welcome Lieutenant Speigner to Cairo."

"How do you do, Lieutenant Speigner." Joe leaned across the bar to shake hands. Max noted the emphasis Joe gave his name, as if filing it away for future reference. "Glad to have you with us. Let's see, I'll think of something to fix you." He rubbed his chin.

"I got just the drink for you to celebrate with," he said. "I came up with it by experimentation the other day when supplies were running low. It's a drink to bring the Americans and British together: bourbon and gin with angostura and lime cordial and dry ginger ale."

"Some welcome to Cairo," said Carminelli. "What do you call it?"

"Lend-Lease," Joe said solemnly. "Or, Over-the-Atlantic. Or, you might call it Sufferin' Allies."

"We'll try it." Carminelli saw Speigner looking around the lounge. "Cairo ain't so different from Washington. Diplomats and pols, bureaucrats and military getting drunk and talking about screwing the competition. Speaking of screwing, you get the most for your money in Cairo. Great exchange rate against the Egyptian pound. I know a class place in the Bulaq. If you're interested."

"Maybe later." Max had never heard of the Bulaq. Brigitte had been all he could handle, and she was from Chevy Chase. Joe brought their drinks. They sampled the bourbon-gin mixture and were relieved to find it unexpectedly tasty. Joe left them with a knowing smile.

Speigner turned to look at the people seated at the tables and immediately noticed a striking woman with a small group of Europeans. Though part of the group she seemed somehow separate from it, more observer than participant. She had a narrow, angular face with prominent cheekbones and dark eyes. Her sandy hair was close-cropped and brushed straight back on either side. It was not her appearance which attracted attention so much as her attitude, aloof yet alert.

"Who is that?" He pointed her out to Carminelli.

"Don't know, but she's with the British Embassy boys and their wives. Drinks before dinnah. Ray-ah roast beef and chitchat about land values in Surrey or perhaps horseflesh—there's a solid topic . . ."

"Can you introduce us? You know the others in the party."

"Say, nothing shy about you, is there, Speigner? I got five pounds says you don't get to first base."

Max followed the aide among the tables. He did not stop to wonder what was drawing him to the woman with the distant expression. Carminelli greeted the embassy officials with a clinging courtesy that would not be denied. The junior diplomats regarded the intruders with studied politeness until Carminelli introduced Speigner as "our expert on Rommel." One of the benefits of Shepheard's was the possibility of picking up information. All three officials became professionally alert as Max briefly explained about having met Rommel, about his research and the consequent invitation to come to Cairo. Across the table the woman's eyes were frankly curious but in an innocent way. He thought she might be a musician or a singer. She watched him with an artist's naked appreciation. One of the diplomats realized that introductions were not complete and presented the Americans first to the wives and then to the woman with the sandy hair. Alone among the women she stood and extended her hand to Max.

"Leftenant Speigner, Captain Carminelli, may I present Anna McAlpin of the London *Times* . . ." Feeling the woman's glance, the diplomat added, ". . . and the New York *Daily News*, of course." Max shook her hand and forgot the clatter of voices around them.

"You are a correspondent," he said.

"Almost," she said with a smile. "I can't claim to be one until I write my first dispatch. I'm very new to the job." Her words were alternately clipped or slurred, like the ripple of a Highland stream.

"You are Scottish!" he said. Her smile was like the sun breaking through after a mountain shower. He forgot about the others around them.

"McAlpin. I've heard that name."

"Where?" she said eagerly.

"In Mississippi."

"Mississippi!" She laughed. "The Mississippi McAlpins!"

The rest of the party, observing that they had launched a private conversation, stirred themselves into small talk to cover such a lapse in manners.

"Do you have relatives in Mississippi?" he persisted.

"I think some of my ancestors emigrated to America before your revolution. Where they went, I don't know. Tell me about my lost relatives in Mississippi."

"I can't remember. Maybe I saw the name on a storefront or in the phone book. Or maybe a McAlpin played fullback on the Ole Miss football team."

"Old what?"

"Ole Miss. Oh, it sounds like an old ladies' team, doesn't it. I mean the University of Mississippi—where I attended college." He hesitated, unwilling to give up the tenuous connection he had established between them. "I'm sure I saw the name McAlpin someplace. Anyway, I'll bet they wore the tartan with distinction and brought honor to your name."

"How kind of you to think so. Perhaps it's not the Mississippi McAlpins who are lost. At least they were not among those left behind." His interest grew and he felt himself drawn to her. She changed the subject. "Mississippi . . . isn't that where you met Rommel?"

"Yes." He did not want to talk about Rommel.

"What was he like?"

"You mean physically? He is of medium height and build, tough and fit. He listens and watches with total concentration. He seems tightly wired. Intense." He saw her glance at a purse on the floor beside her chair. There was a notepad in it.

"Is it commonly known that Rommel visited your country?" She edged toward the chair. "In what year did the visit take place?"

"It was in 1937. I don't know if it is commonly known. I would guess not."

She seemed to make up her mind to leave the notepad where it was. "I must interview you!" Her voice was so forceful that he felt they were eye to eye, even though he was a head taller. "Will you allow it?" she added.

"Yes," he said. She relaxed and took a sip of her wine.

"Will you be visiting the front soon?" When she raised her voice she attracted the diplomats' attention. They automatically assumed an official blandness.

"I hope so," he said. "I want to get close to the action and get a feel for what it's like."

"So do I! I wish my hosts agreed with you. They say no woman has been to the front lines. If we go there—you and I— we will have something in common. The only American and the only woman to have seen the Western Desert battlefront."

"Ah, Miss McAlpin," a diplomat interrupted unctuously. "You would most certainly detest life at the front. There is no water for all-over washing. You could not wash your hair. There is no privacy to be had. One sleeps on the ground. That sort of thing. Much better to interview chaps like—what did you say your name was—oh yes, Speigner here, without giving up the comforts of Cairo."

"You see?" she said to Max with a cutting edge. "My hosts have a rule about women at the front. They say 'too dangerous,' as if danger were a fraternal order with an exclusively male membership."

"Oh-oh, an international crisis brewing," the diplomat joked vigorously. "We'd better go in to dinner." The three wives rose as one.

"Do you see how they treat me?" Anna said to Max. "If you go to the front, promise me you will take me with you!"

"I promise," he said, touching his glass to hers.

"Our table really is waiting," said the diplomat.

"How does one reach you?" she said. He saw nothing but her brown eyes.

"Through the American Embassy."

"You will be hearing from me, then," she said.

The wives were willing Anna to follow them ahead of the men. It was unthinkable that men should precede women into the dining room. Speigner watched her until the party passed through the wide entrance guarded by bronze nymphs holding electric lamps. Carminelli nudged him. They returned to the bar. The captain called for fresh drinks. Their eyes met in the mirror above the bar.

"You said five pounds?" Max said with a grin.

"Egyptian," Carminelli protested.

Max took a sip of his drink and felt the bourbon and gin take hold. Cairo was not such a bad place, and every man at Shepheard's was his friend.

Sufferin' goddamned Allies.

Speigner wiped beads of sweat from his forehead as he followed Carminelli across the courtyard to the officers' mess. The morning air was so tepid, he felt like a fish in a muddy pond. Nevertheless he inhaled another lungful of it to try to shake off the effects of the alcohol.

"What was it you said," he asked Carminelli, taking some consolation at the sight of his companion's pale cheeks and puffy eyes, "about the Aussies being easier to drink with?"

"What I said was, Aussies hate the British more'n the Germans do. They regard us as fellow colonials. I didn't say nothing 'bout drinking with 'em, did I?"

They breakfasted on coffee and eggs in the mess, where Carminelli introduced Speigner to the commander of the marine guard unit. Afterward, the captain escorted him to the attaché's office. Benners was waiting for them. Alert, silver-haired, erect, he welcomed Max with an easy formality. After having made the introductions, Carminelli faded out of the room, closing the high sliding doors softly behind him. Max could feel Benners's appraising glance as he took a seat in front of the polished mahogany desk. The attaché seemed as much politician as soldier, and Benners's opening statement confirmed this opinion.

"We are the guests of the British when it comes to military intelligence, Lieutenant," the attaché began. "Whatever information they share with us is given in the spirit of diplomatic and military protocol. They do not ask our advice, and we are not cleared to attend any high-level briefings. So you see, this invitation to you, a junior officer, is most unusual. What have you got that they haven't?"

That's what everyone wants to know. Including myself.

"I know Rommel," he said, surprising himself. He sounded more confident than he felt.

"You mean, you've actually met him?"

"Yes, sir. He was in the States in thirty-seven, touring Civil War battlefields. I accompanied him to two sites in Mississippi. He was particularly interested in Nathan Bedford Forrest."

"I never heard Rommel went to America." Benners paused. "How does visiting battle sites with Rommel make you an expert on him?"

"I began keeping a file on German staff officers in 1936. Rommel interested me the most, partly because of his book *Infanterie greift an*. Then I met him and got to know him, even though the time we spent together was brief. His subsequent career has kept me busy collecting clippings. You might say I have specialized in Rommel for the past four years, sir."

"What is your background, Lieutenant?" the attaché asked. Seeing Speigner's hesitation he added, "Where did you go to college?"

"The University of Mississippi." Max thought he saw a slight raising of eyebrow across the deck. Nobody gave Mississippi an inch, even halfway around the world.

"Really? What were your major subjects?"

Pellagra and hookworm, sir.

"I took a double major of German and history."

"Very interesting. You seem to be putting your university training to good use. Well, needless to say, the British are consumed with Rommel. He is the very devil to them. The fact that you're here, that they would be disposed to listen to an *American* on the subject of Rommel, is evidence of their obsession. Listen to this memo from the Commander-in-Chief, Middle East!" Benners put on horn-rimmed glasses and began to read.

"'To: All Commanders and Chief of Staff

There exists a real danger that our friend Rommel is becoming a kind of magician or bogeyman to our troops, who are talking far too much about him. He is by no means a superman, although he is undoubtedly very energetic and able. Even if he were a superman, it would be highly undesirable that our men should credit him with supernatural powers.

I wish you to dispel by all possible means the idea that Rommel represents something more than an ordinary German general. The important thing now is to see to it that we do not always talk of Rommel when we mean the enemy in Libya. We must refer to the 'Germans' or the 'Axis powers,' or the 'enemy' and not always keep harping on Rommel. . . .'"

Benners stared at Speigner over the rims of his glasses. "What do you say, Lieutenant. Is the man a god?"

"He has a gift," Max said. The colonel's eyes bored into his, searching.

"Maybe the British are more aware of our resources," Benners observed, "than we are. *I* never knew we had an expert on Rommel in Washington. Come on, *do* we know something the British don't?"

"I don't claim to be an expert," Max said quickly. "I just keep a file on Rommel."

"Just a file," Benners repeated ironically. His tone became brisk. "The British officer who is responsible for asking you here is one Major John Bright-Ashton (they love the hyphenated surname, dont' they?), who works with the D.D.M.I.— that's the Deputy Director of Military Intelligence. In his request he refers to a memo from you, back in forty, predicting Rommel's course of action in Normandy right down to riding his panzer into the English Channel. According to Bright-Ashton's report, nobody at British intelligence took your memo seriously. In fact, it probably was not read by anyone over the rank of lieutenant until some time after the Battle of France was over and they started trying to fit the pieces together. Then somebody found it in the files and they were surprised, to say the least. This major seems quite keen on you, as they say at the Mohammed Ali Club. That's where you're meeting him for lunch today—"

"Today!" Max exclaimed. "Carminelli said . . . excuse me, sir."

"Bright-Ashton is something of a sensation in his own right," Benners continued. "Before the war he was a don at

Oxford College. I'll be interested in hearing a *full* report of your meeting with him. My hunch is that bringing you over here to pick your brain is a clue that the Brits are planning a major offensive soon, and they want all the information on Rommel they can get. Transport is building up at the forward staging areas. A major assault seems inevitable. Middle East Command is under heavy pressure from Churchill to drive Rommel back to Tripolitania. Keep your eyes peeled for us, Lieutenant." He stood and Max rose accordingly.

"Will I see you later . . . sir?"

"I won't be joining you for lunch, if that's what you mean," the attaché said dryly.

Speigner stood in the hallway outside the Mohammed Ali dining room with his cap under his arm. The hum of men's voices from within was punctuated by a subdued clanking of silver and china. Although Speigner's ancestors had emigrated to America after the Revolutionary War, he had the distinct sensation of what it was like to be a colonial. He peered inside the King's Realm to see if he could attract a steward's attention. Two waiters leaning against the wall stared at him without stirring from their posts.

Advance.

He withdrew his head from the doorway and considered what inner voice had spoken. The tone was strong and decisive. Bedford Forrest's face swam into his thoughts, like the painting in Professor Shoemaker's office but with a difference: he was Bedouin. The chin beard was jet black, the eyes dark and unrelenting. White desert robes replaced gray uniform and gold sash. Max wondered at the image and decided that the erect, proud Bedouins he had seen in the streets of Cairo had reminded him of someone. Forrest in Egypt could be nothing if not a desert warrior. Max almost glanced around to see if the obscene old horseman was grinning over his shoulder. Then, like a well-trained member of Forrest's staff, he advanced into the dining room and stood with a Bedouin's natural authority inside the entrance. Englishmen turned to look at him. A steward appeared at his side.

"Major Bright-Ashton's party," he said.

"This way, sir."

His eyes picked Bright-Ashton out of the crowd as he followed the steward between linen-covered tables occupied by British and Egyptian officers. The major stood alertly when he saw Max's American uniform. Another officer remained seated at their table.

"You must be Speigner," said Bright-Ashton. "Welcome to Cairo. I'm John Bright-Ashton and this is Colonel Weathers, of M.I. Please join us."

Bright-Ashton was about Speigner's height but with a scholar's stoop. His neck canted forward as if he had spent too many hours leaning over the O.E.D. Penetrating blue eyes appraised Max behind rimless glasses. A hank of graying hair fell boyishly over a narrow forehead. His khaki shorts, bush shirt and leather sandals made Max feel overdressed in his summer khakis. Colonel Weathers was middle-aged, trim and ramrod-straight with a neat salt-and-pepper mustache. His eyes restlessly moved from one object to another. Max had the impression that he was dissatisfied.

"First, I must say that your memo on Rommel in Normandy was a real piece of work," Bright-Ashton began, "especially considering that it predated the invasion of France . . ."

"Perhaps the leftenant would care to join us in another round," Weathers said. Max realized he was being addressed in the third person.

"Yes, thank you," he said.

Weathers raised a finger and an Egyptian waiter rushed to their table holding a linen napkin over his arm like a white flag of surrender. "Gin and bitters?" Weathers said to Max's shoulder. When Speigner nodded, the colonel held up three fingers and the waiter vanished. Bright-Ashton did not immediately resume his conversation. He seemed to defer to Weathers and lit a meerschaun pipe to allow the colonel an opportunity to reopen the discussion. Weathers glanced around the dining room as if searching for a more interesting conversation at some other table.

"I was referring to Speigner's Rommel memo," Bright-Ashton said around the stem of his pipe. "The one I sent you."

"Quite," said the colonel.

"I understand you compare Rommel to Forrest," the major said.

"They have a lot in common," Max replied, "but the basis of my comparison is that I was with Rommel in Mississippi when he studied Forrest. He seemed well versed on Confederate cavalry tactics."

"Mississippi!" Weathers said, his eyes darting. "Any bourbon distilleries there?"

"Sir?"

"Bourbon. Like Kentucky."

"No, sir. The state is officially dry."

"Dry?"

"Alcohol cannot legally be sold. There is plenty of bourbon consumption, but no distilleries. Not legal ones, anyway."

"Where do people get their whiskey?"

Are we here to talk about Rommel or booze? Why the tension between Weathers and Bright-Ashton?

"Bootleggers bring it in from neighboring states."

"Bootleggers, that's a good one. Ah, our drinks."

The waiter served their gin and bitters on a silver tray, and Speigner remembered Faulkner serving Rommel his cup of coffee. Weathers leaned over the table sociably. He seemed more firmly anchored in the conversation with drink in hand. The major puffed his pipe.

"I bring up the subject of bourbon," Weathers continued, "because, incidentally, I was also in America before the war. In thirty-five. Discovered bourbon on a trip through Kentucky. Marvelous potion. Bourbon and bluegrass. That's a combination a man can live with. No moral embargo on bourbon, is there? I wager you know the origin of your famous bluegrass?" Weathers looked slyly at Bright-Ashton over the rim of his glass, though his question was directed at Max. The unexpected subject caught him by surprise, and he shook his head. Weathers sniffed, rubbed his nose. "The limestone in the soil, of course."

And the defense witness was discredited by the prosecution. What game is he playing?

"Did Rommel like Mississippi?" Bright-Ashton aimed his pipe at Speigner, directing him to continue the discussion of their principal topic.

"Yes, very much, I think. We walked the sites of the

battles of Brice's Crossroads and Shiloh. And Rommel met the writer William Faulkner."

"Who?" said the colonel.

"The fiction writer." Bright-Ashton spoke around the pipe clenched in his teeth. "*Soldier's Pay, Sartoris* . . ." Weathers rattled the ice in his glass, eyes darting restlessly.

"Faulkner invited us—Rommel and myself—to visit his home," Max explained, feeling like a referee. "He gave Rommel his first drink of bourbon." Weathers came alive.

"You don't say!" he said. "Jolly good! Did Rommel like it?"

"I don't think he's much of a drinker."

"Oh, really," Weathers murmured.

"Faulkner challenged Rommel to a tennis match," Max continued. "It was quite an evening." *Night swarms of insects around a spotlight; dew on the grass; pants wet at the knee; tennis balls ponging against racquets; a clock striking in the courthouse belfry.* "Faulkner told Rommel a joke about the RAF. Would you care to hear it?"

Weathers stared impassively ahead, but Bright-Ashton nodded with enthusiasm.

"It concerns a British fighter pilot, an ace, who has been pressed into duty as a speaker to a civic organization back home in Britain—selling war bonds, I suppose. Anyway, here he is, addressing this women's club—oh yes, I forgot to mention that the ace had arrived that very day from the front and is more accustomed to speaking with pilots or soldiers than to ladies—and as he had no speech prepared, he reminisces about his combat experiences. 'I was flying at three thousand feet when I saw a formation of fokkers below,' the pilots says."

Max remembered Faulkner's soft voice imitating a Cockney accent, but he did not have the nerve to try it, surrounded by Englishmen.

"'I am preparing to attack the fokkers,' says the pilot, 'when I see bullet holes rip the fabric of my wings, and I look up'—and of course, he sees the inevitable—'there they are: fokkers to the left of me, fokkers to the right of me . . .' And so on and so forth."

Max saw that Weathers was barely attentive. He hurried to finish.

"The president of the club—the women's group, the civic organization—steps up to the podium and interrupts the pilot, and says, 'For the sake of enlightenment, Captain so-and-so, you might add that the Fokker you have been referring to is an aircraft produced in Germany, isn't that right?'"

A smile tugged at the corner of Max's lip as he recalled Faulkner's snorting laughter and Rommel's expectant grin.

"'Oh no, ma'am,' said the pilot, 'those fokkers were Messerschmitts.'"

Bright-Ashton took the pipe from his mouth with a pleasant expression which Max assumed meant he found the story mildly entertaining. Weathers merely took another sip of his gin. Max glanced around to see if perhaps someone at a nearby table had overheard the joke and was chuckling to himself.

"How tall would you say Rommel is?" Weathers said.

"Sir?"

"Just wondering about Rommel's size, you know, his height." The colonel's tone implied he was not accustomed to having to repeat himself to junior officers.

"He is of medium height, maybe five-seven," Max said. Bright-Ashton stirred solicitously in his chair.

"And so, did Rommel enjoy Faulkner's little joke?" the major asked.

"Yes, he did."

"What conclusion do you draw from this, Leftenant?" said the colonel.

"That Rommel has a sense of humor," Max replied. Bright-Ashton jammed his pipe into his mouth in a satisfied way.

"Did someone say something amusing?" Weathers said. "You S.L.U. chaps have a strange sense of humor, I must say." He pushed his chair away from the table and stood up. Max and John rose respectfully. Max saw that Weathers was well over six feet tall.

"I'm off," Weathers said abruptly. "Carry on with your information-sharing, Leftenant. Must have you over to GHQ to lecture my section when S.L.U. is finished with you."

"I'd be glad to," Max said.

"I thought we were having lunch," Bright-Ashton said.

"Must be off," Weathers repeated. Max thought of the Mad Hatter of *Alice in Wonderland*. The waiter came floating anxiously up to the table to reassure himself that his service was not in question. Weathers waved him away. "Carry on, carry on," he said and stalked across the dining room. They saw him go through the open hallway and into the club bar on the other side.

"I must apologize," Bright-Ashton said as they took their seats. "I had hoped that M.I. would react with more imagination to your . . . being here. Anyhow, have another gin—to celebrate your arrival—and tell me all about meeting Rommel." He held up his glass to their waiter.

"What did the colonel mean, S.L.U.?" Max asked.

"Special Liaison Unit. M.I. takes a rather dim view of us, I'm afraid. We're not regular army, so they consider us amateurs without proper respect for the military. However"— he struck a match—"we do our best to keep up with them."

The waiter brought fresh drinks and, in a more relaxed atmosphere, Max told the story of his battlefield tour with Rommel, recalling that at Brice's Crossroads Rommel had seemed especially interested in Forrest's innovation of bringing artillery unprotected into the skirmish line. He did not mention his motorcycle ride with Rommel and the minié ball they had found. His reticence surprised him, and he rationalized that such information was immaterial to the business at hand. He wondered if Rommel still possessed the minié ball. He pictured him at the Memphis airport holding the tiny souvenir in his hand in farewell. Bright-Ashton was regarding him thoughtfully.

"What's Rommel like?" he asked.

"Physically he's wiry, fit. In thirty-seven he was forty-six but he didn't look within ten years of his age. He had a way of looking at you . . . he seemed to draw your thoughts out of you, whether you intended to say it or not. Spiritually—" Max dropped his eyes. *Why does it seem so personal, an invasion of privacy?* "He was a *force*. That's the only way I can describe him."

Bright-Ashton opened a pocketknife and cleaned his pipe bowl. Max realized that the gesture was a kind of diversion. He appreciated the major's quiet technique of interrogation and waited patiently for him to continue.

"What seemed to interest Rommel the most about Forrest?"

"I think it was the constant pursuit, the exploitation of the enemy's weakness."

"What about the writer, Faulkner? What did he think of Rommel?"

Max remembered a graceful gallery framed by Doric columns, a soft penetrating voice. "They got along well, not because Rommel was interested in literature or writers so much as because Faulkner admired soldiering. I think Faulkner approved of Rommel's sense of history and his—what did he call it—his 'sense of the pathos of war.' He told me he thought Rommel's most dangerous quality was his ability to adapt the lessons of history to any given tactical situation."

"So if one knew history as Rommel knows it, the Fox loses the element of unpredictability, is that it?"

"Maybe," Max conceded. "But wouldn't you agree that most of Rommel's successes are simply the result of his being at the front, where he gets the most immediate information and makes quick decisions based on that information. He probes for weakness, finds it and exploits it. If there is anything 'predictable' about Rommel, it is his instinct for finding your weak spot. His men call it '*Fingerspitzengefühl*,' a sixth sense in his fingertips."

"You're saying that Rommel is unbeatable?"

"Not at all. But I believe that to beat Rommel a commander would have to be in one of two basic situations; one, expose a flank to encirclement and have a counterattack ready to meet Rommel when he takes advantage of it; two, lead Rommel in pursuit beyond his supply line and cut him off when he goes too far. If he has a major flaw it is that he does not know when to stop. If France and England were not separated by the English Channel, Rommel would not have stopped in 1940 until he reached the Firth of Forth."

"You seem confident of your opinion." Bright-Ashton smiled.

"I have spent several years studying Rommel. I'd like that information to be of some use."

"Oh, it already has been. More than you realize. But you of course take into consideration the possibility that Rommel might have changed since you met him?"

"I'd be very interested in learning in what way and how much," Max countered.

"Good!" John held up his glass in a toast. "You're here to learn and not simply to relieve yourself of information like a new don at his first lecture."

"Did I hear somewhere that you had taught history?"

"Yes, at Oxford. In the ice age—B.C., Before Cairo."

Max sensed that he had more in common with this scholarly officer than a mutual assignment.

"I'm afraid I didn't make a very good impression on Colonel Weathers," Speigner glanced in the direction of the Mohammed Ali bar. "I hope that does not create a problem."

"Nothing to worry about," Bright-Ashton said. "We'll doubtless worm our way back into the good graces of M.I., as if that were a state to which any reasonably intelligent person should aspire."

"Where *is* Rommel these days, if you don't mind my asking?"

Bright-Ashton took a pen from his coat pocket and sketched a rough map on his cocktail napkin. "We're building up here, here, and here, along the wire. Our friend Rommel is located somewhere between these points, around Tobruk."

"Isn't that awfully close? What's the actual distance?"

"A hundred kilometers or so, something like that."

"You mean, he's just across the frontier, a short drive by truck, waiting for supplies for his fall offensive. And you're setting up supply dumps almost under his nose!"

"Our camouflage people are quite good, you know. One may operate up there with assurance if not impunity."

Max stared at the lines on the napkin. For some reason he thought of the young Scotswoman he had met the night before.

"When's the last time you set a trap for Rommel?" he said.

"What a remarkable thing to say!"

"I'm serious."

"Yes, I can see you are. The answer is that we haven't found ourselves in a position to be setting traps, other than bogus information given out in radio transmissions now and then." The major scrutinized him. "Let's order lunch. I think that second gin has released your fancies."

"I'd like a chance to get Colonel Weathers's attention."

"This is quite astounding, Speigner. You've been here—what? Twenty-four hours?" Bright-Ashton took a sip of his drink. "What exactly do you have in mind?" he added.

"I don't know. Can we go up to the staging areas and take a look at those dumps?" Max toyed with his glass on the polished table. Then he gave the major his Bedouin look—fierce, proud and enigmatic.

"Certainly, that can be arranged, but . . ." Bright-Ashton hesitated.

"When!"

"In the morning, if you like." The major puffed his pipe vigorously. "Why do I get the feeling that you know something I don't?"

XIII

The tremor of aircraft engines set Speigner's body tingling. He sat beside Bright-Ashton in the cramped passenger space of a Ford Trimotor mail plane making its daily run to the front. Their seats consisted of narrow webbing strung from the fuselage walls. A single crewman held a strap with one hand and put out his cigarette with the other. Bright-Ashton crossed his legs.

Just another day's work, Max thought, grateful for the major's calm presence. Bright-Ashton held a canvas pouch containing tins of cigarettes and chocolate, and half-pint bottles of whiskey for South African pilots at the air base near Sidi Barrani, thirty miles from the Libyan border. "Have to keep one's friends happy," he had told Max. "They're a talkative lot when they come to Cairo. Learn more in one night with them than a week with GHQ." The rest of the plane's interior was filled with mail sacks and cartons. The fuselage shook as the wheels vibrated against the runway of the airfield outside Cairo. Then the aircraft lifted and the wheel noise was replaced by the sound of constant, rushing wind.

After they had been flying for an hour the pilot called back, "Would the Yank like to come forward and get a look-see?" Max squirmed into the tight cockpit and squinted into the sun. The pilot pointed to clouds of dust moving uniformly westward along the desert floor. He identified one cloud as a British tank regiment, others as antiaircraft or artillery or infantry units. Max could make out dark dots moving in some kind of formation under the lacy clouds. They all looked alike to him. The landscape was difficult to read from three thousand feet. He returned to his seat with a feeling of inadequacy.

The crewman announced, "Sidi Barrani comin' up." They held on to the straps of their seats as the plane landed on a dirt airstrip. When he emerged from the aircraft, Max tasted grit in his mouth. He blinked against the dusty wind called the khamsin' and pulled his cap on tight. The air base was, like many scattered about the desert, merely a series of tents at one end of a landing strip, some petrol tanks half sunk in the sand, and two squadrons of fighter planes, Spitfire and Hurricanes, camouflaged under netting. From ropes attached to the wings of planes hung clotheslines and fly nets draped over sleeping cots. The crude domestic arrangements gave the scene a lazy, somnolent look. Max asked an airman how recently the squadrons had seen action.

"Thirty minutes ago," the bearded South African replied politely. A dozen of the sunburned pilots and mechanics crowded curiously around Bright-Ashton and his gift bag, glancing also at Speigner's American uniform.

"Say, the Yanks haven't got into it, have they?" a pilot asked him. He kept looking at Max's pants, and it occurred to Max that he was the only man wearing long trousers. His starched khakis still held their military creases.

"Not yet," Max replied casually. He could feel dust collecting on his cheeks and eyebrows and lining the inside of his collar. The sun struck at his face with the impact of an electric heater held at arm's length.

"We would be obliged for a lift to the forward staging area," Bright-Ashton told the squadron leader and casually added, "Got anyone going that way?" They might have been students hitchhiking on holiday, Max thought.

"Last supply convoy of the day should be coming through any moment now," the squadron leader told them. "They shouldn't mind a couple of extra passengers." His eyes, white against a suntanned face, appraised Speigner's fair skin and fresh uniform. "Rather rough ride," he warned.

A half hour later they were bouncing uncomfortably on

metal seats in the back of an ammunition truck. Max kept
glancing at the crates of explosive shells roped together behind
them. He could hear the crates rubbing against one another.
The rear end of the three-ton lorry was open, and he could see
the other trucks in the convoy popping up over the hill behind
them, radiator grilles pointed at the sky, like so many dancing
rhinos frolicking in the dust. He could never have imagined
dust like this. Following Bright-Ashton's example, he had tied
a handkerchief over his nose and mouth. The fine grit seemed
to penetrate his very pores. He could feel it sifting down his
body inside his shirt, inside the elastic band of his shorts.
Bright-Ashton's sweating forehead had become smudged with
a wavy line of dust turned to mud.

"How much farther?" Max shouted through his mask.

"Perhaps twenty minutes."

Soon the convoys of trucks, jeeps, and half-tracks headed
past them in the opposite direction began to diminish so that
their own small convoy—six lorries led by a single RAF
armored car with its fixed steel turret and machine gun
mounted on top—was alone among the dunes. The sun
hovered like a brown ball behind purple ridges of clouds.

The lorries stopped, and Max was relieved to climb down,
away from the ammunition crates. He looked around for the
supply depot, expecting to see wire fences, armed guards
patrolling stockpiles of materiel. The hills seemed bare and
empty. Then he saw the pits covered by flat roofs built of wood
and sprinkled with sand. The ersatz dunes and valleys bearing
the marks of bulldozers contained petrol, oil, lubricants,
water, food and ammunition in crates and steel drums.

"Welcome to Bir el Khireigat," the major said. The lorries
were being backed into unloading position. "There's the
frontier, about six miles away." He reached into a kit bag.
"With these binoculars we might be able to spot Mussolini's
wire."

"Where are the guards for the dumps?" Max asked,
amazed that so much materiel was left exposed to the enemy.

"See that Bedouin encampment over there? They're
ours." Squinting in the direction John had pointed, Max
gradually perceived camels and men sitting on the ground,
appearing suddenly as if having sprung full-grown from the
desert. He could not understand how he had missed seeing

them. He distinguished the barrels of rifles slung on men's backs. "But our best defense," the major continued, "is disguise. We've set up a series of forward dumps along the wire to get ready for the next campaign. Bringing up more men and machines to protect them would merely advertise their locations and invite air raids. There's little risk of ground attack, though sporadic reconnaissance probes have found a dump or two. Follow me to that ridge over there. Get a look at the frontier."

The two men walked up a long slope blue with shadows. Sand spilled into Speigner's shoes, and he silently resolved to buy some desert boots when he got back to Cairo. At the crest of the hill they came into the dying glare of the sun. The ground was warm under their feet, while the air was growing chill. Max glanced behind him. Walking up the ridge he had a nagging memory of something important. He looked back to see what had prompted it. *Something about climbing a ridge*. John handed him the binoculars.

"There's the border," he said. "The wire stretches hundreds of miles, from the mountains to the Great Sand Sea. The Italians laid it during their twenty-year war with Libya. Your man Rommel is somewhere out there, perhaps as close as seventy-five miles, four or five hours as the panzer goes."

Through the binoculars Max saw a dark line stretching across the desert from north to south.

"Doesn't look like it," Bright-Ashton continued, reaching for his pipe, "but that roll of barbed wire is fifteen feet thick in places. Gazelle carcasses decorate it like brown bunting." With the dying sun behind him, John lit his pipe. Max smelled the tobacco burning and remembered Shoemaker in the dark ballroom and through the window the Mississippi capitol dome burning like a second sun.

Streight's ambush. Rommel's eyes fastened on Shoemaker, his face like Forrest's when he ascended the ridge into Streight's trap—shocked, vengeful, but respectful, too, of a resourceful enemy.

Speigner looked down the slope at the supply dump hidden in the natural basin. Then he stared at the Libyan frontier, at the black thread of wire crawling without end across the desert and somewhere beyond it: Rommel under the same, brown sky.

Something moved in the sky. He saw a single bird sailing high above the desert with its wings spread. He could not identify the type but it floated with a predatory patience. Max wondered at its windblown silences, at the lonely height where it hunted, and a premonition took root in his consciousness. He felt suspended over the desert where tracks of tanks and trucks carved the sand into modern hieroglyphics. He breathed a desert essence of dust, salt, empty oilcans, and gasoline exhaust. Nothing moved beneath him—man, beast, bird, machine—but he could perceive it. The heat of the sand was his body heat. In the north wind he felt as casually violent as a hawk and he shivered, as though having molted the feathers of a previous existence.

Bright-Ashton relit his pipe with match held cupped over bowl. He cut his eyes away from the glowing tobacco to observe his companion. Max stood with his arms stiff beside his body. He searched the horizon for the dust of tracks and wheels. At any moment he expected to hear the whistling of panzer treads and the pulse of engines. The major glanced toward the frontier and turned to Speigner with a questioning look.

"What is it?" he said.

"He won't be expecting it," Max said.

"Who?"

"Commanders who delight in surprising their enemy rarely expect to be served in kind."

"What *are* you talking about?"

"Supplies. The Germans need 'em, and we have 'em." Max flung an arm in the direction of the basin without taking his eyes from Bright-Ashton's face. "I'm talking about British corned beef, Canadian bacon, American canned milk and butter. If your men had been subsisting on sardines, olive oil and hard crackers for four months and there was an enemy dump as well stocked as a post exchange and open twenty-four hours a day, what would *you* do?"

"You think Rommel is going to raid this dump? Whatever gave you such an idea?"

"When he comes, there should be no resistance. Let him come in, then close the door on him."

The former history don, a Wykehamist of Winchester and New College, Oxford, examined the ash in his pipe bowl. By training and by temperament, the major was nothing if not a rational man. When he looked up, his gaze was unwavering.

"Are you serious, Lieutenant?" With his first use of military rank, Bright-Ashton obviously intended to put things into proper perspective. "Are you saying that you *sense* a raid by Rommel? Intuition? Is that it?"

"Rommel is coming." Max astonished himself. He could not explain his premonition because he had never experienced anything remotely like it. John shook his head.

"Do you know what the chaps at M.I. said when they discovered I had managed to push an invitation through channels to bring you to Egypt? They said that I had been too long working on government service, that I needed a leave to get a grip on myself. They called you my 'American seer,' my 'Yankee whizbang,' whom I had dug, mummified, out of the files and revived into a living, tactical savant who could chant mystic words and wave his hand over the desert and *poof!* there Rommel would be. The question is, can one nurture and defend a mystic without becoming mystical?" Even as he spoke, bemused and ironical, he could not restrain a curious glance at the western horizon. Max seized the initiative.

"You said it yourself, today at lunch. The Germans are building up for an offensive against Tobruk. It is reasonable to expect them to probe the frontier to make sure their flank will be secure. The presence of forward dumps like this one also gives them the additional opportunity to raid for supplies, tone their fighting muscle, and give their troops a morale boost: vital intelligence, gunnery practice at moving targets, and free groceries. With minimum losses. What could Rommel be thinking? He can pop in with a division, knock out light resistance, load up his trucks, and get back to the wire before we can react. Here we have"—he gestured expansively at the dump behind them—"a sitting duck."

The two men stood, alone on the ridge, squared off in silhouette against the rapidly darkening sky.

They could hear the lorries staring their engines for their return trip to base.

"And on this . . . *whim* of yours," the major said, "you expect me to propose to GHQ that a brigade of Crusaders be moved up and maintained near the wire to defend against a *possible* sortie by Rommel? They would laugh me off Gezira."

"Not tanks. No reason to risk losing them. Let the RAF handle Rommel's panzers. On a reconnaissance probe, the Germans would ordinarily have minimal air support."

"The RAF is not likely to go on combat alert without hard evidence of enemy movement." Bright-Ashton's face was fierce in the dying light. Yet Max sensed that the major somehow desired to be convinced that his premonition might prove true.

"Okay, let's work it out," Max said. "Routine surveillance should give the RAF enough time to respond if they have already been alerted. Reports of the Germans suddenly maintaining radio silence, aerial reconnaissance sightings—wouldn't that be enough? Have you got any friends in the Air Corps who owe you a favor?"

Bright-Ashton chuckled humorlessly. "Not ten thousand pounds' worth of petrol they don't. All right, there's Squadron Leader Smythe—you just met him—who commands the South African Seventeenth Bomber Squadron. But the regulations one must meet for an alert—" He shrugged his narrow shoulders.

"What about an inspection? Squadron leaders call combat-readiness inspections on a regular basis: planes fueled, ammunition loaded, bomb racks full, pilots standing by, ready to scramble."

"And then?"

"Let's say you get me aboard a recce flight over the frontier. We locate a raiding party headed this way. The pilot radios a warning. Your Squadron Leader Smythe *happens* to have an entire squadron of Blenheims loaded and mounted and engines started. We catch General Rommel with his pants down, and Smythe gets a commendation. If I'm wrong, no harm done. I get a sightseeing tour of the desert, courtesy of the RAF, and Squadron Leader Smythe scratches one inspection off his duty roster."

"May I ask," John said dryly, "when this all is to take place?"

"At sunup."

"Really?"

"It will take Rommel all day to find the dump, secure the area, load his lorries, and get back to his own lines."

The two men faced each other uncertainly. From the far

side of the basin a truck horn sounded, plaintive and imperious at once. The wind whirled up the ridge and a dust devil flitted and danced before dissolving in the particle-laden air. Stars winked overhead in an indigo sky. Bright-Ashton's eyes gleamed in the darkness.

"I would have to manufacture a story for Smythe," he muttered as if thinking out loud, "about M.I. picking up some not-quite-solid but nevertheless intriguing evidence of a possible sortie and would he mind going to the bother of calling up an inspection so he could accommodate a call for air support—just in case."

"Of course," Max said. Elation began to build in him, a feeling of weightlessness.

"But see here," John warned, "even if your scenario were to be played out perfectly and Smythe's boys got to knock hell out of Jerry, there is no way we can admit that we—"

"Squadron Leader Smythe gets credit for being in the right place at the right time. I'm not looking for any bouquets. Are you?" They shared a sudden grin. John shook his head incredulously.

"I don't know what you've got," he said, "but it certainly seems to be contagious. I just remembered that M.I. has been waiting for an opportunity to plant some false information about troop strength and battle order for the Germans to capture. The South African intelligence people have been forging some documents for us. They could send them over by courier tonight."

The truck horn blew insistently. The two officers began to make their way down into the basin, sliding and stumbling over the loose shale. Bright-Ashton touched Max's shoulder and they paused, submerged in a pool of shadow brimming like oil inside the lip of the crater.

"Let us take a moment," he said, "to collect ourselves. I am authorized to pick your brain for clues about Rommel's personality, his tendencies. I am not authorized to *act* on any of your suppositions. It was, frankly, a super achievement to get permission to transfer you to Cairo. To have you here, standing on this ridge, Libya just over the wire, is a terrific coup in itself, and now you want me to set a massive trap for Rommel involving hundreds of men and machines? Isn't there something else I can do for you, such as packing up one of the pyramids and shipping it to Washington for display next to your Capitol?"

"What's the best restaurant in Cairo?"

"What?"

"You know, the best place to eat?"

John brought his face close to Max so that they were almost nose to nose. They could barely see each other.

"The Night-and-Day, at the Semiramis Hotel," John replied curiously.

"I'll bet you," Max said, "the best meal in the house with all the trimmings that we get a visit from Rommel tomorrow."

XIV

"The desert is beautiful at first light," Rommel remarked. His collar was turned up against the cold, and he could see his breath smoking. Thirty miles to the east, sleeping unsuspecting under a fading canopy of stars, was Egypt. Rommel looked right and left at the 21st Panzer Division—the old 5th Light, which had accompanied him to North Africa seven months before—arrayed in battle order. *Can there be a more wonderful feeling than riding into battle at the head of one's army?* He glanced at Armbruster, realizing that his aide had not translated his remark to Major Melchiori.

Armbruster stood behind the two officers in the command armored car bristling with radio antennae, his arms folded tightly against the chill. The general's observation had been so uncharacteristically poetic, Armbruster had assumed that Rommel was merely thinking out loud. In the din created by the idling engines of some 100 panzers, 80 trucks, and 30 armored carriers, he had been inclined to let the sentiment go unnoticed. The moment he felt the weight of the general's glance, however, he turned to the Italian officer and translated quixotically:

"*Il deserto è bèllo chiáro primo.*"

"*Sì bèllo,*" Melchiori agreed readily. Rommel looked

askance at Melchiori's tailored cream-colored combat tunic with green camouflage ascot and matching soft cap. A gleaming leather holster on his belt contained a nickel-plated, ivory-handled Beretta automatic. The Roman was ready for war, Rommel thought wryly; however, there was nothing wrong with a good-looking uniform.

Politics makes bedfellows of us all.

With Armbruster's assistance, Rommel quickly reviewed his battle plan for his guest:

1) They would cross the frontier and penetrate with the main force intact for ten or fifteen miles.

2) The reconnaissance battalion would confuse the enemy by ranging up and down the border, sending false radio signals indicating an attack by the entire Afrika Korps.

3) Ravenstein's battalion would head south, his tanks and armored carriers dragging brushwood to raise enough dust for two divisions.

4) Sixty empty trucks would follow the strike force and proceed to load captured supplies at the Bir el Khireigat dump.

5) The twin pincers of the strike force would knife forward, enveloping the supply dump, and rendezvous at Deir el Hamra oasis to counter any resistance and provide cover for the sixty trucks.

"We'll see a bit of action today, if we're lucky," Rommel concluded. Melchiori was spellbound as Rommel raised his arm, looking at the company commanders ready in their turrets, binoculars trained on him, waiting—in radio silence—for a hand signal from the *Panzergruppe* commander.

"*Los, auf nach Ägypten!*" Rommel cried and brought his arm forward.

Max fumbled with his seat belt as the AT-6's propeller turned over. The engine coughed and sputtered, then caught with a roar. With take-off imminent, he struggled to adjust the obstinate seat belt. He was sweating inside the fur-lined flight jacket and boots, and the bulky parachute trussed to his back made him sit leaning slightly forward. He caught sight of Bright-Ashton standing near the runway, hands jammed in his pockets and his cap pulled on so tight that his ears stuck out. The major's thin, skeptical expression was somehow reassuring, tethering Speigner to a common anxiety. He gave John a thumbs-up signal and was glad to see him repeat the gesture.

Bright-Ashton had worked all night to make the necessary arrangements. While Max dozed on a cot in the squadron headquarters tent, the major had encoded messages, transmitted them, received and decoded replies. Captain Smythe had reluctantly agreed to stage a practice alert that morning, which guaranteed that all aircraft would be fueled, armed, and ready for flight with pilots standing by. A courier had arrived before dawn with falsified documents suggesting that the Eighth Army was not up to combat strength, and an orderly room truck of a South African armored car regiment had been abandoned near Bir el Khireigat, with the false order of battle placed inconspicuously among its maps and weather forecasts.

"I cannot tell you how many people I owe for this mission," John had complained to Speigner, handing him a steaming mug of tea at sunup. Dark circles under his eyes gave the major an owlish look. Bright-Ashton had asked him to choose a code name for their mission on the off chance that it succeeded and was noticed by the top brass, and Max had come up with "Streight's Raid."

The raging storm of their prop wash obliterated the encampment of tents and vehicles, and the AT-6 rushed into the clear blue sky. Soon they were climbing over the stark landscape of the Libyan plateau. Max continued to have difficulty reading the terrain. As the aircraft rose and fell smoothly with sudden currents, his eyes became blurred from trying to identify hills, valleys, and tracks on the bland plateau. He tried instead to sum up the experiences which had brought him 3,000 feet above the desert. Now that he was airborne, suspended, the sequence of events had come to an end. He felt drained of the expectancy that had kept him going. He had been profligate with his confidence in his premonition, had spent his reserves of hope in convincing Bright-Ashton that Rommel would come, and now felt doubt yawn emptily inside him.

"See your supply dump?" The pilot's voice crackled in Speigner's headset, sounding strangely far away. "That's El Khireigat."

Max saw nothing but sand. In a panic he cried, "Where is it?" He realized he had neglected to snap his throat micro-

phone into place, and as he fumbled to secure it his mind
raced: he could not find a fixed position in the featureless
terrain; he saw instead a forest, a mass of dark brown, which
appeared to be moving.

*until Great Birnam Wood to high Dunsinane hill shall
come*

He felt pulled out of sync by the startling sight and yelled into
the mike, "Did you see that!"

"I can hear you, Yank; you don't have to shout," said the
pilot, an affable ex-farmer from the Transvaal. "That cloud
shadow? That what you're lookin' at?"

Watching the vast shadow stain the desert a dull brown,
Speigner felt chastened and naïve, but the pilot had helped
orient him. In a few minutes, when the pilot drew his
attention to the Mussolini wire, Max saw it clearly: a thin,
wavering line stretching across the face of the earth like a black
crayon mark drawn arbitrarily by a giant child.

After following the frontier wire south for thirty minutes,
the pilot turned the aircraft northwest at a 45-degree angle to
the wire. He explained that this was a standard reconnaissance
route and it would give them their best chance of locating
enemy activity. The Great Sand Sea began just south of their
position, and there were no targets in that area for the
Germans to attack. From the new angle, the dune and ridge
shadow streaking the desert floor appeared to Max more
attenuated, stretching longer like a limitless backgammon
board. In its sameness, the desert seemed to take on an
obdurate, secretive nature. Perverse and uncompromising,
the blighted earth spelled out a message for him, drawn in an
ancient language of shadow and windrow: "Not for you, not for
the uninitiated." When the pilot's voice crackled in the
intercom, Speigner's heart jumped and he lurched against his
seat belt.

"Three o'clock. About two miles away. See the dust?"

His eyes burned as he strained to find it: a lacy fringe of
dust like a white puff of cloud low to the ground. That was all
he could see: no panzers, no lorries, just a spot of dust.

"Looks like a whole damned division!" the pilot exclaimed. Speigner was amazed at such deduction based on a

spiral of dust, but he kept his eyes fastened to the spidery windfall. The reconnaissance plane banked sharply and went into a shallow dive.

"We'll get some speed up and give 'em a fly-by," the pilot said. Speigner swallowed hard. His palms were cool with sweat inside the fur-lined gloves. In a matter of seconds they came zipping over the miraculous dust cloud, and Max could discern the dark shapes of panzers with their snoutish cannon among the smaller armored cars and trucks. The machines were spread out over a half mile. The plane overshot the formation in a matter of seconds, and Max was surprised to hear himself snort with relieved laughter into the intercom. They circled and made another pass.

"They're dragging bloody brush! That's no division!" The pilot sounded personally affronted. "It's only a bloody *battalion.*"

As they circled, Speigner noticed black puffs of smoke trailing behind the aircraft. He heard a soft, popping noise. He realized that these puffs of smoke were flak explosions. Antiaircraft fire was tracking the plane. He remained curiously unmoved by this revelation. All of it had the unreality of a dream.

Why would tanks drag brush behind them in the middle of nowhere? Where in the treeless desert had they found brush to drag?

"It's a bloody diversion, raising dust and trying to attract attention," the pilot grumbled. "Let's try a nor-nor'east heading and see if we pick up Jerry's main force a bit north, closer to the dump." While they turned to the new heading, the pilot radioed his base to report the German battalion, giving estimated tanks, bearing, and speed. His clearheaded summary impressed Max, who twisted in his seat to watch the formation disappear behind them. He hated to give it up, now that they had found what they were looking for.

I was right.

He felt like singing "The Star-Spangled Banner," or jumping up and clicking his heels, or walking the wing and shouting to the world, "You see? I was right!" He felt attuned to the plane, to the pattern of their search, to the generous desert which had relinquished its secret. His eyes roved the khaki plain, no longer obscure and unknown but almost homely in its providence.

"Yes," said the pilot. This time Max saw them simultaneously. There was less dust but a larger number of moving black dots spread out in a loose, boxlike formation. Behind it was another group of vehicles moving eastward in an orderly column.

"Help me count 'em!" the pilot cried, his professional detachment swept away by discovery. The aircraft thundered over the formation at two thousand feet. While Max counted, his eyes were also searching for something else: a staff car or some type of command vehicle.

It would be near the front.

"There's an ACV—there—isn't it?" the pilot said. "It looks like one of ours. What's Jerry doing with it, eh?"

"Closer!" Max shouted. He could see something on top of the block-shaped van lumbering along on four-foot-high wheels.

Someone is sitting on top of it.

"Can't go downstairs," the pilot said. "See those tracers? It's too hot down there." Yellow fingers reached out for them, died, and reached out again. Flak smoke ballooned on either side of the aircraft.

"Then circle them!" Max trained the powerful binoculars on the armored command vehicle and focused the lenses.

"Not healthy," the pilot insisted, but he banked the plane.

Under Max's trembling fingers the figure of a soldier sitting on top of the ACV slid into shape, grew fuzzy, then emerged again. There was a familiar cast to the back and shoulders that Max could distinguish even at two thousand feet. Nobody else on earth had such a dominating posture. The figure turned and stared up at the aircraft. Sunlight glinted on his goggles.

It has to be.

From deep inside Max came a fierce cry, the old Rebel yell Shoemaker had taught him and which the pilot later claimed had nearly deafened him through the intercom.

Rommel watched the lone aircraft circling like a vulture. So they had been spotted—not unexpected and of minor consequence. Doubtless the British reconnaissance plane had flown over Ravenstein's diversionary force, and the enemy response, when it came, would be fragmented along a wide front. He glanced at his wristwatch: 7:58 A.M. He estimated that it would take the British two to three hours to mount their troops and another hour or so to find the 21st Division. Since his point was presently a half hour away from the Bir el Khireigat dump, they could have the trucks loaded and headed back to the wire an hour before the first Matilda poked her fat cheeks over the nearest dune.

The British are tentative. That is their major weakness.

He turned and looked back at his antitank battalion trailing closely behind the front rank of Panzer IIIs, the deadly 88s towed by armored half-tracks. One of the gunners, sitting on the back of a half-track, saw him looking and stood up in the moving vehicle with a stiff salute. Rommel could see the boy's teeth a hundred meters away. He waved to the soldier. What magnificent fighters they were! Always ready to do what he asked of them and more.

Perhaps they should not be in a hurry to load the trucks and wait for the British to wake up to them. A good, sharp skirmish with pinpoint firing, a textbook demonstration of the coordination between panzer and antitank units for Melchiori to see, perhaps some prisoners and equipment to take home along with the captured supplies—that would be a shot in the arm for *Panzergruppe* and a nice warm-up for Tobruk. He grinned as he imagined the news of their raid reaching his forces throughout Cyrenaica and their pride in their sister units, as well as their delight in the shared bacon, butter and milk—*don't leave that out!*

He had sent a squadron of sappers and minesweepers ahead to blow gaps in the wire and clear the area for swift passage. His scouts should already have crossed the wire. He heard a muffled explosion a few miles away. He raised his glasses and watched a dust ball rise slowly like a forlorn statement of consent. He heard, or imagined he heard, the faint cheers of German soldiers.

Egypt.

"*Ha già cominciato?*" Melchiori called from inside the ACV. "Has it begun?" Armbruster translated in an identical, nervous tone. Rommel looked down through the open hatch. Their faces were sharply upturned to him like fledglings in a nest. Melchiori held a cup of hot chocolate.

"Not yet!" Rommel brusquely replied. He did not want to

share with anyone his anticipation as they drove through the shattered wire.

Egypt lay open to him, enticing in her grudging acquiescence. He kept a map on his office wall with the printed heading CAIRO. Across the desert terrain he had sketched a broad arrow that drove through the heart of the Egyptian capital and continued beyond it to the Suez Canal. *If only . . . a daring strike with a single, well-trained division creating havoc, GHQ taken with files intact.* He watched a column of panzers grind over a hill, its surface cleaving to their deep-cleated tracks. It was going to be a fine, clear day of only 100 degrees. The khamsin had let up, and there was an acceptable level of dust in the air. His armpits, neck and back were pleasantly cool with drying sweat.

Just before noon, Rommel ordered his escort group to halt and wait for Bayerlein's battalion to arrive at their rendezvous point. For the past two hours he had been sitting with the radio receiver to his ear, listening to reports from recce units. Amazingly, no resistance had been encountered. Where were the British? Tracks and dust ahead indicated a small force had retreated recently beyond their rendezvous location, probably a guard detail defending the Bir el Khireigat dump now twenty miles to their rear, where the support regiment was loading British supplies onto their trucks. Bayerlein reported that there had been no resistance at the dump and that the British had secured about a fourth of the supplies before retreating.

Rommel swept the horizon with his binoculars. The British were cautious and forever fidgeting about to make sure they had numerical superiority, but their probing should have begun at least an hour ago. Rommel resented this tortoiselike hesitation and chafed at being denied the battle for which he had primed his forces, not to mention his very important guest. Many of his panzer companies were low on fuel and were hedgehogged miles away in the middle of nowhere, waiting for their transport to catch up with them. He silently admitted that this circumstance was partly his fault for ordering sweeps beyond operational perimeters in search of the enemy.

Melchiori had at first been excited, then patient, then concerned, and now was concealing his doubts that a battle could be found. With the exigencies of command upon him, Rommel had ignored his guest. Schmidt, however, had thoughtfully provided a lunch of sandwiches and hot chocolate. Rommel was not hungry. Melchiori had taken a single bite of his sardine sandwich when the first bomb struck.

The desert exploded around them. Rommel was furious that his sixth sense had failed him. He glared at the detonations leaping up like a forest of white trees around them and cried, *"Where did they come from!"* Melchiori felt for his crucifix through the cloth of his handsome uniform.

It is impossible that the RAF could have located us and mounted an attack in this strength so soon, unless—That lone aircraft, earlier. The bombers were loaded and ready to take off. How could they have known?

Through the ACV's front periscope Rommel watched the low-flying Blenheims make their bombing runs. The Mammut jumped with the vibrations of the explosions around it. He could see a tank on fire, wheeling madly as if attempting to accelerate out from under the flames. He snatched up the radio headset and jammed it over his hat.

"This is Knight," he said. "AAB commence firing—commence firing at once! Confirm! Over."

Their driver fought the steering wheel to turn the ACV and get up speed down the soft track. Melchiori sat bolt upright in his seat, not moving a muscle, as though it were his responsibility to keep the bombs from hitting them by sitting motionless. With the Mammut temporarily standing still, an easy target, a bomb exploded on the right and blew off the door, armor plate and all. The driver slumped in his seat. Blood spurted from a deep cut in his head. Rommel, standing next to him, was untouched although the heel of his boot had been blown off. The pall of cordite was so thick he could hardly breathe. The ACV rolled gently to the foot of a low incline and stopped.

Rommel glanced around to see about the others. Neither Melchiori nor Schmidt appeared to be injured. The aide was opening a first-aid kit and moving up front toward the driver. Rommel's mind automatically assessed the situation: panzer squadrons 2 and 4 of his escort group had broken north and south—*good!*—dispersal was what was needed, now, and covering fire. A gasoline truck, caught in the act of refueling a tank, had been hit and had exploded. Men ran blazing and died where they fell. Rommel spoke into the microphone.

"Knight to Bishop, over."

"Bishop receiving, over," came the static-ridden reply. But the voice was calm, professional.

"Is this Bishop One?" Rommel wanted to get through to his Chief of Staff, General Gause. "Over," he added.

"This is Bishop Two. One out of town, over." Bishop Two was *Oberst* Otto Fernholz, who assumed Gause's place in case of casualty. Rommel later learned that Gause had a head injury from a near miss that had jammed the turret of his tank.

"Bishop Two, where is AAB, over."

"This is Bishop Two. AAB on working vacation, over." The antiaircraft battery had been hit and was attempting to repair the damage.

"This is Knight. Contact all units for Code Seven, repeat, Code Seven, confirm, over."

"Knight requests Code Seven. Executing, over."

"Very well, Bishop Two, this is Knight. Out."

Rommel yanked the headset off and tossed it angrily aside. Code 7 was a plan for regimental-level withdrawal, requiring certain squadrons to provide covering fire while other units made for the rear in a loose defensive formation. They had to assume that this bomb run was the first wave of an extensive air attack. Code 7 was the only sensible solution under the circumstances. He noticed that Melchiori carefully pressed a linen handkerchief to his shoulder. A dark bloodstain marred his tailored tunic. The Italian was delirious, not from shock but from pride. He smiled and nodded to Rommel as if they were company commanders waiting their turn to pass in review.

Schmidt had dragged the unconscious driver to the rear of the van and was administering a dressing to the man's wound. Rommel slipped behind the wheel. Strangely, the engine had continued to idle, and he backed into the roadway; soon they were rolling along. The blinding dust poured through their shattered open door. They passed tanks which toiled along at twenty miles per hour. Rommel spotted a Mark III motionless in the desert, apparently out of fuel. The crew sat on the hull and waved at each retreating vehicle like spectators at a swiftly passing parade.

* * *

The crackle of static on the radio receiver and the intermittent, harsh voices of the RAF pilots identifying their targets held a dreamlike quality for Max. It was a battle fought in a limbo of electrodes exploding against his eardrums, a battle whose periphery existed in the unknown voice of faceless pilots:

"On the right, Mooney! The lorries, just by that open pit—good shot! By God, look at them go up! That's jerking up the Hun!"

What Speigner had wanted more than anything was happening. Yet, having listened to the one-sided account of the battle from the British pilots' point of view, he was beginning to appreciate the violence he had brought on Rommel.

He had joined the South African mechanics, orderlies, cooks and headquarters staff crowding around a radio at the desert airstrip. Bright-Ashton sat in a folding chair and nursed a cup of coffee, fighting sleep and continually asking if an orderly room truck had been reported captured. Someone pressed a cup of tea into Max's hands, but his mind was somewhere in the clean chaos of the airwaves, where there was no stench of burning oil or screams of dying men. He listened to other reports coming in piecemeal from British recce units. All intelligence indicated the attack had been a border probe aimed at the Bir el Khireigat dump.

"Have there been any estimates of German losses?" Max asked. Hearing the intensity of the American's voice, the radio operator glanced up and shook his head. "I'd appreciate it if you'd let me know right away about captured prisoners and casualties—dead and wounded." He amazed himself.

War meant fighting, and fighting meant killing.

He wondered at the battle being waged inside him as he listened to the pilots' shrill congratulations. The static assaulted his senses, making him jump at each electronic explosion. In his imagination Mark IIIs and Matildas raced for an escarpment and the first to reach it turned hull down to face the enemy.

Rommel was a tourist you met by accident.

We did not meet by accident. He was no tourist.

The file on German officers was a coincidence. It is your business to maintain a professional interest.

There were too many mornings of going to the mailroom with a more than businesslike sense of anticipation. Too many hours spent running a finger down the columns looking for his name.

When you found news of a promotion or assignment or lecture, you felt only professional interest.

It was pride. In him.

Flies were crawling on his teacup, and he set it down. He glanced at Bright-Ashton dozing in his chair. The major had worked all night setting up the mission. He had accomplished miracles of cooperation between RAF and South African units. His mouth sagged open in his sleep. He seemed about to ask a question but was waiting politely for someone else to finish speaking.

This is my ally. This is a man I can trust.

You know Rommel a lot better than you know Bright-Ashton. America is not at war. If you are neutral, where, exactly, do you belong?

"These are for you, sir. Good show."

He looked up in confusion. South African airmen were standing around him. A grizzled veteran wearing a cook's hat and a mess sergeant's stripes was handing a package of Turkish cigars to him. Another airman extended a tin of chocolate.

"I wish we had a bit of brandy," said the sergeant. Max was at a total loss. He looked at their faces, he heard the radio telling of victory, and he could not think of a single word of appreciation or of denial.

Rommel was furious. He had had time as he drove Mammut at top speed through the gap in the wire, crossing into Libya ahead of the slower panzers and lorries, to consider what had happened and why. The sortie was a total failure. He considered himself lucky that early estimates radioed to him in code indicated only six killed and twelve injured, with two panzers and an undetermined number of trucks lost. It could have been much worse. *What is the American expression about taking advantage of wild game? Sitting ducks?* The air strike had hit the dump just as the trucks were being loaded. There would be no Canadian bacon, no American milk, no Argentine canned beef. And there would be no excuses. There was a reason for it. Whatever it was, he would find it.

Von Ravenstein's regiment was waiting at the rendezvous point fifteen miles inside the Libyan border. Rommel slammed on the brakes next to the armored wireless command vehicle. Not wanting to face Melchiori, who sat like a pale, accusing ghost in the back of the ACV, he jumped down out of the van, eager to confront Ravenstein with his frustrations. His leg bumped accidentally into a protruding door hinge. A hard shape inside his pants pocket hurt his thigh. He shoved a hand into the pocket for the offending object. It had a cracked and eroded surface and two indented rings that identified it as Federal, not Confederate. The minié ball seemed to burn his fingers. He felt cheated by the past, by lessons of no value, by wasted affinities. He hurled the bullet as far as he could throw it and turned away, not caring where it landed. Standing in the open doorway behind him, Lieutenant Schmidt ducked away from the sudden, violent motion, then alertly noted where the object struck the sand with a white puff of dust.

Ravenstein emerged from his armored car waving a handful of captured documents. He reported that one of his recce units had captured a South African orderly room truck with two prisoners. Among the maps, weather forecasts and reconnaissance reports had been found classified documents including organizational charts of the newly formed Eighth Army. Quick perusal of the Eighth's order of battle indicated a lack of strength which would take months to build up.

"These secret files," Ravenstein crowed, "are worth a squadron of Mark Fours!"

"If they were not meant for our eyes," Rommel replied skeptically, but he was not displeased.

"Herr General, the truck was still on fire when it was captured," Ravenstein argued. "It apparently had run over one of their own mines and had only just been abandoned when our men found it. 'Midsummer Night's Dream' has succeeded in a way we did not expect!"

"*Miei complimenti!*" said a voice behind him. Melchiori had stripped down to his undershirt. His shoulder was bandaged and one arm was in a sling. With his free hand he held a cigarette and bore his wound with nonchalance.

Rommel looked back at Egypt. He had observed the lack of fortified positions or forward encampments necessary for preparing a major offensive into Libya. There had been no organized pursuit, because the British had no armored forces in the area. The RAF had gotten lucky. While the 21st Division had not come home with bacon, the captured documents were at least *something*. Rommel turned to face his guest.

"We'll have to see that you get the ribbons you deserve," he said. Waves of smiles broke across Melchiori's face. "The panzer combat ribbon and of course the Wehrmacht ribbon for sustaining a wound under fire."

Mussolini will be pleased, after all, and then there will be Tobruk.

Schmidt walked away from the clustered vehicles, squinting into the abrasive dust which rasped at his face. Sighting on a high peak of the escarpment, he climbed a series of outcroppings like shelves until he reached a rocky ledge near the top of the ridge. The wind was not so bad here, and he kicked among the stones until he saw what he had hoped to find. He stooped and gathered up the yellow bullet. The general had shown it to him several times, always with pride and a certain nostalgia. The aide dropped the minié ball in his pocket as he turned to descend the slope. His commander often changed his mind, these days.

XV

Speigner entered the well-kept grounds of the Anglo-Egyptian Union with a slight case of stage fright. Accompanied by Colonel Fellers and Captain Carminelli, he joined the inward tide of guests—British and Egyptian officers and civilians, women in colorful dresses—who converged on the clubhouse surrounded by green lawns, hedges and palms. The occasion was a reception held in honor of the British minister of state, Oliver Lyttleton. Fellers had insisted that Max accompany him, adding somewhat weightily that people expected to meet him.

A week had passed since the ambush at Bir el Khireigat, and Fellers's congratulations had been tempered by objections to Max's having operated on his own, without direct orders. As the attaché of a neutral government embassy, the colonel was concerned about the possibility of official embarrassment over the participation of an American officer in a military action. Speigner had wormed his way out of Fellers's scrutiny by arguing that he had merely cooperated with his British hosts and made a suggestion as to the possibility of a German raid. Otherwise he had kept his distance from the fighting. He had almost convinced himself of his own neutrality, except for a memory of the moment when he had looked past the frontier wire into Libya, seeking Rommel.

"Let's stay in the background," Fellers advised. And there was an end to it, or so Max had thought.

Inside the clubhouse, people stood in small groups sipping sherry, each in his ordered place and not especially happy about it. Fellers adroitly negotiated the crowded room and introduced Max to the American ambassador. Alexander Kirk surprised him by winking as they shook hands. The ambassador seemed to expect him to share in their unspoken secret. Mrs. Kirk further surprised him by coolly slipping her arm through his.

"Come with me," she said. She took him with gentle dominion to meet the British and Egyptian ministers and their wives, who stood in a receiving line near the main entrance. Lyttleton's waxen expression of official goodwill melted into genuine interest as he shook Speigner's hand saying, "*Here* you are!" several times. To Fellers's apparent chagrin, Mrs. Kirk then tugged Max into position at the end of the receiving line. She stood beside him, assuming in her face and bearing a look of permanent delight.

"You're a kind of unofficial guest of honor," she whispered. He took one glance at the medals, ribbons and insignia of the officers making their way down the receiving line and stood at attention. He heard the ambassador's wife saying, "How do you do. I'm Mrs. Alexander Kirk. Please meet Lieutenant Speigner."

A baffling succession of faces passed before him—curious, speculative, skeptical, envious, admiring.

—*Hallo, the Rommel-catcher!*

—*An American with a German name? Were you born in Germany?*

—Didn't catch your name, Leftenant . . .

—Isn't there some notion about Rommel and a Confederate general?

—Good show! Carry on!

—You must consider letting us publish your famous memo in our newsletter, "Soho Times East." Would you like a copy sent round?

—Would you happen to know Rommel's favorite dish? We'd like to put it on our club menu.

—The Dragoons Wives Club would be thrilled to have you address us, Sunday next. Any topic you like.

"They say you are Rommel's friend. What kind of way is that to treat a friend!" Bright-Ashton stood beside him, beaming paternalistically and enjoying Speigner's discomfort. "Hero worship forces the hero to generate a tremendous outlay of social energy, don't you agree?" he added.

"Get me out of here!" Max hissed.

"No you don't. None of that. Took too much doing to get you here. I'm going to squeeze the moment for all it's worth."

"You might explain to me what this is all about," Max whispered.

"Please, no false modesty. Shan't stand for it, not after that twenty-quid dinner I bought you! Anyhow, it's a bit difficult to explain, considering that you're something of an enigma. Nobody is quite sure *what* you've done, actually, or how to categorize you, which is doubtless the major part of your charm. I think the designation 'mystic liaison' might serve to describe your function. You should be assigned an official code name to put your job into proper perspective. How about 'Bedford'?"

Max's grimace turned into a confused half smile for a Black Watch brigadier who pumped his hand in congratulations. Then an Egyptian couple, a diplomat and his wife, passed him with limp handshakes and a perfunctory nod. All the Egyptians he had encountered in the receiving line had appeared cool and indifferent. Before he had time to wonder about this phenomenon, a blond colonel's wife was inquiring if Rommel preferred blondes over brunettes. Max pleaded ignorance in the matter. Bright-Ashton slipped away and left him to cope on his own.

"Excuse me, which side are you on?" The merry, ironic

voice rolled down from the Highlands. He looked into the dark
eyes of Anna McAlpin. Her hair was brushed back severely,
making her cheekbones stand out in clean lines. She wore a
maroon dress with a white lace shawl.

"Glad to see you!" He held onto her hand so that she
could not get away. The line was forced to pause behind her
and a colonel glared at him. It was Arnold Weathers.

"Which side?" she persisted with a wry smile.

"The side of friendship," he said. "A friend of Scotland . . ."

"That is good," she countered, "but so far we have done
all the fighting. We can be friends on an equal basis only when
you Yanks come into the war. Can you please tell me when that
will be? Approximately, I mean."

"Certainly, but over dinner, please." He saw that
Weathers had turned his face away, pretending not to be
listening. "Really, are you engaged this evening?" he added
hesitantly.

"I will accept your kind invitation"—she withdrew her
hand from his—"on the condition that you grant me an
interview. My readers will want to know all about your bonny
deeds." Weathers reluctantly moved in from the right flank.

"We met at the Mohammed Ali Club." The colonel
avoided Max's steady gaze.

"Yes, we did."

"Yes, well—carry on, Leftenant." Weathers's face glowed.

"Thank you, sir."

Anna had moved away to mingle with the crowd. His eyes
followed her, but as he continued to greet arriving guests he
lost sight of her. When at last the receiving line broke up and
Mrs. Kirk released him, he did not see Anna anywhere. He
had decided that she had left the Union when she appeared at
his side—compact, beautiful and self-possessed.

"About that story . . ." she said.

"About that dinner . . ." he said.

The sun was setting when they left the Union together.
They heard cheering from the racetrack at the Gezira Sporting
Club. The distant roar rose and fell like the wind in the palms.
Anna proudly displayed an army car waiting in the parking
area. It had been placed at her disposal by the chief public
information officer, Major Randolph Churchill, son of the

Prime Minister. The driver, an RAF private, was leaning on the fender, smoking. He seemed relieved to have something to do, moving quickly to open the door for them and hurrying around to the driver's seat. They drove along a palm-lined avenue to the southern tip of Zamalik. The air seemed charged with gold flecks which disappeared when they changed directions and crossed the Khasr-el-Nil Bridge, then magically reappeared when they turned south again along the river. The sleek Nile drew copper fire from the sunset. Anna's perfume, mingling with the musty smell of the car's interior, was like fine smoke from burning sky and water. They arrived at Shepheard's too soon to suit Speigner.

Max asked the driver to park down the street and wait for them. They got out of the car and were immediately accosted by sidewalk vendors offering jewelry, watches, shoes, dates, pickled fish and miniature pyramids. Max linked arms with Anna and pushed through the equally crowded foyer of Shepheard's, where another level of business was being transacted à la Cairo. A competitive throng of salesmen wearing burnous, brokers in white linen suits, importers wearing Western-style jackets and Arab tarbooshes milled about, cajoling or shouting or moaning disapproval. Hands gestured continually with cane, cigar or pencil. No women were to be seen here, but as Max and Anna entered the brightly lit lobby, Egyptian girls in their colorful dresses appeared like flowers growing among the drab khaki of British and South African officers. Waiters hurried to tables carrying trays of drinks from the Long Bar.

Speigner saw that all the tables were occupied, and he escorted Anna to the less crowded bar. He felt like an old Cairo hand as he found them an empty space at the counter and signaled Joe. As if he had hoisted Yankee colors, every face along the bar counter turned and stared. He wondered if it was his American uniform. Joe moved toward him with a professional smile.

"Lieutenant Speigner, isn't it," said the bartender. "Let's see, your drink was the Sufferin' Allies, wasn't it?"

"Not this time." Max was inordinately pleased that Joe remembered. "Two whisky and sodas, please." He leaned over the bar as he spoke and Joe's smile froze as Anna came into view. Giuséppe Scialon drew himself to his full height. He was

impeccably attired in white coat, red vest, black bow tie.
Under his close-cropped curly hair his dark eyes were solemn.
On his square shoulders rested the weight of Egyptian public
drinking tradition. He stood flanked by his two black assistant
bartenders in their red waistcoats and tasseled fezzes. The
liquor bottles arrayed behind him were the instruments of his
public service, like an attorney's lawbooks or a physician's
medical journals.

"Lieutenant," Joe said, "I'll be happy to have a waiter
bring your drinks to a table, but we have a rule . . ." He
paused and gave Anna a glance worth a paragraph. "It may
seem unnatural to Westerners, but it's a long-standing custom
here in Cairo: ladies not permitted at the bar."

*Moses brought it down the mountain, bent under the
weight of the stone tablet it was carved on. Ladies not
permitted.*

"I can see Akhenaton trying to sell that to Nefertiti!" Max
exclaimed to cover his embarrassment.

"What?" said Joe.

Max turned to Anna. Everybody was watching them. "I'm
sorry," he murmured. "Didn't know . . ."

"It doesn't matter." Her cheeks were rosily defiant. "As
you Americans say, I have larger fish to fry. I will wait over
there." She went to stand near the wall. Max saw that people
around them who had observed their predicament turned back
to their conversations now that Shepheard's tradition was
secure from assault. Anna looked fiercely Gaelic, a female
Robert the Bruce in maroon and white. She held her purse
clamped tightly under her arm like a gunner with his
ammunition pouch.

"I say, you're not *the* American, are you?" said a captain of
hussars standing next to Speigner at the bar.

"What?" Max said.

"Are you the chap who tipped the RAF about the German
attack at the wire?" The captain's companions were also staring
at Speigner with aggressive curiosity. The glare of publicity
switched from negative to positive like a red light changing to
green.

"I guess so." He dug in his pocket for money to pay for the
drinks Joe placed on the counter.

"Then your money's no good!" the captain exclaimed. "Put
the Yank's drinks on my tab," he told Joe.

"Thanks, but . . ." Max protested.

"Not at all." The captain added effusively. "How'd you do it? Kick Jerry's bum, I mean." The group of hussars crowded around Max.

Anna was waiting for him. He did not want to lead the hussars to where she stood; he wanted to keep her all to himself. But he could not leave her alone. An unescorted European woman received extraordinary attention at Shepheard's. He had no choice but to lead his small group of admirers to her. His expression pleaded for her indulgence. She accepted her drink with an amused smile. Max noted the hussars' admiring glances at Anna and was proud of being her escort and of having a story to tell.

Hubris uncoiled at an alarming rate.

"I had a hunch that Rommel might be primed for an attack," he began. He told about Bright-Ashton arranging for him to go up in the reconnaissance flight, locating the German armored column, seeing an officer with binoculars riding on top of a command vehicle who looked familiar.

"How did you know what Rommel looked like?" they asked.

He told them about meeting Rommel in America. Anna set her drink on a narrow counter along the wall and took a small notebook from her purse. He deliberately slowed his speech so she could take notes. After a while he heard a smug voice and, when he stopped to listen, realized it was his own. He hated to stop telling the story because he had begun to take a detached interest in Speigner-as-hero. Like a frozen frame on a motion picture screen, he left the international troubleshooter in the RAF wireless tent surrounded by South African airmen proferring their small gifts of cigars and chocolate.

"We'd better go," he told Anna. The hussars were calling for another round of drinks. He managed a tactical withdrawal, guiding Anna before him and protecting their retreat with effusive thanks for the drinks. They made their way through the lobby and out into the cool, dusty evening. The driver was standing near the car, arguing with a vendor about the price of pickled fish. He opened the door for them and slid behind the wheel with a small parcel of folded newspaper. A fishy smell filled the car. Max rolled down the window.

"It's early," he said. "Shall we take a spin in your car before dinner?"

Anna was looking at beggars converging in a small stampede toward them. "Let's get out of the city," she said. "Have you been to Giza?"

"Yes," he said. "This past Monday. Carminelli took me."

"I want to see Cheops's pyramid and the Sphinx," she said. "Will you take me?"

"I'd love to," he said, and instructed the driver accordingly.

They drove south along the river, then crossed over the Khedive Abbas Bridge. As the driver negotiated the crowded streets, the honking of his horn lost amid the noise of the city, Speigner sneaked a look at Anna. She was unlike any woman he had known—witty, urbane, beautiful, secure in her own identity; above all, a woman with a cause. Anna stared out the window, lost in thought. He looked past her at Cairo and tried to see it as she must: a place of contrasts and contradictions, of beauty and filth, of historical riches and modern poverty, of ancient streets where pharaohs walked and where now beggars ran beside their car with hands outstretched. At this moment all became inextricably linked for Max—his sudden fame, the sights and sounds of Cairo, the desert where men fought and died bordering the very gates of the city, and now this lovely and brilliant woman at his side.

"What are you thinking?" he asked softly.

"How terrible the smell is," she said.

"Maybe it's the fish." He was as surprised as if she had slapped him. "You don't like Cairo?"

"No, but it doesn't matter, does it?" Her face was pale in the gloom of the back seat. "In fact, it's quite beside the point whether I *like* Cairo."

"What *is* the point?"

"That is something I have observed about you Americans. You don't seem to know what the point is. Look." She pointed at a passing trolley so overloaded with people that it seemed on the point of tipping over. "Do you see human dignity there? I see trapped souls fighting to retain some wee semblance of humanity and losing. And yet they have something Europeans do not: freedom. They are at war, but they are not in prison. No one is torturing them. They can go where they please. You want me to see the *intrigue* of the East? I see a setting for war, that's all. An ancient place of forgotten battles has become a setting for modern warfare. It is *your* place of battle, Egypt. Yes, you are a warrior. Don't look so surprised. You defeated Rommel, didn't you? You are helping to destroy our enemies, aren't you? *That's* the point, that and nothing else. We are riding to the pyramids to get away from your new friends and have a private talk. You will tell me your story so that I can write it and give my people hope that the Afrika Korps can be defeated. *That's* the point. You see?"

They bounced together on the seat as the car bumped over potholes in the road. Her eyes caught sparks of light from passing vehicles and seemed to blaze up. Something in her eyes made him afraid and bold at once. They sat looking out at the derelict shacks on the city limits. The car picked up speed on the road to Giza. A half moon rose over the river which was a silver ribbon between fields of ripe cotton.

Soon they reached Giza. Its main street led directly to the pyramids west of the town. Anna inclined her head ironically at the Cleopatra Night Club and Ramses Restaurant but did not say a word. Max felt inexplicably defensive about the souvenir stands with plaster statuettes of pharaohs and tiny Sphinxes dangling on strings. Vendors closing their stands for the night stopped and stared hopefully at the olive-green military car.

Then he saw the pyramids loom cleanly over the crowded rooftops. A road led into the desert. They followed it until the soft sand made driving impossible. The driver stopped and looked to them for instructions. They told him to wait and got out. Together they surveyed the ancient burial grounds: the three pyramids of Cheops, Chephren, and Mycerinus rode the crest of a low escarpment that rose like a tidal wave out of the Great Sand Sea. Below them, the dark form of the Sphinx presided over a row of crumbling temples.

"The city of the dead," Anna whispered.

Their hands came together as they labored across the sand toward the temples. Lights played intermittently over the battered face of the Sphinx like giant fireflies. Someone was shining a flashlight on it. It occurred to Speigner that tourists were present at all hours, crawling like worms over the tombs, century after century. As if the desert were sending a representative to confirm his thoughts, a ragged child appeared out of the darkness and tried to sell them a plaster statuette of Nefertiti.

"Only two pounds Egyptian." The child was a girl about ten, with a wasted face. Max started to dig in his pocket for money but Anna pulled him on. The child scowled at her as if she were a scorpion.

"Look," Anna whispered in his ear. As they approached the Sphinx it seemed to move against the sky, a living thing compounded of stone, wind and time. They stood silent beneath the statue, which rose sixty feet high. Its face reflected the lights of Giza, so that it appeared luminous against the night. The group of people whose light they had seen moved off toward the pyramids. Their flashlight flickered like a ghost seeking communion among the pharaohs' wives.

"Welcome to Necropolis." Max resisted the intimidation of the statue. Anna continued to stare up at the great stone face with unreserved wonder. He did not know which face was more marvelous.

"The Sphinx is said to guard the tombs," she said, then added in the probing tone of a reporter, "if it stands between the living and the dead, to whom does it speak, to them or to us?" She turned her face up to him.

"To the living," he said after a moment's reflection. No woman he had known would have asked such a question.

"What is it saying?" She was full of life and he held her arm tightly.

"It is telling us that standing here in the sand for four thousand years, guarding the tombs, has been tough duty. It needs a break."

"No!" She laughed deep in her throat. "Please. Look at it. Listen to it. And tell me what it is saying."

He stared up at the great face cratered by shadow, as if the lights of Giza were eroding it as he watched.

"Being alive is getting ready to be dead a long time," he said.

They stood in silence with arms locked together. "They say it has the face of Chephren, brother of Cheops," Anna said brightly, to change their mood. "Did you know it was buried in the sand up to its shoulders for many years, perhaps centuries? Generations of Egyptians believed it was a stone face without a body." Her face became suddenly attentive, as if the Sphinx had whispered to her. "The Arabs call it *Abu el Hal*, father of terror."

"How do you know all this?"

"From books." She shook her head disparagingly. "I have lived in books all my life. Now I must act. I think this is true of you also, Max?" Her features grew sharp with intuition. "The difference is, you have begun to act. Can you help me get to the front lines? Will you talk to your friends at British intelligence for me?"

"You have press credentials, don't you? What's the problem?"

"The British army information office says it is too dangerous for a woman. There are no women at the front. They will not be responsible for me. I want to be the first woman to go to the front!"

"You mean, they won't agree *officially* to allow you to join the other correspondents out there?" he said thoughtfully. "Have you sounded them out about *unofficial* permission? That should be easy to arrange."

"What do you mean?" She clung to his arm with sudden strength.

"I mean, you travel the way I did. It's okay by the British as long as they can turn a blind eye to what you're doing. For the record, they don't know you're going along for the ride. If anything happens, they don't know—officially—how you got there."

"Exactly!" She wrapped her arms around his neck in a fierce hug of gratitude, too quick for him to respond. His eyes searched her face for signs that a possibility had been set in motion between them. She tugged at his hand. "Let us go see the pyramids. And you must tell me more of meeting Rommel in America. Tell me about meeting him and touring the battlefields in Mississippi."

As they walked up the path leading to the pyramids, he saw a shadow move near the base of the Sphinx. He started, then recognized the slight form of the Arab girl. She was following them at a distance.

"Rommel came there with a party of German officers traveling—" He had started to say "under assumed names" but thought better of it. "—to national battle sites. Rommel had an intense curiosity about Forrest. You should have seen his face when he listened to stories of Forrest's adventures. It was like a—wild thing learning to stalk prey. Total concentration. It was incredible. I mean, the idea of his wanting to know so badly—with his whole being. Anyway, we walked the battlefield at Brice's Crossroads, where Forrest defeated a force twice the size of his own. Rommel could see the original battle as if it were still going on. I think that for him all battles are fought forever. We found a motorcycle at a farmhouse and went for a ride."

"You and Rommel!" She released his arm. "Just the two of you?"

"Yes." He wondered why that fact should interest her. The pyramids blocked out the stars above them. "Later, Rommel met the author William Faulkner and visited his home."

"I have read Faulkner's books, *Sartoris* and *Sanctuary*."

"Faulkner took Rommel to Shiloh in the middle of the night. It's in Tennessee, where the Union army won a pivotal battle in the war. It was strange, walking around the battlefield in the dark. Faulkner wanted Rommel to learn a different side of Forrest. I don't know . . . the impatient side. I suppose Faulkner thought Rommel might lack patience. Maybe that's a cavalryman's weakness. Rommel was not a commander of armor then. He was still an infantryman, but his heart was with the cavalry."

Anna abruptly crossed her arms, hugging them to her body and walking apart from him. They had reached the top of the path. The pyramids rose in stark planes like the hinges of the universe. The Sphinx stared obstinately in the opposite direction as if no longer interested in them. Max saw a small, dark form hovering halfway down the long path. He did not know what he had said to upset Anna.

"I was told the four faces of the pyramids are oriented toward the cardinal points of the compass." They looked up at the massive edifice of Cheops. "That is genius." He waited for her to say something, then hurried to fill the silence growing between them. "They say the steps of the pyramids were the means by which a pharaoh was to ascend to meet Osiris, who would grant him eternal life. Maybe the steps weren't just for pharaohs going up. Maybe the gods came down." He grinned hopefully at her.

"Who is a god?" She spoke to Cheops's pyramid, not to him. "Did your friend Rommel come down from the stars?"

"My friend! Wait a minute—"

"He is no god. He is a man like you. He can be defeated."

"Gulliver and the Lilliputian," Max said ironically.

"You speak of Forrest's *adventure*, of Rommel's *heart* being with the cavalry, of battles going on *forever*, as though war is a game to be celebrated with a glass of beer at a place like Shepheard's. But who at Shepheard's entertains the people with stories of whole families herded onto boxcars and taken to camps where they fight for survival each day? Your war is clean and glorious. My war is dirty and miserable. We cannot both be right."

"What I said at Shepheard's—I must have seemed silly to you."

"Oh, no!" She pressed a small fist between her breasts as if communicating with the beat of her heart. "Your story is important. Your advice to the British is important. I am glad to write about what you have accomplished. What I want is for you—and people in the West everywhere—to understand what the war is like in Europe, what the Germans are doing to civilians."

He put his hands on her shoulders as though to convince her that he understood, and his intentions shifted. He leaned down not so much for a kiss as to ally himself with her. She averted her face at the last instant, and his lips brushed her cheek. He drew back but she clung to his hand.

"Thank you." They stood gripping hands like old friends parting. "I am flattered that a handsome young man could admire an old woman of thirty-seven."

He could not believe it. Thirty-seven was middle-aged. His estimation of her age could not have been so far off the mark.

"It is an ancient age, isn't it!" She threw back her head and laughed gaily. He had a wild impulse to kiss her throat. The long beam of a flashlight bobbed primly across the sand. The tourist group had completed their circuit around Cheops. "I am thirty-seven, and you are—what?—twenty-four?"

"Twenty-eight," he lied.

"I don't believe you. I am old enough to be your aunt, or something. I have my job to do. The newspapers that pay for my airplane tickets expect me to do my job, not lollygag about under the pyramids. But if this were the eve of a battle in which you were to fight and perhaps to die and it would give you a moment's peace, I would give it serious consideration."

Speigner squared his shoulders. "I may go out with the RAF on another reconnaissance soon."

She grabbed his arm and pulled him toward the path leading back. "You must take me with you. I would like to see the war from above. But first, please take me to dinner. I am starving. Hiking about these old tombs gives one an awful appetite."

He allowed himself to be taken in tow. They descended the path arm in arm. Halfway down they found the fellahin girl squatting on her heels, clutching her statuette. Max stopped and took an Egyptian five-pound note out of his pocket. With an impossibly wide grin she grabbed the bill, thrust the statuette into his hands, and bounded away before the tall foreigner could change his mind. Max held up the crudely painted replica of Nefertiti so they could see its face.

"She came down from the stars, too," he said and gave it to Anna.

They had dinner at the Semiramis, where Anna was staying. The hotel restaurant was brightly lit and so noisy that Max had to lean across the table for her to hear what he was saying. She ate all of her dinner and part of his. Max enjoyed watching her eat. She cleaned her plate, asking him deft questions between bites and mopping up sauce with pieces of bread. She kept him talking about his role in the counterattack. Their moment beside the pyramids might never have occurred. Speigner marveled at her poise. He still could not believe he had misjudged her age and kept assessing her temples for crow's-feet, her throat for lines. A woman's hands were supposed to be an accurate measure of her age. Anna's hands were smooth, supple, unblemished.

When they finished dinner he suggested a cognac in the hotel lounge but she declined, explaining that she had an early day the next morning. Speigner tried to think of something to delay the inevitable. He promised to ask Colonel Fellers's help in obtaining permission for her to visit the front lines. He escorted her to the elevator, where she waved brightly as the doors closed. With an empty feeling he wandered into the Semiramis bar, and found Carminelli.

The captain, who was more than a little drunk, ordered a

round of drinks and leaning on the counter said, "How about some poontang?"

"Excuse me?"

"What do you call it, then?" Carminelli knitted his brows with some effort. "Snatch? Pussy? Nooky? I say poontang. Y'know that place in the Bulaq I told you? Pretty wog girls. Clean. So?"

"Wog girls?" Max said carelessly.

"Working on government service," Carminelli said out of the side of his mouth, like W. C. Fields. "Local types. Also known as Arabs, a Semitic people scattered widely throughout the Near East, North Africa, and the Arabian Peninsula. An ancient race distinguished by their cemeteries, fine horses, palm trees, petroleum, and poontang. Ever heard of 'em?"

"Okay, okay," Speigner said testily, "but I don't speak Arabic."

"So what kinda conversation you planning to have with 'em? 'Roll over, turn around, do it like this.' You use body English with these girls, believe me. Hey, it's Saturday night. You cashed your travel allotment check, didn't you? So how about it?"

"I don't know." Max toyed with his glass.

"Okay, wait right here!" Carminelli disappeared into the hotel lobby. In a few minutes he returned and, grinning like an ape, handed Max an English-Arabic pocket dictionary.

"Now you're ready for an erudite conversation or whatever fascinating tidbits of information the wog whore wishes to bestow on you. If you learn anything interesting, I hope you'll let me in on it. Only international exchange I've ever heard of, over in the Bulaq, is hashish or gonorrhea. Oh, but these girls are real clean. You won't catch nothing but joy where I'm taking you. So? You up to it or what?"

Speigner thought of Anna averting her face at Cheops.

"Okay." He slipped the paperback dictionary into his coat pocket and drained his glass. "Let's go."

They took a cab and drove to the Bulaq, where military police patrolled the narrow, twisting streets. Soldiers were everywhere, most of them officers, since the Birka district was off limits to other ranks. They paid the cabby and got out at a lane where the buildings seemed to lean together in resignation. Women called to them in various languages from doorways and balconies. Carminelli led the way to a building that stood apart from the rest, a large house surrounded by a fenced courtyard. They passed through the gate and knocked on the door.

The brothel was not at all as Max had expected. Although he had not given it much thought, he had vaguely anticipated a kind of harem: curtains like veils, incense haze, women with eyes painted with kohl swaying to the sound of flute and drum, perhaps guarded by a bare-chested eunuch. A mysterious madam swathed in jewelry would offer him a bevy of girls of all shapes, sizes, and colors, who would pose competitively for him. There would be wine, music, and dancing. Women would drape themselves all over him. At last, he and one of the girls would go to a room together.

"Waiting time is only thirty minutes," Carminelli explained. They lined up behind a dozen men who stood patiently in a kind of foyer or anteroom. Almost all the customers were British officers. Max overheard a conversation between a balding major and a potbellied colonel about a particularly nasty outbreak of diarrhea in the colonel's Royal Horse Artillery regiment. Water supply lay at the root of the problem. Carminelli assured him several times that the house had a reputation for fast service and that he had seen them handle a crowd twice this size with ease.

Speigner was in no hurry. A waiter took orders for spirits, and Max asked for gin. Two men were admitted through the door at the end of the anteroom, and the line inched forward. Eyes glanced with interest at the inner sanctum revealed in the brief parting of the door. Carminelli struck up a conversation with a brigadier about the movie *Gone With the Wind*. Max sipped the warm gin and thought of his Uncle Robert, considered the freest spirit in the older generation of Speigners, a sergeant in the air corps during the Great War. The most memorable event of the war, according to Uncle Robert, was losing his virginity in a Paris whorehouse. "Don't believe what your friends tell you," his uncle had confided over Christmas eggnog, "the first time is the best time." As the gin took hold, it seemed more and more unreasonable for yet another generation of American males to have to cross an ocean and fight a war to get laid.

Photographs of girls (working girls? Max wondered) were

pinned to a kind of bulletin board on the wall, but none of the
officers paid them any attention. Max kept glancing at the
enigmatic, bland faces in the pictures. Why were they all so
irrevocably solemn? Where was the wine, the music, and the
dancing?

Another gin later their turn came, and a woman with a
face like leather, wearing a dark business suit and square-toed
oxfords, escorted them to a cashier, a man with gold rings and a
heavy gold bracelet, who spoke three words: "Five pounds,
please." He took their money and gave them each a ticket.
They entered a softly lighted lounge furnished with divans and
floor cushions. Max smelled cigar smoke, but there was no one
in the room. He heard male laughter and glanced up at a
staircase on the left side of the lounge. Two officers strolled
down the stairs, adjusting a cap or the knot in a tie.

"Here we are!" Carminelli pointed to a descending
elevator whirring to a stop. Max took a swig of gin. The liquor
bit at his throat and glowed in his stomach. Two girls rode in
the elevator like doves in a cage. He observed that the traffic
was handled efficiently.

It's an in-and-out business.

"Ruth," the madam said. "Phoebe." She pointed to each
girl in turn. They stood patiently, dressed in sheer nylon robes
with no undergarments. Max returned the dark stare of
nipples through nylon. Carminelli opted for Ruth, who had
breasts like cantaloupes. Matched by elimination, Max tried to
make some small signal of amiability to Phoebe, a smile, a nod.
Without looking at him, Phoebe took his hand and pulled him
into the tiny elevator. Carminelli and Ruth stepped aboard
with arms wrapped around each other's waists. The madam
closed the door. Ruth operated the control lever. The elevator
ascended with a sudden jerk that made Max's knees sag.

Conveyor belt to paradise.

Carminelli's heavy beard shadow was blue in the dim
overhead light. It made Max feel hairless, prepubescent. He
focused his attention on his groin. Nothing was stirring. He
seemed to have lost all sensation. They passed the second
floor. Carminelli stroked Ruth's hips, and she giggled. The
elevator stopped at the third floor. Ruth led Carminelli to the
right. Phoebe persuaded Max to turn left. Looking over his
shoulder he watched Carminelli swagger up the hall, his arm

cradling Ruth's fleshy shoulders. All the doors in the hallway were closed, but Max had an impression of constant, unseen activity, as in an anthill. Phoebe opened a door and went into a room.

He followed her inside. The small room had two pieces of furniture: a once-white divan with plump red pillows, a high, swaybacked bed. It was also furnished with a quietly insistent odor in which he detected perfume, alcohol, and sweat. He hit the gin. Its kick was becoming less potent.

Where is good old bourbon when you need it?

As she closed the door he heard a stifled moan from another room. He could not tell if it was male or female. It was pitched in a high register and reminded him of speaking in tongues.

Do Moslems speak in tongues? Are there backsliding Moslems, like Baptists in Mississippi? How do Moslems do it? Missionary position? Missionaries had converted the Copts. Maybe she was a Copt.

This was going to be a cultural exchange he could take home to Brigitte, like a reusable urn from Cheops's era. He did not let himself dwell on what else he might take back to Brigitte.

The girl was looking at him attentively. She appeared to await instructions. He had been depending on her initiative. Yet the unexpected sensibility was worthy of interest. He studied her face. She had delicate features—high cheekbones, curved eyebrows, long lashes over eyes like anthracite, a fleeting smile. Though he lacked confidence in his ability to judge a woman's age, he guessed hers to be eighteen or nineteen.

Could she be new to the business? This might explain her hesitation. Or am I her first American? That would put us on a kind of equal basis. She is probably wondering how Americans do it.

"Fuck me," she said.

It's a start.

He sat on the divan and sank into it. She knelt and slipped off his shoes. Her hair was jet black and fine.

"Where are you from?" he said.

It was a mannerism acquired in Mississippi, where there were plenty of clichés to fall back on. One sought common ground. She might be a runaway from a red-roofed village beside the Nile with olive trees and dogs dozing in the street. She gave him a blank stare. She wore a lot of eye shadow. He hauled out his pocket dictionary. The lights were low for reading. "*Manzil* [home] . . . *madiyna* [town]?" Her expression did not change. He wished he were a burning bush.

Why shouldn't there be amenities? Her civilization is a lot older than ours.

He glared at his dictionary through an alcoholic haze until he found what he was looking for: "*Ayn* [where] . . . *inti* [you] . . . *min* [from]?"

She rewarded him with a dazzling smile of understanding. She had small but perfect white teeth. "*El Qâhira*," she said. Cairo. She stroked the bottom of his foot, her eyes glancing at his dictionary as though to see what would come next.

She wants me to try again. She is starved for companionship. Do they own her? Does she get off weekends or holidays? What was it Anna had said, "Egyptians are born slaves"? . . . Anna.

"This is a beautiful country," he said. She knelt at his feet with a fixed smile. If her tongue had lolled like a puppy he would not have been surprised. "*Gamiyl a* [beautiful] . . . *bilaad* [country]."

"Okay, you fuck me," she said. She looked very pleased with herself for constructing an independent clause. She turned her face half away and gave him a sidelong smile.

"Phoebe, listen," he said, riffling the dictionary. "*Ahraam* [pyramids] . . . *tamaam* [quite] . . . *murattab* [lovely]!" He glanced up for some confirmation, perhaps a *shukran* (thank you), only to see her frowning in confusion. "No, wait— mistake. *Murattab* means moist. I mean *bâhir* . . . [incredibly beautiful]. Do you understand? I mean, your pyramids are really terrific!" He grinned at her. This was almost like having a conversation.

She opened her robe and her breasts swung free. The nipples, painted pink, glared at him. She took his hand and pressed it against her. Her nipples were soft. Brigitte's had been as rigid as pencil erasers.

"Let's work up to it," he said. "What's the rush?"

It occurred to him that she had a schedule to meet. *How many men can she service on a good night? Do you*

*pay by the hour? The price is five pounds sterling. If she
services one customer per hour during, say, a six-hour shift,
she is knocking down a gross of . . .*

"*Laa* [no] . . ." He went back to his dictionary. "*Yisri'*
[hurry]." But she was already moving toward the bed.

"Phoebe?" he said.

She dropped her robe. Her body was lightly powdered.
Her olive skin had a dull sheen. Her pubic hair had been
shaved, giving her the appearance of a child with unusually
precocious breasts. The pink nipples renewed their imperious
stare. He could not just leave her standing. He put down his
gin and his dictionary and began to unbutton his shirt. She lay
on the bed, her body curved at the hip, leaving a space for
him. He took off his pants and folded them over the arm of the
divan. The gesture made him feel more in control. He picked
up his dictionary and his glass and took them to bed. He left
his shorts on, noticing, as he crawled into bed, that the olive
drab clashed with the purple sheets. Phoebe pressed herself
against him. She nodded once, gravely. He had seen someone
nod like that before. He remembered an Ole Miss receiving
line, college boys in their ROTC uniforms, girls in evening
dresses. It had been his first college formal, and a professor's
wife—Mrs. Shoemaker—had tried to put him at ease.

*Ole Miss. A hundred thousand years ago. And the Chi
Omega beauty queen—Alice something? If Alice were here
. . . It would be complicated.*

He thought of smiles and poses and primping and
chiseled profiles and gartered thighs and white cigarettes with
lipstick stains and heavy perfume and "Blue Moon." Phoebe's
hand slid up his thigh. She lightly massaged his groin and he
became erect, straining against the thin material of his shorts.

"What's Arabic for foreplay!"

She was pulling his shorts down. The elastic waistband
caught on his stiff penis and released it so that it sprang back.
"What do Egyptians do about kissing?" he persisted. Determination to have it his way—he was the paying customer if it
came to that!—made him grope for his dictionary on the
bedside table. He turned the pages to the soft lamplight which
came from across the room. Phoebe crouched beside him on
all fours. He located the Arabic word for *kissing*.

"*Bowsa?*" he asked.

She gave him a level glance, then leaned forward and gave his member several stiff pecks like a housewife welcoming her husband home from the office. His soul cried out for ceremony.

"Dammit, you people have had thousands of years to practice! You're leaving something *out*. At home we build up to it. You know, dancing, holding hands, sharing a Coke at the corner drugstore. I realize that under the circumstances . . ."

"Coke?" Phoebe looked surprised. "American?" Max sat up in bed. "You not British?" she added.

"You speak English!"

"Of course." She tossed her hair disdainfully, and he loved her for it. She was coming to life. "British soldiers in Egypt long time. All girl here speak English except ignorant *fellahin* girl. House rule say fuck not talk. Better for everybody. Talk take time, cause trouble." She glanced solicitously at his penis. It stood at attention. Max was hypnotized. It was like seeing life breathed into a mannequin by the creator. It was the cry of Moses in the bullrushes.

She spoke, therefore she thought, therefore was she sentient and desirable.

"How can talk cause trouble?" He fed her the question greedily, like a boy nourishing a small campfire with sticks.

"One must take care what one say to British."

"Why is that?"

"They hate Egyptian."

"Why!"

"Because we hate them." She shrugged. "*Inshallah*."

Inshallah was a common Islamic expression meaning "If God wills." So Phoebe was a Moslem. Another twig and the fire blazed brighter.

"Why do you hate them?"

"America should understand. Did not you win freedom from the British? Did you not fight the British?"

"Yes, but that was a long time ago."

"You hate the British, too." It was a statement, not a question. She glanced at his penis. It nodded attentively.

"No, they are my country's allies."

"You are friends with the British?"

"Yes. We help them in their war against the Germans and Italians."

"Then I must treat you like British. No more talk politics." She buried her face between her knees and presented her rump. The twin moons with their patina of talcum glistened above the purple sheets.

"I'm an American."

"We fuck now, okay?" Her voice was muffled against the bedclothes.

"I'm not like the British. I'm different."

"You want me on top?" She twisted her head around and regarded him expectantly. It was exciting to see her thinking.

"I mean, you should not hate Americans just because you hate the British." He gave her bottom an affectionate pat. Foreplay. She sat back on her heels and placed her hands on her knees. The gesture seemed demure. He knelt in front of her, taking both her hands in his. She smiled with understanding. Americans played strange games. Talking politics and fucking, usually anathema to each other, were to be combined. She squirmed closer so that their knees touched.

"America should not help British," she scolded. "Let German win war and come to Egypt and set my people free from British." Her knees spread outside his. She pushed closer.

"You want me to go home to America? Is that it?" Max was experiencing a shortness of breath. It was up to her to keep the conversation going.

"I have a brother in New Jersey!" She converged on him.

"A brother!" Max cried with feeling.

"He work in a gas station." They became preoccupied with the common arrangement of limbs.

"Gas station . . ."

"I go to America someday." She rested her hands on his shoulders.

"You'll love it." He spread his fingers against her back as though they were dancing.

"My brother save money to buy a store." She rose to mount him, lifting one thigh gracefully, then the other.

"That's a *wonderful* idea."

"He sell Egyptian goods to our people that live in America." She guided him inside her.

"*Unbelievable*."

"I forget what you call store like that." She thrust herself down on him.

"Ah . . . im . . . ah . . . port . . . ah."

"What is it?" She moved against him slowly.

"Im . . . im . . . im . . . porter."

"Importer, that's it." She thrust hard as if convincing him of her plans. "I buy *goods* for him *here* and send to *him* in America. He send *me* the *money* to *pay* for it."

"Money. Pay."

"I *get* best *goods* for him, at best *price*."

"Best."

"I buy for him *wine, liquor, cheese, dates* . . ."

"Buy it!"

". . . *bread, cotton cloth, tea* . . ."

"Buy it!"

". . . *blended coffee, syrups, leather goods* . . ."

"Don't stop buying!"

". . . *crockery, Coptic prayer beads* . . ."

"Buy everything!"

". . . *sandals, toys* . . ."

"Buy it all!"

". . . *small statues of the pyramids and the gods!*"

"God!"

"When we are rich, I will go to New Jersey and live in America for good."

"Good."

She allowed him to rest his head on her shoulder. He dozed and found himself in a commodious, hospitable bazaar. He browsed and window-shopped and looked upon the fine things of life. There was no hurry, no responsibility, no pressing engagements. He saw Rommel in the bazaar. They greeted each other in brotherly fashion. He nudged Rommel's shoulder and asked him when was the last time he got some.

XVI

Rommel balanced a tier of packages in his lap and watched a custom shoemaker dressed in a 50,000-lira silk suit trace the outline of Lucie's foot on a sheet of paper. He wanted to put the packages down, but there did not seem to be anyplace to put them. Lucie was finding Rome to be a shopping bonanza for Christmas presents. She had bought Manfred a ready-made suit, a cap and a scarf. One of the parcels contained a present for Rommel, and he suspected it was a pair of gloves. Now it was Lucie's turn to buy something for herself. She intended to have a pair of shoes made and sent to her in Austria. Yet his meeting with Mussolini was only two hours away. He needed time to compose his thoughts.

We have every confidence in you, Herr General.

That is most gratifying, but frankly any success we gain will be due in large part to your supplying my troops with petrol, ammunition and other materiel.

You will achieve success. I know it.

With all respect, one must not expect miracles. Am I supposed to win on cussedness alone?

Ha-ha-ha. Cussedness! I like it. Very good.

My cussedness without Il Duce's support is worth about as much in the desert as a Tiger tank without ammunition or petrol.

"Red or white?" Lucie held up two leather samples.

"What?" he said.

"I can't decide. The shoe would look elegant in either." Her smile was brilliant, a bride's smile. She knelt before him with the swatches in either hand. The shoemaker squatted next to her in his expensive suit. The high-priced cobbler's obsequiousness offended Rommel. It reminded him of Comando Suprèmo hoping to win his sanction for another withdrawal.

"Why not take them both?" He tried to appear interested for her sake.

"Oh, no," she replied quickly. "They're too dear. I think I'll take the white."

Money matters confused him. It was a constant nuisance, all the paying for meals, tipping porters or waiters. He had grown accustomed to having a meal simply appear before him. Civilian life was a thousand times more complicated. The meals were so elaborate: antipasto, pasta, soup, meat, bread, vegetables, two wines, dessert, coffee. During lunch at a café along the Via Veneto he had found himself wondering what Bayerlein and von Mellenthin were saying over their biscuits, sardines and tea across the Mediterranean. He imagined Bayerlein angrily brushing the flies away and was startled by a sharp pang of nostalgia. He had only been gone four days. Perhaps it was not civilian life that bothered him, but politics. He thought again of Mussolini as he handed Lucie a sheaf of the oversized lira notes with which to pay the man.

We have every confidence in you, General Rommel.

Please appreciate our morale situation, Duce. While my troops fight with enthusiasm when they have a chance to seize the initiative, they grow increasingly bitter when the supply train fails them.

You will find a way to succeed.

(No, no, no, you puddinghead, the equation is: no supplies equals certain defeat. Can't you get that through your thick skull!)

I have every faith in you . . .

(Give me strength. Don't let me say it to his face.)

Every confidence . . .

No, no, no. Your "Roman legions" are not worth shit. When I came to North Africa they were throwing down their weapons and piling onto overloaded trucks in wild retreat, every man for himself. Your Italian soldiers are useless mouths to feed. There are supplies enough, if they are channeled only to the D.A.K. and my panzer divisions. Give me priority on supplies and I will take Tobruk in a week, thus proving worthy of your confidence—mein Duce.

"I am not political," he said out loud.

"What, dear?" Lucie said. They were standing on the sidewalk outside the shoemaker's shop, waiting for their embassy staff car to fetch them. People were staring at Rommel's dress uniform with the red general's stripe on the trousers leg. Lucie wore a conservative navy-blue traveling suit, white blouse, and black hat with floppy brim.

"Nothing," he said, recovering. "It is not important. What is important is that we are together." He linked arms with her while balancing packages against his chest.

"You are worried about your meeting with Il Duce, aren't you?" Lucie's dark eyes were solemn.

"Let us not talk of it now." He willed the shine to come back into her eyes.

"I know you have much on your mind," she said thoughtfully, "but it is just as important for you to relax and give yourself a rest."

How does one tell one's wife that ninety-eight hours of vacationing is about all he can stand?

"Oh, our lunch in the country yesterday was great," he said. "I mean, that and four nights with you, my love."

The Mercedes pulled up smoothly to the curb, attracting much attention from pedestrians who stared uninhibitedly as the general and his wife got inside the limousine.

"I want your birthday tomorrow to be perfect." Lucie settled herself on the luxurious leather seat.

"Don't remind me," he joked. Actually, he felt no different about turning fifty than he had at forty or thirty. It was all of a piece. One kept fit and did his work the best he could. With the exception of his recurring jaundice and upset stomach he felt fit as a fiddle. "Where would you like to go, my sweet?"

Lucie whipped out her travel guide pamphlet. "The Baths of Trajan, the Forum of Julius Caesar, the Temple of Saturn, the Coliseum—"

"My God, dearest, are you collecting ruins, too? If you want ruins, come back to North Africa with me. I'll show you some ruins."

"They're all near the Venezia Palace," she protested. "Oh, and St. Peter's. We're meeting the von Ravensteins there at two."

Rommel sank back glumly against the soft leather. It had been wonderful to be with Lucie again, to draw strength as always from her certainty, her delight in the simple concerns of domestic comfort. He had washed off the grit of North Africa, had slept between clean sheets in an airy (if cold), high-ceilinged suite at the Hotel Eden, had dined very well, had made vigorous love—twice—to his wife. And then there had been his favorite time of the vacation: yesterday they had driven out of Rome along the Appian Way. They had passed through the Arch of Constantine, through which conquering Roman legions had returned, as promised, brandishing their shields or lying on them. He could almost hear the beat of the war drums, the rattle of spear and shield, the tramp of sandaled feet.

They had found a rustic country inn which reminded him of the Swabian taverns of his youth. They sat in a sunny, cobblestoned courtyard under a grape arbor, where the innkeeper served them a lunch of bread and butter, thinly sliced prosciutto, smoked salami, pastrami, hot mustard, olives, and a delightful *vino di campagna*. He had actually drunk a second glass of it.

But that was yesterday. Today he was ready to get back to work, and his duty roster listed a single item: politics. He had to persuade Mussolini to bring stockpiles up to attack levels. On November 8 every ship in an Italian convoy with 40,000 tons of supplies had been sunk, and the Italian navy had halted convoy operations. No ships had arrived in Libya since October 16. Secondly, he desperately needed Mussolini to override *Comando Suprèmo* reluctance to attack Tobruk because of fears of a possible British offensive. Of course the British were going to attack eventually, which was the reason for assaulting Tobruk as soon as supplies reached them. It should be emphasized that the documents captured during "Midsummer Night's Dream" indicated that it would take several months for the enemy to bring his forces up to combat strength, but time was running out. He believed that he had convinced OKW of the need to assault Tobruk. All that remained was to obtain Mussolini's approval.

"Erwin, look!" Lucie said.

The limousine had neared the end of a street which opened up on the Coliseum. The massive curve of the outside wall loomed without warning, growing more awesome the closer they came. Rommel was subdued by this sudden presence of antiquity, so clean and strong that his heart seemed to stop. He sat like a stone in the Mercedes, poised between the living and the dead.

There was a nobility about the dead. They had ceased to

scramble for daily bread or possessions, ceased to argue, to worry, to cajole or to apologize, to pray or to hope. They were free of responsibility. They stood on their record. It would seem that death had its advantages.

Rommel and his wife got out of the limousine and went up the nearest ramp leading to the arena. The embassy driver followed at a discreet distance. The air inside the ramp tunnel was rank with a thousand years of urine.

"This place needs a good cleaning!" Lucie sniffed.

"When in Rome, my dear," he teased.

They emerged into the great amphitheater and heard in its intimidating silence an ancient cry for blood. Rommel could imagine the seats filled with a gray sea of Romans in homespun tunics with whitecaps of citizens' togas dotting the waves of shouting, screaming, laughing, arguing, eating, drinking, vomiting spectators. The great arena was still, its walls lined with twentieth-century trash. Wastepaper fluttered in the wind. Yet he imagined a door opening in the wall, just opposite, and two gladiators marching out abreast, approaching the emperor's box to raise their weapons in salute.

"We who are about to die," he muttered.

"What, dear?" Lucie said.

Then the clash of broadswords, the crowd's roar at a clean kill. Then perhaps a lion's growl and the slap of a condemned criminal's sandals against the hard-packed sand, running in terrible silence, saving his breath until the end when there was no point in holding back the screams.

Rommel shut off his imagination. He did not care for spectator sport, preferring the solitary pleasures of swimming, mountain climbing, skiing, hunting, or cycling.

"Look at the quaint little garbage troughs," Lucie was saying. The driver came forward to explain that there was a vomitorium at the end of each row for the spectator's convenience. The waste matter was pulled by gravity through an intricate pipe system which emptied into underground cisterns.

"Oh my, I'm sorry I asked," she said.

Rommel could not comprehend such excess. His soul revolted against it. No self-respecting German would gorge himself to the point of nausea, stick his finger down his throat, and throw up in public. What kind of a civilization would condone such ludicrous behavior? He strove for a pleasant thought and remembered New York, the Polo Grounds, and baseball. A clean sport played by polyglot teams of Irish, German, Polish, Italian, and Jewish ancestry.

Have you ever been to a baseball game, Excellency?

No, I don't think so.

It's a very complicated game. My plan to attack Tobruk, on the other hand, is quite simple. All I need is supplies.

When we met last August I gave you permission to attack Tobruk. What happened?

Comando Suprèmo refused to cooperate. They wanted to abandon Sollum and Tobruk and fall back. That's no way to build an empire, Excellency, if you will permit me to say so.

"Now we've seen the Coliseum," he told Lucie. "I cannot be late for my meeting at the Venezia Palace."

"What about St. Peter's!" Lucie cried. "We're to meet General and Countess von Ravenstein there."

"It can't be helped," he said. Lucie followed him back to the car in dutiful silence. He was sorry to deprive her of the small joys of further sightseeing, but there would be time later for further holiday pursuits. He ordered the driver to take him to the Venezia Palace. His watch read 1:40. Twenty minutes seemed plenty of time to make the drive across downtown Rome. Traffic careered dangerously close on either side of the car. Italian drivers, he noted, drifted in and out of lanes like a school of crazed minnows going after a single floating crumb. They passed the time at stoplights cursing each other and making obscene gestures.

Italians were loud, period. Rome was the loudest city in the world and the dirtiest. Rommel agreed with Lucie. Rome could use a good washing, starching and ironing. The Italians were careless, disorganized, unpunctual. They laughed and cried too easily. If he had to volunteer a single, beneficial influence of his trip to Rome—other than being with Lucie, of course—it would be that now he understood the failures of his Italian generals in North Africa better. Understanding did not mean sympathizing, but perhaps it would help him cope with them.

The car had not moved in several minutes. The four-lane avenue was bumper-to-bumper with cars. Every driver except theirs seemed to be riding his horn. It was bedlam. Rommel leaned irritably over the front seat and asked the driver what was the problem.

"There is a fistfight going on, Herr General," said the driver laconically. "Up there where the street enters the plaza. A man has dragged another from his automobile, and they are going at each other. It happens often. We have no choice but to wait."

"How far is it to the Venezia Palace?" Rommel snapped. The driver straightened up in his seat.

"Seven or eight blocks, approximately one and a half kilometers, Herr General."

"I'll walk." Rommel opened the door. "You will take Frau Rommel wherever she likes. My meeting will be over between fifteen hundred and fifteen hundred thirty hours. Pick me up at the Venezia Palace at that time."

"*Jawohl, Herr General!*"

"Lucie, I am going to walk."

"I heard."

"Don't worry, we will see St. Peter's another time."

"What shall I tell the von Ravensteins?"

"Tell them I had to drop in on Mussolini. They'll understand."

She gave him a dark look—from the Italian side of her family—and said in a level but not unkind voice, "Last night when you put your hand on my breast and said, 'That reminds me—we need to strengthen our position above Tobruk on Hill 209,' I knew you were not joking. You miss your command. But give me one more day."

Rommel glanced in shock at the back of the driver's head.

"Oh, don't mind him," she said. "He sees and hears only what he is supposed to. Go on, go to Mussolini. But remember—twenty-four hours belong to me."

Rommel eased out of the car, nodding dutifully, and closed the door carefully behind him. When Lucie was in a mood like this, he was used to walking softly. He left his wife staring out the opposite window in chagrin or amusement or both, he could not tell. When he reached the end of the street, he observed that the "fight" was more of a fist-shaking contest, with dozens of drivers vacating their cars to take sides and appreciate the *fúria bella* of the combatants. Some music lover had turned up his car radio at peak volume to provide an operatic background to the squabble. At some point, Rommel thought, the would-be brawlers would decide that honor had been satisfied, hug, kiss—*abbracci, baci*—and make up, to the applause of their audience. Such was the fighting temper he had observed in the Italian soldier, an anger that was an end in itself. It was too volatile and burned itself out quickly. It was no good in battle, where a cold fury was needed. Too bad there were no street corners in the North African desert. If he could set up a traffic jam between Eighth Army and Ariete or XX Corps, maybe he'd get a bit of action from Mussolini's legionnaires.

At the Venezia Palace the duty officer at the reception desk escorted him to Mussolini without delay. Their footsteps rang in the polished marble corridors. Rommel felt at home in the ancient palace, seat of empire, and approved of Mussolini's choice of Venezia as his chief administration building. Like the Reichstag, Venezia possessed a grand air of formality and ceremony which burned here like a well-kept flame. Rommel approved of such places wholeheartedly. The battlefield was the fire which lit the torch of government. He had come to offer Mussolini some matches.

Il Duce came forward to greet him, effusive as always in his greetings. The generals Bastico and Cavallero were conspicuously present, as Rommel had expected them to be. Their hostile glances told him that they had been filling Mussolini's ears with reasons for not attacking Tobruk. Perhaps they had gone too far, and His Excellency had tired of their excuses.

He was never prepared for Mussolini's size, the thick shoulders, the girth. By comparison Rommel felt shrunken. He drew himself to his full height and squared his shoulders. Il Duce wore an impressive black uniform with a wide leather belt. His only decoration was the gold seal of office on a silver ribbon around his neck. Rommel experienced the ambivalence he often felt in the presence of a head of state: on one hand, he respected the political savvy and the ability to think on a grand scale; on the other, he retained a stubborn, Swabian independence which refused to kow-tow to another man and remained determinedly democratic.

"Have you enjoyed your stay in Rome?" Mussolini was asking in serviceable German. "Your hotel has been satisfactory?"

"Very much so," he said with feeling. "And the accommodations are quite luxurious compared to my quarters at Gambut. It's hard to get used to the lack of flies in Rome. I keep thinking I should be brushing them away, and they are not there."

The mantle of affairs of state settled over dictator and general, and each became alert to the other's every nuance.

"*Wie geht's in Afrika?*" Mussolini said.

"Your Excellency, it is imperative that we attack Tobruk. The Führer has approved my plan, and with your permission I can mount an attack by November twenty-one."

"You feel that such an attack would be successful?"

"The fortress will fall in forty-eight hours at the most." Rommel knew that Mussolini admired his confidence, a quality in which many of the Italian generals were sadly lacking.

"And what about the counterattack from the south?" Il Duce spoke without looking directly at him. In this he differed from Hitler. To Rommel, the Führer seemed more personally involved, quicker to agree or to contradict, ready with a joke or a compliment, his eyes penetrating as if trying to read one's thoughts. Mussolini struck Rommel as aloof, brooding his titanic thoughts of empire, a man to be treated with respect but also with caution. One was reminded of the awesome silences of the Coliseum.

"The British will not attack and risk having their retreat cut off." Rommel felt Bastico's eyes burning into him. "The operation called 'Midsummer Night's Dream' showed that the British needed several months to build up to combat strength."

"Ah, yes, 'Midsummer Night's Dream.' Major Melchiori gave me most glowing reports of that mission," said Mussolini, actually smiling.

I'll just bet he did. God bless you for remembering. I entertained your courtier, and now it's pay-back time.

"Let us walk a bit," Il Duce said. "I like to move when I talk. It helps me think. You, too, do a lot of thinking on your feet, eh, General?" They moved away from Bastico and Cavallero, following a sunlit corridor which ended on an open balcony with a view of the glistening Tiber and the distant white dome of St. Peter's.

"What is your opinion of morale?" said Mussolini.

"Our troops are in high spirits, your Excellency. Field exercises show them combat-ready in every strike unit."

"What is your opinion of morale among Italian forces?"

"Surely your generals are more qualified to report to you in that area."

"I am interested in your opinion."

What is he getting at?

They had reached the balcony at the end of the corridor. Rome gleamed before them like a many-faceted jewel. Rommel saw Bastico's head appear in a hallway behind them, then just as quickly disappear.

"From all appearances," he said carefully, "I would say morale is high among the Italian forces."

"What is your opinion about the fighting quality of the Italian soldier?"

He wants me to say something good about the Italians.

"Excellency, the Bersaglieri units are magnificent fighters, as good as any soldiers anywhere. General Gambara's Twentieth Corps is a capable, rapid-strike, motorized force. Many of the units that make up Pavia, Trento, and Bologna divisions are equipped with Austrian artillery captured in the Great War which are useless against the modern British armor. If they were properly equipped, they would follow me to Suez and back again." He could feel a fine sweat on the back of his neck.

Mussolini was silent for a long moment, then nodded profoundly and turned to Rommel with the beginnings of a smile. "I hear you are having a birthday, your fiftieth? Congratulations. I have a little present for you. I am going to give you Tobruk, but you must go there yourself to pick up your gift, no?"

Relief flooded through Rommel's veins. Rome was the most beautiful city he had ever seen. Mussolini was a benevolent ruler. He almost reached out to shake Il Duce's hand, then remembered himself and saluted.

Cavallero and Bastico immediately smelled a rat when Mussolini and Rommel returned from their stroll. By way of retribution, they invited Rommel to view a newly released documentary film, *Onward From Benghazi*. A screen and projector were quickly set up and the lights turned off. He was then treated to the Italian version of the capture of Benghazi on April 3, 1941. Determined Italian infantry were shown storming the city to resounding strains of martial music. He clearly remembered that a single German battalion under von Wechmar had taken Benghazi that day. As far as he knew, there had not been an Italian soldier within miles of Benghazi at the time. The projector was turned off. Cavallero and Bastico glared at Rommel, daring him to contradict the contents of the film.

"Most illuminating," he said carelessly. "I often wondered what went on in that battle."

XVII

Through his goggles the world appeared as a nightmarish fusion of sand and sky, as if the very elements had joined in battle. All the surfaces of their moving jeep, from windshield to seats to floorboards, were coated with a uniform mantle of grit. Bright-Ashton, who had pulled off the track to keep from being run over by a rampaging column of caterpillars towing artillery, was less a man than a sand monster. The dust rooster-tailing from the half-tracks attacked them like a living swarm intent on filling their lungs. In self-defense the major wheeled to the left, shifted into second and pressed the accelerator against the floorboard. He did not stop the jeep until the air was fit to breathe. They sat still, recovering. The Rover's engine idled efficiently as if the dust had improved its octane. Bright-Ashton opened his canteen, wiped off the mouth, and offered Speigner the first sip.

"Desert may get us before we get there." John leaned close to be heard above the din of engines and grinding gears. Max handed back the canteen and watched Bright-Ashton drink greedily, Adam's apple bobbing. He took off his goggles and brushed away the sand encrusted on them.

"How far is it now?" he asked. It was the middle of the afternoon, and they had been driving for several hours. The major had been relying on a map and a compass for directions to General Cunningham's headquarters at Fort Maddalena. There were no direct roads, or tracks, from their point of origin—an RAF landing strip near an oasis called Bir el Khamea.

"About ten miles, or another hour at the rate we're going—if we don't get lost." Bright-Ashton grinned under his goggles like a maniacal insect. "It's just across the wire, you know!" He held up the canteen in a mock toast to Max. "Going to Libya, old boy. I must say, it's a novel experience riding an American junior officer's coattails. If it weren't for you, they certainly would not consider allowing a GHQ rat like me to scratch around up here. So, here's to you!"

Max would not acknowledge such a sentiment. It had to be the other way around. He was entirely dependent on the major's ability to deal with the desert on its own terms. His brief trip to the frontier two months before had ill prepared him for what he now witnessed: the maelstrom of the Eighth Army moving west toward Libya. From where their jeep was stopped, on a slight rise, he could see a staggering amount of transport—tanks, lorries, heavy machinery, armored cars; a vast armada setting sail across a beige ocean. A line of lorries plunged through waves of dust parting over their radiators like the sea wings of a ship's bow and billowing on either side in a tan wake. Bright-Ashton had told him that 700 tanks and 100,000 men had been assembled for the campaign code-named *Crusader*. Amid this war storm of men and machines, they were two men in one jeep. Max did not have to remind himself to stick close to Bright-Ashton.

They were on their way to Fort Maddalena, which was being used as Lieutenant General Alan Cunningham's advance headquarters. Cunningham had recently been appointed Eighth Army Commander by Sir Claude Auchinleck, Commander-in-Chief, Middle East. From newspaper clippings in Fellers's embassy office, Speigner had learned of Cunningham's successful campaign against the Italians in Somaliland and Abyssinia. In July 1941 Cunningham had restored Haile Selassie, Lion of Judah and King of Kings, to the Ethiopian throne from which the Italians had driven him in 1936. As a result of his victories in East Africa, Cunningham had enjoyed a great deal of favorable press in England and had been the popular choice for Auchinleck's appointment.

Fellers had had his reservations: "Cunningham was fighting the Italians, not the Germans. He's got a tiger of a different stripe now, but his honeymoon will last for a while and he has invited you up as a kind of mascot-observer, a good-luck charm. My advice is that you'll do best in that role if you keep your opinions to yourself and speak when spoken to. *I'll* be very interested in your observations, however, so keep your eyes and ears open, Lieutenant!"

Bright-Ashton had a more colorful explanation of Cunningham's interest in Max: "You're like an American artifact, a Navajo cooking pot which turned up unexpectedly at an archaeological dig at some obscure pharaoh's tomb up the Nile; an American *Wunderkind* who foiled a German raid by pure instinct, the reclusive Rommel scholar enticed out of his cloistered cell by that renowned star-maker, Major John Bright-Ashton!"

Refreshed by the drink of water and the relatively breathable air, they got under way again, proceeding along the periphery of the armada's dust storm as much as possible. The November sun was slanting directly in their faces when they reached the great roll of wire at the frontier. John guessed that Fort Maddalena lay to the south, and they turned left, parallel to the wire. Max squinted west at the enemy territory of Libya. The desert floor appeared as black and flat as asphalt. It held no revelations for Max as it had seemed to do in September, when he had stretched himself like a human net to catch the wind. He felt shrunken and inept bumping along in the heat and the grit, existing merely for the sake of physical discomfort. Did they expect him to sniff the air and point Rommel like a bird dog?

"There it is!" Bright-Ashton blithely made a ninety-degree turn through a gap in the wire and they were in Libya. Tracks fanned out across the sand in several directions and disappeared. A single wooden post with a crudely painted "8" on it told them which track to follow. After driving steadily for five minutes they saw the white adobe walls of Fort Maddalena. The nineteenth-century British outpost was surrounded by a city of tents and machinery: lorries and tanks of various types: Stuarts, Matildas, Valentines. They passed a landing strip which had been created by erecting two parallel rows of oil drums along an area of flat, hard-packed sand.

John asked a sergeant for directions to the adjutant's office, and they threaded their way through what looked to Max like a military county fair. Uniformed men with an assortment of weapons and vehicles mingled with Arab vendors in filthy galabiehs hawking fried bread, coffee, and Italian caps, insignia, pistols, and bayonets. In the adjutant's tent Bright-Ashton was given two tent halves and informed of the commander's press conference and staff meeting to be held shortly. They found a space to park their jeep and put up their two-man tent. They arranged their fly net so that it trapped fewer flies than it kept out. Then they made their way to the fort.

Max stopped to admire a brand spanking-new Crusader. Like everything else the tank was covered with dust, but the fresh paint underneath gleamed dully and its rubber treads showed little wear.

"We've been waiting for a shipment of these to arrive," John said. "Hundreds just off the boat. Tip the balance, now."

"Not for my money." The voice belonged to a young tank commander, a lieutenant with grease on his uniform and a wrench in his hand. "These new jobs all need adjustment terribly. The bolts are hand-tight from the factory. The tracks are loose. This one"—he whacked the hull with his wrench—"I couldn't defend against a bloody nutcracker in it." He stood there glaring at them, and they simultaneously shoved their hands into their pockets.

"Carry on," John said lamely. They joined a small procession of officers and correspondents entering the fort. Max saw a familiar figure among them—jaunty, long-legged stride, shoulders narrow but square, sandy hair curling out from under a camouflage cap tilted at an angle. Heads were turning to look at Anna McAlpin. Half the soldiers appeared delighted to see a woman at the front and half disapproved. Max felt his adrenaline kick in. He hurried through the crowd to catch her. Her smile, when she saw him, spoke to his soul. She seemed almost as glad to see him, hugging him tightly and introducing him to her companion, Major Randolph Churchill.

"Yes, he's the prime minister's son, in case you're too polite to ask," she added mischievously. "And he has broken precedent like so many shattered bone teacups to get me here." She linked arms with Max. "The only woman at the

front must ally herself with the only American, no?" They
introduced Churchill to Bright-Ashton, who recalled a previous meeting between the two in Cairo at GHQ, and the two
British officers fell in behind Max and Anna as they strolled
through the open wooden gates of Fort Maddalena.

"Look at them," she whispered, indicating with a quick
slant of her eyes the men turning to stare at her. "They're
dying with curiosity as to what I'm doing here, wearing British
fatigues, but now I'm here, there's nothing to be done about it
and not a one of them would condescend to ask openly about
me."

The firm pressure of her arm, her smile, her good nature
fortified him. He was ready for anything.

Inside the fort an awning had been set up for the briefing.
Men swarmed to one side where a bar had been set up. Bright-
Ashton pointed out Cunningham to Speigner. The dapper
general was half hidden behind orbiting satellites of junior
officers. Max squeezed through the crush to get drinks for
Anna and himself. The bartender poured whisky neat into
paper cups. There were no mixers, scotch being more plentiful
and less valuable than water. When he returned to her, they
raised their cups in a silent toast. He watched her cheeks
hollow out as she sipped the whisky. Dusk rapidly filled the
corners of the citadel walls, transforming them into dark
cisterns brimming with shadows.

"If my role here is to be the only woman," Anna said to
John, "and Max is the token American, what, exactly, do *you*
do here, Major?"

"Keeper of the mascot!" Bright-Ashton puffed his pipe for
emphasis.

"When you write about this," Max said to Anna, "what
will you say?"

They listened to the deep murmur of male voices. Among
the field commanders, liaison officers and headquarters staff
were correspondents from the London *Times,* the *Daily Mail,
the New York Times, Chicago Tribune* and other newspapers
or radio networks. Not many months before, these men might
have jostled for counter space in bars and pubs from London to
New York. The bar table against which they now congregated
was set up between two European armies poised to do battle
in a Middle Eastern desert. Soldier and correspondent drank,
smoked, and chatted with guarded indifference.

"Should one say," Anna said quietly, "that whisky helps?"

In unspoken endorsement, Speigner and Bright-Ashton drained their cups. Cunningham's aide joined them and asked if they would like to greet the general. They approached Cunningham's party. His subordinates stepped aside to allow them access. The Eighth Army commander received them with conscientious charm.

"I see we have a lovely infiltrator in our midst." Cunningham smiled at Anna. "Breaking the sex barrier on behalf of the *Times?*"

"And the New York *Daily News*," she said. "We mustn't leave them out." She glanced at Max.

"Yes, here's our Rommel man." Cunningham offered Speigner his hand, appraising the American with interest. "What is old Rommel up to, these days?"

Max could feel their eyes on him. He heard someone whisper, "El Khireigat." Anna also looked up in anticipation. People in high places enjoyed a brilliant, concentrated ability to coin the memorable phrase. Here was the moment, yet Max did not feel equal to it.

"He's at Tobruk, driving his artillerists crazy with round-the-clock inspections, sir," he said.

"And his panzers?" said the general.

"Hedgehogged at Sidi Omar." Speigner relaxed. "But Rommel rarely does the expected."

"Well then, what's Rommel reading these days, Civil War tactics?" The general's voice was hoarse.

"I gave him a book once," Speigner said.

"Oh, what was that?"

"*The Sound and the Fury*, by William Faulkner."

"Faulkner? Faulkner? Not familiar with the name." Cunningham inclined his head toward his aide. The colonel whispered an explanation.

"Novels, eh?" the general dryly observed. "Rommel will have plenty of time for novels in P.O.W. camp, won't he! Leftenant, glad to have you up! Come along later and let us know if you get any mysterious signals from Tobruk. It's all one and the same, you know. One and the same."

A dismissal had been given, and the guests withdrew. Max continued to study Cunningham. He liked the general's confident manner, his immaculate desert uniform, the way he stood erect as a sapling. Cunningham reminded him of Major Shoemaker: the sensitive eyes framed by dark eyebrows, firm mouth under a graying mustache, lines of fierce concentration, a man who gave the impression of being a listener and a learner as well as a man of decisive action. Here was a general worthy of Rommel.

But he looks tired.

An adjutant rapped on a table, calling for attention. Lieutenant General Alan Cunningham, C.B., K.C.B., D.S.O., M.C., stood before them.

"Crusader," said the general. "An historic name for an historic battle. Eighth Army is in position, and tomorrow, November Eighteen, Crusader will begin. We estimate that our forces will have numerical superiority of four to three over the Germans and Italians combined, and two to one over the Germans alone, which is the more important ratio. I have talked with our tank commanders, and I can tell you they are ready and eager for the battle." An aide produced a map on a portable stand.

"Our enemy is concentrating his forces for an attack on Tobruk, here." Cunningham jabbed a stiff finger at the map. "He thus is in a dilemma. Should he turn and fight us coming up in his rear and leave off attacking the fort? It becomes a two-front battle for him. We know his defensive dispositions. His forward defense line stretches from Bardia to Sidi Omar, heavily mined, manned by the Italian Savona Division and German antitank units. At Bir el Gubi, here, the Ariete Division is dug in to threaten the flank of our march on Tobruk.

"Relief of Tobruk is our primary objective, of course, but it is of paramount importance to seek and find Rommel's armor and win a decisive tank battle. Thirtieth Corps, under the command of Willoughby Norrie, will lead in this respect. And we hope to engage Rommel's three armored brigades here, at Gabr Saleh. Thirteenth Corps, under Godwin-Austen, will envelop the frontier defenses in a holding action until the tank battle has been won, then push through the Sollum-Omar line and on to Tobruk."

Cunningham sketched the broad outlines of the campaign, speaking in a voice rusty with fatigue but full of determination. Max could scarcely conceive of the staggering logistics of moving 100,000 men and 2,500 machines to the edge of battle. He sensed the armada poised across the desert—ammunition racks heavy with shells, fuel tanks topped off, extra water cans, food and gear strapped on the hulls of tanks and armored cars. Men squinted into the dust and waited for the final command. Max glanced at the fair, windburned faces around him. There was an unholy calm about these men, yet also a smell of adrenaline compounded of sweat, tobacco, brass, leather, hair oil, and gasoline. A sweet scent rose above the man-smell, a fragrance of civilization. Anna stood on tiptoe beside him, trying to see Cunningham over the shoulders of the men in front of her. She felt his eyes and turned her face up to him with an impish grin.

Cunningham finished his briefing. He paused, then said with quiet deliberation, "I am going to seek old Rommel out and destroy him and his armor." Spontaneous applause broke out, but at the same time there was a rumble, a predatory growl, of thunder. The soldiers glanced at the rain clouds visible under the eaves of the awning. They could smell the rain coming. The storm had swept down from the Mediterranean while no one was looking. Having steeled themselves against the concussion of exploding shells and whine of bullets, they were taken unawares of a rainstorm in the desert.

It was not coping with rain and thunder and mud that affected their spirits so much as the fact that nature seemed to be conspiring against them. The thunder was like the advance artillery barrage of a German raid, as if Rommel's Afrika Korps were out there lying on the clay dunes or snaking unscathed through the camel thorn, as if at Rommel's command a jagged spear of lightning split the heavens and a cataract of thunder burst on the Eighth Army.

Someone had turned on a radio, and the men milling about, uncertain whether to make a dash for their tents, stopped to listen. Amid the thunder and the pop of static, Winston Churchill came on the BBC to address them. Whatever a man's commitment or perspective, the familiar voice reached out to him. They listened motionless, faces pale in the lightning or momentarily illuminated by the glow of a cigarette lighter cupped against the wind. The voice rolled to a conclusion:

For the first time British and Empire troops will meet the Germans with an ample supply of equipment in modern weapons of all kinds. The battle itself will affect the whole course of the war. Now is the time to strike the hardest blow yet struck for final victory, home and freedom. The Desert Army may add a page to history which will rank with Blenheim and Waterloo. The eyes of all nations are upon you. All our hearts are with you. May God uphold the right!

The first heavy, pelting drops exploded in the sand. The Desert Rats turned up their collars, pulled their caps on tight, said their good nights, and walked briskly out of the fort with shoulders hunched against the rivers of lightning flooding the sky. Max and Anna were among the last to leave the tent. Bright-Ashton had disappeared into the rain ahead of them. Max noticed a pint bottle of scotch someone had left behind on a folding chair. He slipped it into his pocket.

"Churchill made some patriot forget his whisky," he said. "How about a nightcap?"

She grinned out from under her jacket, which she had pulled over her head. "Your tent or mine?"

"We have some tin cups in our mess kits," he said.

They ran through a barrage of thunder, ducking to make as small a target as possible for the raindrops. Max became quite lost among the city of dark tents, and Anna alertly led the way to her tent. She had an unerring instinct, guiding them down a broad boulevard, up a side street, down an alley and, finally, inside the flap of a shoulder-high tent. Max half expected to find a liaison officer or another correspondent waiting for them, but they were alone, stooping and dripping. A cot took up most of the available space.

"Don't touch the inside of the ceiling," Max warned. "It will drip on you all night."

"Oh, I don't think it will rain all night," she said. "Let's enjoy the storm while it lasts. Help me turn the cot around so we can look out the flap on the leeward side."

She pulled back the flap. The rain overshot their window, giving them a cozy and unobstructed view of the storm. Anna found a piece of a candle among her things. Max stuck it in an empty bottle and lit it. They sat on the hard cot. Anna wrapped herself in her jacket and pulled her feet up under her. Without a cup, they passed the bottle of scotch between them. A skeleton of lightning bared its bones. They sipped the fiery whisky and waited for the thunder. Water dripped in puddles under the sides of the tent.

"I'm glad you're here," Max said. "You look great!"

"What!" She shook her hair, and flying droplets made the candle fizz. "My hair is gray with sand. And I'm wearing these borrowed fatigues because I've run out of clean clothes. One of the true horrors of war is that one never has a clean thing to wear. I'm down to one pair of stockings and must wash them every night and hang them out to dry, but there's no water to wash with, out here." An idea dawned on her. She unfolded her legs in a lithe movement. She dug in her suitcase and found her stockings. She reached out into the rain and knotted the nylons over the guy rope of the tent. "There. Let nature do my laundry."

"Doing your wash at a time like this?" Max wore a whisky grin. "That reminds me—a woman's place is in the home . . ."

". . . baking cookies with a baby on her hip?" She grabbed the bottle of scotch out of his hand with an ironic grimace.

"There's a saying in Mississippi: 'Keep your woman pregnant in the summer and barefoot in the winter.'" Anna punched him in the arm and his face grew solemn in the candle glow. "I think you are very brave to come to the front."

"Not brave at all! There are women doctors and nurses right now this instant enduring danger and hardships on the open seas, in the convoys. What I do is nothing compared to them."

"Still, you're the only woman here with the Eighth Army. That says a lot about you."

"Understand me!" She turned to face him, her body curled up like a girl's. "I am doing very little—with my typewriter—to join the fight. If I can play a small part in helping our side win the war, I will go anywhere, do anything that is asked of me. I do not know the first thing about writing a dispatch, you know. I asked the 'real' correspondents how one goes about it."

"Anna McAlpin." Max raised the bottle. "I salute you. Here's to your first dispatch."

"Oh, I've already filed my first one," she said dryly. "It was about you."

He paused in the act of swallowing. The liquor burned his throat. He wiped his mouth with the back of his hand. Rain pattered steadily over the sides of the tent.

"What was it about?"

"Oh, an American lieutenant whom the British invited to Egypt as a sort of Lend-Lease Rommel-catcher."

"You didn't say that!" Max straightened up and the cot rocked precariously.

"No, don't worry. I simply sketched out your story, about the brilliant memo you wrote in 1940, before the invasion of France . . ."

"Not so brilliant." The candlelight felt hot on his face.

". . . and how the British were interested in it and in your having met Rommel during his trip to America. And how you are also an expert on the American Civil War . . ."

"No, not an 'expert'!"

". . . and how you have a theory about some kind of connection between Rommel and the Confederate general Bedford Forrest. And about the German raid on the supply dump which you foiled . . ."

"Not by myself! I shouldn't get the credit."

". . . and of course how you have become a kind of pet of the British brass—and I wanted to use our discussion that night at the pyramids, but it was not strictly a part of the story."

"Colonel Fellers is going to go through the roof," he said, thinking out loud. "I'm supposed to be staying in the background. When will it be published?" He saw her face grow solemn as she appreciated the possibility that her article could get him sent home. Lightning flared, and thunder came from a long way off.

"I don't know," she said. "Soon, perhaps."

"In the New York *Daily News and* the London *Times?*"

"I suppose . . . I thought you would be glad."

From a nearby tent came raucous male voices singing about the Afrika Korps to the tune of *She'll Be Comin' Round the Mountain:*

They'll be comin' through Qattara when they come,
    When they come!
They'll be comin' through Qattara when they come,
    When they come . . .

"I just had to show off that night at the Sphinx, didn't I?"
He drank sparingly, realizing that he was getting a little drunk.

"I am sorry. I did not mean—oh, and also, in the dispatch,
I said that you consider Rommel to be your friend."

"Where did you get *that* idea?" He was stunned.

"You told me."

"I did not."

"Oh yes, but you did. About going motorcycle riding
together, about studing battlefields together, about the book
of Faulkner's you gave him, and how he signed his own book
to Faulkner for you, about drinking American whisky—
bourbon—and roaming a battlefield in the dead of night. You
shared time and adventures together, did you not? Perhaps
you did not state categorically that Rommel is your friend, but
everything you told me spoke of friendship. Tell me now, do
you deny it?" She was sitting cross-legged on the cot, facing
him with eyebrows raised. He could make no denial to an
interrogator who demanded the truth and paid in kind.

"Why do you hunt him if you respect him so?"

"To stop him."

"To destroy him?"

"To stop him from making war."

"To kill him?"

"To stop him."

"Max, I must tell you what I think: You are oversensitive,
you feel things deeply, and your feelings color your perceptions. You extend your senses to embrace all perspectives, and
you try to understand the other man's point of view. In time of
peace, that is the way of the artist or the scholar or even the
advertising copywriter, but we are at war. Do you think the
Nazis will try to meet you halfway? Or will they simply shoot
you? Their way is so simple and effective. And you, would you
shoot back? What would you fight for? Your life, your country?
You wear a uniform. Are you then a soldier? Don't you see, I
would have you protect *me*, to save me and my country, you
Americans!"

The candlelight was slightly behind her, and Max could not read her face masked by shadow.

"I want to stop him," he said defensively, "but why must I want to kill him to do it? He *is* an artist. The battle is his symphony. He has an artist's temperament. He can't *not* fight any more than Beethoven could keep his hands off a piano and a blank sheet of composition paper. He listens to the battle ebb and flow, raises his baton, and a new movement begins. . . ."

"Words!" Anna cried. "Such talk makes me so angry! Don't you know what the Germans are doing in France and Holland and Poland, putting people into camps, making war on the Jews? Out here, the desert is a great polo ground, where war is played by nice rules. Civilians are not caught in the middle, here. It is pure war in an arena that was made for the Rommels of this world and their 'symphonies'—soldier against soldier, machine against machine. They call it the last gentleman's war: Rommel telegrams Eighth Army headquarters requesting better treatment of German P.O.W.s, and Auchinleck agrees to 'do the right thing.' Compared to Europe, this place is a boys' playground! Your Rommel makes war seem palatable, a giant polo match with guns, in which men die cleanly and honorably, and their enemies stand at attention over their graves while the honor guard fires a salute. And because of Rommel, all the *rest* can go on. He makes people focus on him, and they forget about the women and children being killed. That's no fun, is it! How much more interesting to open your newspaper over a cup of coffee and see what 'Old Rommel' is up to, the wily fox, the rising star of the desert. It's fun and games. Deadly to its victims, no doubt, but after all, they *are* soldiers, and it's their duty to die for home and hearth." Her voice became so husky that she seemed to speak from the bottom of her lungs, the words torn from the center of her. "All your Rommel means to me is misery, and I want you to help make it *stop*."

Things between them had changed. She had challenged him in a way that made him confront himself at his core. He wanted to tell Anna that he would fight, that he was capable of fighting, and of killing, their common enemy. He was afraid, not so much of war or of killing or of death as of some central fact of human existence buried in his psyche. He struggled to find an answer but there were no words. She watched him with a sheepish grin as if apologizing to herself for him.

"You want me to be more than I am," he said at last.

"You are here. You must do what you can."

"I'm not what you've made me out to be."

"Then you must try."

XVIII

Rommel held the stiff salute while the bugle call echoed over a rocky hillside slick with rain. The clear, ringing notes and the sight of open graves forged another link in a chain of memories: all the military cemeteries, unpretentious and out of the way, in the lowlands of France, on mountain peaks in Italy, and now here, in Beda Littoria.

They will break your heart, these quiet places. The grass will not even grow on this slab of rock to form a decent covering for them. I will come back again, when everyone is gone. At the Bloody Pond, Faulkner quoted Forrest: "War means fighting, and fighting means killing." It is never so simple. Unless during the battle.

The honor guard presented arms. The four coffins were lowered into the graves, three for German soldiers killed in the abortive assassination attempt, the fourth for Major Geoffrey Keyes, who had led the raid. Impressed by the British commando leader's bravery and daring, Rommel had insisted that Keyes be buried with full military honors. As he stood at attention among his staff members and listened to the chaplain read the services for the dead, he was aware of his subordinates' attitude of mixed sorrow and relief. If his return flight from Rome had not been diverted to Athens due to bad weather the commandos might have found him at home, though their intelligence was way off the mark. He had long since moved his headquarters from the Prefettúra building at Beda Littoria, where the raid had occurred, to Gambut, fly-blown but at least free of assassins.

"If they had got me," he joked with Schmidt after the ceremony, "this funeral might have been better attended." Schmidt did not find it amusing. Rommel was entertained by the added thought that among the corps leaders of *Panzergruppe Afrika*—German as well as Italian—there were those who would not have missed him. The British had paid him the ultimate compliment. It was as if they were saying, "We cannot defeat Rommel on the battlefield and must try to get him any way we can."

We've not heard of any Soviet commandos trying to knock off Guderian.

As they returned to Gambut, soldiers along the road turned to stare and salute Rommel's speeding staff car flying its red and black command flags. Transport moving east in front of them was heavy as assault units moved into position for the attack on Tobruk. Rommel tried to ignore how few petrol or ammunition trucks there were among the artillery and armored units moving sluggishly up the Via Balbia. They were chronically short of stockpiles but the attack had to go forward.

At Gambut Rommel strode through the muddied entrance of his headquarters and went directly to his office. They were laying for him. He could tell it by their bland expressions concealing antagonism, dissembling, and obstinacy. All his division commanders had begun to look alike to him— Ravenstein, von Mellenthin, Cruewall, Summermann, Bayerlein. They stood grouped together on one side of the map table with the model of Tobruk. Mellenthin held a folder prominently before him. Rommel guessed that it would contain more aerial photographs. He moved to the opposite side of the table, took off his hat, and casually tossed it on top of the cardboard and plaster model of the fortress. His generals stared at the hat as if it had become a military objective. They spread out around the table in simultaneous flanking movements.

"Well?" said Rommel. Their eyes slid sideways at von Mellenthin. The chief intelligence officer cleared his throat optimistically.

"Herr General," Mellenthin began, "my staff has been receiving hourly requests from our field units to the east and southeast to be informed as to the possibility of an enemy attack from those sectors. Allow me to present evidence of the British buildup."

He laid a photograph on the corner of the table nearest to Rommel so that he could glance down and examine it if he chose. Rommel kept his eyes fixed on Mellenthin's face.

"This photograph was presented to me personally," Mellenthin added, "by Colonel Augustin—chief Luftwaffe reconnaissance officer."

Why the citing of sources? Why the need for certification?

"It shows a new British airfield constructed south of the Qattara Depression. Over 100 aircraft have been counted there. These are aerial photos of a military railroad being built from Mersa Matruh toward the frontier wire. This is a radio intercept report, dated November 17, indicating a South African division moving southwest from Mersa Matruh into the desert. And today, the enemy suddenly commenced radio silence." Mellenthin concluded, "Since *Panzergruppe* headquarters has not issued an alert for British attack, our forward units rather routinely reported this radio silence."

They watched him expectantly. Rommel lowered his eyes to the fort with his hat on it and cautioned himself to be patient.

They think I am obsessed with Tobruk because I failed to conquer it the first time out. They think it is mainly a matter of pride, and that my "obsession" causes me to ignore reports of a British buildup. It is immaterial what they think of me, as long as they obey my orders; but it is imperative that they not allow caution to divert us from our true objective.

General Cruewell shifted his weight with the heavy deliberation of a Mark IV turret turning. "Wechmar reports," said the Afrika Korps commander, "that his Thirty-Third battalion ran into enemy reconnaissance in force as early as ten-thirty this morning." When Rommel did not reply, Cruewell added gloomily, "At 5 P.M. this afternoon, the third recce battalion was attacked by as many as two hundred armored vehicles."

Cruewell was staid and self-possessed. Rommel resented Cruewell's equanimity which he felt derived in large part from Cruewell's personal fortune. Cruewell was from Dortmund, where his family owned a printing company with a monopoly on Protestant hymnbook publishing.

I protest.

"I know the British are building up their forces," Rommel said at last, forcing a conciliatory tone; "of course, they are continually building up for an assault. But we must take Tobruk *before* they attack from Egypt in order to avoid a simultaneous, coordinated breakout through our siege line. A combined two-front attack could trap our fighting units between Tobruk and Sollum and drive them into the sea. We naturally will expect the British to stage some kind of relief attack in the rear of our assault force at Tobruk. Sufficient motorized units will be deployed between Capuzzo and Bir el Gubi to defend against this possibility. The Twenty-First Panzer and the Ariete divisions should be more than enough for that purpose. We must not divert emphasis from where it belongs: *Tobruk*."

"I refuse to stand idly by and watch the enemy advance unmolested on Tobruk," Cruewell growled.

"We mustn't lose our nerve!" The thin veneer of Rommel's patience dissolved in the heat of his anger.

If it ain't mosquitoes, it's something else. Bedbugs and Cruewell.

"Herr General," Bayerlein interjected, "Fifteenth Panzer informs Afrika Korps that British attack intentions are possible in the south." Bayerlein was Cruewell's chief of staff. Rommel refused to acknowledge his remark. Ravenstein now made his move.

"I propose that my regiment move south to Gabr Saleh to guard the southern flank." Ravenstein glanced at Cruewell for support.

Aristocrats always stick together.

"Let us remember," Rommel said stiffly, "that 'Midsummer Night's Dream' showed that the enemy needed much more time to build up his forces. I do not believe he will attack us yet." He almost smiled to see the wind going out of Ravenstein's sails. It was his 5th Panzer Regiment that had captured the South African orderly truck with the Eighth Army order of battle. Now they came at him from all sides like a swollen stream breaking through a dam, attempting to erode his conviction. Rommel stood fast, deaf to their entreaties. He raised his finger for silence.

"We must not show our hand to the enemy too soon," he said. By way of dismissal, he left the room.

War by committee stinks.

Rommel went outside and circled the building, pulling his cap tight against the misting rain. Mud oozed over the toes of his desert boots. If the British did try to mount a major attack, they had picked a bad time for it. The weather, however, would also ground the Luftwaffe. *Panzergruppe Afrika* would be forced to rely solely on motorized reconnaissance units and radio intercepts for intelligence reports. It couldn't be helped. Once he heard Boetticher's artillery open up against Tobruk, everything would be all right. He had concentrated a powerful siege train under Boetticher's Artillery Command 104: nine 210-mm. howitzers, 38 150-mm., and 12 105-mm. Rommel was looking forward to deploying the 104's guns personally.

He heard automobile and armored half-track engines start up on the other side of the building. The generals were leaving. He would give them another minute to clear out and let him get back to work. His fingers strayed to the pocket of his tunic. He got out the newspaper clipping and turned his back to the rain to keep it dry as he read it for the fourth time. Someone in the German embassy in Lisbon had noticed the piece in the London *Times* and had sent it to him by diplomatic pouch.

YANK DIRECTS AMBUSH
OF AFRIKA KORPS
by
Anna McAlpin

The Yanks have landed in North Africa.

At least, they have arrived in the person of one Lt. Maxwell Speigner, U.S. Army Intelligence. Speigner enjoys the unique distinction of having met Erwin Rommel in America before the War. Rommel was then a colonel and was traveling with a small group of German general staff officers studying Civil War battlefields. According to Speigner, Rommel showed an especial interest in the flamboyant Confederate cavalryman, Gen. Nathan Bedford Forrest, sometimes called "The Wizard of the Saddle." Lt. Speigner escorted the German visitors to the battlefields of Brice's Crossroads and Shiloh.

It was Rommel's interest in Forrest which, strangely enough, brought Speigner to North Africa. A memo by Speigner predicting Rommel's tactics during the German invasion of France in 1940 received belated attention from British intelligence. By comparing Rommel to Forrest, Speigner was able to forecast many of the actual tactics and maneuvers Rommel used in the German march to the Channel. Subsequently, Speigner was invited to Cairo as a military observer and lecturer.

The American had an immediate effect on the war in the Western Desert, as his advice to prepare for a surprise German raid on forward supply dumps along the Egyptian-Libyan frontier proved accurate. On Sept. 14 just such a raid occurred, and RAF fighters successfully bombed and strafed a panzer division in the act of loading captured British materiel. The German force was beaten off with losses of several tanks, trucks, and men wounded or captured.

The ambush was the first in which Rommel's Afrika Korps has been foiled, and no doubt resulted in a good deal of embarrassment for the Desert Fox with a corresponding boost in the morale of the Western Desert forces.

It is one of the odd coincidences of war that the paths of two soldiers who met in a neutral country— one which is not at war, yet—have thus crossed again. Lt. Speigner is currently the toast of Cairo society and continues to aid British intelligence with his expert information on Rommel.

One cannot help observing that perhaps Nathan Bedford Forrest is not the only wizard in American military history.

The reconnaissance aircraft, that day at the wire, September 14. Speigner. The article credited Speigner with having "foiled" the raid. Sheer propaganda. The British would never allow an American lieutenant such authority. And yet . . .

* * *

As their plane taxied to the runway for takeoff, Max saw a ground-control officer running beside the moving aircraft, frantically signaling to the pilot. Max asked Bright-Ashton what was going on.

"Wheels picked up too much mud," John explained. Max was impressed by the major's ability to comprehend the situation. "Scraping off the excess before we're allowed to take off."

The narrow Blenheim bomber shuddered as its engines revved for takeoff. Max and Bright-Ashton sat in the rear of improvised seating in the bomb bay of the Eighth Army Headquarters staff plane. In the forward compartment Cunningham and his senior officers sat in more comfortable seats. They were flying to General Norrie's XXX Corps headquarters. Max had hoped to be allowed to travel with the press corps— and Anna—to an observation point near the front lines once the main battle had begun, but his assignment was to stay with Eighth Army HQ. "*Here's* where the action is!" John had exclaimed, amazed that Max would consider wandering around the desert.

Speigner had left McAlpin after an unsatisfactory goodbye in front of the Press and Censors tent with confused promises to meet somewhere, sometime, on the battlefield or at Fort Maddalena. Back with Cunningham's staff, Max had spent the morning watching unending columns of machines crawl westward into Libya. The most exciting event of the day so far had been a football match in the camel thorn between the South Africans and the Indians. British lorry drivers cheered while their column halted for refueling. Everywhere Max looked, soldiers gathered in small groups near vehicles and brewed tea. Their kettles were suspended over fires built in cans holding gasoline-soaked sand. The Eighth Army Operations caravan had been equally quiet. Cunningham's staff made a great fuss over decoding a routine radio transmission, especially when the general himself was nearby to see them doing something. So far there had been no news from Gabr Saleh. The armored car screen in advance of XXX Corps tank columns reported no contact with the enemy. All day nobody at Eighth Army HQ had dared to ask the question that was on everyone's mind: *where were the Germans?*

The Blenheim's engine vibrations rolled in waves as it slithered in a lingering takeoff over the muddy desert. Airborne, Max watched the brown earth come alive with crawling things that seemed to have come from nowhere, like creatures which came out of their holes when it rained. In less than fifteen minutes the Blenheim began its descent. At XXX Corps HQ Cunningham was received like a tribal chieftain by Norrie and his staff. There was a flurry of saluting and hand shaking. In the confusion of men, vehicles, and tents Bright-Ashton seemed to know where he and Max belonged. They spent the morning sitting on the running board of an orderly room truck, drinking tea. Nearby, XXX Corp HQ tent hummed like a beehive. Men came and went on unknown errands. Max imagined Cunningham and Norrie as co-regent queen bees, wings folded and wary, radiating perpetual heat at the inner core of the hive. For his part, Speigner was content to remain quietly in the shadows of the caravan, where he listened to sergeants trading tins of bully beef for canned puddings, tea packets for cigarettes. Tea was constantly being brewed all around them. Soldiers wrote letters home or shaved while looking into a lorry's rearview mirror. Each of them, however, seemed to have invisible antennae tuned to receive signals from the pulsating center.

Not equipped with such natural apparatus, Max was tying his shoe when an orderly appeared at his shoulder bearing a request for him to report to headquarters. Max looked to Bright-Ashton for advice.

"You're on your own," the major said. "I'm not a privileged character like you."

Max eased inside the Battle Control tent. No one paid him the slightest attention. He found an empty corner and stood with his hands clasped behind him, feeling foolish. The hive was, as he had imagined, a controlled dynamo of radio operators, decoders, and intelligence officers studying maps spread on a makeshift table cluttered with teacups. Cigarette butts littered the sand floor. At the center of the buzzing drones the king bee leaned solemnly over the maps. Norrie hovered beside him. Gradually Max began to feel less self-conscious, extended his own antennae, and listened to the generals arguing.

"It's a great waste," said Norrie, who was built like a bear,

with jowly cheeks and a no-nonsense jaw, "to let Fourth
Armored go over to Thirteenth Corps. If the Fifteenth and
Twenty-First Panzer come at the Seventh Brigade at once
. . . Why can't Thirtieth Corps, intact at Gabr Saleh, serve as
a sufficient flank guard for Thirteenth Corps?" Cunningham
did not look up from the map table. His chief of staff,
Brigadier-General Galloway, nervously eyed Cunningham
askance.

"Gabr Saleh means less than nothing to Rommel," Norrie
persisted. "Why should he come at us there? The only way to
force his hand is to have a go at Tobruk. Thirtieth Corps should
drive north straightaway."

"Give it time." Cunningham spoke in a thin rasp. "We
must protect the infantry. When it becomes clear that Thirteenth Corps is not threatened, then we can decide in what
direction to move."

"Exactly," Norrie fumed. "'In what direction.' Whoever
heard of forcing a decisive armored engagement by sitting and
waiting?" Cunningham looked up warily. Norrie added, "The
situation hardly lifts one's spirits, does it?"

Norrie's casual mention of Rommel put it all into perspective for Max. It was a game played by generals. He wished he
could be a similar fly on the wall at *Panzergruppe* headquarters
but, on reflection, decided that Rommel would not be there
leaning over a map table. He would be in the saddle roaming
the German positions around Tobruk, perhaps directing an
artillery bombardment. Or perhaps he was stalking the Eighth
Army across the trackless desert. Why had he waited? Why
had he not attacked, as the British had hoped? Speigner tried
to picture what Rommel was like now, after four years of war,
of success, of nearly unlimited power. How impatient he
would be with failure—above all, with his own failure at
Tobruk seven months before. He remembered only a smiling
Rommel leaning on crutches beside the Confederate statue in
Oxford, Mississippi, lips purple with blackberry juice; or his
unaffected grin when they waved goodbye at Memphis
Airport. Now he was only hours away, somewhere out there
where thousands of soldiers waited in armored vehicles for
battle. If Cunningham's headquarters was a beehive, Rommel's
command post—the hard seat of a racing half-track—was a
white flame blistering the desert.

"Leftenant Speigner?"

Cunningham was speaking to him. A number of faces—it seemed every face in the tent—had turned toward him. The general had obviously been obliged to repeat himself. He flushed and met Cunningham's intense gaze.

"Are you with us, Leftenant?" The Eighth Army commander was smiling.

Speigner report for comic relief.

"I trust you have been busy divining what Rommel's up to out there." Cunningham's smile faded as a chain-smoking aide near him lit another cigarette. "Do you mind?" the general said. The aide dropped the offending cigarette and ground it out with his heel. Max remembered Bright-Ashton saying, "Cunningham is frightfully tense these days. He's had to give up smoking. Doctor said smoke irritated his eyes. Experiencing nicotine withdrawal."

He screwed up his courage. "I agree with General Norrie, sir. I think Rommel is at Tobruk, waiting to see what we . . . you will do next." Cunningham frowned and turned back to the map table.

"What do you think he'd like for us to do?" His question, delivered without looking at Speigner, had the attention of all.

"His favorite tactic is divide and conquer," Max replied. "If he can get the bulge on you, he'll try to split your forces and whip each half at a time." He saw Norrie's bearlike head nod in agreement. Cunningham did not react. He seemed relieved when the radio operator called him to the console to take a call. The general gingerly put on the headset and held the microphone before him as if it were an ice-cream cone.

"Very well," he spoke into it as if it were an ordinary telephone. "I said—hello? Do you receive me? What's the matter with this gadget!" The general's face flushed. It was obvious he did not know how to use the equipment. His staff tried not to watch as the radio operator showed him how to depress the button on the microphone when sending, and to say "over" when his message was concluded. The unspoken question on everyone's mind: if the general is unfamiliar with the use of standard equipment, how can he successfully lead an army in mechanized warfare under adverse conditions?

The hive resumed humming. Field commanders reported, took orders back to their units, or—curious like the rest—poked around, adding to the illusion of activity inside the tent. No one spoke to Max again. After a while he slipped out of the tent and made his way through the caravan of vehicles to the adjutant's truck. Bright-Ashton was in a fever to find out what Max had heard at Battle Control.

"That's all right," he said when Max related what had happened. "Acquitted yourself admirably. Not your fault the old bugger can't take criticism. Now, however, I think we may have become rather a pair of orphans up here."

For the rest of the day they kept abreast of events like other men watching Command Center from a distance: by gossip and rumor. Max learned from a lorry driver that the following day's orders had been issued. All units were to secure assigned battle positions and reconnoiter in strength toward Trigh Capuzzo and Bir el Gubi. In other words, as Bright-Ashton observed, nothing new was happening. Throughout the evening and all the next day, Max's concerns grew simple. He learned how to scrounge a cup of precious water with which to brush his teeth, wash, and shave—and then to bathe his socks and shorts in the soapy liquid remaining. He found where he and Bright-Ashton could count on a cup of tea at any hour. He grew adept at ritual barter. Men established goodwill by swapping cigarettes or candy or food along with information, all with an intense politeness which exceeded even that of Mississippi society.

The afternoon of November 19, he learned that the first real battle had taken place. The 22nd Armored Brigade had engaged Italian tanks near Bir el Gubi and had gone on to attack the Ariete Division in full strength. The South Africans had been beaten off with a loss of fifty-two tanks.

"Those territorial troops have only been a month in Egypt," Bright-Ashton complained. "Imagine making a charge like that on a strong, well-dug-in antitank battalion! What did they expect?"

Max later ascertained that Cunningham's forces had become widely dispersed: one armored brigade, the 22nd, had been defeated and was licking its wounds to the west; another, the 7th, had pushed north into the Sidi Rezegh area and was dangerously exposed on three sides; a third, 4th Brigade, remained inactive at its original position to the south at Gabr Saleh, waiting for the Germans to attack.

This is made to order for Rommel. He's just beginning to

turn his face from Tobruk and is seeing the British hovering like a swarm of mosquitoes at his back.

The German attack came on the twentieth in late afternoon. John interrupted Max's sixth tea of the day and related the news: "The Fifteenth Panzer Division attacked at Gabr Saleh, as Cunningham had hoped they would. However, instead of waiting for them with three armored brigades, Cunningham had only one brigade in position, the Fourth, with 120-odd Honey tanks. The Fourth Brigade was driven back. The Germans characteristically camped on the battlefield. At this point, Cunningham's wireless broke down, and he is flying back to Fort Maddalena with his staff. Max, old boy, we have suddenly become unassigned."

Speigner felt relief and frustration. Having followed the events of the battle from a distance, like watching a championship chess match from the back row of an auditorium, his interest had been whetted. He wanted to creep closer to the front now. All morning of the twenty-first he provoked and cajoled Bright-Ashton to find a way for them to travel to the forward observation area, where Anna had gone, near the wire at Sidi Omar some twenty-five kilometers east of Gabr Saleh. In early afternoon a solution presented itself when a recce patrol arrived in a half-track. Max traded cigarettes and chocolate with the driver and learned that there were two empty seats in the vehicle.

The half-track headed north along the wire at 4 P.M. Speigner and Bright-Ashton sat next to the steel tailgate, which rattled like a machine gun. Max did not notice the hard seat or the choking grit. He was going to the front.

XIX

Rommel stood alone on the northern escarpment. Covered with dust from head to foot, he looked like a human outcropping. The lines of his face were etched like chisel marks in stone. In the distance, spilling in an avalanche of winking light into the black Mediterranean, was Tobruk. Red flashes of artillery and yellow tracers pierced the smoke haze which hovered above the city like fierce and possessive ghosts.

Cruewell was out of gas. The Afrika Korps had stalled out somewhere near Sidi Omar in pursuit of scattered British units. They had not encountered the 7th Armored Division as had been hoped, although Oberst Stephan had led elements of 21st Panzer in a successful battle against 4th Armored Brigade at Gabr Saleh. It was inconceivable that, having mounted a major offensive—as was now clearly evident—the British would split their forces in this manner. Not until the previous night, when he had listened to an open news broadcast from the BBC, had Rommel accepted the fact that the British were beginning a major campaign. The bulletin had been succinct:

> Eighth Army, with about 75,000 men excellently
> armed and equipped, has started a general offensive
> in the Western Desert with the aim of destroying the
> German-Italian forces in Africa.

So they were coming. Earlier than he had expected. He had put too much stock in "Midsummer Night's Dream" and the captured South African orderly room truck. Had the British set him up? He had thought so all along.

"Herr General, headquarters requests that you return to Gambut immediately. You are needed for . . ."

Rommel waved away the signals officer hovering at his elbow. Headquarters could wait. He had come to the front lines to get a feel for the battle that was forming. Raising his glasses, he saw what he had been looking for. An angry cloud of dust, like a running sore on the earth, was pushing out from the perimeter of Tobruk's defense network. The 70th Brigade was breaking out in an attempt to form a salient. The garrison's sally port appeared to be some 4,000 yards wide and deep and was directed at El Duda, four miles northwest of the ridge above Sidi Rezegh airfield. Rommel could see a thin line of Mark IIIs running before the breakout forces. *Panzers in retreat*. He turned abruptly to the signals officer.

"Find me some eighty-eights!" he snapped. "I want the nearest antitank company here on the double-quick." The subordinate did not flinch at Rommel's abrasive tone but moved like a well-oiled machine to obey the order.

While he waited for the antitank unit, Rommel searched the terrain below for a logical spot to lay a barrage. He made a rough estimate of the point where the salient would come within effective range of the 88s, about 11,000 meters. The signals officer reported that an antitank company was on the way and that the recce wireless operator was intercepting British transmissions, as tank commanders broke radio silence in the heat of battle. Rommel went to the wireless truck. Listening to intermittent bursts of English conversation, he guessed that the attack on the airfield to the south was the other half of a pincer movement closing with the garrison breakout. Instinct told him that he had to make a stand and seal off the salient before the enemy forces made contact, or the Afrika Korps would have its work cut out to dislodge them.

In spite of his concern he felt a growing strength, an exalted state of alertness in which he was able to forget everything and concentrate on the single task before him. It was like being granted a reprieve from his larger responsibility. Towed behind half-tracks, twelve 88s bounced and swayed regally up the ridge like princes in chariots of steel. Rommel sent a motorcycle courier screaming down the escarpment to alert the regimental commander fighting a holding action against the breakout to assign them a forward observer and to exchange battle frequencies and code names. Rommel had chosen the name Wolf One for his gunnery command post, while the observer would answer to Hawk. He noted with satisfaction the efficiency with which the antitank crews sprang into action, unloading and positioning the 88s, anchoring them and stacking the shells. The company commander approached with an importunate salute.

"I wish to point out, Herr General," the captain complained, "that we have no infantry support. This close to the front we—"

Captain Morton, artillery was meant to be taken.

"What is your name, *Hauptmann?*" Rommel interrupted. "Dietrich."

"Don't worry, Dietrich. The only question that should interest you, as it does interest me, is: how accurate are your gunners?" He watched Dietrich wrap his mind around the thought, eyes dark with resolve. The wireless tapped out a coded message from their forward observer.

"Wolf One, this is Hawk. Four targets in Sector Five-A: three Matildas and an armored troop carrier. Fire for adjustment. Over."

It had begun.

Arriving at *Panzergruppe* headquarters several hours later was like crossing a burning field and entering a barnyard filled with stampeding animals alarmed by the smoke. Rommel found his staff hurrying in and out of the Casa Bianca, transferring files and maps to a wireless armored command vehicle nosed snugly up to the front door. Oberst Siegfried Westphal, whom Rommel had temporarily placed in charge of HQ staff, paused to explain.

"New Zealand Division is moving west in heavy numbers," he panted, slightly out of breath from carrying boxes under each arm. "We're moving to El Adem." He shifted his eyes. "Just in case."

Rommel looked at Westphal's intelligent face with its prematurely receding hairline and long nose. He trusted Westphal's judgment, even if the colonel tended to act on his own initiative. He was reminded of a remark attributed to Percy Hobart, the father of British armor: "The secret of success in the Army is to be sufficiently insubordinate, and the key word is *sufficiently*." Westphal reminded him of himself.

"I should have waited for you to approve the move to El Adem," Westphal was saying, "but we had trouble locating you at the front, which reminds me that Cruewell and Ravenstein have repeatedly requested that HQ stay in direct contact with you at all times. Do you think it would be possible—"

"No I do not," Rommel said irritably. His generals would tether him to HQ with an umbilical cord of regulations until it reached its natural conclusion: slow strangulation. "Move HQ wherever you like, but don't expect me to sit and tap my fingers waiting for reports from the field. Now that I'm here, however, have Cruewell and Ravenstein stand by to receive further orders, and then bring me up to date on what happened this afternoon." He stalked inside the building, leaving Westphal to retrieve maps and files already packed inside the armored car. The colonel's long-suffering expression became one of blank efficiency as he reentered Casa Bianca.

While Westphal smoothed out a large map of eastern Libya, Schmidt appeared with a cup of hot chocolate. Rommel absently sipped the bracing liquid. He could not remember whether he had eaten or drunk anything in the past twenty-four hours. Westphal stuck numbered pins in the map, indicating the last-known positions of German, Italian, and enemy units. The situation defied description. If Rommel had carefully designed such maneuvers to simulate battlefield chaos, no one would have taken it seriously. *Panzergruppe* and Eighth Army units were layered across the desert like stratified crusts in a Greek pastry: the top layer was the Tobruk garrison to the north, bounded by a semicircle siege line of the 90th Light and Italian infantry, which had been attacked below the Sidi Rezegh escarpment by 7th Armored Brigade, which had turned to confront the Afrika Korps, which had swung north away from 30th Corps, leaving the Ariete Division to fight 1st South African at Bir el Gubi and the Savona Division to repulse XIII Corps near the wire at Sidi Omar; meanwhile, New Zealand Division was striking west along the northern escarpment plateau.

Yet it was a situation made to order for Rommel. Unlike the careful, plodding Eighth Army, the Afrika Korps had been schooled in his favorite lesson: no battle plan could accommodate every combat condition, therefore one went into battle armed with superior weapons and training and the willingness to improvise. All plans were meant to be abandoned in the heat of battle, if necessary. If such was chaos, then this was his element. He drank his hot chocolate and studied the wild assortment of pins in the map. Inevitably a pattern emerged like escarpments evolving, pushing up plateaus and creating depressions, as though the earth itself were bending to his will.

"Ravenstein must attack from the west side of the airfield." His conviction riveted Westphal beside him. "Five Panzer will make a wide turning movement to the north. We'll borrow Boetticher's heavy artillery and turn them around from the seige to face south in support of the Twenty-First." Westphal glowed with appreciation. Rommel did not look at him. "I'm going back up there to observe." He meant: to the

Sidi Rezegh escarpment. "Advise Boetticher to begin his bombardment at 0530."

Away he rode in his open *Kübelwagen,* wrapped in a dusty greatcoat against the evening chill. He slept sitting up. At first light he was perched on the spare tire mounted on the front of his jeep, watching the battle begin. At first the British had the upper hand: 7th Armored Division attacked in concentrated fury, inflicting heavy casualties on the lorried infantry manning positions above the airfield. In his glasses Rommel saw a Mark II shot down by a direct hit with an armor-piercing shell. Flames shot twenty feet out of the turret, catapulting a body— the tank commander, or perhaps the loader—into the air. The dying man bounced and rolled like a moving torch off the blackening hull of the Mark II. Oil smoke followed the flames like an exhalation of agony. He lowered his glasses. He thought he heard the screams of the men trapped inside.

Then the pounding of Boetticher's big guns began to tell. Seventh Armored retreated in a raging hurricane of smoke and dust, leaving behind the charred remains of tanks, lorries, and half-tracks. Twenty-First Panzer, under Ravenstein, swept triumphantly in from the west. Sidi Rezegh airfield again belonged to *Panzergruppe.* Satisfied, Rommel turned his attention to the east. The 361st Afrika Regiment was desperately clinging to Point 175, a natural fortress created by a bend in the escarpment, against repeated charges by the New Zealanders. Earlier that day the 6th New Zealand Brigade had captured the Afrika Korps headquarters, which lay in their direct line of march. Luckily Cruewell was with his armor at the time, but most of his staff, documents, and HQ equipment had been lost. With his light escort of Mark IIs and fast armored cars borrowed from Baron von Wechmar's reconnaissance battalion, Rommel set out on the run, moving eastward parallel with Trigh Capuzzo. At one point his motorcycle scouts spotted an enemy support column several miles away, but they left it alone and made for Point 175. Engines laboring, they inched up the steep northern gap in the escarpment.

Rommel leaped out of his still-moving jeep. He was met by the regimental commander, who reported the situation. The 361st had only light tanks, Mark Is and IIs, which were no match for the heavier Shermans and Valentines of the 6th New

Zealand, and their heavy weapons company had 5.0-cm and 3.7-cm antitank guns which, though sturdy and serviceable, lacked the range and striking power of the 88s. The enemy had to be drawn within range of the smaller antitank weapons.

"Throw out an armored car screen," Rommel ordered without hesitation. "Make them commit to us with a hit-and-run flank attack and draw them in. Once they get their blood up, they'll keep coming. Then it's up to your gunners!"

When the attack came as predicted, he personally deployed the antitank guns—much as he had done the day before to blunt the Tobruk garrison salient. The New Zealanders struck in battalion strength in successive waves, but the 361st gunners performed splendidly. Rommel could not discern what motivated them more: survival instinct or the desire to impress him, but by nightfall they had inflicted heavy casualties and turned back the enemy. He went among the grimy, sweat-streaked gunners and shook their hands. He stood before their smoking-hot guns and looked down from the heights. Lorries hauling away the enemy wounded cast long shadows over the land. Enemy fire had diminished to lonely, defiant thumps of artillery. Silence haunted the battlefield.

Now is the time to advance.

He was flushed with a sudden fever to get back to his headquarters at El Adem, or wherever Westphal had moved it. He knew how to end the campaign with a single stroke. In his mind's eye a wheeling movement formed with the grace of a bird. He could not wait for his escort to mount up, and took off in an armored car ahead of them. He sat in the open turret as they rocked and bounced down the escarpment trail.

Night came in a rush. Stars began to appear, singly then in clusters, spreading from the east and suddenly, violently, conquering the sky. The air was cold and clear. The armored car meandered west among the myriad tracks of many vehicles. They drove without headlights at a steady 20 mph, navigating by starlight. To Rommel, the imprints of treads and tires took on a life of their own, crisscrossing busily as if making war on the sand. From the open turret he called down occasional instructions to the driver to avoid a pile of rocks or clump of thornbushes or to change to a smoother set of tracks while maintaining their due-west heading.

He began to notice dark spots on the horizon, dull lumps

under the sparkling sky. The spots came and went in the way of all mirages, then remained in view. He distinguished squat shapes of tanks like a herd of sleeping elephants, an armored battalion leaguered in a circle against night attack, gun snouts facing outward.

"They're ours," he called down to the driver and gunner inside the armored car. "You can tell by the looseness of the formation. Probably part of Fifth Panzer."

Real estate of the Reich.

Farther on, a glow lit up the western horizon. As they came closer they could see a light blazing openly like an amiable beacon. Rommel guessed it was a hospital company and it was: set up just south of Trigh Capuzzo and operating full blast. Within a mile of the hospital company, he could see figures entering tents and spilling light among previously invisible vehicles parked helter-skelter. The driver prudently changed course to avoid the hospital. He and the gunner had identified the vehicles as British.

"Let's check it out." Rommel was in a proprietorial mood. "They belong to us, now. Our units are leaguered all around. This is obviously a captured hospital company."

As if to support his theory, no one at the field hospital paid much attention to them when they parked the armored car nearby. Rommel instructed the driver and gunner to stay with the vehicle while he went inside a tent to see if any German soldiers were being tended. He noted that British officers lounging beside a staff car had been allowed to retain their side arms, an oversight that would have to be corrected.

Inside, doctors and orderlies moved among cots arranged in two rows with a single aisle in the middle. Rommel moved down the aisle with an alert, paternalistic air. His greatcoat was covered with dust and no insignia showed. He held his cap tucked under his arm. From the names on the charts tied to the cots he surmised that German soldiers were interspersed among the British patients. Otherwise it was impossible to distinguish between pale faces equal in pain. He felt a rush of humility at being in their presence.

There was something indomitable about a field hospital. On one hand there were the doctors and nurses quietly taking pulses, changing dressings, attaching plasma bottles to portable racks, wrapping limbs in gauze; on the other there were the wounded, intent on bearing their pain with dignity, smoking cigarettes, dictating letters home, attempting to shave. Here was the life force at its core, an indefatigable will which never failed to inspire Rommel. It permeated the air along with the ether and sulfur and rubbing alcohol.

A man with bandages over his eyes was moving his lips. Rommel could not determine whether he was trying to sing or pray or tell his life's story. Intent on the man's silent struggle, Rommel did not notice a doctor turn away from a cot and approach him.

"Welcome to our hospital, General," said the doctor. *"Witamy do szpital,"* he repeated, tucking a clipboard under his arm.

He thinks I am Polish?

Rommel's first impulse was to laugh it off. Instinct told him to play along. Above the medicinal odors he smelled a familiar stink. Sniffing, he realized it was himself. He had not had a sponge bath in—how long?—a week? An all-over bath, three weeks? No water, no time. Perhaps he *smelled* like a Polish general?

Man stinks the same stink, no matter where in time.

"Would you like me to show you our hospital?" The doctor spoke English slowly and distinctly.

"Thank you very much."

"This way." The doctor gestured for Rommel to accompany him on his rounds. They moved to the next cot. The patient stirred when the doctor felt his pulse. The soldier had been badly burned and was swathed in bandages. Rommel glanced at the man's chart, a single sheet of paper stapled to the wooden frame of the cot. His name was Heinrich, a panzergrenadier. Rommel noted with satisfaction that he had given only name, rank, and serial number, even if the hospital *was* under German control.

Rommel gazed over the doctor's shoulder with admiration. The panzergrenadier's lot was a hard one. He was continually exposed to physical danger as he moved outside the tanks in coordinated armor/infantry attack. His job was to destroy or capture enemy infantry after their trenches had been overrun by the charging panzers. He emerged, time after time, from the searing, choking dust of machines to face the bullets of a well-dug-in enemy. As an ex-infantryman converted to armor, Rommel held his grenadiers in the highest esteem. The young soldier grimaced, revealing strong white teeth with a gap in the center. At that moment Panzergrenadier Heinrich was the very soul of the Afrika Korps for Rommel, who compulsively edged closer to him as the doctor turned to the next wounded man. Heinrich's eyelids fluttered open. Rommel was reminded of his son, Manfred, waking disoriented from a nap. The panzergrenadier's eyes bulged in recognition. His face contorted with what Rommel perceived to be intense pain. Seeing the soldier's lips move, he leaned down to hear what he was saying.

"Herr General," Heinrich whispered in German. "You are in danger. You should not be here."

"I came to see how you are doing," Rommel replied cheerfully. Hearing German spoken, the doctor left the other patient's bed and came to listen. Heinrich motioned for Rommel to lean very close.

"Enemy hospital," he whispered. "You will be captured."

"Thank you." Rommel spoke English for the doctor's benefit. "We all wish the war to be over soon, and then you can go home." He muttered in German, "Don't worry."

He glanced at the exits. It was true that no German soldiers were on guard. Could the fighting units have overshot this support company in pursuit of enemy armor? Through an open flap he saw a guard wearing a New Zealand bush shirt and khaki shorts. A Sten gun leaned against a tent post. A lorry's mud flap bore the printed illustration of a Desert Rat. The grenadier's eyes burned with alarm.

"Where are you from, Heinrich?" he asked, attempting to speak German with a Polish accent.

"Adenau. Please do not waste time. The doctor is watching you!" The grenadier's eyes were haunted.

"Adenau. I think I have been there. Refresh my memory. Where is it?"

"Please, Herr General. Oh, near Koblenz. Only a village . . ."

Only a village! And how glad will you be to see it again? It glistens like a diamond in your dreams.

"The Rhineland must be very beautiful this time of year. In the hills the leaves have turned their most brilliant colors."

The grenadier's eyes grew moist. Rommel had made the soldier forget his pain for a moment. He felt extraordinarily pleased with himself.

This must be why I felt compelled to stop here.

"I hope to see it again, when the war is over," Heinrich said.

"For you, that will be very soon," Rommel replied. "Rest well, grenadier. You have earned it."

"Who can rest when his general is in danger?"

"Do not trouble yourself," Rommel said. "We will all come through this alive, God willing." The doctor smiled approvingly. Rommel was not afraid, but it seemed sensible to take precautions. He followed the doctor down the aisle, intending to duck out the nearest exit. He saw the goggle-eyed expressions of other German patients. His was too famous a face not to be recognized, insignia or no insignia. He looked at the narrow back of the doctor in front of him, expecting at any moment for him to turn with a dawning awareness. Rommel paused beside the cot of a British soldier whose chart identified him as a member of a support unit with Eighth Army HQ. The man was propped up in bed, smoking. He looked at Rommel with a distracted gaze as though seeing the unwounded move about like tropical fish in an aquarium, without context in his own tightly contained world of pain. The man's eyes were clear. Rommel impulsively spoke to him.

"Excuse me," he said, in English. "Would you know of an American lieutenant traveling with your staff headquarters?" He startled himself with the question, and he realized now why he had lingered at this hospital.

Speigner.

He had not put the American out of his mind after all. "Midsummer Night's Dream" had caused him not to take the British threat seriously. Now he was paying for it. Had Max been responsible? He had to know.

"American? You mean, a Yank?" The soldier spoke slowly through cracked lips.

"His name is Speigner," Rommel said. The doctor turned back to join them. His face lit up with understanding.

"I've heard of the chap." His chatty tone seemed incongruous among the moans of the wounded and the murmur of orderlies. "The 'mystic' Yank who outfoxed the Fox at Bir el

Khireigat? That one?" Rommel remained impassive. "Has the Polish Brigade heard of him?"

"Yes, a little," Rommel said cautiously. "I am curious, how did he do it?" The wounded soldier watched them and smoked his cigarette patiently, enjoying the diversion.

"They say he is a crystal-ball gazer. But who knows? They say he heard Rommel coming on the wind. I read about him in the *Times*. It's marvelous . . . takes us outside all this"—he swept an arm disdainfully at the tent and all its occupants— ". . . bloody reality! He's a bogey man. It's magic, don't you know?"

"Yes, I see," said Rommel. "Thank you very much. It is a very interesting story." He snapped his heels together. "Poland salutes you." He had heard enough. He needed to escape the young doctor and his romantic fantasies. He walked through the exit. The doctor followed him outside.

At the fringe of the light, the armored car engine started and it emerged from the gloom a moment after Rommel stepped out of the tent. Light from the open flap shone on its side where the Afrika Korps emblem of a palm tree with swastika imposed over it was clearly visible. The doctor stared at the emblem in astonishment. Rommel nimbly climbed on the hull and swung his legs into the open turret. He saw his driver and gunner staring anxiously at him. In the dim glow of the instrument panel their foreheads gleamed with sweat, despite the chill temperature.

"How do you like my captured vehicle?" Rommel called to the doctor. "Very good machine."

The doctor relaxed, then came to attention in his white smock and unexpectedly saluted. Rommel grinned as he responded with the open-palmed British salute.

"Good luck!" The doctor watched the armored car disappear into the gloom, then reentered the tent.

Rommel looked back at the hospital company he had considered his own property. The clustered brightness grew smaller and smaller, a brave island of light in a sea of darkness.

Tomorrow is Totensonntag, the Day of the Dead, our national day of mourning. Many will die. We need luck. The doctor wished us luck. Heard it on the wind? Outfoxed the Fox? Oh, my American friend, I hope that we meet again.

XX

Speigner's joints ached from the constant jolting, and his throat felt like sandpaper. In camp he had failed to notice the relentlessness with which the desert parched a man. Soldiers and airmen spent the day brewing tea. One drank liquids at short intervals all day long, so that a steaming mug of strong tea had seemed merely an anchor for conversation. Out here one hugged his canteen to his chest. He tried not to think of the comforts of Cunningham's headquarters. Bright-Ashton nudged him and pointed to a clutter of vehicles crowding like sheep against the wire.

The half-track engine guttered down, and they stopped while an officer checked the formation through field glasses. The riders shared a tense moment of suspense. Sand hissed against the metal sides of the half-track. Speigner experienced a shock of vulnerability.

"British," the officer announced over his shoulder. An audible sigh passed among them.

They approached the stationary vehicles. Tiny figures were visible between the truck and jeeps. Max recognized a familiar small form among them, and his heart jumped. Anna was running toward their open truck before it came to a stop.

He leaped down, but before he could say a word she clutched at his coat in the manner of a child tattling to her father.

"This is terrible. I'm so glad to see you. They won't let us go any farther. We heard artillery. There's a battle going on. They are waiting to get an all-clear from the base at Sidi Omar. But now you are here, you must help me persuade Major Churchill to lend us a jeep and let us drive closer to the front. I want to report to my papers that I have been to the front!"

She was like a miniature desert gladiator, her hair blond with sand, her skin ruddy from wind and sun. Her spirit was contagious. He turned questioningly to Bright-Ashton to see if he had heard.

"I don't mind asking for the major's jeep," John said mildly, "but you'll have to accept responsibility."

"I'll be glad to." Max's bravado was fueled by Anna's bright gaze. He completely forgot about the desert.

John went to confer with Churchill. The correspondents crowded around the newcomers, grateful for any bits of information they could pick up, even a description of the uneventful ride from Cunningham's headquarters. When they found out that Speigner was the famous intelligence officer who had contributed to the RAF attack on 21st Panzer Division, they fairly besieged him with questions. Bright-Ashton broke up the press conference by dangling the ignition keys to a jeep in front of Max.

They drove into a claret sunset. John tacked the jeep back and forth across the uneven terrain, seeking firm ground. Max watched the needle of the compass affixed to the dashboard swing wildly from northwest to northeast. There could be no doubt that they were headed for the fighting. They could hear the thump of heavy guns in the distance. Anna leaned forward and gripped the brace bar with such delight that Max hummed a few notes of a Highland fling. She burst into nervous laughter and reached back swiftly to caress his cheek.

Night came at them in a rush. John said, "We're going to have to go back in a few minutes. Can't use the headlamps in this direction, you know. Useless to try to get much farther. You can say you were *almost* at the front!"

Anna begged and coerced, and they went on. In the sudden darkness, John ran over a heap of rusting metal, the remains of a wrecked vehicle. There was a sharp report. The jeep slewed around and came to a halt, leaning precariously to the left. Max thought they had been hit by enemy fire.

"Blowout!" John said angrily.

They got out to assess the damage. They felt the still-warm flat tire. There was a large, ragged hole in it. Max took off his jacket and helped John unbolt the spare tire. He set up the jack and pumped the lever to raise the jeep. Max had noticed that the vehicle leaned toward them, but the jack seemed to hold. He loosened the lug nuts and unscrewed them, dropping each into his shirt pocket so he would not lose

them. John was struggling to unseat the wheel from the lug
bolts when the jack slipped and the jeep collapsed. The major
cried out. He was caught under the wheel. Speigner felt his
way up John's arm until he came abruptly to the rim of the
wheel. His fingers encountered a sticky wetness. The wheel
was crushing John's hand against the ground. Immobilized by
confusion, Max bent close to him as if for advice. John had
passed out.

"See if there's a shovel in the back of the jeep," he shouted
to Anna, although she was squatting beside him.

He felt for the jack. It appeared to be pinned crossways
under the axle. He decided to try to dig around the wheel and
hope that the jack handle, flush between the ground and the
axle, would support the weight of the vehicle long enough for
them to work John's hand free. Anna brought the folded
shovel. Speigner unsnapped the blade and slid the handle into
locking position. He began to dig, carefully at first, then more
rapidly. He stopped and felt to see if the rim had shifted. It did
not seem to have moved, and he continued to dig until he had
cleared a narrow area on either side of the rim. Then he began
to dig with his fingers at the base of the rim, where it cut into
John's hand. As gently as possible, he worked the arm free. He
dragged John clear of the listing jeep.

They worked over him as a team, silently and efficiently.
Anna had found a medical kit in the jeep. They cleaned the
wound after a fashion and liberally powdered it with sulfa,
then wrapped it in a gauze bandage. Max rubbed the flesh just
below the elbow to restore circulation. He knew the bones
were broken. The hand had already swollen to the size of a
small catcher's mitt.

He tried to decide what to do. Night filled the cavities of
the land like a black tide. The jack was bent under the dead
weight of the jeep axle. There was no way to change the tire
now. They had been driving some forty-five minutes, at an
average rate of about 20 mph. They might have come as far as
fifteen miles. He did not think he could carry the major that
far, even if they were able to find their way back. He felt Anna
watching him.

"We'd better stay put," he said. "Churchill will come after
us at first light."

"How will he know what direction we took?"

"He knows we headed northwest."

"If he is one degree off, he could miss us by miles." Anna's voice was devoid of emotion. She cradled Bright-Ashton's head in her lap and stroked his forehead.

They both looked at the major to see if he showed any signs of waking. Consciousness bubbled up in him as they watched. He gasped as though releasing a bit of it. He tried to sit up. Anna supported him with her arm and brought the canteen to his lips. He swallowed some water but immediately gagged it up.

"It hurts," he said in a tone of apology.

"Are there any pain tablets in the medicine kit?" Max said. Anna handed him a square metal container, and he found a vial of pills. "See if he can get these down." John managed to swallow them. He had begun to shiver in the night wind. So had Anna, in spite of her heavy coat and fur-lined collar. Speigner looked in the jeep and got out a rolled tarpaulin, which turned out to be a two-man tent with pole halves, pegs, and guy ropes packed inside. He set it up quickly, pegged tight, with the closed end facing the wind like the bow of a ship. They helped John creep inside and stretch out on the ground. There were no blankets, but Anna emptied her leather handbag and put it under John's head for a pillow.

Max heard a rumbling like thunder. On the horizon the light show of a night barrage began. "Look at this!" he cried. She crawled out and knelt beside him. Yellow and white tracers of artillery shells arched lazily back and forth, delivering red balls of explosions. Green flares like falling stars hovered over the earth. "Night bombers," he said. Anna was shaking with cold, and he put his arm around her. Red streams of antiaircraft fire hosed the sky, seeking to extinguish the enemy bombers.

Each side seemed to be working in concert with the common purpose of staining the sky red, yellow, white, or green. It was as if soldiers of both armies were flailing together at a vast incompleteness, and in so doing incidentally maiming or killing one another. Max turned to Anna, eager to share her perceptions.

"What do you think?"

"I hope we win," she said angrily. "I hope the British get the best of it. I hope we make better holes in the desert than they do and that our holes are in the right places and theirs are in the wrong ones. And the major is going to catch pneumonia, if I do not lie down close to him and keep him warm."

She crawled into the tent. When Max looked back at the artillery light show, a cloud moving like the hand of God swept up to the red and yellow tracers and blotted them out in a moment. He was stunned by this phenomenon until he felt the rush of silt and understood that a dust storm had rolled in like a solid wall between them and the battle. Blinking against the dust he moved backward into the tent so he could fasten the canvas flaps behind him without turning around in the cramped space. He felt with his hand to see where Anna lay so he would not tread on her with his knees. She lay in the middle facing John, who lay sleeping on his back. His breath whistled in the dark.

"I'll keep him warm if you'll keep me warm," Anna murmured without turning around.

He lay down beside her. The ground was as hard and cold as a sheet of ice. He curled chastely against her, shaping himself to the curve of her hips. For the first time in his life he had become responsible for the safety of other human beings. The tent flap blew open and he inched forward to button it tight. He could feel the weight of sand piling up outside the canvas. As he resumed his position beside Anna he had an instinctive awareness that they would never be this close again. Shaking with cold, he settled down and put his arm around her.

Max raised his head, awakened by a pearly silence. The rattle of sand against the canvas had ceased. He felt groggy from a fitful night of half dozing, half waking. His head poked against the ceiling of the makeshift tent, and he heard a solid sheet of sand slide down the outside surface. A soft weight moved against him. Anna had curled up next to him during the night. The discovery of their closeness passed through him like a cool draft of water. He stretched his aching neck and licked his lips. The tip of his tongue rasped against mustache stubble and he tasted dust. Fine silt had filtered through the canvas and transformed the three of them—hair, faces, clothing—into creatures of camouflage, uniformly tan. John was sleeping on his side. His good arm was crooked under his head, the bandaged right hand resting on top of his thigh.

Speigner pushed open a flap on the leeward side where the sand mound was only a foot high. He stuck his head out of the tent. The sun was well above the horizon. The sky was clear, and a steady breeze rose from the south.

Out of the corner of his eye he saw a large, dark shape. His subconscious identified it as a dune he had not noticed during the sandstorm. With a calm, robust curiosity he turned and looked into the gun of the tank. The cannon was smooth-ended, with no blast deflector. It stared straight at him, a black and bottomless eye some 40 feet away. He became hard and still. The machine waited patiently. He was a small, defense-less animal, caught in the hunter's shadow. Instinct told him to remain motionless until the tank made him move. He breathed in shallow pants. His heart drummed against his rib cage. He stared at the tank through slitted lids. It seemed impossible that a huge, noisy armored vehicle could appear without warning. He hoped madly that he was dreaming or seeing a mirage.

The fact that the tank did not move was temporarily reassuring. It's engine was not running. He listened intently for any sounds from inside it. The wind sighed against the hull with a hiss of grit. John moaned in his sleep, and Anna stirred. Her hand reached behind her to feel instinctively for him. He felt the feathery touch of her fingers. He could not take his eyes from the tank.

Anyone at home? Home. British or German?

No markings were readily visible on the mud-colored hull. His mind sorted through mental drawings of tank models. He recognized the type at the same time that he saw the insignia stenciled just below the turret: a palm tree emblazoned with a swastika.

Panzerkampfwagen III, Ausf. B, 1938. Armored fighting vehicle, type III, model B. Armament: 3.7 cm Kampfwagen-kanone, 150 rounds ammunition, three (3) 7.92 mm machine guns, 4500 rounds. Weight: 18 tons; length: 18 feet, 11 inches; maximum speed 20 mph. Somebody please help me.

How had it appeared without his having heard it coming? The noise of the sandstorm could have covered it. When had it arrived? Surely they would have noticed it—18 feet and 18 tons. Was anyone inside it? Perhaps the crew had abandoned it. Out of fuel? Where was its support unit? Maybe it was lost. Had the boundary of the front lines surged back and forth around them while they slept?

He noted, with a strangely detached curiosity, that the panzer crew had draped a piece of mosquito netting over the hull so that if formed a skirt over the clearance space between the tracks, rounding the hard square shape of the tank into something resembling a rounded dune. The skirt gave the tank a lived-in, customized quality. Max was convinced the Mark III was occupied. He remembered that it had space for a crew of five.

His armament consisted of a .45-caliber automatic, which had slipped half out of the holster John had dropped on the sand. Max saw that Bright-Ashton carried it at full cock with the safety on, combat style. Bronzed by silt, it reminded Max of an antique dueling pistol.

Max was filled with sudden resentment for the unprovoked threat. He was an American, a neutral, irrelevantly dressed in military uniform. The blank eye of the *Kampfwagenkanone,* however, did not discriminate among uniforms or insignia. He reached for the automatic. His fingers curled around the grip, and he hefted the heavy pistol. In reaching across Anna, he awakened her. She opened her eyes, blinked, yawned, sat up and stretched. She began to brush sand from her hair.

"Good morning!" Her normal tone startled him.

"Shhhhhhhhh." He put a warning finger to his lips. She stared in surprise. The presence of the panzer seemed merely to offend her. She put her fists against her hips, a dusty blond moth.

"What is happening?" she demanded. He clamped his hand over her mouth lest the tank reply with a searing blast.

"We've got to get away," he whispered hoarsely. "Wake John and collect the water bottles and let's get the hell out of here."

She stared at the tank defiantly. "Perhaps no one is inside. Max, it is surely abandoned. You must capture it."

He was confounded by her indifference to being imminently dead. At the same time, he was grateful to her for diverting his fear into impatience.

"Be reasonable. How would I capture it? With John's pistol? Like Tom Mix? I'd need a horse, then. Where's my horse? If they see us, they will blow us to pieces. We've got to get out of here." His voice trembled.

"We are at war," she said, dark eyes shining.

He had known from the start that she was a brave woman. Now it seemed that he had also known that her valor would get him into trouble.

"*Who* is at war!" he hissed furiously. "Me, an American? You, a news correspondent? John—does he look belligerent?" He glanced anxiously at the Mark III, expecting at any moment to hear the whine of its starter motor or the solid snick of a 7.92-mm machine gun lever being cocked. He had the impression that the gun snout was a sensor, listening in on their conversation and sternly poised to rebuke them.

"I want you," she said, "to make war on the Nazis."

"I rather agree with Speigner." Bright-Ashton had crawled to the open flap and was peeking out at the tank. "Discretion's the better part and all that," John added. "If I weren't indisposed, I might open the hatch and have a look-see, but there's absolutely no point in Max taking the risk."

"Give me the gun!" Anna said. Speigner stared at her. It seemed insane to give the tank so much time to shoot them. "Give it to me," she repeated.

"No," he said dully.

"All right, I don't need it anyway." Her eyes were leaden. He forgot his fear.

"I'll go." He crawled away before he could change his mind. He angled away from the machine, circling it, listening and watching for any sign of life. The sand chafed his hands and knees. He stood and walked bent over, to make a smaller target. The pistol was almost forgotten in his hand. He saw a gaping black hole in the side of the tank just above the treads. He smelled charred metal. He straightened up, moving more confidently around to the back of the tank.

Took a direct hit, drove into the desert as far as possible out of the battle zone, got out while they could, put out the fire, were picked up by another unit. Recovery vehicle will come to pick up the disabled panzer. Germans very efficient at recovery.

He turned to glance into the open desert, hoping to spot

the crew walking away from them. He felt rather than saw the turret move.

He glared at the tank. The turret was motionless, but he could see that the gun tube angle had changed by perceptible degrees, the snout having turned as if to catch his scent. Incredibly, with a thin grating sound of metal, the turret moved again. Beyond it he noted Anna and John's horrified faces, recording their reaction as proof that his eyes had not deceived him.

Someone. Inside it. Hand-cranking the turret around. Alive and dangerous. The enemy. Must do something. Engine dead. They can't move anything but the turret. Must be weak or they would crank it faster.

The turret continued its rotation, an inch at a time. He moved along the circumference it described, staying ahead of the snout's search. Through the walls of the tank he could hear an elbow bumping against metal as someone clumsily rotated the crank handle. When the cannon canted 45 degrees from the front, it stopped. Speigner also hesitated. The gun pointed blankly to the east without a target. Something moved inside Max.

He took several quick steps and leaped on the hull, grabbing at one of the cables holding the basic load in place. Empty jerry cans clattered off the hull. He flailed over an obstacle course of water and gas cans, extra road wheels, tarps and boxed tools. Clutching the pistol in one hand, he jerked at the hatch release with the other. The hatch swung open and he ducked, expecting a hail of bullets. Nothing happened. He pointed the gun into the darkness and squeezed the trigger. Something was wrong with the pistol. It would not fire. A pale face floated below him like a bass under a log. He heard John's voice calling from far away.

"Safety catch *off!*"

He fumbled with the pistol. Features swam into focus—a pair of eyes, a smear of a mouth. He could not find the catch. Further hesitation would be a sign of weakness. He resolutely aimed the useless gun at the face.

"*Ergeben Sie sich, sonst werde ich Sie totschiessen!*" Max shouted fiercely. A dangerous silence filled the dark tank.

"*Du sprichst Deutsch.*" It was a ridiculously boyish tenor voice, hopeful and fearful. "Do you have any water, please? I am very thirsty."

"Come out! All of you!"

"My comrades are dead." The voice was resigned.

"Come out with your hands on your head."

"I am very sorry. I do not think I can."

"What is the matter?"

"I have not the strength remaining. Can you help me?"

A grimy hand rose toward the light, followed by a man's face. Max leaned down through the open hatch, still pointing the pistol. His enemy's face had lean, oil-smeared cheeks. A fringe of singed eyebrows spread across a wide forehead in a burlesque of surprise. The eyes were vulnerable and haunted. Max's fingers closed around the hand. When the German locked his grip, he tensed to repel an attack. He strained to catch sight of any other crewmen inside the tank. He saw a leg sticking out from the machine gunner's space. It angled, toe down, with an awful awkwardness. The driver was not to be seen. The loader, likewise, had disappeared. A human hand lay on the floor of the tank, palm down, an apparition of war.

"Can you help me?" the German repeated. His grip loosened. Max sensed how weak the man was. He tightened his hold and heaved the soldier up. They looked each other in the eye and then glanced away. In that glance each had announced his role—captor and captive—though neither appeared prepared for it.

"I am sorry," said the German, squinting against the glare, "but I have had no water for two days. Also, since the tank was hit, I cannot hear so well." He pointed at his ear apologetically. Max helped the soldier climb off the hull. He was young, blond, and slender. He wore a peaked cap with a red, white, and black bull's-eye on it. His light green uniform was dirty and oil-stained. He wore the insignia of a noncommissioned officer.

"Were you tank commander?" Max asked.

"*Was?*" The German cupped his hand to his ear. Anna and John cautiously approached the tank. The prisoner did not appear surprised to see a woman in the desert. "*Kann ich etwas Wasser haben?*" he asked Speigner.

"Can we spare some water?" Max said. John went to fetch the water bottle. Anna grinned wildly at Max.

"Welcome to the war!" she cried.

Max realized that she believed he had acted bravely. In

his own mind, he had had no real choice in the matter. Besides, the German had been ready to be captured, and Max did not count it much of an accomplishment to have taken him. But he frowned at the prisoner to hide his pleasure. John returned with the water bottle. Max let the prisoner drink only a few swallows.

"Naturally, we can't take him with us," John said. "Let him go back to his own people, if he can find them . . ."

"Wait." Max turned to the prisoner. "*Sprechen Sie Englisch?*" The captive shook his head. Max motioned for John to continue.

"We don't know how long it will take us to get to the wire," John reasoned. "We have to make our water last."

"He is Max's prisoner!" Anna exclaimed.

"I don't think I'm authorized to take prisoners," Max said with a grin. "I'm neutral, remember? Maybe the Black Watch would like to have him."

"You've never been stranded in the desert . . ." John began.

"I don't think he could make it on his own," Max said solemnly. "Besides, we couldn't just send him off in the desert without any water. We have to share with him. Don't we?"

The prisoner watched them warily, aware that his fate was being decided. Max still held the pistol. He tried to give it back to Bright-Ashton. John waved it off.

"No, if he's to be your prisoner," he said, "*you* must guard him. By the way, let me show you how the bloody catch works." Max glanced self-consciously at the prisoner as they turned their backs to shield the demonstration from view. "See, there it is. Got it? Oh no, you keep it. It's your show." John added in afterthought, "How about the others? I mean, inside."

"All dead."

"Are you certain? Better to be absolutely positive."

Max looked up at the open turret. Moments before, the panzer had seemed so dangerous. Now it had become a mausoleum on caterpillar tracks. He hated reentering the tank. Handing the automatic to John, he climbed onto the hull. He peered into the hatch. The first thing he saw was the severed hand. It seemed to move. He started, then realized that flies were crawling over it.

He lowered himself into the panzer. An overpowering stench of decay, cordite, and burnt oil made him gag; but he found the silence more unbearable than the smell. He made more noise than was necessary, bumping against the seats and the shell-deflector plate behind the cannon breech. A black cloud of flies lifted and resettled on a drying pool of blood. Breathing through his mouth, he counted pieces of four bodies. Shreds of clothing and flesh stuck to the walls and instruments.

The only human corpse he had ever seen close up had been that of his grandfather, resting formally in a flower-draped coffin beside a church pulpit. The only way he could tell that his grandfather was dead and not sleeping was that his hair had been parted on the wrong side.

These were angry dead with frenzied eyeballs and gaping mouths. The odor of death roared from them instead of screams.

Question: Why did the British call prototype tanks "cisterns" or "reservoirs"? Answer: To keep the Germans from discovering what they were building, they claimed the machines were built to carry water. Correction: They were reservoirs after all, built to hold blood.

It seemed impossible that men could be killed inside so much steel plating. He saw the holes where an armor-piercing shell had entered one side of the hull and exited through the other, missing the few live shells stored in the racks. Apparently most of the tank's ammunition had already been expended, leaving empty shell casings when the panzer had taken the hit. This undoubtedly had saved his prisoner's life.

Speigner wondered how long the man had kept company with his companions. Their silence was devastating. He abruptly clambered out of the hatch as if pursued. Bright-Ashton raised his pistol in alarm. Squatting on the hull, Max breathed in deep gasps and shook his head incredulously.

Anna went to gather the gear. She looped water bottles tied to strings around her shoulders. Max gave the soldier another drink of water and two milk tablets. Color began to seep back into the man's cheeks.

"I didn't know them very well." The German seemed to need to explain. "Georges and Alph were killed by the impact. At the time, they were arguing over whose fault it was the machine gun had jammed. We never found out. Fritz lost his hand and bled to death. I hardly noticed him bleeding, he was so quiet. I don't know what killed Friedrich. Shrapnel, I suppose. My ears won't stop ringing. We had sardines and hardtack and tube cheese, but I couldn't find it after—"

"How long did you stay in the tank—with them?" Max asked.

"I don't know," said the prisoner. "I was thinking. I had to make up my mind what to do." He shrugged.

"Let's get going before it's too hot to travel," John interrupted. "Have you checked your man for any hidden weapons? He might have a bayonet strapped to his leg." Max blushed to acknowledge his lack of experience. He made a thorough frisk search of the German. There were no hidden weapons.

They set out in a northerly direction walking abreast. John's plan was to reach either the wire or a British unit believed to be in the Omar range some fifteen or twenty miles ahead. Heat shimmered in liquid waves over the sand. Speigner looked back at the panzer. Its mud-colored paint and cross-hatching of white and green blended with the beige background like a desert toad in hibernation. He thought of the silent crew in no hurry for spring. Something of himself remained with them.

Movement at the rear of the tank startled him. A fire bucket blackened from cooking and exhaust fumes swung by a wire handle from the hull. He had not noticed it before. It had been constructed from a 30-gallon petrol can, similar to those of British tanks crews, by cutting it in half. At every stop, the crew made a paste of sand and gasoline for fuel and brewed ersatz coffee or fried hard biscuits in olive oil. All armies traveled on their stomachs. A sudden breeze swung the bucket on its hook. He turned away and caught up with the others.

A cloud bank rolled across the sky. Max watched the welcome shadow streak the sand. Bright-Ashton, however, complained that they must not fix on some spot on the horizon to guide them. Without a compass, he had been depending on their shadows for direction.

They were alone with the shuffling of their footsteps. For the next hour Max scanned the horizon until his eyes burned. It seemed impossible that the British armada had vanished into thin air. Where were the guns and tanks that had fired the tracers they had watched the night before? He wished that he had counted their rations before rolling them up into two bundles. He hefted the tent half he carried. It was disappointingly light. The German prisoner carried a similar bundle of cans and ration packets wrapped in a tent half. They had breakfasted on biscuits, milk tablets, and a bit of chocolate. John had taken charge of rationing. Speigner wondered how long their food and water would have to last. It seemed inevitable that they would be picked up within a half day's time, at the outside. John seemed alert and in good spirits in spite of his injured hand. Max had dressed the wound before they set out on their march. Angry red streaks had formed on John's wrist. Max knew the infection was painful. John would not be able to lead them much longer. Anna was beginning to limp, though she gamely kept pace. The prisoner, while weak from his vigil in the tank, marched with a slouching stride and the vigor of relaxed responsibility. For him the war was over.

Speigner saw a black tree growing out of the sand, about a half inch above the horizon. He thought greedily of shade and a cool well surrounded by palm trees. The others saw the tree, too, and increased their gait. After a while, John determined that it was a column of oil smoke from a burning vehicle. They debated whether it was the scene of the night barrage they had witnessed. Regardless, now they had something to guide them.

They stopped to share a drink from one of the water bottles. John rationed two sips each. Max noted that the major was rapidly weakening. He wondered if the slender German was strong enough to help him carry John. He knew he could not carry him by himself.

A dot swam in the distance. He tried to catch it, to hold it with his will. Like the bouncing ball in a sing-along cartoon, it played tricks with his vision, appearing and dissolving, sliding from right to left. What were the words to the song? His throat was too dry to swallow. The water sloshed in the bottles around Anna's neck.

"It's a U-S lorry," John murmured.

"U.S.?" Max said hopefully.

"Unserviceable. There may be shade."

The prospect was cheering. Four pairs of eyes fastened on

the dark spot, which grew into the angular shape of a wrecked vehicle. A half hour later they found that it was indeed a lorry, with a smashed cab and no wheels. They huddled in a sliver of shade beside the lorry, protected also from the wind. Anna unwrapped a bonnet she had fashioned from a strip of cloth torn from her dress. Her face was blistered in spite of her precautions. She saw Max looking at her and flashed him the V sign.

"*Du bist polnisch?*" The prisoner had been studying Speigner's uniform.

"*Amerikanisch.*"

Having digested this information, the German added, "Then has America entered the war?"

"Not yet." Max studied his prisoner. He did not seem typical of the Afrika Korps stereotype: proud, elitist, scornful of the enemy. "You are not a career soldier." It was a statement to be confirmed.

"No. I am a conscript. I was a teacher before the war. Science and nature was my subject. After the war I hope to return to teaching." They shared a biscuit, chewing in silence. "May I ask, what does an American do in Libya?"

"Did you ever meet Rommel?" Max asked impulsively.

"Me? Only a sergeant? I saw him once, reviewing the troops in Tripoli."

"What do the troops think of him?"

The German shrugged. "They—we—are proud to serve under him. He is a soldier's general. He is not afraid to die. He is not like the rest of us. That is why we follow him . . . followed, that is."

"Do you know where he is?"

The prisoner grinned at him. "Out there!" He gestured toward the sun in the west. "Where the battle is."

So the prisoner was not without Afrika Korps pride, after all, he thought.

Almost killed him. Tried to pull trigger. Alive because of a fluke. Because of a safety catch.

He imagined a Movietone News replay in which he stood over the panzer turret, holding the pistol to the German's head. The martial theme music swelled, then the narrator's nasal voice:

"*American military observer in Egypt almost precipitates*

U.S. entry into war! November twenty-four: In Western Desert action, G-Two Lieutenant Maxwell Speigner single-handedly captured a German Mark III panzer using a .45 automatic which failed to fire. In the first unofficial action by a U.S. serviceman abroad, a Nazi tank commander was captured by the special liaison officer with the American Embassy in Cairo. Of the risky business, the young lieutenant would only say: (Tight shot of Max, who holds the pistol up to the camera with a modest shrug) 'I couldn't find the safety catch.' (Narrator's voice returns.) Up to now, American machines and know-how have contributed to the Allied war effort in North Africa. Now an American fighting man has stepped in to show what the Yanks can do, in person!" (Up music, dissolve to fashion news.)

"What are you thinking?" Anna has been gingerly plucking at her socks but now gave up trying to take them off. The blisters had burst, and the blood-soaked material stuck to her feet. "What were you saying to him?"

"Did you know," Max said airily, "that slave owners in America often felt more responsible for their slaves than for their own children?"

"What are you talking about?" She looked at him sharply. "Do you suffer from heatstroke?"

"No, ma'am, I've just gone into the slavery business, that's all."

"What do you mean?"

"I mean, he's mine." Hearing the cognate, the prisoner gave him a questioning look. "Yes, you are *mein Kampf*," Max added. "My own African war, my own African slave."

"Max, don't fail me, now," Anna said nervously. "We will reach the wire soon, you'll see. Someone will pick us up."

"Ha-ha-ha, it's not heatstroke, lady. I have contracted an atavistic urge to save my own skin. I squeezed the trigger when I opened the hatch. And now he's mine. I bought him with a bit of pressure with this finger, this one." He crooked his index finger in the air. "He belongs to me."

"Don't be silly. You did what you had to do."

"But he's not for sale. I'm taking him back to Mississippi after the war, and we're going to plant cotton, and sell it down the river at Vicksburg, and maybe build a railroad together."

"What are you talking about?"

"I'm talking about killing people, Young Miss. Or almost killing them."

Anna angrily pulled on her shoes over the bloody socks. Speigner stared into the distance. It took several seconds for him to realize what he was seeing. A dozen or more columns of heavy smoke had sprouted on the horizon. It was impossible to tell which one had served as their guidepost. They stretched across a wide area—perhaps twenty-five miles—and Max could only guess at the extent of the battle or the direction of advance or retreat.

"Are we winning?" Anna said.

Max stood abruptly. Her Scottish belligerence was as uncompromising as the sun. The prisoner obediently got up and waited for instructions. John had become too feverish to walk. Max showed the German how to form a cross-carry "chair" by gripping one's own forearm and holding onto the other's arm with the free hand. Anna helped settle John between them, and they started again, moving slowly.

The man appeared without warning, popping up over a slight undulation that had hidden him from view until he was within several hundred yards. They set John down and suspiciously watched the man come. With his dark head and large, flat ears he moved toward them like a moon man on a lunar surface. Then they recognized the one-piece khaki flight suit with zippered pockets, flier's helmet with earphones, and leather jacket bearing RCAF insignia. The Canadian, however, apparently had his own misgivings when he saw a German, an American, and a woman carrying a British officer. Max pulled back his jacket to show who wore the pistol, and the pilot cautiously approached.

"Hallo," the pilot said hoarsely. "Got some water to spare? Haven't had a drop all day. Been walkin' since yesterday afternoon." They gave him a drink and he said, "Pilot Officer Green here." It seemed somehow appropriate that he was Canadian. After he had drunk, he patted his pockets to find something to give them in exchange. "Afraid I don't have anything to offer you except these cigarettes."

"How marvelous!" Anna cried. The airman immediately produced a cigarette lighter. Her smile reminded Max of the first time he had seen her, at Shepheard's.

"Do you know who is winning the battle?" she asked.

"Haven't the foggiest," the pilot cheerfully replied.

"How about giving us a hand with the major," Max said. "And let's get going."

"Isn't the wire in *that* direction?" The airman pointed east.

"Yes, but it's too far."

"Only twenty or twenty-five kilometers," said the pilot.

"We have to carry the major," Max said impatiently. "At the wire we would still be miles from Maddalena, with Italian minefields to contend with. I say, head for the smoke columns and at least we have a chance of being picked up by our own people."

"I'm with you!" the pilot suddenly agreed.

Speigner and the prisoner lifted John and they set out. The presence of the talkative pilot was diverting, and with an extra pair of hands they made faster progress. The Canadian told them how his fighter plane had run out of fuel after he lost his bearings in a cloud bank. He had been flying a support mission during the South Africans' attack at Bir el Gubi. He could not tell them very much about the battle, except that the South Africans seemed to have gotten the worst of it. They had broken off the attack.

The party struggled up a sloping ridge. When they reached the top, they saw a sight that stopped them in their tracks. The desert was alive with British vehicles streaming eastward in retreat, hundreds of them in an uneven column stretching for miles. There was no order to it. Jeeps and lorries ran side by side with heavy guns towed by half-tracks; armored cars, vans, and motorcycles passed foot soldiers caught like unlucky pedestrians in a gigantic avenue with a perpetual green light. Tanks with cannons pointing behind them crawled over the sand hills. Max heard their tracks whistling as if making shrill excuses. This could not be the same armada he had glimpsed from Cunningham's aircraft.

Rommel has won.

The airman and the German carried Bright-Ashton down the slope behind Max and Anna. They changed course in an easterly direction to converge with the pell-mell retreat. An empty ammunition truck drove alongside them, canvas top flapping desperately against its metal frame. Max tried to hail the driver. He stopped only after Speigner had jumped on the running board and shouted at him through the open window.

"We need a doctor or a medical corpsman!" Speigner shouted above the grinding noise of engines. "Is there a mobile hospital anywhere?"

"Don't ask me!" the driver shouted back. "I've got the bleedin' Afrika Korps on my bleedin' trail!" The driver noticed the prisoner's German uniform and let in the clutch, forcing Max to jump down. He fell to his knees, stood and irritably dusted himself off.

The party moved along the periphery of the fleeing mass. Speigner continued to try to flag down every vehicle that came close. The first lorry to stop was an open-cab 1500-pounder hauling ammunition racks and towing a heavy gun. Four German prisoners perched like birds on the wooden wheel base supporting the weapon. They looked defeated and tired, covered with dust. Speigner thought what a huge joke it was that the comrades of such as these were in pursuit of the Eighth Army.

"Shall I take him off your hands?" a sergeant in the lorry asked, pointing at Max's prisoner. "Do you a favor. Room for another one back there."

"Why are prisoners riding when our people," Max indicated Anna and John, "are afoot?"

"Why, indeed. Well, we must put them somewhere, mustn't we! Come along, then, Jerry," the sergeant called officiously to Speigner's prisoner. "That is, if it's all right with you, sir?"

Max hesitated. He was not ready to let his prisoner go. The crazy image of them plowing Mud Island and sowing cotton had become almost too real. He saw that his prisoner was looking at him for permission. Max nodded brusquely, and the German climbed aboard the gun carriage. The other prisoners did not speak to him. He did not look back as the lorry drove away in a cloud of dust.

Soon Max saw what he had been searching for: a convoy of white trucks and vans with red crosses painted on the sides. All four of them, including John with his good arm, waved frantically at the ambulance company. The medical convoy proceeded amid the rout with the dignity of a mother duck with her ducklings in tow. They flagged down the lead driver, who directed them to the second from the last truck in the convoy. There was stretcher space for John and room in the cab for Max and Anna. The Canadian airman rode on the running board until he hailed a ride in a passing troop carrier.

"See you in Soho!" he shouted and disappeared as blithely as he had come.

XXI

It was chaos. It was armored warfare at its best. He had created it.

Rommel stood in his open car gripping the back seat and swaying with the movement, oblivious to the dust. The engine labored as they ascended the steep bank of the wadi. The wireless truck followed, struggling through the deep sand. In the distance he could hear the dull thump of artillery. Somewhere beyond the long afternoon shadows 21st panzer was bombarding XXX Corps. On all sides of them soft-skinned transport streamed eastward. The British fled before his panzers like gazelles before the wolf—generals and clerks alike, mechanics with wrenches sticking out of their pockets, intelligence units with gasoline cans handy to burn their files, pilots scrambling to clear the ground before the air strip was overrun. It was a lovely afternoon and Egypt was not far ahead. He strained to catch his first glimpse of the wire.

One bold stroke. An arrow slicing through the soft belly of 7th Armored. Then for the heart. Cruewell disagrees, of course. Wants a methodical cleanup of the battlefield, a salvage operation. What would Forrest have said? Better to operate on the grand scale rather than to creep about the battlefield anxiously. Harry the enemy and deny him the ability to regroup.

"The wireless truck is stuck," observed his chief of staff, Gause, who sat in the back seat beside him. Rommel glanced impatiently into the wadi, where the back tires of the radio truck spun vainly in the dry riverbed.

"We'll go on to the wire!" he snapped to the driver. "Let them catch up the best way they can."

He would allow nothing to delay his rendezvous with Ravenstein near Bir Sheferzen. He silently cursed the incompetency of the truck driver. If Westphal tried to raise him on the wireless from *Panzergruppe* HQ, let the signals officer explain that Rommel was the only one maintaining his schedule.

Ravenstein better be there.

When they reached the rendezvous point, a gap in the wire about thirty-five miles south of the sea, Ravenstein was waiting. He was parked near the wire in a single truck. Rommel surmissed that Ravenstein had also been forced to drive ahead of his straggling forces in order to meet at the appointed time. He watched the young general approach with swift, impatient steps. Ravenstein was doubtless set on arguing him out of his plan. Rommel spread his map emphatically on the fender of his car.

"As I told you this morning," Rommel said, "you have a chance of ending this campaign with one strike. You will move your group here, to the Halfaya Pass area. Twenty-First Panzer is to cross the frontier and attack Fourth Indian Division from their rear, while Fifteenth Panzer moves in from the south along the wire. Ariete will conform from the east, and our panzer divisions will drive the enemy onto the minefields of our Sollum front and force them to surrender."

Ravenstein stared morosely at the map. He would be exposed to capture if he proceeded alone behind enemy territory. To Rommel the risk was minimal compared to the prospect of sudden victory.

"Verstehen Sie?" He folded the map abruptly.

Ravenstein glanced at his commander. Swallowing his objections like a bitter pill, he saluted ceremoniously. He got into his truck and drove through the gap in the wire.

Rommel watched the truck disappear inside its own dust trail. He felt a deep satisfaction. Ravenstein's obedience was the key: one man moving to the Will, followed by a dozen, then a hundred, then a thousand, then ten thousand. Rommel could envision the military tableau unfolding as clearly as if he were flying above the desert, riding the thermals. The movements of men with their sweating faces, of five thousand machines grinding and clanking across the desert, were reduced in his mind to the blazing progress of arrows roughly sketched on a map. His divisions would thrust and wheel past the static lines of XIII Corps, then attack from an unexpected quarter and pound the enemy like a mailed fist.

Soon it will all be over. Then Cruewell can sweep up to his heart's content.

Out of the corner of his eye he detected movement. An alarm sounded in his brain. A group of British stragglers strolled along the wire, careless of mines. There were eight of them. They did not appear to be armed. Where were their weapons? Behind their backs, under their clothes?

"*Achtung!*" Rommel whispered to his driver, who cursed silently and grabbed the machine gun mounted under the dashboard. Gause quietly took his pistol out of its holster.

The enemy soldiers stared. It occurred to Rommel that they probably had never seen a German general before. They gawked at the palm and swastika on the side of the car. Rommel watched hands and arms for sudden movement. The driver braced his automatic weapon to fire at the first provocation. Rommel merely rested his hand on his holstered side arm. In a situation like this, bold authority was worth a platoon of infantry. He sensed defeat in their dusty faces. One of them stepped forward.

"*Haben Sie Wasser?*" he said.

"No," Rommel replied. "Keep moving." They seemed relieved to hear English spoken.

"We have gotten lost," said their leader. "Could you help us?"

"I'm sorry. Go away!" He waved his hand at them as if shooing flies.

"We've been walking since yesterday, and you're the first people we have seen. We're awfully thirsty."

"I am not interested in you. Go away."

The leader reached in his pocket and the driver gripped his weapon, preparing to fire. All of the enemy soldiers raised their hands except for the leader, who held out some cans.

"We've some chocolate and tinned beef. We'll trade you for water." He came forward and laid his handful of cans on the sand, then stepped back respectfully. Others among them added items to the little store of goods.

"What have we got?" Rommel asked over his shoulder.

"I do not know," said Gause.

"Some sandwiches and a thermos of coffee," his driver whispered between clenched teeth, never taking his eyes from the British. "Also two gallon cans of water."

"Give them a can," said Rommel.

"But, Herr—" The driver caught the word *General* lest he reveal his precious charge to the enemy. "We may need extra water for the radiator."

"Geben Sie sie ihnen!"

The driver set a water can beside the pile of goods while keeping his submachine gun pointed at the British.

"That is all we can give you," Rommel said. "You may keep your food."

"May we walk along behind your car, sir?" The leader's tone became deferential. Rommel half-expected him to doff his cap like a peasant.

"You are not my prisoners," he said curtly. "You must take water and go."

"Where, sir?"

"I don't know—wherever you like! I am busy."

"We are lost."

"Find someone else to surrender to, not me."

"Don't you see?" the soldier persisted. "We wish to be put in the bag."

"I cannot help you. Go away." Rommel took his pistol out of its holster and cocked it. He held it against his shoulder, pointing at the sky. The leader stared at him steadily.

"You must accept my surrender," said the leader.

Rommel raised his pistol and fired it into the air. The British ducked their heads at the flat report of the gun.

"Pick up cans and go away!" he commanded.

"Where can we go?" said the leader.

"I don't care," Rommel cried. "Just go away." He flung his arm in a westerly direction. "There!"

"Will we be picked up soon?" the man said.

"It is no concern of mine. I am very busy!" The British soldier faced Rommel, will against will. Both were equally determined. Gause cleared his throat diplomatically.

"We really must be going," he said.

The enemy soldier hesitated, overcome by Gause's politeness. Rommel got into the car and sat staring in the opposite direction. The whole episode had dampened his spirits. He could stand anything except procrastination. If the British did not go soon, he would shoot them for interrupting his schedule. Gause faced down the enemy leader, who directed his men to retrieve their goods and head off into the desert. As the driver started the engine and drove through the gap, the stragglers veered back to the wire and continued to the south, as before.

We are in Egypt.

The thought temporarily appeased Rommel, but something was lacking: he did not feel the exhilaration upon crossing the wire that he had experienced in the past. The British stragglers had taken the edge off, and Rommel wished to get it back. At this moment, the driver unfortunately chose to slow down and ask Romnmel if he wished to stop and wait for his escort. Gause, too, added a note of caution.

"We're too far in front. You should not expose yourself like this."

"Drive!" Rommel shouted. "Go!" He glared ahead as though willing the vehicle to move faster. Gause turned up his collar. Dusk darkened the hills, and the wind was cold in the open car.

They wound among endless dunes. Rommel leaned over the seat and complained to the driver about the petty pace. He refused to accept the soldier's argument that the track was too uneven for speed. He ordered him to accelerate and relished the sharp jolts the suspension system was taking as if each represented impediments he had overcome: lack of fuel for his tanks, delays in reassembling after a battle in order to pursue the enemy, wireless breakdowns that made it impossible to send amended orders based on changing conditions.

A sharp crack came from the right front wheel. The driver stopped the car. Rommel sat very still while the driver crawled under the car to assess the damage. Earlier in the day he had seen a captured Crusader tank with a crudely painted replica of the Egyptian god of the sun, Horus—a hawk's head with an all-seeing eye. A panzergrenadier Oberleutnant had told him what the design represented. Egyptian warriors of old prayed to Horus as their god of battles.

Would it do any good to send up a request? After all, we are in Egypt.

"*Herr General,*" the driver reported, "the steering column has snapped."

"Now we *must* wait for the others to catch up with us," Gause said immediately. "What is the enemy's last known position?"

"Isn't there a way it can be fixed?" Rommel said. He got out of the car and gained some small relief in fussing with the tire, although the tire had little to do with the problem. He kicked the tire with the misgivings of a used-car buyer. He noticed that it turned an inch and stayed there. He kicked it again, harder.

"Kick the one on the other side!" he told the driver. "Make it straight. And let's go. When it begins to veer off track, we can straighten them up again." The driver's look of incredulity melted into obedience when he saw his commander's determination. Rommel jumped on the running board and held onto the windshield. The driver let in the clutch.

"*Gott im Himmel,*" Gause moaned.

The track rose in a gradual incline, with fewer dunes and firmer ground, but ruts stood up like waves. The car had gone twenty meters before a bump turned it. The driver immediately braked. Rommel leaped off to put his theory into practice, kicking the tire straight while the driver did the same on the opposite side. Gause looked on in silence. They proceeded as before, but this time the car began to veer before it had traveled twice its own length. After repeating the operation a dozen times, they had advanced only two hundred meters in five minutes. Rommel cast about for improvements. He looked pointedly at Gause.

"May I help?" the chief of staff said halfheartedly.

The two generals jogged alongside the vehicle kicking the tires each time the car stopped. To a distant observer it might have appeared that they were attacking the car. The driver operated only the gearshift, clutch, and accelerator. There was no point in attempting to guide the automobile with the slack steering wheel. The generals trotted to keep up during the brief, exciting periods of free motion. Their lengthening shadows bobbed over the desert floor like giant jumping jacks. Gause was panting heavily. Rommel had not yet begun to breathe hard, but his temper was deteriorating.

"How do the shits in Berlin expect me to conquer Egypt

with equipment like this!" He viciously kicked the tire. His outburst confused the driver, who hesitated at the controls in case the general expected him to answer either for the broken-down mechanism or for Berlin. "Go on! Go on! Go on!" Rommel cried in a frenzy. The car lurched ahead, weaving like a frightened animal. At last it veered sharply to the right. The driver slammed on the brakes.

"What difference will a few hundred yards matter!" Gause screamed.

"It matters to *me!*" Rommel's face was brick red. "Get out and let me drive!" The corporal leaped out of the car as if the seat were burning him. Rommel grabbed the steering wheel. He would have jerked it clear of its column if he could. He slammed the lever into first, grinding the gears with a spine-rattling screech. "You've been going too slow!" he accused the corporal. "At a higher rate of speed, the wheels may run straight."

He let in the clutch with a jerk and the back tires kicked gravel. He gripped the steering wheel out of habit, infuriated by its treacherous loose play. Gause and the driver trotted behind him, heads down to avoid the dust. The track led across a flat plain, and as the car began its capricious turn, he spun the broken wheel in the opposite direction, leaning as if body English might bend the machine to his will. When the speedometer reached thirty-five, the car settled irrevocably into its manic circle. The chief of staff and the corporal stopped and watched in amazement as Rommel whipped by them. They caught a glimpse of him spinning the steering wheel, his face a bitter, dusty mask. They glanced speechlessly at each other. It dawned on them that Rommel was not going to stop driving in a circle.

The speedometer rose to fifty. Rommel whirled the steering wheel against the centrifugal pull. His hands moved with machinelike dexterity. There was no room in him for reason. Rage consumed every part of him. He allowed it to burn clean through, unchecked, glorying in its purifying power. His foot depressed the accelerator pedal to the floorboard. The speedometer rose to sixty-five as the car slewed and careered through alternating patches of sand and gravel. A hurricane of dust boiled from the wheels. He became lost in a private frenzy. A series of whanging, thumping sounds came from the overheated engine. It stopped running. The car glided to a halt. A pall of dust hung over it.

When the air cleared, Rommel sat motionless behind the wheel. There was something wrong in his stillness, like rain on a cloudless day. Gause and the driver were loath to enter the charmed circle of the car's tracks. Having hung back for nearly a minute, Gause finally went forward. The driver loitered behind. The chief of staff stood beside the car as though awaiting orders. Rommel did not look up. The only sounds were the engine ticking and the crunch of the driver's footsteps as he tentatively examined the car. Rommel broke the silence.

"It is getting cold."

Night had fallen. Stars twinkled in the Egyptian sky. The temperature rapidly dropped to near freezing. He wrapped himself in his greatcoat. There was nothing to do but wait for Cruewell's scouts. Mere chance would determine which side would find them first, advancing Germans or retreating British. In the starlight Rommel's face was like stone.

Over the dunes headlamps glowed and disappeared like marsh gas. They heard the whirr of tires on sand, then the growl of an engine. When the lights found them, dazzling in their intensity, the vehicle came straight toward them. They listened for a familiar engine sound, strained to identify the shape of the vehicle behind the lights. It loomed close, larger than an armored car, and stopped. Its motor idled smoothly. The door opened.

"Herr General!" The voice belonged to Cruewell himself. Rommel recognized the square shape of Mammut. Men of the Afrika Korps piled out of the ACV and surrounded them with relieved murmurs, offering cigarettes and cups of cocoa.

"Where is Twenty-First Panzer?" Rommel's crisp tone commanded instant silence. The friendly forms froze, silhouetted against the headlight beams.

"Out of gas," Cruewell said.

"You are forever running out of gas!"

"I am afraid so."

Rommel was stung by a sharp suspicion: Cruewell knew something he was not telling. Had his orders been countermanded again? Would they leave him, as usual, to discover the facts for himself? He angrily entered Mammut. The rest of them piled in behind him, five officers and two enlisted men.

There was barely room for all of them. Cruewell ordered his driver to head back to the frontier. The desert lay silent and unrelenting before them.

It can still work. Our tank commanders are notorious for squirreling away unreported cans of water and fuel. We can always squeeze out another sixty miles in a pinch. That is all it will take. Italians attack from the east, 21st Panzer sweeps to the north, behind the frontier, 15th Panzer rolls them up along the southern flank. And we've got them!

He realized that it was too quiet in the ACV. The driver had slowed down. They had been riding for what seemed like an hour, although the staff car had broken down only some twenty kilometers from the wire.

"What is it?" he asked irritably.

"We're having trouble finding the gap," Cruewell explained.

Rommel said loudly, "A driver's first obligation is to know his route." *He should be court-martialed.* "Drive south along the wire. We'll come to it eventually."

All conversation ceased; every face followed the headlight beams; no one budged an inch in the cramped space. At the periphery of the light, the wire gleamed in ironic reflection, endless. Occasionally a dune or wadi forced the driver to detour away from the wire.

"I think we passed the gap back there," he said, glancing at Rommel for permission to turn around. Rommel nodded curtly. The slow, blundering circle drove him crazy. He stood with his hands on the dashboard, his breath frosting the windshield. After ten minutes he could stand it no longer.

"Stop!" he demanded. "I will drive now."

He grasped the steering wheel as if strangling a live creature. His sense of direction told him a gap lay to the south, but that would mean retracing their path for the third time. Surely there was another gap farther on. He drove north, his eyes clinging to the wire. The ACV rocked as rough ground appeared without warning. It was no small feat, he discovered, to drive the heavy van over trackless desert and watch the wire at the same time. Unspoken criticism emanated like warm breath from the men hovering behind him. Their silence rubbed his patience raw. In the glow from the instrument panel the lines in his face were harshly exaggerated, his eyes shrouded in black sockets.

"It has to be here somewhere." He spoke more to himself than to the others.

Cruewell replied ironically, "Perhaps the British have spun wire and plugged all the gaps."

"Then I will make a new one," Rommel said grimly. He swung the ACV east, brought it about to face the wire, and revved the engine; then he roared toward the wire at top speed. With a screech of metal tearing against metal, the van rammed the caterpillar of barbed wire. It buckled but refused to break, rising nearly to the Mammut's windshield in a fierce embrace.

"I do not think we can get through this way," Cruewell argued.

Every eye was fixed on the man at the wheel. He backed up and tried again. They all reached for something to hold onto as the vehicle collided with the wire. It wrapped cozily around Mammut. His face maniacal, Rommel rammed it again and again. No one had the courage to argue with him. On the sixth attempt, the van became tangled in the wire so that the back wheels spun and began to dig in. Rommel gave up.

"We'll find the gap when it gets light," he said. The anger had gone out of him. He pulled his coat around him and closed his eyes. Within minutes he was asleep.

The ambulance company limped toward the frontier with its load of misery. The dust was thick as fog. During temporary breaks when the convoy stalled behind an abandoned vehicle, the driver climbed out of the cab to wipe the windshield clean. Then Max could see a surrealistic landscape of retreat. The long columns of fleeing vehicles were guided by solitary beacons of burning aircraft or lorries. Beside the track were the smoldering remains of a Crusader, left like a reminder of the Eighth Army's failure. Groggy with fatigue he sat half awake, half asleep next to Anna. No one had spoken for the past hour. Anna dozed with her head on his shoulder. The driver hunched over his steering wheel, straining to see the rear of the lorry in front of them. Among other wounded, Bright-Ashton lay on a stretcher in the back of the lorry. A medical corpsman had given him morphine and sulfanilamide. He assured Speigner that the major would be all right, although he had developed an infection in his bloodstream that would require a doctor's attention at Fort Maddalena.

A courier on a motorcycle pulled up beside their lorry and shouted a question. Max could not hear him over the steady roar of all the engines. He shook his head and the courier accelerated soundlessly away. The presence of so many shapes passing silently, as it were, warped the present into a waking mirage.

Poked my face into an enemy tank. Was it twenty-four hours ago or longer? Not killed. Anna says I won. Won the battle but lost the war? Why are we retreating? How did it happen?

He thought of the artillery bombardment lighting up the night, the columns of smoke the next day. His friend John had wounded his hand changing his tire. *A combat casualty?* A beaten enemy had been glad to surrender to him. *A tactical victory?* He had seen the ways men reacted to defeat. Some withdrew, became stoic or depressed; some were bitter and vengeful; others were cheerful, happy to have come out of it alive. He felt none of these emotions.

Anna stirred beside him. She would be leaving soon on assignment to Lebanon. He knew that he would never see her again. He bounced on the hard seat and tried to piece together the fragments of memory.

The convoy halted. The driver shouted something to him. Anna woke up and sleepily relayed the information that they had reached a gap in the wire. When the dust cleared, Max saw an hourglass shape of hundreds of headlamp beams converging on a point in the roll of wire. On the other side they fanned out in all directions as if a dam of light had burst. When their turn came, the lorry squeezed through the hole in the dam and followed the flow south toward Maddalena.

Wide awake and refreshed by her nap and the prospect of their return to civilization, Anna became chatty. She lapsed into a Scottish brogue as she reminisced about Edinburgh, where she had worked as a reporter before the war; and about the next stop on her tour of the Middle East theater—Beirut— and, above all, a bath in a hot tub with scented soap and lots of fresh water. Max tried to pay attention to her words, her gestures, the lilting cadence of her language. He was aware that he should be storing up memories, like a squirrel facing a long winter. Yet he was also frustrated by her excitement about flying on to Beirut and disappointed that it did not matter to her that they would soon be saying goodbye.

The convoy passed a dark shape against the wire. There was something familiar about its boxlike outline. He observed that it was a lorry or van butted up against the barrier and apparently abandoned like so many other vehicles. The fact slid away from his mind like smoke though a faint flavor remained. He listened to Anna and watched the wire seem to uncoil as they passed. Maddalena appeared as an irregular contour on the horizon, blotting out the fading sprinkle of stars. Then he remembered.

A *stiff-backed figure riding on top of an armored van. Seen from high above. Boxlike shape. Rommel. His command vehicle. Against the wire.*

"Turn back!" he shouted at the driver. "We must go back. That van parked by the wire, did you see it?" The man could not hear him. Max shoved Anna forward toward the dashboard, leaned behind her close to the driver and repeated his demand.

"What about it?" the driver shouted.

"I think it's Rommel's staff vehicle!"

"That's daft. Begging your pardon. Rommel himself? There's Fort Maddalena just ahead. Don't you worry."

"Turn around!" Max cried.

"I got wounded to deliver."

"You must do as I say. This is an order. I am an officer . . . attached to Cunningham's headquarters."

"Cunningham's out! I heard Auchinleck's taking command." The driver grinned like a leprechaun.

"Do you think it is really Rommel?" Anna said.

"It's his command vehicle, or one just like it," Max replied. "It has to be checked out."

"Yes. You must do it!" Her expression was as determined as when she had asked him to hand over Bright-Ashton's pistol so she could search the panzer.

"I could use John's help." He was thinking out loud. "They've got him all doped up . . ." The convoy stopped at the edge of the tent city around the fort. He was out the door instantly, looking up and down the dark avenues of tents.

"You will find a way," Anna cried. Framed by the open door, her face was livid with expectation.

He loped past the column of lorries until he came to Eighth Army Headquarters. Light spilled from the tent as couriers and staff went in and out. He stopped to think. During the time he had been at Maddalena he had made a few acquaintances on the staff. No one was likely to remember him or to respond to his request. If Cunningham had been replaced, he had no strong ally left at headquarters. His eye fell on a motorcycle parked near the tent entrance.

He sidled up to it and picked up the leather helmet dangling from the handlebars. Buckling the strap under his chin, he straddled the machine as if it belonged to him. He had never driven a motorcycle. He remembered strong, sure hands flicking a starter switch and gripping the throttle, a practiced foot folding the stand and flipping down the starter pedal. Regardless of the make and model of the motorbike, the switch, throttle, and kick starter were approximately where they should be. He brought his weight down on the pedal. The warm engine caught instantly. Relying partly on memory, partly on inspiration, he fumbled with his toe for the gear lever while his left hand released the clutch. He was off and running and nearly collided with a lorry. Its horn rebuked him. He heard shouts and glanced back to see a courier dash out of the headquarters tent after him. A twist of the throttle provided an instant solution. He zipped ahead with a burst of power. He quickly passed the stationary line of lorries and rode north against the continuing flow of vehicles spread out for miles. He concentrated on getting the feel of the machine as he dodged clumps of camel thorn. After a few kilometers he stuck close to the wire. His eyes watched the barbed wire caterpillar crawl just ahead of his bobbing headlamp.

It was Rommel. He knew it. A song of discovery thrummed in his veins, setting him free. It did not matter how he knew. The important thing was to act on his intuition.

After a while, however, he began to suffer doubts along with the freezing cold. Dawn was a gray tinge in the east. What could Rommel have been doing on this side of the wire? Out in front of his troops. Lost? Out of petrol? And what could be done if he found Rommel? Shake hands? Reminisce about old times? He had no weapon, though it would hardly matter if he towed a twenty-five pounder behind the motorbike. He was one man, with no radio, no way to call for reinforcements. His determination began to seem as thin as his light jacket. His hands felt frozen to the handlebars. The desert rapidly

changed from purple to lavender to ocher to beige. Then the
sun exploded over the horizon like a dazzling orange bomb.

   *Brice's Crossroads. Bouncing over thick pasture. Spin-
ning wheels in a red clay bank. How Rommel had loved the
speed, the rushing air. That daredevil dash down the straight
road across the marsh. The same road where the sun had
beaten Sturgis's troops. Riding into the past. Gathering speed
to penetrate time itself. Had Rommel forgotten?*

   How far was it to the gap? Thirty kilometers? If the ACV
had been parked less than halfway between the gap and
Maddalena, it should appear any moment. Far ahead he saw a
wrinkle in the wire. His eyes clung tenaciously to it. He was
frustrated whenever the rough terrain hid it from view. He
crossed a wadi, bogging down in the soft sand, changing to a
low gear and kicking on either side with his feet to struggle
clear and accelerate up the opposite bank. The wrinkle was
distinctly visible, now, as a large dent in the wire; yet there
was no ACV in sight. He drove faster. The motorcycle left the
ground over a shallow rise, forcing him to slow to a more
manageable speed. When he reached the spot, deep tire
tracks leading up to the battered wire indicated that a large,
heavy vehicle had rammed the barrier and pushed it out of
position some ten or twelve feet. A fresh set of tracks led
north.

   He raced his engine anxiously. There was nothing to do
but follow the tracks. When they began to veer to the right,
toward the beaten path of the convoys, he tried to will them to
stay clear, to keep his only link with the ACV intact. But the
snakelike tracks seemed to have a life of their own, disappearing with a vengeance among all the rest. All he could do was
follow the heavily traveled route and hope for the best.
Anything was possible. The ACV could have broken down or
run out of gas. He opened the throttle until the bike reached a
speed of 55 mph. Its front tire vibrated madly over the pitted
surface. All the tracks suddenly swerved left together. Like
trained creatures they went directly to the gap in the wire.

   Speigner stopped in the gap and pushed back his helmet.
The desert was empty except for a thin trail of dust on a far
ridge. It could have been a dust devil.

   Blasting up beside the ACV. Steel panel slides back.

Rommel's face appears in the opening. Van going faster. Bike cresting its wake like a surfer on a wave.

Hello, Max, how are you?

Not too bad. How are you?

I should not complain. I have a supply problem, of course. They are turning me into a goddamned quartermaster.

Can you tell me which side is winning?

It is too early to tell. What part do you play in this?

Stop the bus and I'll tell you.

If I stop I must capture you.

Do it. Let's see what happens.

We are inside Libya. What is to keep me from capturing you?

Stop the bus.

I cannot stop.

I think you can.

It is impossible. If you think it can be done, you stop the bus. Stop it if you can.

XXII

It was the wrong time of day. They scheduled it at an unsuitable hour.

Speigner passed through the gate of the fenced courtyard. The man at the door recognized him and admitted him without delay. There was a short waiting line during the midafternoon lull, but Speigner had not come early to beat the rush. For some time he had been making appointments with Phoebe. It cost double, but he was spared the inconvenience of waiting and of enduring the feeling of being shuffled in on a conveyor belt. He walked past the queue of officers making small talk and went to the cashier, whom he paid without a word. The madam greeted him with what passed for a smile, a twisting of her mouth, and said, "I will ring Phoebe. She is expecting you."

A month had passed since the battle. Inexplicably, Rommel had pulled back just when it seemed he had won. General Auchinleck had kept after him all the way across Cyrenaica. The British had regained all the Libyan territory lost in 1941. The panic-stricken retreat in which Max had participated had somehow translated into victory. He was hard put to understand a misconception of such dimensions. In the meantime, America had entered the war and orders had come through for him to return to Washington. He had had one final service to perform in Cairo. Colonel Weathers had invited him to give a lecture for Military Intelligence.

They scheduled it at a time when people could not come. After the lunch hour was an awkward time. It should have been during lunch, not after it. Who was responsible for that?

He had given the lecture. Now there was nothing left for him to do in Cairo. Anna had gone out of his life so swiftly she seemed like someone he had read about or seen in a movie. Despite promises to get together before she left for Lebanon, she had departed without seeing him. There had been a note at the Semiramis when he called for her. It was scribbled on the back of a postcard.

Dear Max,

    I am so sorry to have to go without saying goodbye. I have to dash to catch my plane. Please know that my prayers go with you. I am so happy that America has joined the fight. Your experience and knowledge of Rommel will be indispensable, and I expect great things of you. I will send you a clipping of the dispatch I wrote about you when I get back to New York.

    You are a warrior now.

au revoir,
Anna

He had many memories of her—arguing at the Sphinx, mopping her plate with a piece of bread, demanding that he hand over John's pistol, pulling on her shoes over bloody socks—but his abiding memory was of her pale face in the cab of the lorry, exhausted but indefatigable, when she said, "You will find a way."

The elevator was descending as he entered the lounge. Phoebe rode in the wire cage. She wore fresh makeup and was smiling. She danced out to meet him.

"Hello, Max! I am welcoming you."

"Hi, Phoebe." Distracted by his thoughts, he allowed himself to be kissed and petted and towed into the elevator. Phoebe's open affection was unusual. She did not ordinarily indulge in such public display. He saw the cashier watching them with an expression of bored detachment before he returned to counting his money.

There were six in the audience. Six. Why did they have to have it in such a large room? Surely there were seminar rooms available. Who was responsible? Weathers.

They got off the elevator and went down the corridor. Phoebe put her head on his shoulder, which made walking difficult.

"Today is the day," she said.

"What day?" They had reached the door to her room and she flung the door open.

"The day we go on the date. Not a date to eat but the other kind, like you say in America. I am so more excited."

"Date?" He balked in the doorway. She tugged at his hand.

"Yes, date. Boy-girl. You know what you said."

"Aren't we together now?"

"This is nothing—only fucking. But afterwards . . . a real date. You promised." She prepared to become petulant, a relaxing of the facial muscles he recognized.

Wasn't it announced in advance? There should have been a notice posted on GHQ bulletin boards, or maybe a memo sent around. Whoever organized it did one crummy job.

"Promised?" He tossed his hat carelessly on the divan.

"To take me to the bazaar." She helped him out of his coat, her dark eyes feeding on his face. She loosened his tie.

"The bazaar?"

"I have money from my brother. I buy things. You take to America on plane with you. My brother get it from you in America." She plucked his shirttails out of his pants and began unbuttoning.

"You think I can avoid customs duties?" he said, lifting his arm so she could pull the shirt off. "Phoebe, there's only so much merchandise a person can take into the U.S. duty-free. After that, I pay as much tax as anyone else."

"Soldier have special privilege, yes?" Phoebe was un-buckling his belt. In the past, this gesture might have heralded an erection. Today, nothing was happening.

"Oh, no they don't!" Max was down to shoes and shorts. Phoebe glanced at his crotch. She raised her hands above her head and went into a leisurely bump-and-grind routine. Max kicked off his shoes and lay on the bed.

"The goods they arrive okay if you take to America." She emphasized this theory with a series of hopeful bumps. Max stared at the ceiling and pictured six faces surrounded by the empty seats. Bright-Ashton had squirmed in his seat, restless with embarrassment. "They don't take so more space. Jelly, spice, leather good, clothing—they fit your duffel bag okay."

He was sorry he had told her that he had been recalled to regular duty. He could not have foreseen her request, however. Phoebe had always been full of surprises.

"Phoebe, good God. This is our last time. Do you have to . . . ?"

"Maybe not last time. Maybe I visit you in America. Do you want the oil?"

"No oil today."

She stripped off his shorts, lightly raking his thighs with her nails. Then she began to peel off her scanty garments, one by one. Max watched her out of consideration for her feelings.

That bald-headed brigadier had the gall to ask for a short biography of Rommel. Said he "just got over and needed a spot of briefing." It was degrading, like an oral midterm exam from a prof too lazy to grade a written test.

Phoebe crawled into bed and began stroking and kissing him. He lay still. After a minute she sat up.

"Something bother you, Max?"

Max sat up too. "Nobody came to my lecture." She opened her eyes wide with sympathy, and hurt feelings gushed from him. "Worked a week on my talk. Last hurrah. Some-thing for the Brits to remember. A summary, based on Rommel's known movements during Crusader. His tendency toward dispersal of his forces, spreading himself too thin in flanking movements, outrunning his fuel supply. In Normandy he was commanding a single division and could coordinate his battalions like muscles attached to his nervous system. But in the desert, where climatic conditions play havoc with radio transmissions, he runs a risk of breakdown in chain of command when he leads from the front." They sat eye to eye. Phoebe frowned to match his intense expression. "His acceptance of this risk tells me he is frustrated with failure to achieve his immediate goals and with the incompetence of his Italian allies. Rommel is out of patience. The way to beat him is to keep him at bay while building superior reserves and then let him come on. There will come a point when he can't wait any longer. Then he will say, 'To hell with the odds.' And you'll have him at a disadvantage. That's the only way you're going to beat him."

Phoebe returned to her stroking and kissing momentarily but gave up when she saw that he gained more relief from talking. She listened attentively.

"But in the middle of my prepared lecture, I got sidetracked on a vindictive appraisal of the concept of British armor. How the caste system has hung on there, with a cadre of gentlemanly amateurs and an enlisted body of peasants. Instead of armor per se you have a horsey lot of ex-cavalry regiments known as lancers, hussars, or dragoons. The RAF concepts of organization and warfare are as modern as their planes and equipment; yet British tank strategy is eighteenth-century in concept, except armored machines have replaced horses. Armor cannot function as freely within the British army as the technical panzer arm of the Wehrmacht, which is manned by professionals recruited from all classes of an industrial society unencumbered by caste traditions. Consider the very jargon of British armor: one commands from his 'charger,' instead of his tank; supply trains go forward at the order 'Lead horses.' The cavalry's mind is as armor-plated as its body, where tradition is concerned. Until British armor reorganizes along the same lines as the Germans, they will wage a battle against themselves as well as the enemy, tethered to the past while facing a superior opponent held in check temporarily by sheer weight of numbers." He paused, hungering for a packed gallery erupting in stunned denial and angry rebuttal. Phoebe cocked her head. Actually he had delivered no such inflammatory opinions to his audience of six, though now it almost seemed that he had.

"Well, I can't claim it's all original with me," he murmured, and slumped back down.

"Now, now." She chastely stroked his forehead.

"They wanted to know Rommel's *hobbies*, his preference in field sports, whether he liked horses!"

"Now, now."

"They asked if Forrest was a bandit, a kind of Robin Hood, who had learned hit-and-run tactics by robbing trains."

"Now, now."

Max began to experience an odd, post-coital languor.

"Now we go to bazaar," Phoebe said.

It felt strange to be with Phoebe out of doors. Among the people crowding the alleyways of the ancient marketplace called Bab el Sharia she appeared shorter, rounder. He saw people staring at them. Phoebe's makeup, hair style, and extravagant clothing identified her as a prostitute. A rich G.I. and his woman, they were thinking. He did not mind if Phoebe was thought to be his woman. But in the bazaar he did not relish having shopkeepers mark him as rich. The bazaar had been created for the purpose of parting fools with their money. He nervously followed Phoebe through twisting alleys so narrow that shops were stalls wedged into crevices. Phoebe browsed with the lazy expertise of a shark escorting a slow freighter. She absently slapped away begging children, of which there were a great number. Max smelled food cooking, incense, spices, leather, charcoal smoke, and rotting waste. Phoebe lingered in a tailor's shop, dallied at a crockery stall, trifled with a jeweler, dawdled at a spice stand.

At a leather shop, she got serious.

Max did not like the look of the fat leather merchant. His beady eyes did not inspire confidence. Phoebe entered into a litany of haggling over a dozen leather bracelets. She bargained by rote, mechanically, with periodic invocations of *Inshallah*. Their singsong bartering flowed together, so that they seemed to be completing the last line of each other's song lyrics.

There was a teamwork to it, like Rodgers and Hart. Max watched them with the dull expression of a halfwit.

"Is only three pounds!" Phoebe turned to him flushed with triumph.

"Egyptian?" he brushed flies away from his face.

"No, sterling." She was disappointed he did not share her elation.

"That seems high to me," he said dubiously. "Are you sure you want to pay that much?"

"But Max, I hope this to be your goodbye present to me. Something to remember you by."

Like my lecture at M.I.

"A dozen leather bracelets? Six for each arm! I thought this was strickly business, for your brother's shop."

"It is for shop. Strictly."

The leather merchant had turned away to allow them a moment of private discussion.

"Then it's for business and should be done in a businesslike manner," Max said, although he did not feel especially businesslike. "Can't we shop around? There must be other leather merchants."

Phoebe spoke brusquely to the merchant, who sagged before her attack, a broken man.

"Is now one pound sterling. A great bargain!" she told Max expectantly. When Speigner reached for his wallet, the merchant had already scooped up the bracelets and was depositing them in Phoebe's voluminous shopping bag.

They wound through the alleyways until Phoebe found a clothier she fancied. There were many cotton stalls with fabrics just as bright. Max could not understand why she was so determined to do business with this particular shop. He listened to her begin haggling with the shopkeeper and became alert when he heard the word *akhuw*, which meant a relative—he was not sure which: cousin or uncle. It might have been a complimentary term, but why would Phoebe be nice to a guy who was trying to take her/his money? He noticed a leather shop across the alley. Since it was only steps away, he moved closer and saw a bracelet identical to the ones she had bought earlier.

"Kem?" How much? he asked the shopkeeper.

"Ishriyn piastriyn." The man's shrug implied the price was nonnegotiable. Even so, it was half what he had paid Phoebe's leather merchant. He turned back to the clothier and saw that Phoebe had been watching him while she continued to haggle.

"Two and a half pounds per square meter, Max," she said, holding up a bolt of fabric. "Egyptian, not sterling."

"Don't tell me," he said. "A bargain."

"It is good price, Max." Her eyes grew melancholy at the doubt in his voice.

"Then *you* pay it," he said.

"Max, I am ask for too much? Then I pay you back. My brother—"

"In New Jersey."

"Yes. He send money right away, and I pay you back any day."

"I'm leaving Friday," he said.

"Just a small loan," she said.

"To remember me by? Look, you're not kin to this guy, are you, Phoebe? *Akhuw*—cousin, uncle? Or the other one, who sold you—us—the bracelets? Is he a member of the family—or maybe just an in-law?" Phoebe's face clouded over as she comprehended what he was saying. "There are identical bracelets across the alley for less than half what we paid your bargain-basement dealer back there. I like to be remembered, but not as a sap."

They squared off in the alley with an audience of urchins. The clothier appeared at Phoebe's side. Together they launched a shrieking defense spiced with many references to Speigner's ancestry. He noticed that Phoebe and the clothier bore a marked family resemblance when they became angry, the same hook of the nose, same slant of the canine teeth. He looked enough like Phoebe to be her brother.

Is this the way it ends, Phoebe? Not with a bang but a shriek?

Smiling ruefully to himself, he made his way through the tortuous alleys of Bab el Sharia. He had one final obligation, a farewell lunch with Bright-Ashton, and then, he thought, I will have run my course in Cairo.

He had not been to the Mohammed Ali Club since the day after he arrived, four months ago. It seemed more like a year. He could not get used to the idea of going back to Washington. It was hard to recall what his apartment looked like. His little cat was probably long gone, no doubt having taken possession of some other lonesome, unsuspecting person. He did not know whether he could stand to sit in his office and supervise the operation of his files department. In his heart he knew what he would do as soon as he returned. He would put in for transfer to a combat unit. If there was to be an Allied invasion of North Africa, he wanted to be part of it. With a feeling akin to nostalgia he followed a waiter to Bright-Ashton's table near a window. The major's smile was quick and genuine. He gestured for Max to take the seat opposite and moved a white lily in a slender vase to one side so they would not have to talk around it.

"Join me in a drink?" John said. "Gin and lime?" Max nodded and the waiter went away. Bright-Ashton gave him a sensitive glance. "Are we having a celebration or a wake? Are you glad to be going home at last? I wish *I* could."

"Are you kidding? Hot dogs, hamburgers, apple pie, everything that Cairo hasn't got," Max replied with false enthusiasm.

"*And* telephones that work, shopkeepers who don't haggle over the price, no flies, no dust, no muezzin's call to prayer every time you go for a stroll."

"Heaven on earth . . ." Max paused.

"But what?" John twisted his glass on its hand-crafted coaster.

"Well, I'd prefer to leave here feeling better about my job."

"I'm sorry about the turnout for your lecture," John said quickly.

"It's not that. I don't think I've made much of a contribution." Max shrugged.

"Don't talk such nonsense! The Khireigat dump alone—"

"That was sheer luck and you know it."

"Bloody nonsense! It was all your show from the very start. And your insights into Rommel, his borrowing from Forrest, have been very enlightening."

"GHQ has been amused," Max said ironically. "I provided 'a bizarre example of American intelligence.' I believe GHQ thought of me as droll."

"You are oversensitive," John protested. "I think you've done a marvelous job, and I should know—better than anyone. I'm the one you carried out of the desert, remember? If it weren't for you, I might not have this." He flexed the fingers of his right hand.

The waiter brought Max's drink. They raised their glasses to each other.

Max changed the subject, determined that their last meal together should be pleasant. "What news from the front?"

"You've heard about the convoy that got through to Tripoli?" Bright-Ashton nervously toyed with his glass again. "RAF boys at Malta can't get them all. Still, I suppose it could have come at a worse time. If the Afrika Korps had been fattened up while the battle for Tobruk was going on in November, our chaps would likely be holding the El Alamein line instead of El Agheila."

"Getting a convoy shipment is as good as a victory in battle," Max observed. "How's the line holding at Agheila?"

"Am I speaking with the U.S. State Department or my personal stretcher-bearer? All right. Of course we have a supply problem. One thousand miles across the desert—who wouldn't? And as you doubtless have surmised, troop strength is not up to par. So many troops and materiel have been diverted to the Far East now that Japan's come in. Lucky that Rommel's holed up for the winter."

"If Rommel knew how thin we were out there," Max reflected, "I wouldn't be surprised if he would be tempted to counterattack, would you?"

"This soon after withdrawing?" John raised his eyebrows. "Well then, we shan't tell him about out troop strength."

"I imagine it's plain enough," Max said. "All he has to do is fly over in his Storch and see for himself. He came close to beating us during Crusader, didn't he?"

"Too true." Bright-Ashton took a stiff swallow and smacked his lips at the bite of lime. "Information from German prisoners indicates he was with Fifth Panzer in the surprise drive through Seventh Armored to the wire."

Max glanced up. "What date?"

"November twenty-five or twenty-six. I think it was. Before the second battle for the Sidi Rezegh high ground."

"So he could have been there," Max said, thinking out loud.

"Where?"

"Across the wire."

"You mean, with Twenty-First Panzer southeast of Halfaya?"

"No, near Maddalena."

"What would he have been doing there?"

"I don't know—leading a spearhead behind the lines. Out to capture Eighth Army headquarters. Creating chaos. The usual."

Bright-Ashton assumed an expression of mock incredulity. "Speaking as a mystic?"

"All I've ever done here is guess what's going on," Max countered. "*You're* the one with the answers, you tell *me*."

"You think I have nothing better to do than stay up poring over battle reports so I can graph Rommel's frenetic path through the scrub? Really, Speigner."

The waiter came to take their order for lunch. They ordered the daily special—fish with mayonnaise—and more gin and lime juice.

"I wonder," Max said, "if he knows—I'm in Egypt. He probably wouldn't care even if he . . ."

"Rommel? Oh, he knows, all right. Been knowing."

"Are you sure?" Max tried to suppress his excitement.

"Can't reveal my sources," John said blandly, "but we had a decoded transmission from Tripoli to Berlin some time ago that mentioned you, although not by name."

"Tripoli?" His mind was racing. "You mean, after the Germans' recent withdrawal?"

"No, ages ago."

"When?"

"I'd have to look it up. Mid-September, I'd say."

"Right after I arrived?" Max was amazed. "What did the message say?"

"It's been a long . . ."

"Try to remember, *please!*" Max leaned over the table. The major gave him a searching look.

"Well, I *was* keen on it, since it rather justified my having got you over here. My stock went up around the office when we found that Rommel had taken notice of your arrival."

"*What did it say?*"

"Something to the effect, 'American liaison officer personally known to me arrived Cairo yesterday.'"

Max was lost in thought. "There's only one way," he said slowly, "that Rommel could have gotten that information. The State Department cipher—what do they call it?"

"The Black Code," John said. "You should know that better than I."

"He's got it!" Max cried. Heads turned to glance at the American officer who showed such small regard for decorum. Doubtless, their expressions were saying, he could not hold his liquor. "The Germans have broken it!"

". . . he said, as he leapt to a conclusion," Bright-Ashton joked.

"I'm serious," said Max. "Look, where else would that information have been available? Did your side report it to London? I hardly think news of my arrival was worth their while to encode it. There's only one way—and if I can get into the embassy transmission files, I can verify it."

"Perhaps it's only coincidence." John grew solemn.

"Do you see what this means? It's possible there is a connection between our embassy reports and German strategy."

"My dear Max, proving your case would result in cutting your embassy off from Allied intelligence."

Max reflected for a moment. "What if Colonel Fellers, or Mr. Kirk, has recently relayed to Washington an assessment of the current low levels of troop strength in Libya? An intercepted report like that would have Rommel raring to attack."

"But he'd have to attack to prove your point."

"Exactly."

"There are other factors, surely?" John persisted.

The waiter brought their fish salad. As he set the food on the table, Speigner placed his napkin beside his plate and stood. The waiter and Bright-Ashton stared at him.

"I'm sorry," Max apologized to both of them, "but I've got to get back to the office."

"Can't it wait thirty minutes?" John asked. The waiter seemed to second the question.

"I've got to get into those files," said Speigner, shaking his head. At this mention of private information the waiter discreetly withdrew.

"When is your flight to America?" Bright-Ashton asked.

"Friday." Max sat on the edge of his chair. "Look, if I find what I think I will, can you help me get to Agheila?"

John looked at the salad arranged on a bed of lettuce leaves with symmetrical wedges of tomato and lemon. "Must it always be business before pleasure?" he sighed.

"If Colonel Fellers is doing his job," Max said eagerly, "his report on the current British position has gone out."

"So?"

"So I believe Rommel will act on this information . . ."

"Surely not this information alone!"

". . . coupled with his own observations. If an attack is coming and our code is in any way responsible, then the American liaison office must try to secure advance warning."

"I am to exhaust every RAF favor I've got coming for the next two years ferrying you a thousand miles to the front, so you can—what?"

"I want to fly reconnaissance behind enemy lines."

John pushed back his plate and lit a cigarette. "To think how I argued with my superiors about having you over. I creep in from my shaky limb and find you clinging to the main trunk, shooing me out again as far as I can go."

"Don't be so modest," Max said with a grin. "I'll bet my next paycheck you'll come through."

"Why do I suddenly feel like your Birka girl—Phoebe? Aren't I to be paid in advance, rather than much, much later?" John tapped an ash elaborately. "All right, I've gone this far, and"—he held up his healed right hand—"I do owe you. But remember, I can't promise anything beyond getting you a hitch to Benghazi. From there, you're on your own."

"Will you be at your office this afternoon if I phone?" Max stood up to leave. John nodded wearily. "Thanks for the lunch, anyway. And, major," Max added mischievously, "no more gin while you're on duty."

The embassy office was nearly deserted during lunch hour. Besides the marine guard at the door and the duty officer, there was a single receptionist in the anteroom.

Speigner recognized her as the wife of a newly assigned marine lieutenant. She was bright, cheerful, and eager to please. He approached her with an ingratiating smile. He could not recall her name.

"Hi, Beth," he guessed.

"It's Betsy." She tucked her chin in a deprecating way. "You're back early."

"Betsy, oh yeah, how's it going?" His casual attitude, which had the flavor of home, seemed to please her. *We Americans stick together over here in the land of camels and crocs.* "I need to look something up in the files. Just take a minute." Her bright smile faded. "I've got clearance. I'm trying to get Colonel Fellers that commendation from the British he was hoping they'd give him before Christmas."

"Can't it wait until after lunch?" The young woman glanced at the locked door of the filing closet. "Martha keeps a strict log on who goes in and who comes out."

"It'll only take a minute," Speigner coaxed. "I need to double-check some information for a two o'clock meeting at GHQ, and I've got a taxi waiting. I'll be in and out before you know it."

"Well, if *you'll* take the responsibility," she said hesitantly. "You'll have to sign the log." She opened a brown notebook and laid it on the desk.

"Glad to." He scribbled his name with a flourish. If he was right, Colonel Fellers might not get a commendation, but it could save the State Department a great deal of embarrassment, not to mention British lives. If he was wrong, what could they do—reprimand him?

She let him into the files room, flicking on the light for him before retiring to her desk. Cabinets lined the walls. Max felt perfectly at home among them. Even the dust seemed familiar. He searched the headings on each drawer and soon found what he was looking for: the radio transmissions log file, a drawer of note cards summarizing each transmission and bearing a cross-reference number for carbon copy files of original messages. When he found the number, or numbers, he needed, Betsy would have to unlock another cabinet and locate the classified documents for him. He started with the section dated "Dec. 31, 1941," reading the notations and flipping quickly through the cards.

Egypt   12/13/41
From: Kirk   Tel. 1, 9 am

Bank buying rate per dollar (daily figure for the—)

Egypt   1/1/42
From: Kirk   Tel. 1, 9 am

Attack on the VALIANT and the QUEEN ELIZA-
BETH in Alexandria Harbor (Info. re: submarines
used in—)

Egypt: 1/1/42
From: Kirk   Tel. 2, 10:30 am

Meatless days. Info. regarding 3—now ordered by
Govt. Comments on rise in price in fish.

Egypt: 1/1/42
From: Kirk   Tel. 3, 11 am
                            Confid. File

Weakness of present position in Middle East Theater.
STRICTLY CONFIDENTIAL FOR THE SECRE-
TARY AND UNDER SEC. (submits estimate of—)

Max copied the reference number on a slip of paper, closed the
drawer, and gave Besty the piece of paper. She produced
another notebook, headed "Confidential File Log," and had
him sign his name. Then she opened a locked cabinet and
withdrew. Speigner found the file he wanted and devoured it:

SECRET

From: Egypt
Filed: 11:00 am, 1/1/42

The following estimate of current British military situation in the Western Desert is based on
information received from GHQ in Cairo.

The British position in Cyrenaica is overextended, with tenuous supply lines and skeleton
forces manning forward posts between Benghazi and
El Agheila. Fresh replacement troops have been diverted to the Far East Theater; for example, 7

Armored Brigade, 18 Infantry Div., 6 and 7 Australian Div., and 17 Indian Div. (previously assigned to Iraq), including additional RAF fighter & bomber squadrons and several artillery and antiaircraft regiments.

Weakness on land is exacerbated by simultaneous British naval losses which inhibit control of Mediterranean shipping lanes. German attacks on Malta have curtailed British reconnaissance patrols, allowing Axis convoys to slip through. British ships sunk or damaged in the past 60 days include: carrier Ark Royal; battleships Barham, Queen Elizabeth, and Valiant; cruisers Galatea, Neptune, and Aurora; destroyer Kandanhar.

Regardless of territorial gains made by the British because of recent German retreat, their current military situation is precarious. German forces remain intact and dangerous. The British have contingency plans for withdrawal in case of sudden German attack, which is not expected, however, before spring. In the meantime, the British are stockpiling for a spring offensive of their own.

Kirk

. . . *skeleton forces . . . plans for withdrawal . . . German attack not expected.* . . . He could feel the heat such information would generate in Rommel. Strike when the enemy was weakest! Good strategy, certainly, but more importantly it was Rommel's nature to do so. He could no more resist such an opportunity than an owl could withstand its biological imperative to attack a wounded crow. Speigner handed Betsy the file, thanked her, and hurried downstairs to use the lobby phone. He rang up Bright-Ashton. In a voice trembling with excitement, he asked if they could meet within the hour. John understood that the American had information he did not wish to repeat over the phone. Max could hear doubt, resignation and something else—envy?—in the precise voice made flat and nasal by the wires. Bright-Ashton suggested a bar near Shepheard's. Speigner caught a taxi and went there immediately. He had been nursing a tepid cup of tea for twenty minutes when the major arrived.

"Not enough evidence to warrant the trouble." John lit his pipe after listening to Speigner's account of the transmission he had discovered.

"It's my neck, not yours," Max argued. "Besides, America is in the war now. Don't you think I have a duty to perform?"

"Listen," John said, "I can't tell you how we do it, but if Rommel plans to break out, we'll know about it as soon as his friends the Italians. None of our sources have picked up the slightest indication that he plans to attack."

Max wondered whether John was referring delicately to the Enigma code. Could the British have broken it?

"Don't forget, Rommel achieved surprise last spring by ignoring Italian general orders not to attack," Max persisted. "He simply attacked without informing the Italians. One thing I remember Rommel admired about Forrest was that he kept his own counsel and revealed his plans only at the last possible moment."

"Granted," Bright-Ashton said. "Still there's not enough. . . ."

"You told me at lunch about the supply ships getting through. Remember?" Max's voice rose indignantly. He lowered it when John glanced around to see if anyone was listening. "Two things have happened: one, he's got evidence that British positions are weakly defended, both from intercepted transmissions by our embassy and from his own intelligence sources; two, he has finally received a big shipment of supplies that he's been expecting for months. Can't you feel it! It's like the quiet before a storm, when the tingle in the back of your neck tells you lightning is going to strike."

"This is no supply dump you're talking about," John said quietly. "No raid to capture stores along the frontier. This is the beginnings of a major campaign, right? Even if we knew for certain, this minute, he was coming, I doubt there's very much that could be done about it."

"Equipment and troops could be saved! Why give up without a struggle?"

"You are marvelous, Max, you truly are. Here you are, talking as though Rommel's counterattack were a *fait accompli*. How do you drag me into these things?"

"All I'm asking is . . ." Max's face lit up as he realized that he had heard acquiescence in the major's voice.

"You'd ask for the sun and the moon." John smiled. "I've talked to a chap in the mail service. It's highly irregular, but I've got you a place on the mail plane to Benghazi as a diplomatic courier. It's the most direct route other than a bomb run on Tripoli. Perhaps they should fit you out in a parachute and drop you off over Panzer Group HQ. This time, if anything happens and you're found out, I can't help you and will not vouch for you. In the absence of written orders from your embassy liaison—"

"Two plane rides!" Max turned inside out with elation. "One to get there and one to fly reconnaissance."

"All I can do," Bright-Ashton cautioned, "is get there and put you in touch with an RAF squadron leader I *think* is near Benghazi—classmates at Winchester. The rest is up to you. And may I say, Max, that your service to the Crown has exceeded my wildest expectations."

XXIII

War with America. The Führer had announced it during a recent speech in which he had some kind words for me. One must take the bad with the good. No point in worrying about it. Leave national policy to the politicans and let the generals do the fighting. There is enough to think about, with the British diverting their crack units to the Far East and weakening their front lines. Opportunity not to be missed . . . but war with America?

Rommel tried to concentrate on the intelligence reports piled on his desk. Memories flooded over the printed lines and filled in the contours of his imagination. He stared at the White House through an iron fence in the still of the night, wandered among the fortresses of democracy alongside the Washington Mall, entered the Lincoln Memorial and looked upon the craggy face of freedom itself, read the immortal words inscribed on the walls: ". . . this government of the people, by the people, for the people, shall not perish . . ." He heard Speigner translating Faulkner's story and cursing as he stumbled over an unseen brush pile in the haunted woods of Shiloh. He sprinted over the Brooklyn Bridge above gulls white against the green river. He climbed the rocky battlements of Gettysburg. He learned that America's natural resources, its steel and petroleum and wheat, were less formidable than its spirit. A sleeping giant has been awakened. Someday it would surely rise before him.

"Herr General," Schmidt stuck his head through the doorway. "We just received a call from Comando Suprèmo. General Cavallero will arrive shortly."

I don't have to take any more shit from Cavallero.

"Very well," he said.

His surprise attack would not be leaked by the Italians' faulty security *this* time. Field Marshal Kesselring was playing it hands-off as far as the idea of excluding the Italians was concerned. But now that *Panzergruppe* had been elevated to *Panzerarmee* and Rommel had been promoted to *Oberbefehlshaber*, army commander, he did not have to answer to Cavallero. Thus he had given strict orders regarding distribution of the battle plan to field officers in 90th Light and 21st Panzer. Neither OKW nor Comando Suprèmo would learn of the counterattack until the assault had been launched. Messages from Comando Suprèmo to Rome had a way of getting around to British ears. He had determined that orders would be posted by his quartermaster in all Panzerarmee road maintenance depots the day of the battle, January 21—today. He planned to lead a support unit with the *ad hoc* title of Group Marcks. They would achieve perfect and total surprise.

Rommel shuffled through the papers until he found the U.S. State Department report from Cairo dated 1-1-42. It had been a major factor in his decision to counterattack. His eyes raced over the typewritten copy, pausing over crucial phrases: "British position . . . overextended . . . troops . . . diverted to the Far East . . . British naval losses . . . inhibit control of Mediterranean shipping lanes . . . current military situation . . . precarious . . . contingency plans for withdrawal . . . German attack . . . not expected . . . before spring. . . ." Along with the Axis supply convoy that had gotten through, this intercept provided the best of omens for a successful attack.

On impulse he went into the bedroom of his quarters. He opened the footlocker under his bed and peeled away uniforms and underwear, socks and shirts. In the bottom was the small wooden box in which he kept his medals. He placed the box on the shelf under his shaving mirror and switched on the light. Inside the box, among the tarnished brass buttons and multicolored ribbons from three nations, was his minié ball. Schmidt had surprised him by presenting it after the withdrawal had been completed. It felt slightly dusty to the touch.

Kept his own counsel.

He looked at his face in the mirror. Jaundice flirted at the corners of his mouth and in the hollows of his cheeks. December had taken its toll: the retreat across Cyrenaica, his first major withdrawal, had been a tough but necessary choice. His divisions needed to regroup, to mend their wounds, to rearm their strike units. The Führer had stood firm behind him against inevitable criticism from OKW and Comando Suprèmo, hence this invaluable shipment of January 5, which included fifty-five tanks and twenty armored cars, antitank guns and all kinds of ammunition and supplies. Now he had a chance to regain all the ground he had given up and more: Tobruk.

Cavallero, the Italian commander, was coming, full of *tempèsta*. Battle notices had not been posted for twenty minutes yet and here came Comando Suprèmo with demands. Cavallero would accuse him of exceeding his authority and of undermining the Axis alliance by withholding information. He would scream about the need to hold back, go slowly, reduce the mission to a reconnaissance in force—just the sort of thing the British had come to expect from the Italians. Rommel planned to listen, keep his mouth shut and let his *Oberbefehlshaber* title do his talking for him.

I've got the British by the short hairs, and I am going to tear it out by the roots.

He dropped the minié ball into his pocket and went out to meet Cavallero.

At 4 A.M. the RAF jeep crept through the streets of Benghazi. Antiaircraft spotlights swept the sky with infinite patience. Plundered by three armies, Benghazi's ruined buildings gaped like open graves. First the Italians had been driven away by the British, blowing their supply dumps and burning the docks as they retreated. Then the Germans had retaken Benghazi and the British had hauled away all the petrol, ammunition, wine, oranges, and sheep they could carry, systematically destroying what they could not. A few months later it was the Germans' turn to repeat the ritual. What British bombers left intact, German demolition squads blew up. They had been quite thorough, Max thought. Twisted railroad cars lay in monstrous heaps beside newly laid tracks shining in the glow of the spotlights. Tree stumps lined what had once been wide, shady boulevards. Storefronts were boarded up. Piles of debris and rubble lined the sidewalks.

Speigner wondered at such casual destruction. A salty breeze off the Mediterranean swept through the tattered town as if to say, Yes, but none of this will endure.

He had been on the move constantly for the past twelve hours, having left Cario at 4 P.M. the day before in a Ford Trimotor mail plane. It had touched down at six airfields on its way to Benghazi. He had dozed in his harness seat only to be jolted awake by the shock of landing at Mersa Matruh, or Tobruk, or Gazala, where bags of mail were thrown out and exchanged for return mail, fuel was taken on, and the Trimotor revved for another takeoff. Now, riding in a jeep, he felt he was in the wrong element, too near to the ground. He was going to an airstrip south of Benghazi. In his pocket was a slip of paper with the name of Bright-Ashton's friend, Squadron Leader Arthur Rosenberg. He secretly rebelled against the slow pace of the jeep, which weaved among armored cars parked beside an occasional camel or donkey-led cart. From the tent cities erected on the perimeter of the town came the strangely normal smell of food frying and the sound of dogs barking. Speigner felt an overwhelming sense of disaster to which the sleeping town was oblivious. The jeep headlights illuminated a road sign:

DO NOT EXCEED SPEED LIMIT
YOU ARE BEING TIMED

Although the airstrip was only fifteen kilometers south of Benghazi, it was 5 A.M. when they arrived. The duty officer of the squadron was asleep with a book of poetry in his hand. He sleepily told Max that Rosenberg was not to be disturbed and suggested that he get a cup of tea and come back at 0530. In the mess tent, Max drank some rusty-tasting tea, ate a bully sandwich, and listened to two mechanics argue about which food they missed the most: apricots or apples, kidney or pork pies, fresh baked bread, fish and chips, a pint of bitters. In spite of his preoccupation with his mission, Max became homesick. Food meant home: jambalaya in New Orleans, barbecue in Memphis, fried chicken in Mississippi. Red streaks appeared in the east as he made his way back to the operations tent. Rosenberg was awake.

On an empty petrol can behind the tent, the squadron leader had laid out his shaving kit and was busy with his shaving brush. Wearing an undershirt and a towel draped around his thick neck, Rosenberg gave Max a noncommittal glance, then returned to his mirror. He soaped his blue-bearded jaws and stropped his razor. "Yes?"

"I've come from Cairo on a matter of extreme importance," Max said. "We have a mutual friend—"

"Who are you?" Rosenberg methodically began to shave.

"Lieutenant Maxwell Speigner, U.S. Army Intelligence, assigned to military liaison office, U.S. Embassy, Cairo. Major John Bright-Ashton told me to look you up."

"To what purpose?"

After you get there, the rest is up to you.

"I have information which indicates Rommel may be mounting a counterattack."

Rosenberg compressed his lips against a fringe of white suds. "Where did you get that notion?"

"From a top secret source."

"I haven't heard any reports about a German buildup." Rosenberg shaved over his upper lip.

"Bright-Ashton gave me your name . . ."

"So you said."

"He mentioned you were fellow Wykehamists . . ."

"In another life." The squadron leader wiped his razor on the towel. "What do you want?"

"To fly with your next reconnaissance patrol." Max tried to keep the impatience out of his voice.

"Quite impossible."

How did one explain four years of clipping German newspapers, a trip to Shiloh, a night of star shells, an enemy tank with a ghostly crew, a Scottish woman's fierceness, a motorcycle chase to a gap in the wire?

The razor rasped against Rosenberg's beard. "Don't you think if an attack was being mounted our patrols would spot the increased activity?"

"I think it will come from the south, from the desert," Max said, "with a simultaneous attack along the Via Balbia."

"What gave you that idea?" Rosenberg stopped shaving.

"Because that's what Nathan Bedford Forrest did at the Battle of Brice's Crossroads, and I accompanied Erwin Rommel to the site of that battle in 1937."

The squadron leader wiped his face clean, glancing over his towel at Max. "May I see your papers, please?" Speigner handed them to him. "If Bright-Ashton is behind this, you must have some cause," Rosenberg said after studying the papers. "But I prefer not to hear any more theory about Rommel and Nathan or whoever. I have enough on my mind as it is. We have a recce flight scheduled for noon—"

"There's no time to lose!" Max broke in.

"We don't have petrol for two midday flights," Rosenberg continued unperturbed. "You'll have to talk to the pilot. If he wants to go up a bit early, that's his lookout. Check with the duty officer to see who's next up on the flight line."

Rosenberg gathered up his shaving kit and walked back to the tent. Thinking that Bright-Ashton might have better prepared him for such a reception, Max went around to the front of the operations tent. The duty officer referred him to a pilot named Murphy, who was drinking a cup of ersatz coffee in the mess and working a crossword puzzle. Max sat beside the pilot and stated his request, apologizing for the inconvenience. Murphy was a ruddy-faced Irishman with a handlebar mustache. He squinted at Speigner as if observing the enemy from two thousand feet. Murphy leisurely finished his coffee. He tried to erase a word in the puzzle but smeared the writing and tossed the paper aside.

"Let's go," he said.

Sitting in the back seat of the AT-6, trussed in bulky flight jacket and parachute, leather helmet strapped tight with hard earphones pressing against his ears, Speigner felt isolated from the rest of the world. He watched an industrious ground crew perform their duties efficiently. Firemen and ambulance crews sat in open cabs with casual watchfulness. The violent noise of the engine warming up isolated him further, and he found himself remembering unrelated events. On Beale Street he had heard W. C. Handy play the blues in a nightclub packed shoulder to shoulder with whites and blacks. On the last night before college graduation he had sat at the foot of the marble Confederate monument waiting for dawn, while a sheriff's deputy circled the courthouse square and regarded him possessively. He thought of his mother sewing while she listened to her favorite radio show—her fingers as restless as her dreams. Inside this Lend-Lease aircraft, all that had happened to him in the past was like water dreams in which he swam leisurely from one event to another, floating free to the surface of the present, where he now emerged with a single duty before him.

The AT-6 blasted down the dirt strip and they were airborne, rising into the wind from the west. Below them spread the tent city of the 4th Indian Division—rank upon rank of lorries, half-tracks, light tanks, and artillery pieces— and the railroad track and supply depots along it. As they gained altitude Max could see the red-and-white checkerboard of Benghazi to the north. When they circled he could see silver-domed mosques among the red roofs, seemingly pristine and untouched from this height. He imagined the street vendors setting up their vegetable stands amid the rubble, the twenty-four-hours-a-day brothels serving coffee to the late departing and the early arriving. The black line of the Via Balbia traced the coastline, which cleaved to the dark sweep of the sea. The time was 7:30 A.M.

They flew south. The pilot tersely identified for Max the towns of Beda Fomm and Agedabia and the 1st Armored Division camped east of the latter. An hour passed with no sign of enemy activity. Even with his binoculars Max could not, at 2,500 feet, distinguish whether the scattered vehicles moving up the Via Balbia were British or German. Murphy readily identified petrol convoys or motorized infantry. "If it's got a red eye on it, see, it's ours." His voice sounded indifferent over the intercom. He did not speak again until they were passing over the town of Mersa Brega. This time, his tone of interest made Max's heart skip.

"What have we here?"

"What is it!" Max looked on either side of them, but saw nothing moving on highway or desert.

"Smoke," Murphy said. "Behind enemy lines. You can't see it from where you sit. The Germans are burning something. Lots of black smoke."

Forrest had a trick: set fire to wagons to simulate retreat, wheel in a wide circle, and strike the flanks of an unwary, advancing enemy.

"Can we fly over it?" Max's voice vibrated through his own earphones.

"We'd be too low. We need another 2,000 feet of altitude, if we try it." Murphy sounded almost bored. Then Speigner heard the engine throttle down and felt the nose of the plane drop. "Wait a *minute!*" Murphy said.

"What is it?" Max cried. "I can't see." He felt the plane level off.

"Holy mother. They're comin' right up the highway like they was on parade."

"The Germans?"

"It ain't your bloody mom, is it?"

"Can we go down and take a closer look?"

"My God, the whole bloody Afrika Korps is pot-shotting us. Look at the tracers! We're goin' home," the pilot shouted.

A hole appeared in Max's windshield like a raindrop. Air whistled through it. The right wing suddenly grew tattered. Loose shards of metal flapped untidily behind it.

Someone did a poor job of checking out the plane this morning . . . no, we are taking hits.

The aircraft slanted in a gentle, banking turn toward the sea. Speigner could see nothing except the open highway to the north, which they had passed minutes ago. As the Advanced Trainer completed its turn, he craned his neck to see behind them. On the sun-blanched Via Balbia stood a column of vehicles which seemed to spill down the highway, like black pebbles strewn in perfect alignment. Lights winked from them, and yellow tentacles waved at the plane. Max felt the thump of bullets piercing the fuselage. He fumbled to press the voice-operated microphone against his throat.

"Can't we go any faster!" He did not recognize the strangled sound of his own voice. There was no response. "Murphy? Can you hear me?" The plane continued its gentle circle. They were now turning into the sun. Something was very wrong. His mind was not working. He felt dizzy. He wanted to say something, but he could not remember what it was. He saw a bloodstain growing like a crimson flower on his left leg. He stared at it uncomprehending until the pain came, burning his brain clear. The sun was shining over his left shoulder. That meant they had come full circle. More holes appeared magically in the wings. The plane continued to turn, although it seemed to him they were losing altitude.

The Afrika Korps is using us for target practice.

He took off his scarf and tied it around his thigh to stop the bleeding. The wound was just above his knee. The pain was a steady throbbing. He was reasonably sure it was a flesh wound. The plane did not have dual controls. He had no way to change speed or direction, even if he knew how to fly a plane. He looked at the back of the pilot's seat, which rose within six inches of the ceiling. Murphy might have been on the other side of a mountain, but he had to try to reach him.

With awkward fingers, he unbuckled his seatbelt and slipped out of his shoulder harness. Ignoring the pain as he moved his leg, he pulled himself forward. There was not room enough to stand. With one hand gripping the back of the seat to support his weight, he groped with the other for Murphy's head. Cracks appeared in the glass on the right side of the cockpit. Holes ate into the wings as if metal-eating moths were at work. He felt the top of Murphy's leather helmet. His fingers delicately traced the hard shape of the pilot's head, which tilted to one side.

"Murphy! Murphy! Murphy!" He was nearly sobbing. "They're shooting us to pieces. We're falling apart in the air." He tried to shake the pilot's head, but it dropped farther to one side, eluding his reach. "Straighten up. Murphy, straighten up or they'll shoot us to pieces." There was no reply. He had heard the same silence somewhere. His leg hurt very bad. It occurred to him that there might be shrapnel buried in his flesh, a minor inconvenience under the circumstances. He couldn't support his weight any more and fell back in his seat.

Sweat ran into his eyes, and he fiercely wiped it away, thinking it was tears and embarrassed to be weeping.

Unmanly to cry. Infants cry. Men don't . . . Going to die.

Something was different. The earth had stopped revolving around the aircraft. On his left, the Via Balbia ran unswerving and steady. The plane had stopped turning.

"Murphy!" he called. "Are you all right?" He waited but did not expect the pilot to reply. He remembered where he had heard such a silence: inside the German tank. The cockpit of the AT-6 was *his* place of silence.

They had lost a great deal of altitude. The rate at which the plane slid groundward told him that they were in a shallow dive. He smelled smoke. His racing thoughts turned radically, like horses in a burning barn. The cockpit was on fire. Electrical circuits shorted out with an insidious, chalky stench.

"Pull up!" he yelled. "Pull out of it. Murphy!" To combat his helplessness, he grabbed the top of the pilot's seat and heaved himself forward as though to lighten the plane's load. "Pull up! Pull up!"

The earth moved toward the plane with a patient hunger. He had heard pilots talk about "picking your spot" or appraising the ground rushing to meet them, exercising the one option left open to them—choosing their place to die. He fell back into his seat and watched the rising earth with a terrible indifference. His body, however, began to tense for impact. His feet were braced against the floorboard; his hands gripped the edge of his seat. He could see clumps of camel thorn flying beneath the wings, each withered stalk clearly distinguishable among the rocks and wind patterns in the sand. Just before they hit, he felt the nose of the plane lift in an eloquent motion, so that the aircraft bounced on its wheels— once, twice—before it tipped over onto the propeller, which disintegrated as the nose plowed into the sand.

Speigner was thrown forward. His parachute jammed against the ceiling so that he was caught upside down between the back of Murphy's seat and the top of the aircraft. He had the breath knocked out of him, and he fought for air. Instinct made him grope for the door handle. The cockpit was full of smoke. With the first breath he took he began to cough and retch. He unlatched the door and tumbled out, catching himself on the edge of the wing. He forgot about the pain in his leg when he saw Murphy was slumped against the instrument panel. He pulled himself back into the blinding smoke to unbuckle the pilot's seat belt. A weight on his back interfered with his movement, and he slapped furiously at it before realizing that it was his parachute.

Murphy was crimson from neck to groin. He did not appear to be breathing, but Max was determined to get him out. He unbuckled the seat belt and tried to pull him bodily from the plane. Murphy's arms and shoulders were slick with blood, and the weight was too much for Max. He was rapidly losing strength. He took hold of Murphy's parachute straps and with one last heave yanked the pilot over the sill of the open door. Together they fell heavily to the ground.

Max could not breathe. The plane seemed to rest on his chest, crushing him vengefully under its motheaten wing. Then he perceived that the pilot's body lay on top of him and struggled to free himself. He grasped the slippery red hands and began to drag Murphy away from the burning plane. The cockpit had become engulfed by flames. He was afraid the aircraft would explode at any moment. He tried to move faster as he walked backward, bent against the weight of the body, and fell over a clump of brush. Disoriented, he picked himself up and began to dust himself off, then noticed Murphy lying at his feet and remembered what he had to do. He continued to drag the body until they were about 100 feet from the plane. The pain in his leg had returned, and he was aware that his left shoe had filled with blood. It squished with every step he took.

He heard engines muttering and turned hopefully in their direction. He forgot about the Germans. Machines meant men and men meant help. He watched the motorcycles plunge across the sand, and waved his arm to show them where he was.

Through binoculars Rommel watched the downed airman signaling for help. He wondered whether the Tommy had intended to give himself up all along. Why else would he have circled that way? Along with the rest of his troops, Rommel had been diverted by the suicidal aircraft. At first he had been irritated with his antiaircraft batteries for not bringing the target down at once and made a mental note to increase their practice time, ammunition permitting. Then he had felt a growing respect for the British plane. There was a lovely defiance in the way it took the fire and kept coming back. He had begun to fear for the pilot's safety. He did not know why.

Although he had more important things on his mind, he kept his glasses trained on the doomed aircraft. He saw the copilot pull the injured pilot from the cockpit, tumble to the ground, and drag him to safety. Something was familiar about the tall, lanky airman waving to the recce motorcyclists. He ordered his wireless operator to obtain the identity of the prisoners. In a few minutes the reply came back.

"They say it is an American, Herr General. The British pilot is dead." Rommel's burning glance made the radioman hesitate. "The American's name is Speigner."

Speigner. Here. How did he know? We obviously caught the British by surprise. When their observation posts at El Agheila were taken, the wireless operators still wore their headsets. Intercepts show that Support Group of First Armored Division is disconcerted and falling back in confusion. Field guns and transport vehicles are being abandoned all over the place. If Speigner knew, why did he not warn the British?

"Send to reconnaissance: I want the American brought to me when we reach our rendezvous south of Agedabia," he told the radio operator and turned his attention back to the battle.

On a cot beside a medical corps truck Speigner lay in a morphine stupor. He was aware that a doctor probed his thigh with a sharp instrument, though he felt no pain. He heard the doctor mutter, *"Die Wunde ist sauber. Ich finde keine Metallstücke in der Wunde."*

"Das ist gut," Max sighed. The doctor glanced up from his work.

"Du sprichst Deutsch? Amerika hat schon angegriffen?"

Yes, Max thought, America has attacked. The doctor's voice seemed to come from a thousand miles away. Max wondered if perhaps he was speaking on the phone. Transoceanic calls were expensive, and he wished to be as accommodating as possible. *"Was macht mein Bein?"* he inquired about his leg, which had been bandaged and taped.

"Du hast viel Blut verloren." The doctor pointed at the glucose bag suspended above the cot and attached to his arm

by a tube and needle. Speigner had not noticed it. *"Wir konnen eine Infektion vermeiden, wenn du von den Füssen bleibst."*

There would be little chance of infection if he stayed off his feet. He relaxed, hearing the concern in the man's voice. The doctor's admonishment signified that the universe was, after all, benign. Max closed his eyes.

"But how do you rate special treatment?" the doctor was asking. Speigner swam up into the light.

"What do you mean?" he said.

"General Rommel has ordered that you receive immediate attention and, as soon as you are well enough, you are to be brought to him."

"That's nice," Max said drowsily.

"Perhaps it is because you are an American," the doctor prompted. "The novelty?"

But Max had curled up in a warm cocoon of sleep. Occasionally he rose to semiconsciousness and eavesdropped on the orderlies who tucked a blanket around him or checked the needle taped to his arm. They were debating nightlife in Stuttgart versus the girls of Hamburg. When he awoke, the truck—or was it an ambulance?—was moving. Speigner raised himself up and looked out the rear window. Behind the truck, winding around a long curve of the Via Balbia as far as he could see was a mass of transport. On either side of the highway were tanks and half-tracks. He observed the efficiency of the convoy. There was no wasted motion. All vehicles moved at the same speed, every soldier of the *Panzerarmee* in his ordered place.

He realized there was something he should remember. Still in a daze he thought of the crash landing, the lifting of the aircraft's nose—had Murphy's hand moved on the controls?—his pulling the pilot out of the burning plane. *No, after that. Rommel asked to see me.* What did he feel? Curiosity? Dread? Envy—because it was Rommel who was calling for him and not the other way around? Had he actually daydreamed about visiting a P.O.W. compound for Very Important Prisoners and bringing Rommel some fruit, a magazine, perhaps a rare pint of bourbon for old times' sake?

Anna was right. I was playing a game. Until now.

The morphine had worn off. The pain in his leg was a

constant reminder of his failure. He felt very thin. His pants were too big for him. They were new pants of light green wool, two sizes too large but they fit over his bandage. There were bloodstains on his khaki jacket. Murphy's blood or his own? Murphy. So obliging to take off a few hours early to accommodate the Yank. He wanted to feel remorse but was suddenly hungry instead.

The truck made a right turn off the highway and bounced over a rough track, which did not do his leg any good. Then it stopped. The back doors were opened. Hands helped him stand. Someone gave him a crutch. He was escorted to a Kübelwagen and put in the back seat. Someone gave him a sausage roll and a cup of coffee which was very good and lifted his spirits. He dozed for a time—it could have been minutes or hours. A guard and a driver got into the car and drove back to the highway. They turned right, which he assumed was to the north. The wind was cold and smelled of rain. The guard gave him a blanket and asked him to empty his pockets.

Max was surprised that the contents of his old trousers' pockets had been transferred to his new ones. The items he withdrew, one by one, were like an inventory of his former existence: twenty-five pounds Egyptian, some loose change, a pack of chewing gum, a wallet with identification cards and a picture of his mother, a vial of pain pills with printed instructions on the side: "Nehmen Sie zwei alle sechs Stunden." The guard seemed primarily interested in American cigarettes and was disappointed that Max did not have any. He gave the guard a five-pound note and a stick of chewing gum.

The gray afternoon merged indistinguishably with evening as they drove north. They passed fewer support vehicles and more armor, artillery, and infantry. In spite of his pain and thirst Speigner felt a buzz of excitement when the Kübelwagen turned off the highway. They stopped near several lorries and motorcycles, a light tank and an armored wireless command vehicle. He saw a British ACV like the one he had seen at the wire. He was not, however, taken to the ACV, but was put in one of the lorries. The truck bed was empty except for some dirty straw mattresses. Max lay down and rolled up in his blanket. Protected from the wind he soon became drowsy. His thoughts ran together and he slept.

An icy mantle of light rain was falling when Rommel went

to the truck where Speigner was being held. The battle was going better than anticipated, and he had decided to move on Agedabia before the British could reorganize. The village lay some fifteen miles northeast of their present position. He had only a few minutes to spare before they pushed off, but he was concerned about Speigner's condition. The guard told him that the prisoner was sleeping. He pushed back a canvas flap and shined a flashlight into the truck. Speigner was sleeping so soundly he did not awaken when the flashlight beam struck his face.

Max had changed. Even given the limitations of his present circumstances—the pallor and hollow cheeks and drugged breathing—Rommel perceived a different man from the one he had met five years ago. The long nose seemed more narrow, the jaw leaner. The hairline was beginning to recede. Rommel felt the passing of time, as one gauges his own aging by the maturing of one's children.

I did not let the Italians know my plans, which means that the British spies in Rome did not learn of it. Yet here Speigner is, having left Cairo—when?—a week ago? He anticipated my attack on the border dump in September. Now he has advance knowledge of my counterattack. How? I must be doing something obvious. Something connects us. There is a key. Speigner had access to British intelligence. But why would they open up to him, when America was not officially in the war, at least not in September when he arrived. . . . That's it. I learned of his arrival from the intercepted embassy transmissions. That is the key. It joins us like twins. Speigner has learned we have the code. He found the New Year's Day analysis of the weakened British front lines, put two and two together, and here he is. To what purpose? To warn the British? Too late. To confirm that his theory is correct? What would confirm it? My attacking. I must assume that he operated with British approval. If so, they know I have the American cipher. If he acted alone, however, it is still possible that they do not know I have it. My "little fellers" are worth an extra panzer division. Speigner could cost me a great deal. Was that what I sensed in America? That my future enemy was Speigner?

Max stirred in his sleep and Rommel snapped off the light. He stared down at the dark figure, determined to interrogate Speigner as soon as possible. In the meantime, he had a battle to fight.

During the night Max felt the truck move. He lay awake wondering where they were going. The vibrations of the wheels told him they drove over desert and not the highway. He heard distant artillery, possibly from 1st Armored Division, which was east of Agedabia. He thought of the mighty battle to come and felt helpless and frustrated. His leg ached but eventually the drumming of the tires and truck motor lulled him into a troubled sleep. When he awoke, the truck was not moving. Dull light slanted through the canvas. Rain tapped on the roof. He was cold and hungry. He hobbled painfully to the rear of the truck and looked through the canvas door.

He saw the same motorcycles, lorries, and light tanks as before, but the surrounding terrain was different—muddy and bleak. Then he saw Rommel standing in the rain. Several officers were grouped around him. They appeared to have paused between the ACV and an armored personnel carrier to settle an argument. Rommel listened impassively. His face was heavily lined. It was almost a physical shock for Max to see him again. In his greatcoat Rommel appeared shorter and more heavy-set than Speigner remembered him, perhaps in contrast with his taller staff members. It seemed against the laws of nature for large men to defer to a smaller one. Yet there was an irresistible quality of command in Rommel's erect posture. His short-billed cap with its abrupt crown was pugnacious. Oblivious to the rain, surrounded by his generals and his machines of war, he was like a god.

Red collar insignia distinguished two of the other officers as generals. Max thought one might be Cruewell, commander of the Afrika Korps, another possibly von Schwerin—no, he had been replaced and Ravenstein captured—perhaps Bayerlein or even Kesselring?

Is the Luftwaffe uniform blue?

There was also an Italian officer, who seemed to dominate the discussion by filibuster. Rommel listened with crossed arms and lowered head.

"I have an order signed by Il Duce himself," Cavallero was saying to Rommel, "directing you to limit this action to a sortie. Then you must return to Mersa Brega."

Glancing at the directive, Rommel ironically remarked,

"The mail plane from Rome must have stopped on its way to Tripoli." He thrust the paper back at Cavallero. "I plan to advance as long as I am able. If the British do not stop me, no one will." They glared at each other while the other officers watched nervously.

"Why did you not inform Comando Suprèmo of your plans!" Cavallero could barely restrain his fury. "It is highly irregular—"

"German troops are doing most of the fighting." Rommel shrugged. He glanced about and saw the canvas cover parting at the rear of the truck where Max was being held. Speigner opened the flap wider and their eyes met. "I have to get back to work," Rommel said abruptly. "I must interrogate a prisoner."

Cavallero spun on his heel, followed apologetically by Kesselring, who had gone to the trouble of flying the Italian in his private plane to meet with Rommel. The German officers lingered behind. Rommel had developed the habit of ending a meeting by walking away from it, but they were unsure whether they had been dismissed.

Speigner's guard, observing the general coming toward him, noticed that the flap was open. He yanked it shut and barked, *"Treten Sie zurück!"* Speigner stepped back obediently. Seconds later, however, the canvas was thrown back. Rommel stood before him.

"Speigner," he said heartily, "so we are at war! How are you feeling? Are you able to climb down?" He motioned to the guard, who put down his rifle and helped hoist Max to the ground.

"Thank you, Herr General." To his own astonishment, Max made an awkward little bow. He covered his embarrassment by fussing with his crutch to make it fit comfortably under his arm. He was furious with himself for being *grateful* that Rommel had paid him some attention.

"Come and have some cocoa." Rommel was surprised how glad he was to see the American. He could not help smiling at the mismatched pants which drooped low on Speigner's hips. A belt would have to be found for him. He adjusted to the funereal pace with which Speigner hobbled after him toward the ACV. The faces of his officers bore long-suffering expressions. Rommel gestured for Max to enter

Mammut ahead of him, relishing his staff members' chagrin. He loved it when an unexpected event jolted them out of their circumspect manner. He dismissed the guard and ushered Speigner inside the van, where Schmidt warily regarded him from the driver's seat. Alone among the officers von Mellenthin followed them into the van. Rommel gestured for Max to sit at a compact, fold-down table. He clumsily slid onto the bench seat, holding his injured leg straight. Adjacent to the table was a radio console with headset and microphone. Across the rear of the van was a padded seat. A machine pistol was mounted on brackets set in the wall. Spread on the table was a map of the area. Someone had drawn bold marks on it with red and blue crayons. Speigner tried not to stare at it.

"May I take the map?" Mellenthin spoke German under the assumption that the prisoner could not understand him. Max stacked his crutches on the floor.

"If you like," Rommel replied. "However, I was thinking of asking Speigner's opinion of my plan. We knew each other before the war. He was my host during my trip to America. Schmidt—get the prisoner a cup of cocoa."

Mellenthin folded the map, put it in his pocket, and stepped back deliberately as if to disengage himself from his commander's folly.

"It has been a long time," Rommel began genially. "May I call you Max? Did you give Herr Faulkner my book, after all?"

Speigner smiled nervously. "Yes. Major Shoemaker took it to him. Do you remember Shoemaker—the storyteller?"

"Of course. I wonder what Faulkner thought of my book?"

"Shoemaker wrote me that he was honored to receive an inscribed copy."

"Yes, but what did he think of the book itself? He seemed quite knowledgeable about military history."

Rommel's tone was bantering but his eyes were fanatical. This was not the man who had walked the fields with Speigner at Brice's Crossroads. Max thought of a sun-brazened priest, hair severely trimmed around the ears, mouth taut and ambitious, gray eyes impenetrable. Behind the general's elaborate courtesy a predator was at work.

"You must come back to Mississippi and ask him yourself some day," Max countered.

"I do not think I will visit your country again."

"Why not?"

"Is it not obvious?" Rommel could not restrain a thin-lipped smile of pride. "At any rate, if I asked Herr Faulkner what he thought of my work, he might ask me the same question. I confess I did not finish his book. The one you gave me. I found his characters and plot obscure. Quite mad. Ah, here is your cocoa."

This is sanity? What would Faulkner's character, Dilsey, say?

Schmidt brought Max a cup of steaming cocoa. Von Mellenthin glared at Max as if accusing him of violating protocol. Was the prisoner a guest of the Reich or its captive?

"Excuse me," the intelligence chief said to Rommel. "If you are going to reminisce with the prisoner about your trip to America, I hope you will not object if I leave you to it."

Rommel waved at him without taking his eyes from Speigner's face. Mellenthin coldly left the ACV.

"So you were at the dump before me," Rommel said.

"At the dump?"

"Please. Do not insult me. The Khireigat dump. For you the war is over. You must be candid with me."

Gray eyes stalked him.

"All right," he admitted. "Yes, I was there."

"Of course I would like to know how." Rommel pretended to relax. He took a seat on the bench opposite Speigner.

"That is a trade secret."

"Someone told me—someone from your side—that you heard it on the wind. Such fantasy. How did you do it?"

The watchful eyes drew pride from Max. "I remembered the raid of Streight."

"Streight?"

"The story Major Shoemaker told, that day at the hotel. The Union raid across Alabama. Cavalry mounted on mules. Forrest pursued them across Sand Mountain. Streight laid an ambush for Forrest."

"I remember," said Rommel, "but it explains nothing. How did you know I was coming?"

"Your forces were spotted by a reconnaissance plane."

"I know that," Rommel said impatiently, "but the RAF counterattacked so swiftly. We were expected."

"It was luck." Speigner shrugged.

"I do not believe in luck like that. Tell me how."

He wants to tie it up in a neat package. War has meaning if there is a lesson to be learned. Something positive to carry forward in the name of the dead. It is also efficient and guarantees top performance.

"When we were at Brice's Crossroads that day," Max said, "you made me see courage and genius but not waste. After being in the desert I think I understand how quickly a life can vanish, but I cannot truly comprehend it. Can you?"

"It is all part of a piece," Rommel replied brusquely.

"Is it?"

"Let us return to your role as military liaison to the British. What information did you share with them? How was it that they brought you to Cairo?"

"Maxwell Speigner, First Lieutenant, serial number . . ."

"Come now, Max. Let us not play games. The war is over for you, now. What difference can it make?"

"I do not know," Max said levelly, "but you would not be asking these questions if it were not of use to you."

"I know about your memo about me," Rommel said. "You are surprised? Give us some credit. We have our sources. You predicted my style of fighting in the invasion of France. The British were greatly impressed—"

"That is incorrect. No one paid it any attention until the Afrika Korps came to Tripoli."

"Someone must have appreciated it or you would not be here." Rommel leaned on the table. "What I want to know is, what am I doing that is so obvious?" He waited for a reply, but Speigner was silent. "What made you suspect I was planning to counterattack?" Max lowered his eyes. Rommel became angry. In the driver's seat Schmidt shared his commander's anger and glowered at the prisoner. "When did you begin to suspect it? You must tell me that!" Rommel was suddenly furious. *"Are you acting alone?"*

Speigner stared straight ahead. Rommel impulsively ordered Schmidt to leave the van. The aide left reluctantly.

"All right, I will tell you something that will ensure your close captivity for the remainder of the war," Rommel said. "For you there now can be no prisoner exchange. I have your State Department code. Yes, you know it. I see it in your face.

That is how you guessed I was counterattacking. Your Colonel Fellers is most thorough. I highly approve of his work. He has become one of my favorite authors. Who else on your side knows I have the code?"

Speigner shook his head.

"You can be persuaded to talk, if it comes to that." Rommel's jaw muscles bulged. "You must cooperate and make things easier for us all."

"I did not realize there were S.S. units operating within *Panzergruppe*," Max said coldly.

"There are not!" Rommel was horrified at the idea.

"Then who is going to make me talk? Torture is not your style."

"We all change," Rommel said.

"You have not changed that much. Your style is to fight fair. Your fairness is legend. You are a hero to the Eighth Army, did you know that? They have an expression for chivalry in battle. They call it 'doing a Rommel.' Your fairness is what makes you dangerous. Both sides respect you. You make war honorable, so that all the rest—Hitler's persecution of Jews and Free French and Poles, the camps where civilians are interned—all of that can go on."

"You will be silent!" Rommel cried.

"Surely you have heard of the camps," Max pressed the offensive. "Everyone has heard of them. Why do you think Hitler supports you? In the beginning it was because of your book. That got his attention, did it not? Then it was your victories in Normandy. You became a national hero. But now, what makes you so valuable to Hitler? The strategists agree that the real struggle now is in Russia. And after that it will be the Allied invasion to liberate France. Comparatively, the North Africa campaign is a sideshow, except for you. *You* make it important. You make headlines. You make Germany proud. You balance out all the rest. That is why you must be stopped."

Rommel jumped to his feet and slammed his fist down on the table. "Who will stop me?" he shouted. Schmidt rushed back into the van—he had been hovering just outside the door—and stood behind his commander. "I do not care if the British know I have the American code. I have got them down, and I am going to tear their hair out. After I take Agheila, it is on to Benghazi. Then Tobruk. Then Sollum. Then Egypt and the Suez Canal—" His hands reached involuntarily to throttle Speigner. He forceably returned them to his side, as though standing at attention, and took a deep breath. "You are correct. It is not my style to beat information out of a prisoner. I will fight fair, and I shall win."

Anna was right. He must be destroyed. He is too strong.

"Herr General, should I remove the prisoner?" Schmidt asked.

"Not just yet," Rommel said. "I will keep him here for a while."

"The men are wondering," Schmidt hesitated, "will we be moving out, now?"

Rommel stared thoughtfully at Speigner. "Pass the word," he told his aide, "we will take a short break. The men need a rest. Tell them to catch forty winks, and I will let them know when it is time to advance again." He almost grinned to see the recognition light up in Max's eyes. Schmidt was perplexed. "Now that you have reminded me of Forrest's pursuit of Streight's Union cavalry, I will take a page from Forrest's book. He had them on the run but stopped to allow his troops to rest up for the final battle. Do you remember? I can see you do. It worked for Forrest. It will work for me. No one here can appreciate it as well as you. How ironic that an enemy should comprehend the significance of my order better than my own men."

Schmidt shot Max a jealous glance as he went to relay the order. He paused and asked hopefully, "Shall I return the prisoner to the Military Police?"

"*Nein*. He is going with me to Benghazi. Tie his hands, Schmidt. He's not going to escape."

Rommel snatched a folded blanket from an open locker, shook it out, wrapped it around him, and stretched out on the padded bench. Schmidt made Max lean forward so he could bind his hands behind his back. Assured that the cords cut into the American's flesh, he pushed Speigner down beside the radio console.

"*Bleiben Sie still!*" Schmidt muttered. He went to the door to relay Rommel's orders to the runner outside. Max seized the moment to scrutinize the van for anything that might be of use to him. His eyes passed over the open locker adjoining the bench seat where Rommel lay, then returned sharply to an object in the bottom of it. Rommel had uncovered some type of small tool when he lifted the blanket. Max could see a handle. It looked like a screwdriver. He craned his neck to get a better angle of vision. Rommel lay still. Max could hear Schmidt giving orders to the courier. He strained to see inside the locker. The handle ended in a canvas sheath. Blood pulsed in Max's temples. He eased back into his corner just as Schmidt returned to sit at the map table. The aide glanced suspiciously at the prisoner, who had settled back against the wall with eyes closed.

Speigner listened to the sounds of Group Marcks obeying the stop order. An engine was shut down, a hatch was closed, a radio squawked as it was turned off abruptly. Soon all was silent except for the scribbling of Schmidt's pencil. Max opened his eyes in a squint and saw the aide reading from a handbook, then writing on a pad. Max began to work his wrists inside his bonds.

If it is a knife if it is a knife if it is if . . .

For a very long time Max rotated his wrists to stretch the cords around them, ignoring the pain of chafing. His heart made a steady thumping as though keeping time with the secret movements of his hands. He felt lightheaded. His wrists were so numb he could not feel whether he was making any progress. He had lost track of time when he heard Schmidt's pencil cease scratching. The aide had crossed his arms on the table and lowered his head on top of them. Rommel began to snore lightly.

Max held his breath and willed Schmidt to be at peace. The rope was loosening rapidly, and he worked with renewed strength. His bonds had grown slick with his blood. Tears filled his eyes as he slid raw flesh under the knots and pulled his hands free. He rested for a while and considered what to do next. If he tried to stand without his crutch, Schmidt would hear him. He stretched his body flat on the floor and writhed by inches toward the locker. His fingers groped for the handle. He pulled it free of its sheath and revealed the stubby blade of a utility knife. Relief put a new edge on his fear.

He crawled by degrees toward Schmidt, paralyzed momentarily by a shooting pain in his left knee. It felt wet. He knew the wound had reopened. The aide's head did not move from his arms. There was no way of knowing whether Schmidt was indeed asleep. Max looked at the holster strapped to the aide's belt. Everything depended on quickness. If Schmidt cried out, all was lost. When he was directly behind Schmidt, Max lifted his good knee, got his right leg under his weight. Rommel's snore rattled reassuringly from the rear of the van. He gathered his courage and rose behind the aide.

Hand over his mouth and shove the blade into his neck. He smelled Schmidt, an honest stink of sweat and dirty clothes. *Quick. Then take the pistol.* As he started to clamp his hand over the aide's mouth a fateful memory interposed—of Schmidt handing him a mug of cocoa with an ironic smile. *How to kill a man who is jealous of his commander's attentions to someone else?* He could not make the blade dig for the spinal column. Instead, as Schmidt awoke in panic and struggled under his hand, he pressed the point of the knife lightly into the neck, drawing blood. He forced the lieutenant's head down against the table. With his other hand squeezing Schmidt's mouth shut he whispered, *"Seien Sie still oder ich werde Sie toten."*

Pinning Schmidt against the table with the knife, he groped for the aide's holster, unsnapped it quietly, and took out the Luger. It felt huge and alien in his hand. He whispered again, "If you wake the general, I will shoot him first. Lie on the floor." He stuck the pistol in his belt and pressing the knife to the aide's neck guided him into a prone position. With his injured leg extended to the side and hurting badly, he knelt on the aide's back with his right knee and pressed him against the floor. He laid the knife down, took the piece of rope from his pocket and trussed Schmidt's hands behind his back. He glanced at the padded seat where Rommel was a dark, unmoving lump. The snores had ceased, however, and the rustle of rope and flesh sounded violently loud to Max. Schmidt, too, was watching Rommel. Max could almost hear the aide's mind frantically searching for a way out. He rolled the German on his back, held the knife at his throat, and undid his belt buckle. The aide's eyes gleamed liquidly in the dark. He worked the belt through its loops, rolled Schmidt onto his back, and used the belt to secure Schmidt's ankles. Finally, he tied a handkerchief around the aide's head, forcing it between his teeth.

Satisfied, Speigner limped slowly toward the rear of the

van. From Schmidt came a stifled groan. Rommel lay on his stomach, his face pressed into the crevice formed by the seat cushion and the padded back. His fabled *Fingerspitzengefühl* had failed him, Max thought, when he most needed it. Speigner cocked the Luger with a metallic snap like a pistol report. Rommel uncoiled like a released spring. He came to a half-sitting, half-crouching position and stared incredulously at the gun barrel in his face.

"Do not move," Max said. "I must take you, alive or dead. If you resist, Schmidt dies too."

Rommel had tensed to strike out, to slap the pistol away and grapple with the American. The mention of Schmidt made him hesitate. From the darkness came a flapping noise. Schmidt struggled against his bonds as though to explain or perhaps to apologize. Max took a step back, just out of Rommel's reach.

"Now, do as I tell you," Max said. Rommel sat stiffly, attempting to judge the American's will. Speigner's face was hidden in shadow. Only the gleaming metal of the Luger was visible against his silhouette. "Go sit in the driver's seat." Rommel hesitated, his mind groping for a solution. "Now! Get up!"

Rommel stood. As he moved forward, the American stepped aside to allow him to pass. At that moment, Schmidt doubled his legs and lashed out with his feet, knocking Speigner off balance. Max reached out a hand to catch himself against the wall, and Rommel leaped at him with hands like claws. He did not see Max swing the Luger in a swift backhanded motion, nor did he feel the blow to his temple. There was a searing flash of light and he found himself on his knees. He tried to spring to his feet but his brain refused to cooperate. Pain rocked him, and nausea flooded his throat.

Max listened for a guard's footstep outside Mammut but no one came to the door. He pulled Rommel to his feet, pushed him to the front of the van and forced him into the driver's seat. Rommel blacked out for what seemed only a few seconds. When he came to, he was slumped over the steering wheel, his head resting on his arms. He breathed deeply and tried to shake off the grogginess. His arms felt heavy. He could not lift them. Slowly he stopped straining his muscles. His wrists were tightly bound to the wheel with thin cord which was someone's shoelaces. A canteen appeared before his lips.

"*Trinke!*" Speigner commanded. He tilted the canteen. Rommel angrily twisted his face away so that some water slopped onto his tunic. Max poured water on a handkerchief he had found in Schmidt's pocket and mopped the cut on Rommel's temple where a bump had swollen to the size of a golf ball. Rommel shook his head. "Be still!" Max gripped the crown of Rommel's head with one hand while he finished wiping the wound clean.

"You surprise me, Max," Rommel said with a steely composure. "I did not think you had it in you."

"You would expect one of your own officers to try to escape, wouldn't you?" Speigner's voice shook with strain. "Would *you* give up without a fight?" Rommel stared ahead in unspoken acknowledgement.

"What are you going to do?" he said.

Max looked out the open visor at the sleeping battle group. Motionless hulks of tanks and armored cars were silhouetted against the horizon.

"You are going to drive us to the British lines." Max tried to sound confident. Rommel searched the American's eyes for weakness.

"Even if I were to cooperate," he replied calmly, "how do you know where to reconnoiter enemy units?"

"There's a garrison at Antelat. We'll go there."

"You won't get past my night patrol," Rommel snapped. "My armored cars will stop you." He glared at Speigner with fierce satisfaction.

"Then you will be dead, Herr General," Max said quietly.

"I thought you were a scholar, a military historian." Rommel kept smiling as though they shared a grim joke.

"*Jawohl*, Herr General, history is on my mind." Max reached down and started the engine. Rommel immediately pressed the accelerator, racing the engine to attract attention. Max alertly turned off the ignition. Rommel was grinning savagely. Speigner lurched to where Schmidt lay, dragged the aide by his collar to the front of the van, and stuck the Luger barrel behind his ear. "Alive in British hands or dead now." Max's voice trembled. "You choose for the three of us!"

Schmidt made a strangled cry. His teeth gripped the handkerchief cutting into his mouth. The pistol barrel forced his ear to stick out like a circus clown's. The aide shook his head, his eyes beseeching his commander. Rommel knew Schmidt meant for him not to do as the American ordered, to disregard the threat to the aide's life, but he also read fear in Schmidt's eyes. Speigner's stare was unwavering.

"All right," said Rommel.

"Thank you, Herr General."

"Call me Erwin, if you like. You outrank me with that Luger."

"I will operate the gears." Max switched on the ignition and pressed the starter button. "Is reverse down and back or up and back, this way? Yes, thank you. If you will depress the clutch pedal? Here we go."

Rommel backed up, waited for Max to shift into first gear, spun the wheel by rotating both his arms at once and bending his body with the unusual motion, then straightened out and drove away from the leaguered armor. He looked for movement, light, a curious face—*anything*—but their departure went unnoticed. He had ordered Group Marcks to go to sleep and sleep it did. Still, one expected some vigilance. The ACV lumbered into the open desert. The intermittent rain had created a slick surface, but the 18-inch-wide tires of Mammut were equal to the terrain. In the dark it was impossible to pick the smoothest path. The vehicle bumped over unseen clumps of brush or shallow undulations in the sand. Speigner turned the dash lights on just long enough to get a compass heading of north-northeast, then turned them off again. The American was very much in control. Rommel remembered how Max's finger had tightened on the trigger and his face had set itself against the explosive report of the pistol. There was no question that he was committed to a life-or-death effort. He had underestimated Speigner and had become careless. Now he was in a hole, with few options. Certainly they would soon be missed by Group Marcks. Pursuit was inevitable. But would Speigner shoot them at the last moment? If he could work his hands loose, he could jump the American at an opportune moment. The shoelaces would stretch if he put enough pressure on them. He flexed his numb wrists and his fingers tingled and prickled.

Max watched the rearview mirror for a light moving against the gloom. In some truck or armored car at Group Marcks, a guard was reporting to the duty officer that the command vehicle of *Oberbefehlshaber* Rommel had been observed leaving the area. The duty officer would be loath to break radio silence, but the safety of the C in C would override normal security precautions. Max moved haltingly to the radio console and flipped the power switch to *Auf* and the receiver switch to *Empfang*. A red light appeared on the dial. If a call came through, it would have to be answered. Schmidt would have to do it. Even if the aide ignored or altered the call signs in an attempt to warn headquarters, failure to reply would guarantee immediate pursuit. Without lights to guide them, however, the pursuers would not know which direction to take.

While Speigner moved back to the radio, Rommel subtly changed course. He turned by degrees, so Max would not notice, until he judged they were headed east. The Afrika Korps was somewhere out there, perhaps thirty minutes away. Surely there were no British units this far south of Antelat. When Max limped to the front of the van he was preoccupied with his thoughts. Rommel was hopeful that his new heading would go unnoticed. The American remembered to check the compass. As he leaned closer to the dashboard to try to read the unlit dial, Rommel stepped on the brakes and caused him to lose his balance. Max caught himself on the dash.

"Sorry, I thought it was a ditch ahead," Rommel explained, then added, "I am driving with my wrists. My hands have lost their feeling and I cannot grip the wheel."

A voice spoke through the headset. For a second Max thought someone else was in the van with them. When Speigner turned away to deal with the radio call, Rommel went back to work on the shoelaces. His wrists were raw even though the cloth of his sleeve protected them. He kept twisting and pulling while listening to Speigner instruct Schmidt.

"The general is a dead man if you say anything to warn HQ," Max told the aide as he pulled away the gag. "I want you to take the call as though nothing out of the ordinary is happening. Tell them the Oberbefehlshaber has decided to make a recce of tomorrow's route and is checking condition of the ground for heavy transport. He is sweeping perimeter and will return presently to Group Marcks. No escort is required.

If they ask our position, tell them we are five miles east of them."

Rommel smiled. *We are getting there, anyhow.*

Speigner held the headset between them so that he and Schmidt could listen to the earphone receiver at the same time. A disciplined German voice said, "This is Rainbow to Gold. Over." Max flipped the console switch to *Senden* and nodded to Schmidt.

"This is Gold. Over," the aide said.

"This is Rainbow. What are your instructions regarding current maneuver? Over."

"This is Gold," Schmidt replied, staring into Speigner's eyes only a few inches from his own. "Sweeping perimeter. Will return to original position presently. Over."

"This is Rainbow. Request Gold position. Over."

"This is Gold. Position five miles east of Rainbow . . ."

Max put his hand over the microphone and whispered, "*Sign off.*"

". . . Gold out," said Schmidt. There was a long silence; then the headquarters operator came back on the air.

"This is Rainbow. Confirm security Gold prisoner. Over."

"This is Gold. Security satisfactory," Schmidt said. "Out."

Max nodded in relief. The aide's tone had been appropriately authoritative. Max hung the headset back on its hook and considered the probable reaction at Group Marcks HQ. They were accustomed to their C in C doing the unexpected. It was possible they would not send a patrol after them. If they did, it would be headed in the wrong direction.

Reflected glare lit the interior of the van. Max whirled to see that the headlights had been turned on, lighting the muddy desert like a prolonged, silent explosion. Rommel had hooked the sole of his boot under the headlamp switch and turned the lights on with his foot. Max hobbled over and slammed the switch with the heel of his palm. In the second before his eyes readjusted to the darkness, Rommel was a black shape hovering malevolently beside him.

"It won't work," Rommel said. "They will soon be after us. It is only a matter of time. There will be no escape."

Max did not reply. Instead, he checked Rommel's wrists and discovered that the laces had been loosened. Gripping Rommel's arm with one hand, he laboriously untied the knot—

picking it apart with his fingernails—and started to retie Rommel's wrists to the wheel. He hesitated and began rubbing Rommel's hand to get the blood circulating. He heard a telltale rustle from the center of the van and ordered Schmidt to lie still. He leaned close to Rommel as he chafed his hand.

"Either you drive or I untie you from the wheel and drive myself," Max said.

Rommel thought of the compass. He could not allow Max to drive and thus to check their directions. "I will drive," he said.

As Speigner considered Rommel's sudden acquiescence, the wireless headset vibrated insistently. He finished tightening Rommel's bonds to the wheel and hurried to listen to the message.

"This is Rainbow," said the same precise voice. "Were those your lights just now? Acknowledge. Over."

My God, they saw.

"Tell them," he ordered Schmidt, "Gold copies. Negative on lights. They saw someone else. Gold cannot confirm lights." He anxiously listened to Schmidt repeat the message into the microphone, his finger on the send switch to cut the aide off if he tried to warn HQ. There was no reply from Group Marcks. Max hung up the headset, dragged Schmidt closer to the front where he could keep an eye on him, and released the hand brake. Rommel waited patiently—too patiently, Max thought. It occurred to him to check the compass. He turned on the dashboard light and lit the dial. The needle pointed due east. Rommel glowered at him in triumph and frustration.

"Engage the clutch!" Speigner ordered. "We're turning north." He put his hand on the gear-stick knob. "When did you do it? When I was retying Schmidt's hands behind him?" Rommel did not move. He stared straight ahead. "Let in the clutch!" Max repeated. He forced Rommel to one side with his hip, sitting on the seat beside him. Max pushed in the clutch pedal, rammed the gear lever into first, and started the vehicle moving. When he began to turn the wheel to the left, Rommel resisted with all his strength. They struggled over the wheel while the ACV stubbornly headed east. Speigner put on the brakes.

"You will drive north!" he cried.

"No," said Rommel. Their faces were only inches apart.

"Drive!"

"No."

Bracing himself, Speigner stood up, pulled the Luger from his belt, and turned to Schmidt, taking aim at the fleshy part of his thigh. Schmidt's eyes widened in horror. Max pulled the trigger. It did not move. He realized he had forgotten the safety release. He examined the Luger and released the catch. Schmidt was crying, *"Nein, nein!"* and kicking at him with both feet, which were still tied together by the belt. The aide humped like a landed seal toward the rear of the van. Rommel twisted around in his seat to watch in disbelief. Max limped after Schmidt, aimed and fired.

Speigner was overwhelmed by the report of the gun, Schmidt's screams and the stifling smell of cordite. He pulled himself together and turned back to the driver's seat. He laid the barrel against Rommel's head.

"I will not hesitate to shoot you," he said. "With you down, I can drive without further interference. Schmidt requires medical attention now. It behooves you to drive north as quickly as possible. British doctors will take care of him."

"I will not," Rommel said angrily. "You are a coward. You will not remain alive much longer, I promise you."

"Then neither will you," said Max. "Drive."

"No."

"I am going to put a bullet into Schmidt's other leg," Max said coldly. "Then his arm. And so forth, until you change your mind." He moved toward Schmidt, who lay curled up beside the table. The floor was sticky with blood. Tortured by indecision, Rommel screwed his head around to see. When Max raised the pistol, he cried out.

"All right!"

Speigner returned to sit by Rommel. He grasped the gearshift lever. "Operate the clutch," he said.

"You *are* a bastard." Rommel depressed the clutch pedal and let it out as Max shifted into low gear. The ACV was under way again. "How badly is he hurt?"

"He needs a doctor. Do not waste more time. We want to go due north, remember? Veer left."

"Is this the way you American shits plan to fight the war?" Rommel glanced furiously from the uneven path ahead at Speigner. Max shifted into second.

"We will fight it the way you do—any way we have to."

"Including shooting unarmed prisoners?" Rommel stamped on the clutch as Max shifted to third. "That qualifies as a war crime in my book!" The speedometer read 20 mph. Rommel gradually eased back on the accelerator and slowed down.

"You might have done the same thing, in my place," Max said.

"I fight fair, as you yourself observed."

"What about your boss?—You're going too slow. Speed up!"

"Kesselring?"

"*Der Führer*. Do you want to discuss war crimes?"

"That is not at issue here."

"You're off heading again. See that hill standing by itself? Go straight for it. I want to see it in front of us continually, while I put a tourniquet on Schmidt. Understand?"

"*Ja.*"

Speigner limped to the center of the van, where Schmidt lay incoherent. Ignoring the pain in his own leg, Max freed the belt binding the aide's ankles, then cut away the trouser leg from the wound. He examined the bleeding. Satisfied that the bullet had not pierced an artery, he fashioned a tourniquet with the belt, glancing occasionally toward the front to see the designated hill through the windshield.

Rommel drove as ordered and took out his frustration on his bonds, twisting and pulling his wrists continually to loosen the cords. The increased pressure on his wrists shut off the circulation even more. His fingers were too numb to grip the wheel. He tried to think clearly. Would Max bind up Schmidt's wound only to shoot him again? It did not stand to reason. He resolved to test the American by stopping the van. They would find out what the American had in him. He had shown he was a fighter—Rommel respected that—but a desperate one, like a cat in a corner which fought out of fear, not courage.

Something in the rearview mirror attracted his attention, a bobbing black dot emerging, growing more substantial, then coming up fast. His heart leaped. It was a motorcycle. He recognized the round helmet and square handlebars. In less than a minute the motorbike was edging alongside. Speigner would hear its engine any second. Rommel wrenched the wheel to the left as though to ram the bike. The cyclist sheered away and accelerated like an angry bee. As he passed the van the soldier strained to see through the armor-plated visor who was in the driver's seat. Rommel struggled helplessly against the laces. He had no way to signal, other than to swerve back and forth like a drunken driver.

As soon as Max heard the motorcycle, he grabbed the machine pistol off the rack, checked the ammunition clip, and lurched to the front of the swaying van. He crouched next to Rommel and gripped the steering wheel with one hand to hold it steady. Rommel slammed on the brakes, left foot depressing the clutch pedal automatically. The engine continued to idle as the motorcycle circled warily in front of them and stopped abreast of the passenger door, about fifty feet away. Max cocked the firing mechanism and threw open the door.

"Look out!" Rommel shouted.

Max aimed from the hip and pulled the trigger, wondering—in a frozen instant of detachment—whether he had again overlooked the safety catch. The automatic weapon leaped in his hands, spraying a burst of bullets in the general direction of the cyclist, whose machine fell on its side as he hit the ground. Rommel raced the engine and engaged the clutch. Mammut grudgingly clunked into motion in third gear. He spun the wheel to the left as far as he could turn it. The sudden movement threw Max off balance. Dropping the machine pistol to the ground he fell out of the van, clutching the door. His feet slithered in the mud. Rommel locked the steering wheel in a tight turn and stood on the accelerator. Max's feet slipped out from under him and he held on with all his might. He could feel his fingers sliding off the edge of the door. The van tilted crazily as it completed a full circle around the fallen motorcyclist, who crouched beside his overturned machine and watched them in confusion.

Max desperately kicked at the ground and swung his lower body toward the van, managing to hang one foot on the first step. He reached inside the open door and caught hold of a metal loop bolted to the dashboard. In less than a heartbeat he pulled himself safely inside. He made for Rommel. They fought to control the steering wheel. With his hands tied to the wheel Rommel could only bump at the American like a rag doll, slamming him with head, shoulder, and hip, kicking at

Max's foot now depressing the accelerator pedal. Max hacked at Rommel's stomach with his elbow and knocked the wind out of him. While Rommel gasped for air, the ACV bumped northward. Its door banged on its hinges. Gray light began to leak over the eastern horizon.

"Now they will know our position," Rommel said grimly after he had caught his breath.

They drove in silence, side by side. After a while the headset began to buzz. "Someone is calling you, Herr Speigner," Rommel gloated. Max kept driving. The desert was coming to life in the light, and the empty miles stretched before them. He tried to ignore the headset, but it seemed to hum inside his brain.

"Aren't you going to answer it?" Rommel said coyly.

"It's time I put out an SOS," Max said, thinking out loud. He stopped the van, pulled up the emergency brake, and staggered to the radio. He put on the headset, started to change the transmission frequency, then decided to leave it where it was in the hope that when they broke radio silence earlier, their calls had been intercepted by the British, who would continue to monitor the same frequency. He flipped the switch to *Senden*.

"Mayday, Mayday, Mayday. Calling all British units in the Antelat area. Mayday, Mayday. This is Lieutenant Maxwell Speigner, U.S. Army Intelligence. Please listen carefully. I have commandeered an enemy vehicle and have escaped from a German assault force north of Agedabia. I was captured January twenty-one when my RAF reconnaissance flight was shot down. The pilot's name was Murphy. I estimate my present position as ten miles south of Antelat. I have taken prisoner a high-ranking German general officer and request nearest British units to rendezvous with us. This is a Mayday, Mayday. Acknowledge . . . somebody. Over."

They would not believe it if I said the prisoner was Rommel.

He waited at the console. Rain pattered on the steel roof. Rommel watched the dawn breaking over the dunes. Schmidt appeared to be unconscious. Max tried again.

"Mayday, Mayday. This is Lieutenant Maxwell Speigner, U.S. Army. Calling any British unit. Acknowledge. Over."

He thought of Group Marcks scrambling and vehicles

streaming after them. As he was reaching for the dial to try another frequency, the earphone vibrated in his ears.

". . . copy you, Speigner. Say again. Over." The voice faded in and out. He thought he detected a slight brogue which could have been Welsh or Scottish. He hurriedly duplicated his message. For the first time he began to hope that he might succeed. Relief surged at the edges of his self-control.

"Identify your prisoner, over," said the unknown voice.

"This is Speigner. He is a high-ranking officer from Panzerarmee Command. That is all I can say. Over." There was an electric pause.

Max stared helplessly at the back of Rommel's head. They were wasting valuable time. This must be a listening post at a comfortable distance from the front lines, perhaps Benghazi.

"*Where are you?*" Max cried into the microphone. "Can you help us?—Over."

"Leftenant," said a new English voice, calm and reasonable. "Drive your vehicle to the nearest high ground and give us a look at you. Face your transport north and flash your lights. One slow, two quick, and repeat every thirty seconds for three minutes. Over." Max was stunned at this orderly proposal. The voice made it seem so routine. He had a wild desire to shout huzzahs over the air to British and German alike.

"This is Speigner. Understood! Proceeding to high ground. Out!"

Max took his seat beside Rommel, who hitched himself over to make room for both of them. Max shifted into first and began to drive. The only high ground he could see was a low ridge about a half mile away. Rommel had made good progress in freeing his hands and hoped Speigner did not notice the stretched laces.

Max's thoughts swarmed with hope: there was a British unit close enough to make visual contact, probably a recce unit of scout cars. Whoever it was, they could escort the ACV safely behind British lines. He glanced in his rearview mirror, dreading to see German armored cars behind them, but the muddy plain was empty. Against his side he felt the solid weight of Rommel's body, which seemed to collapse against him in defeat. He grasped the wheel next to Rommel's wrists.

Whenever he turned it, Rommel's hands moved in tandem with his.

Soon they reached the top of the ridge and faced north across a shallow valley several miles wide. Max pulled up the emergency brake and began to flash his headlights: one slow, two fast. He counted to thirty and repeated the process six times. He watched for a similar signal from the opposing ridge. Instead, the crackle of the headset claimed his attention. He went to the radio.

"This is British Reconnaissance. We have your position, Leftenant," said the new voice. "Do you see a plateau ahead of you? If so, make for it. We will meet you near the base of the plateau. Over."

"This is Speigner. Will comply. Out."

Max grinned at the flat, muddy valley as if the rains had caused it to break out in wildflowers. He drove as fast as the rough terrain would allow.

Rommel began to gather his strength. The American's attention would have to be diverted if he were to have a chance. All he wanted was to free his hands.

Let us start even. Victory will go to the one who wants it most.

Rommel glanced at the outside mirror and found his diversion. An armored car popped over the ridge a mile behind them, then another, then a light tank. Group Marcks had found them. He swiveled his eyes at Max. At that moment Speigner was engrossed in crossing a wadi. Mud spattered the visor as the ACV groaned up the slippery bank. Speigner's eyes fastened on the plateau looming above them. He strained for the first glimpse of a friendly vehicle. He saw what appeared to be a magic wand waving above the sand. It whipped merrily back and forth, growing taller and taller. A gray RAF armored car emerged beneath the radio antennae. Out of the same depression appeared a motorcycle with a sidecar. Speigner recognized the turret of a Rolls-Royce armored car.

We're going to make it.

Max did not observe the German armor storming across the valley behind them. Rommel had eyes for nothing else.

Come to Erwin.

As Speigner drew within 200 meters of the RAF car, a column of gray smoke sprang up beside it. Another column bracketed it between them. The Rolls spun around and disappeared into the depression, followed by the motorcycle. Another explosion erupted at the spot where they had been. In the mirror Max saw a line of German tanks spitting fire. The valley heaved with mud-colored machines swarming like disturbed beetles closing on the intruder in their nest. Max drove as fast as he could, but there was no catching the Rolls. It leaped over the rolling terrain, antennae thrashing madly.

The motorcycles were the first machines to catch the ACV, crisscrossing in front of it in a droning throng. A jeep with mounted machine gun swerved in front of them. The weapon was pointed at the open visor. Max could see the eyes of the soldier manning the machine gun. He pointed the Luger at Rommel's temple and waved the jeep away. It slowed to retard the van's progress, and Speigner rammed it from behind. As the jeep veered out of the heavier vehicle's path, Max could see a soldier shouting into a microphone. Armored cars came up on either side, followed by fast, light Mark IIs, their turret cannons pointing at the ACV in an empty threat. Speigner knew they would not fire on Mammut with its precious cargo. The roar of engines and caterpillar tracks four deep around them made Max feel as though he were being squeezed by a massive vise which conformed perfectly to his body. He was determined to delay the inevitable as long as possible. The boxlike van with its armored escort proceeded north at a ceremonial pace, like an aging queen mother attended by ladies-in-waiting.

"You cannot win," Rommel said.

"Neither can you." Speigner's reply echoed somewhere on the far side of his soul.

"No man can kill me," Rommel said. He felt a strange sense of peace. "It profits me little to think someone can."

They rode in mutual silence, besieged by the rumble of the escort.

Max heard a scratching noise. Rats were eating at the corners of his mind.

On the roof. They're on the roof.

He raised the Luger and fired at the ceiling. The bullet could not penetrate the heavy plating, but there were quick, pounding steps toward the rear of the van. He fired again and heard a weapon clatter off the roof, along with the palpitations of elbows and knees against the hollow steel surface. A soldier leaped clear. At the first shot Rommel jerked to pull free, but his wristbones caught in the laces. Max steered with one hand, pistol ready in the other. Rommel froze at the sight of a pondlike crater before them. The American obviously did not recognize the salt marsh. Its whitish, ridge-marked surface like furrows in a field was actually a dry crust covering a slough of stinking slime.

In his rearview mirror Max saw the armored motorcycle drop back on all sides. Why were they giving up? His eyes frantically searched the horizon for a miracle—a line of tanks from First Armored Division blocking their path. Then the world tilted. The desert heaved in a cataclysmic act of nature.

We are drowning in sand.

Panzergrenadiers poured into the marsh, sinking up to their knees. Their boots made sucking noises in the muck. The ACV settled into the slime up to its underbelly.

"Well, here we are," said Rommel.

In the hooded eyes Max read simple courage. Max turned the gun on Rommel. His finger tightened on the trigger.

He is the enemy he is enemy he is enemy enemy enemy—

Shuffling footsteps made Speigner turn his head. Schmidt tottered toward him, a pale Lazarus in a bloody German uniform. The aide shook his fist in the air as if reprimanding a child. Max readily shifted his aim to Schmidt. With all his strength Rommel yanked free of his bonds and wrapped his arms around Max, pinioning his elbows against his waist. Schmidt snatched the Luger and fell backward clutching it in both hands. Max fell on his knees with Rommel hugging him. He bucked free and groped for the gun. Rommel tore at Speigner's pants leg. A shoe came off in his hand. The door was ripped off its hinges, and a huge panzergrenadier filled Mammut like a murderous genie, his carbine aimed at Speigner's stomach. Rommel flung himself on top of the American, facing the startled grenadier.

"ER IST MEIN!"

XXIV

On January 27, Rommel sat on the padded bench seat in Mammut and went over the latest intelligence reports. Benghazi was defended to the south by XIII Corps, while 4th Indian had begun to pull out on the eastern highway, slipping away with valuable war supplies. A plan took shape: He would send 90th Light up the coast road and the Italians through Soluch, while he would take Group Marcks with 3 and 33 Reconnaissance units and cross Jebel Akhdar. The range was thought to be impassable because of its treacherous, rain-slick trails. The British would not expect to see him in their rear. He would strike them swiftly and decisively. The order of the day was "Mount up!"

There will be no more retreat.

He took satisfaction in his sore wrists. He thought with fierce pride of his fight with Speigner. The personal combat had driven away the lethargy of retreat. It had put a new edge on his imagination.

At first he had been angry with Speigner for using the threat to Schmidt to get what he wanted. It would never have occurred to Rommel to wound one man to get another to obey. The aide's injury had proved to be a minor flesh wound, however, and it was now clear that Speigner had aimed carefully. In retrospect he could appreciate that Max had done whatever he had to, in order to get the job done. He was a fighter. One had to admire that. If Max had said, "Drive or I shoot," Rommel would have made him shoot. Max understood that and had given him an option.

That is why Speigner will be allowed to go on our last ride together.

Max heard the guard talking with another soldier about *der Amerikaner.* To be discussed by strangers was to exist, however tenuously, in the real world. He huddled under his thin blanket and regarded his discomfort with a kind of awe.

For the past twenty-four hours—or was it forty-eight?—he had known nothing except the bounce and rattle of the truck. He had wrapped himself in his failure and refused to come out. He had been visited often by a cold eye sighting down a gun barrel. The genie's eye promised death.

The guard who sat across the truck had not spoken the entire time of their journey, and Max, in his cocoon of misery, had not asked any questions. On a primitive level they knew each other very well. Their relationship was well defined. They both were expected to sit still or go wherever they were told, though for different reasons. They both were subjects of the Third Reich for the duration of the war, barring a miracle. For two meals a day—hardtack, sardines and ersatz coffee—and a blanket, he was required merely to be still.

When they had first dragged him out of Rommel's van, he had assumed from the guards' rough handling that he was to be summarily shot. He had sat in the truck waiting for someone to haul him out and stand him up against a wadi bank. When the truck convoy began to roll—he could hear other vehicles moving with them—he realized they were not going to shoot him, at least not right away. He wondered how far they had driven. Could it be as far to the rear as Tripoli? He had never asked Bright-Ashton what the Germans did with their prisoners of war, whether they shipped them home to Germany or kept them in a desert compound. The most economical arrangement would be to drop them off in the Great Sand Sea and wish them *viel Glück*. Forrest had called it "paroling" the prisoners, but west Tennessee was considerably better suited for walking than south Tripolitania.

"*Kommen Sie*," said the guard.

Accompanied not only by his silent comrade but also by two military policemen with carbines at the ready, and feeling very conspicuous, Speigner made his way down a muddy avenue between two rows of tanks. Rain fell steadily and mud caked around his shoes in heavy patties which he swung between his crutches with difficulty. Hostile faces appeared at open hatches. Soldiers stared vengefully at the assassin who had attempted to kill their commander. Max struggled against mud and hatred. He had no idea what they were going to do with him, but from the looks of Rommel's "Afrikans," it would be some kind of Judeo-Teutonic justice, an eye for an eye, efficiently. He saw a familiar squat shape—Rommel's ACV.

The van was empty except for the driver, who slumped in his seat smoking a cigarette. His sullen glance told of demerits received for having left a sheathed knife in an open locker. The guard motioned for Max to sit on the floor. Speigner settled down and glanced around the interior. It seemed smaller, ordinary and functional, with the utility which its British designers had built into it. The wireless set would never again hum with possibility for Max. The driver's seat would hold one driver, not two.

As if reading Speigner's thoughts, the driver sat up straight and ditched his cigarette out the visored port. Rommel entered the van.

He folded his wet poncho and stowed it under the table. He ignored Speigner and instead leaned over his maps. The only evidence of their fight was a bandage on his temple. He covertly regarded Max, who sat on the floor at his guard's feet.

The American looks like a wet rat.

After several minutes of preoccupation with his charts, Rommel nodded to the guard who pulled Speigner to his feet. Max balanced on his crutches and waited blankly for sentencing. The driver also got up and stood protectively behind Rommel.

"It is no problem." Rommel waved the driver back to his seat. He continued to study his maps. Max waited, glancing in embarrassment at the floor where mud drying on his shoes fell away in clumps.

"Here is the situation," Rommel said without looking up. Max was startled to be addressed as though nothing had happened. Rommel pointed at the map. "My attack group is here, between Msus and Benghazi, which is defended by Fourth Indian. First Armored has left the flank exposed by responding to the Afrika Korps' feint at Mechili, to the east. We are the main attack force, but the British are not sure whether we are a mere reconnaissance in force; thus they offer us their flank. So here it is: part of our group is being blocked by Fourth Indian's defense line along the coast road south of Benghazi; the rest of my force is swinging inland for a flank attack southeast of Benghazi. Directly east, the city is protected by rough country, a series of mountain ridges considered impassable for armor, especially in this weather. And behind this barrier is Fourth Indian's escape route. Tell me, what would Forrest do?"

Their eyes met for the first time. Max was astonished to see no malice or vengefulness in Rommel's gaze, only a lively curiosity.

"You are not going to shoot me?" he said.

"My God," Rommel said impatiently. "It was your duty to escape. If not for the shooting of an unarmed, trussed prisoner, your efforts would have been completely honorable. You should be relieved to hear that Schmidt is recovering and will soon be in the pink. He was so proud when I pinned the wound medal to his pillow myself, this morning. Now, to return to my question—"

"Will I be sent to the rear with the other prisoners?" The words seemed to rasp from inside Max's rib cage.

"Don't be in such a hurry for internment—you'll get there soon enough," Rommel said reproachfully. "My question, please!"

Max forced himself to concentrate on the map. The situation was made for a Forrest or a Rommel: a static defense line south of the coastal city, a natural barrier of mountains to the east of Benghazi. He replied without hesitation, "Forrest liked to split his forces and knock on the front door while sending some surprise visitors around to the back. In this case, he would swing around the defended positions south of town and cross the mountains to the east. The enemy will not expect him to attack from the rear, while the bulk of his forces attack from the south and southeast."

"Interesting," Rommel said. "By a strange coincidence, that is exactly what I plan to do. What would you say if I invited you to come along for the ride? On the condition that you refrain from poking a Luger at me. Your guard will come along to make sure you and I don't take any more early morning drives." Rommel looked around for his new aide, who was standing in the door. "Haas? Pass the word—ready to shove off at seventeen-thirty hours, inspection in fifteen minutes!"

He turned and saw Speigner's naked expression of uncertainty and hope. Rommel shook his head reassuringly.

"I do not blame you," he said. "It all turned out for the best. I admit to a bias in my favor. We'll take a ride over the mountains. It may not be as exciting as our previous ride, but perhaps it will be something to remember."

They went out into the rain, a mere inconvenience for Rommel in his poncho and peaked cap but sodden misery for Max. From a distance, he watched Rommel inspect his escort group of five armored cars and six tanks. Then they climbed into an armored radio car whose rectangular, halolike antenna suspended above the roof was covered by a canvas tarpaulin. The three crew members stared inhospitably at Max and his guard as they wormed into the seating space inside the vehicle.

"Mount up!" Rommel sang out. One by one, the tank hatches clanged shut. In Max's soul a door clanged shut and a strange excitement took hold.

The raiding force drove north over rolling dunes resembling an ocean storm with 20-foot-high waves. Twice they had to stop when their advance scout car reported enemy units crossing in front of them, heading east. Rommel reasoned that these were part of 1st Armored Division responding to the Afrika Korps feint toward Mechili. By dawn the raiders were ascending the foothills of the low Jebel Akhdar range, which stretched 150 miles along the coast between the port cities of Benghazi and Derna. Max sat bent over in a cramped corner and listened to infrequent snatches of conversation between Rommel and the armored car commander, concerning their location.

Then Rommel ordered Max to join him in the open hatchway. Speigner's guard asked to be allowed to keep an eye on his prisoner. He climbed on the hull and sat alertly behind them. On the point were two heavy tanks, and behind were four Mark IIs and four armored cars. About a quarter of a mile ahead Max saw their scout car disappearing around a bend. The two-rut road wound through brown and purple hills dotted with surprising patches of meadow and scrub trees. Max had forgotten how shiny and green leaves could be on a rainy morning. Against the gray sky twin peaks rose in the distance. The road wound through a gap between these great horns.

What is this, a lark? Why not go whole hog and ask if they can rummage up a spare Wehrmacht jacket to go with the green trousers and you'd be all set! What about the pilot, Murphy? What about Bright-Ashton, Colonel Fellers, Anna? What would Anna say? "I want you to perform an act of (say 'war' in place of 'love')." Verily, Miss McAlpin, it has come to pass. Why this feeling of—happiness? Because one night we got mosquito-bit and inebriated while tramping around Shiloh with a writer who claimed to have been wounded in France and have a silver plate in his head?

He stole a glance at the blunt, weathered face beside him. Water dripped from the peaked cap and Perspex goggles. Mist sheered off the raised hatch like ocean spray off a ship's prow. Engines groaned up the steep trail. Caterpillar tracks wheezed and clanked. Rommel leaned forward as if he owned the wind.

At noon they rolled through Charruba and received a frenzied ovation from a pack of village dogs, the only creatures to be seen outside the stone buildings. Past the village the road forked and the column turned west. Soon they crested the gap between the peaks and began to descend the treacherous clay track carved into the side of the mountains. Brakes overheated in the armored cars. Rommel gave the order to dismount for a short break. The tanks stopped in the narrow road, protected from air attack on one side by a bluff, exposed on the other. They could see cottages in a valley 1,000 feet below.

"Reminds me of Italy," Rommel remarked.

"One white flare and three green," Max said. Rommel stared at him in amazement. "I read your book," Max added with a smile.

Everything took on an air of enchantment. A herdsman's hovel stood in a ravine beside the road. The shepherd could be seen driving his flock up a tortuous path. White sheep moved lithe as birds against the red mountain. Soldiers filled water cans at a spring-fed cistern. Rommel dipped a cupful of cold water and offered Max a drink. Down the mountain road an Arab and his donkey waited patiently. Although there was room to go around the parked vehicles, the man had elected to wait for them to pass.

"Perhaps the ass is suspicious of panzerkampfwagens?" Rommel said.

"It must be accustomed to British Matildas," Max suggested.

"One is tempted to make a correlation," Rommel said. His grin faded. "I could have had you shot, you know."

"Yes, Herr General."

"I am equally concerned for all our prisoners. Thus the British have little to fear of ill treatment after their capture. Is that not so?"

What does he want?

"Except perhaps for the Italians." Max shrugged.

"That is a different story," Rommel said irritably. "I am talking about *my* Afrikans."

Does he want me to say something good about the Germans?

"The British have long thought we outnumber them. The truth is, we usually fight against odds of two to one. We make up the difference with training and well-maintained equipment." Rommel's eyes beseeched him and demanded at once. "You were wrong to say I do not feel the loss of my men—or of brave enemy dead!"

"I did not say . . ." Max was perplexed by the sudden show of emotion.

"You implied it, in so many words. There will be a lifetime to mourn the dead, after the war. You were wrong."

They faced each other beside the cistern. Some soldiers stood close by, ready for their commander's slightest signal of alarm. The gray eyes would be satisfied with no less than total surrender.

"*Ja, ich habe unrecht*," Max said.

By midafternoon they had crossed the Benghazi-Barce railroad and descended to the coastal plain. The Via Balbia was only sixteen kilometers away. The horizon to the southwest had a rosy glow.

"The British are burning their stores in Benghazi," Rommel noted.

"Maybe it's a feint." Max unconsciously took Rommel's part.

"If *I* were occupying Benghazi, perhaps," Rommel replied ironically, "but the British? Not in a hundred years. Look!" He handed Max his binoculars, pointing toward the Via Balbia. A line of lorries stretched for miles. The column moved

sluggishly in spasms, like a giant snake aroused from its winter
sleep. The retreating British had sent their motorized transport ahead to escape the German pincer closing from the south
and southeast. They obviously expected no resistance. No
armor was to be seen along the rain-slick Via Balbia.

"I dream of lorries fat and saucy like these," Rommel
exclaimed, "but never so many, like grapes in clusters." He
snatched the field glasses out of Speigner's hands and appraised
the column which he already regarded as his property. He
automatically began to select a place of ambush. There was a
section of highway elevated above the marshy plain, with
drainage ditches on either side.

"We'll block the road where they cannot turn and run,"
Rommel spoke without lowering his glasses, like a commander
conferring with a junior officer whose opinion he respected.
Max noticed nothing unusual about being addressed in this
manner, although he was to remember it long afterward.
Rommel called the armored car commander topside to have
him relay the order. The young captain stared enviously at
Speigner.

"I could operate more efficiently if I were riding up here
with you, Herr General," he said. Rommel replied with
innocent abrasiveness.

"Not enough room. You can sit back there with the M.P.,
if you like."

The *Strassenpanzer* commander glared at Speigner and
disappeared into his car. Rommel's tanks rolled stealthily
behind a row of dunes. Twilight crept over the slate-gray
Mediterranean like a smoke screen. Max smelled the sea, cool
and salty. Rommel, too, sensed its invitation. He leaned into
the hatch and said, *"Angreifen!"*

The raiders surged like steel leopards toward the unsuspecting column. Rommel repeatedly pointed toward the lead
truck with a chopping motion of his hand. The panzers
bounded across the open ground and turned onto the Via
Balbia. Speigner could see the driver of the first lorry gaping at
the white Wehrmacht crosses on the panzer turrets.

"Surprise!" Rommel said cheerfully.

A Mark III blocked the road, its cannon aimed squarely at
the lead truck. The lorry driver ducked out of sight. While the
heavy tanks blocked the path of the column, the Mark IIs

cruised south to seal off any escape. They sailed down the empty southbound lane like highway patrolmen monitoring commuter traffic. The armored cars crept in predatory fashion along the line. Their commanders directed drivers to step out of their trucks, give up their weapons, and sit down on the seaward side of the road. The scene held a sorcerous quality for Speigner, like an eclipse of the moon. It was highway robbery on an epic scale and Rommel was the greatest of robber barons.

A tally was reported to Rommel. He had captured over a thousand Indian Division trucks loaded with food, medicine, ammunition, weapons and spare parts, but the materiel was scarcely more valuable than the lorries themselves. The armored car radio operator informed Rommel that von Mellenthin was calling. Group Marcks had taken Benghazi, but 4th Indian's motorized infantry and armored support units had broken out and escaped with the bulk of their men and equipment intact. Rommel was adamant that Group Marcks and 90th Light consolidate their victory by capturing all remaining British dumps before they could be blown up. In afterthought he told Mellenthin, "Have Berndt set up some cameras to record my entry into the city. This will be good news back home."

With a light escort of a Mark II and one armored car they swept into Benghazi. Max realized that they were exposing themselves to fire in the open hatch. Scattered British units were still armed and dangerous. He would not have been surprised to hear the whine of bullets at any moment. Rommel, however, was in a sportive mood. He stylishly returned the salutes of couriers shooting past on motorcycles or tank commanders rounding up enemy troops. They rolled unopposed down boulevards bordered by palm trees as graceful and incongruous amid the rubble as a woman's feather hat in a minefield. British troops sat disconsolately on both sides of the road, waiting to be taken. Rommel saw some British tank crews setting their Crusaders on fire, and he ordered his armored car commander to get on the radio and put a stop to it.

When their car stopped at a public square, a smartly attired British colonel recognized Rommel and begged to be allowed to surrender to him in person. Rommel, munching on a hard cracker, saluted and waved the officer away when he lingered beside the vehicle. The rooftops were outlined against a burst of flame as a nearby dump exploded. Max ducked but Rommel pointed to a minaret sihouetted against the red clouds.

"God help us, it can be lovely!" he shouted above the bedlam. Max stared at the spire as though at a half-recognized face in a crowded bazaar. Rommel turned away to order a captain to reconnoiter the dump and catch the British demolition crews before they did any more damage.

"The bastards are burning my petrol!" he yelled happily. "Get their asses."

A major of military police appeared beside the radio car to report that an airfield and a railway yard would be used as detention areas for prisoners. Rommel nodded and glanced at Speigner.

Rommel and Speigner awkwardly looked away from each other. Max watched British soldiers being herded across the road by a single M.P. Rommel agreed to pose for a film crew setting up camera and lights in the square. A press corps photographer raised his bulky camera and Max started to move out of the picture. Rommel touched him lightly on the arm.

"One photo of us together, Max. To mark the occasion."

The camera flash extracted the two figures from the smoke-filled night: one of them bluff-faced, wiry, aggressive; the other vulnerable, lanky, questing. The photographer lowered his camera and took a step back, as if releasing them. Rommel abruptly shoved his square hand into Speigner's grasp, then turned to face the klieg lights. An M.P. told Max to get down. In confusion Max inched down the hull and handed his crutches to the M.P. The armored car pulled away. Max saw Rommel give the camera an Axis salute.

Among hundreds of captured British soldiers, Speigner crouched in a railway yard and waited for the train. He nodded with fatigue but was afraid to fall asleep. His stomach churned with hunger and his leg ached. The rain had stopped. He had no idea what time it was. It seemed he had been waiting all night. He shivered in his thin jacket and hugged himself against the cold. The Germans apparently had made no provision for feeding the prisoners, and Arab vendors had appeared to remedy the situation. They set their carts on the other side of a fence, selling oranges, dates, rice balls and fried bread. The P.O.W.s queued up with the same patient, chagrined expressions they had worn in chow lines from Alamein to Derna. Max remembered the money in his pocket and joined the line, leaning on his crutches. The vendor refused his Egyptian coins but was quick to accept the sterling. Max wondered if the man would have been as eager to deal in deutsche marks. Returning to his place beside the tracks, he hunkered painfully and shared his handful of dried dates with the Black Watch sergeant next to him. They ate and watched the railroad tracks gleam copper-bright in the glow of burning warehouses.

Transport rumbled through the streets of Benghazi. The smell of exhaust fumes mingled with oil smoke. A plane flew low over the city, its red and green lights winking with an insatiable curiosity. Artillery thudded far away, where 4th Indian continued to break out of Panzer Army's grip. Max felt a sharp stab of envy.

An armored car slowly cruised the railroad tracks, its spotlight sweeping over the mass of soldiers. Speigner paid little attention until the beam flashed over him, hesitated, then fixed on his face. Blinded by the glare, he heard a murmur rise from the crowd. Feet crunched the gravel and Rommel stood over him, accompanied by two armed guards. Max swallowed a mouthful of half-chewed dates.

Rommel signaled the armored car commander to turn off his spotlight. He was intensely happy and smiled at Speigner as he searched for the words with which to share his good news. The Führer had just promoted him to Colonel General, a rare achievement for an officer his age. Also, a wonderful telegram from Lucie had arrived. "All Germany kneels at your feet," she had reported ecstatically. The American struggled with his crutches. His face was pale and greasy. Dried date crumbs stuck to the corner of his mouth.

"I did not think I would find you," Rommel said in German. "There are so many prisoners here." He gestured diffidently at their audience of British soldiers. "But things have a way of working out." He hesitated. "Can you walk a bit?"

He strolled down the center of the track, bobbing on his

toes with nervous energy. Max swung along beside him. Rommel's face became contorted with happiness.

"They are calling the Via Balbia the 'Rommelbahn'!" he said. Speigner could only nod his head. Rommel realized it was foolish to expect the American to share in his good fortune. That was not why he had come to find him, anyway. "I put in a word for you with the officer in charge of the prisoner detail."

"Danke, Herr General."

"Do not worry," Rommel replied, as if Speigner had somehow posed a doubt about his future. "You will be taken care of. They tell me our P.O.W.s eat better than the Afrika Korps. I will be kept informed of your destination. Please feel free to visit me and Frau Rommel after the war. My home is in Wiener Neustadt, near Vienna. I will not be hard to find."

"Danke schön."

Rommel turned on his heel, and Speigner maneuvered himself about on his crutches. Hundreds of British eyes followed their slow progress along the tracks.

"What did Forrest do after the war?" Rommel asked suddenly. "I mean, what was his occupation?"

"Forrest?" Speigner hesitated, then the zeal for historical fact bubbled up in him. "He raised cotton. He made a good deal of money but lost his fortune when he tried to organize a railroad. He invested his savings and went bankrupt when the railroad company went under. He died penniless."

Rommel shook his head sympathetically. "That is too bad, but then it does not matter, not really. They could not take his victories away from him, could they?" He thought for a moment. "If he could have chosen an end for himself, he would have wanted to die in battle. I am sure of that. How old was he?"

"When he died?" Max did some calculations. "Fifty-six." Speigner hardly noticed the pain in his leg. He felt outside of himself, as he had when he and Rommel had fought for control of Mammut or when the reconnaissance plane had circled the German ground forces. They came to the armored car. The guards waited nervously. The prisoners watched intently, as if there were a collective awareness of the responsibility to record the scene for retelling in pubs from Scotland to Wales:

how each man had seen Erwin Rommel—the Desert Fox himself, in person—after the battle for Benghazi.

The cynosure of this Axis-Allied attention dug his hand into his pocket and produced a tiny package. Men craned their necks to see what it was. Rommel handed it to Max.

Speigner felt a familiar shape and weight inside the neatly rolled piece of newspaper. He started to tear at the paper, and Rommel said quietly, "The paper is part of it."

Then Rommel clambered up on the armored car, boots scraping against the steel hull. His armed guards relaxed noticeably. Max shook a small, heavy object into his palm. By the light of burning buildings he saw the minié ball with its patina of Mississippi clay. He raised his eyes to Rommel, who was crouched on the hull, watching him.

"*Viel Glück!*" Rommel said brusquely.

The wheels of the *Strassenpanzer* began to roll. Rommel climbed to the open hatch and sat in it. Max unfolded the newspaper clipping and saw its heading and byline in the faint light:

YANK DIRECTS AMBUSH
OF AFRIKA KORPS
by
Anna McAlpin

Max looked up to see Rommel in retreat, his back ramrod-straight, sturdy shoulders swaying gently as the armored car bumped over the railroad tracks. He might have been Hannibal riding the lead elephant through an Alpine pass.

Rommel turned and waved goodbye. The M.P. company in charge of the prisoners, thinking Rommel was saluting them, erupted in a spontaneous, boyish cheer. He belonged to them, and they would go wherever he asked.

Max trembled strangely. Then he realized that the ties were vibrating under his feet. The train was coming. A guard motioned him off the track and back into line. The prisoners parted to make room for him, regarding him with curiosity and suspicion. When he looked back, Rommel's radio car was gone.

Epilogue

"Hey, Rommel," Ramey said. "Walden says the commandant wants you."

In a way, the Alabama lieutenant was like the cat Max had once lived with. His hatred was an inflexible standard on which Max could always rely. Ramey stood over Speigner's bunk and glared at him. Hostility leaked from him like gas from a broken oven. Max could almost smell it. Ramey's paranoia seemed tailor-made for life at Stalag 87. Speigner had become his special target the day the photo came. Max would never have shown it to anyone if the Luftwaffe censor had not spread the word among the guards. Eventually Major Tillman, the senior Allied officer, had heard about it and had asked to see the unusual picture: an American lieutenant and a German field marshal together in North Africa.

He pushed past Ramey and went out the barracks door. Eyes followed him with an unspoken question. He had straddled the fence at Stalag 87 for two and a half years, ever since he had arrived there in early 1942. His German-speaking ability had been exploited by both sides. He helped the prisoners by negotiating for free flow of Red Cross parcels. He helped their captors by explaining camp policy, especially in matters of indoctrination. He had developed a neutral attitude when performing for either side. While the Germans admired his detachment as a means of achieving efficiency, the prisoners marked it as deviousness just short of conspiracy.

He walked across the bare prison yard to the gate. The guard, a middle-aged private named Walden, waited with a confidential grin. A mechanic before the war, Walden was not cruel like some of the other guards but was nevertheless a bully in his own way. Speigner saw the guard eyeing his pockets, and he self-consciously felt to see if he had any cigarettes. There was a package of Lucky Strikes in his shirt

427

pocket, along with the minié ball. He had become so accustomed to its solid weight that it seemed like part of his body. He had never shown it to anyone, prisoner or captor. They had given him no choice about revealing the photo, but they would never know the story of his "*Viel Glück*" charm. It remained a secret part of himself, like a private garden behind a ghetto wall. Walden's eyes were fixed on his pocket.

"*Wie geht's,*" said the guard. He unlocked the gate and swung it open with a flourish, as if doing Speigner a favor.

"*Ganz gut,*" Max replied automatically. "What does the commandant want?"

Walden started to speak, then paused to let Max know he would have to pay for the advance information. "There is a film. *Zigaretten?*"

"What film?"

"*Eine Zigarette.*"

"Is it *Victory in the West?*"

Speigner had heard of the 1940 German propaganda film "*Sieg im Westen,*" in which Rommel was said to have appeared and even to have directed a scene. The film had become immensely popular in Germany, particularly now that the war was going badly on the Eastern Front.

"How should I know!" Walden said impatiently. "The officers do not invite *me* to see it. *Zwei Zigaretten?* I have important news about your man."

"Who?"

"Rommel, who else?"

Max immediately took out the package and shook out two cigarettes. They disappeared into Walden's pocket like magic.

"*Er ist kaputt,*" said the guard and turned back to his post.

"What do you mean?"

"He is dead, finished. It is in the papers." Walden shrugged.

Max shook his head angrily. "How?"

"The paper says he died of wounds received when his car was strafed in France."

It was common knowledge among the prisoners that Rommel had been in command of coastal defenses in France, the Germans' "Atlantic Wall." But Max had not heard anything about a strafing. There was a new rumor every day. German newspapers were notoriously unreliable these days.

"Was it during the invasion?" he said.

"For two cigarettes you get Rommel is dead. For the rest of the packet you get how the invasion is going."

"Save it for the Russians!" Speigner snapped. His feet crunched defiantly against the gravel walkway to camp headquarters. Heads turned among guards and P.O.W.s alike. Prisoners were supposed to walk quietly, never to draw attention to themselves.

No man can kill me. It profits me little to think that someone can.

Max entered the dayroom with hat in hand. The company sergeant looked up from his paperwork and jerked his head in the direction of a hallway. The commandant was standing beside an open door. Speigner saw a movie screen in the room. Captain Battnegel waited with his characteristic pose: head tilted slightly back so that he appeared to be looking down on all he surveyed. His camp nickname was "the Clerk." Before the war he had been an accountant.

"There is a film," the commandant told Speigner. "You have the privilege of attending a showing only because I think he would have wanted you to. Sit in the back."

Max tentatively entered the room, where folding chairs had been arranged in front of the screen. Several administrative officers in blue-gray Luftwaffe uniforms glanced at him without surprise. They had all seen the photo of Speigner with Rommel on the armored car in Libya. A sergeant fussed with a projector in the back of the room. Max sat near him. He overheard a snatch of conversation between two of the officers:

". . . did it so his wife would get his pension."

Did what? Who? Rommel?

"Ready?" Battnegel asked the sergeant. "Lights, please."

The sudden darkness caused a deferential silence in the room. Max felt that he was being squeezed into another dimension, a dry place of grieving without tears. The projector whirred and images flickered on the screen.

A military band played a dirge. Companies of infantry, Luftwaffe, and Waffen S.S. paraded at slow march past a town hall. Worshipful crowds jammed the sidewalks. Max could not tell whether it was a staged demonstration. Girls waved small

Nazi flags. A narrator spoke in melancholy German: "The funeral of *Generalfeldmarschall* Erwin Rommel was held at Ulm on October 18, 1944."

The camera cut to an interior shot of the town hall. An open coffin stood in the center of a meeting room with vaulted ceiling. As if from an usher's point of view, the camera panned pillars surmounted with eagles and approached the coffin, which was attended by an honor guard of four officers. Max recognized their cuff brassards with the emblem of a palm tree and the word *Afrika*. The camera cut to a closeup of Rommel's corpse draped with a Nazi flag.

He holds them all in contempt.

The hooded eyes were closed. The wide Swabian mouth was cemented in perpetual disapproval. Deep lines stretched from nose to the corner of the mouth in a scowl for eternity.

"The *Feldmarschall* died of wounds sustained on July 17, 1944, when enemy aircraft strafed his car outside Paris," the narrator said.

The camera panned to a velvet cushion where Rommel's medals were displayed, among them the Knight's Cross and Pour le Mérite. Then it returned to the coffin, which had now been closed and decorated with Rommel's helmet, sword and marshal's baton. Four generals had replaced the Afrikans. The band played the funeral march from the *Götterdämmerung*. The mourners entered the hall.

Speigner recognized General von Rundstedt from his photos. Rundstedt accompanied a woman and a young man, who Max guessed were Frau Rommel and Manfred. He had often tried to picture what Lucie Rommel looked like. She was small, dark-haired, with handsome features masked by grief. Manfred was tall and vulnerable. He resembled his mother more than his father, yet Max saw Rommel in the son's bearing. Rundstedt stood to deliver the oration.

"Our Führer, Adolf Hitler, has called us here to say farewell to his Field Marshal, fallen on the field of honor . . ."

no man can kill me

" . . . A pitiless destiny has snatched him from us, just at the moment when the fighting has come to its crisis . . ."

it profits me little

" . . . This tireless fighter in the cause of the Führer and the Reich was imbued with the National-Socialist spirit . . ."

inbued with winning
"His heart belonged to the Führer."
belonged to honor
"I present this wreath," Rundstedt reached out and touched a large wreath placed at the foot of the coffin, "in the name of Adolf Hitler."
I am not political I am a soldier
The band played *"Ich hatt' einen Kameraden."* The camera cut to a street scene outside the hall. Rommel's coffin was placed on a half-track gun carrier. Hitler's wreath was draped conspicuously in front. An honor guard sat stiffly on either side of the coffin. An infantry company presented arms. Generals saluted. A soldier carried Rommel's medals before the half-track like an offering to the gods. The band played a dirge, and the mourners paraded through the streets of Ulm. Girls waved Nazi flags.

Speigner involuntarily touched the minié ball in his shirt pocket. He remembered the last time he had seen Rommel: sitting in the open hatchway of his armored car at the Benghazi railroad depot, his wiry form ramrod-straight, expectant, determined, defiant. Grief ballooned blackly inside Speigner and he clamped down on it and held it back.

The lights were turned on. The officers stirred contritely and looked at each other to see if anyone was prepared to make an appropriate remark. Battnegel glanced at Speigner. The fan in the projector continued to run, cooling the hot bulb.

They think because my face is in a photograph with his that I was his friend. Don't they know I was his enemy? The reason I am here is that I tried to destroy him. It does not matter that I failed. The point is, I tried to kill him.

The moment had passed. The sergeant rewound the film. Boots scraped on the floor. Battnegel tilted his head and archly regarded Speigner. "The prisoner is dismissed," he said.

Max stood and moved toward the door. In the hall he stopped and turned back. They were all looking at him.

"Danke, Herr Kommandant," he said formally, "for allowing me to see the film."

He walked stiffly up the corridor, leaving a murmur of voices behind him. The company sergeant gave him an officious glance but Max did not look at him. He went out into the chill air, automatically feeling for his cap in his back pocket. His feet crunched on the gravel walk. His footsteps sounded far away. He set his feet down carefully, as if he were treading the narrow surface of time itself. He did not want to stray off the straight path of the present and lose himself in the past or the future.

"*What's the German for 'Lost Cause?'*" Faulkner asked.

He could see the author standing in the tiny military cemetery at Ole Miss, his hair blazing silver in the moonlight. "*Verlorene Sache,*" Max translated mechanically.

He felt the dead weight of the minié ball in his shirt pocket, hard against his chest. The good luck charm had failed them both. He took it out of his pocket and curled his fingers around it. He could feel the worn grooves.

Three rings for Confederate two for Federal no man can kill me it profits me little

Max stopped at the gate and stared out over the gray fields surrounding the compound. Walden, who had watched Speigner walk solemnly away from the headquarters building with the stiff, uncertain steps of a convalescent, stirred himself solicitously to open the bolted latch. Without warning, Max turned in a single, violent motion and hurled the minié ball over the field as far as he could throw it. Walden ducked his head at the unexpected movement, his hand on his holster. In the field a pair of grouse, startled from their hiding place, beat quick and low across the heath.

"*Was ist das!*" Walden cried.

"My *viel Glück* charm," Max said fiercely. "I have no need for it, anymore."

The guard stared at him as if he were mad. To reassure Walden Max reached for a cigarette, but on second thought gave him the whole package and made the man smile.

Acknowledgments

I would like to thank the following people for their suggestions, advice or encouragement: Jack Maxey, Colonel (Ret.); Val L. McGee, Lieutenant Colonel (Ret.); Clinton McCarty, Willie Morris, Hanne Gaycken, Carolyn Blakemore, my editor, and Chaucy Bennetts, copy editor.

For historical facts and figures I am indebted to these authors and their works: Shelby Foote, *The Civil War: A Narrative;* Joseph Blotner, *Faulkner: A Biography;* Claude Gentry, *The Battle of Brice's Crossroads;* David Irving, *The Trail of the Fox;* Ronald Lewin, *Rommel As Military Commander;* Desmond Young, *Rommel the Desert Fox;* Friedrich W. von Mellenthin, *Panzer Battles* and *German Generals of World War II;* Heinz W. Schmidt, *With Rommel in the Desert;* James S. Lucas, *Panzer Army Africa;* David Kahn, *The Code Breakers;* Matthew Cooper, *Panzer: The Armoured Force;* Great Britain Air Ministry, *RAF Middle East;* Eve Curie, *Journey Among Warriors;* Correlli Barnett, *The Desert Generals;* Keith Douglas, *Alamein to Zem Zem.*

I would also like to thank these research facilities and organizations: the University of Mississippi Library, the Library of Congress, the National Archives, the National Park Service (Shiloh and Gettysburg), the Dale County (Ala.) National Guard, and the Patton Museum of Cavalry and Armor.

L.W.

Oxford, Mississippi
Spring, 1985

ABOUT THE AUTHOR

LAWRENCE WELLS was born September 14, 1941, the same day Erwin Rommel led his panzers into Egypt on a raid code-named "Midsummer Night's Dream." A native of Ozark, Alabama, Wells attended the University of Alabama and "Ole Miss" and taught English at Murray State University in Murray, Kentucky. He has edited several nonfiction books, including *William Faulkner: The Cofield Collection*. He lives in Oxford, Mississippi, where he and his wife, Dean, operate a regional publishing company, Yoknapatawpha Press. Wells's second novel, *Let The Band Play Dixie*, will soon be published.